CONVERSION

C⊕NVERSION

KATHERINE HⓞWE

G. P. PUTNAM'S SONS
An Imprint of Penguin Group (USA)

G. P. PUTNAM'S SONS
Published by the Penguin Group
Penguin Group (USA) LLC
375 Hudson Street, New York, NY 10014

USA | Canada | UK | Ireland | Australia
New Zealand | India | South Africa | China
penguin.com
A Penguin Random House Company

Library of Congress Cataloging-in-Publication Data is available upon request.
Printed in the United States of America.
ISBN 978-0-399-16777-5
1 3 5 7 9 10 8 6 4 2

Design by Ryan Thomann. Text set in Adobe Caslon.

For my friends

CONVERSION

PRELUDE

*H*ow long must I wait?

His tongue creeps out the corner of his mouth while he writes, the tip of it black with ink, the blacking in his gums staining his teeth. He looks like he's got a mouthful of tar. I've been waiting for some time, but Reverend Green's still writing. His quill runs across the paper, scratching like mouse paws. Scratch scratch, dip, scratch, lick, scratch.

My feet ache, and shifting my weight just makes the one hurt worse than the other. I'm leaning in the door frame, and in my mind my mother prods me in my back to make me straight. It's so sharp, the prodding, I could almost swear she was really there.

"Ann?" he says.

I'd gotten so used to the waiting that I don't hear him at first.

"Ann!" He's tossed his quill down.

"Yes," I whisper.

He turns a chill eye on me, an arm over the back of his chair. His elbow's worn the turkey-work well away, 'til it's so threadbare, it shines. Reverend Green's the kind of man who's always being inter-rupted. A harassed look about him, as if he can never get time to concentrate on one thing altogether. Spends his whole life turning around in his chair.

I take a step back, thinking better of my errand. He gives me a long look. He's none too eager to hear what I've got to say either.

"Well, you'd best come in," he says at length, returning to his paper.

He hunches over his desk, free hand clutching bunches of his hair like he's anxious to finish whatever he's writing. Scratch scratch scratch.

I should've gone when I had the chance; he'd never've known I was here. I glance over my shoulder, through the parsonage hall. Goody Green, his wife, has got the fire going all right, but the door's open to the yard, as it's a warm day. The patch of sunlight on the floor is so bright, I have to squint. A long stretch of shadow, and a cat wraps around the doorjamb and flattens himself out in the sunshine with a yawn. He rolls on his back, batting at ghosts.

Goody Green's at the table wringing out cheesecloth. She looks harried, and no wonder, with the baby hiccoughing so. She was bouncing him up and down the hall when I arrived, beating him over her shoulder. I said she should hold him upside down and give him a little shake, but she glared and said, "If you'll just wait for Reverend Green over there."

I not being a mother, I suppose she'd ignore my advice, though it's common knowledge how many Putnams I raised myself. Now I see she's given up. The baby's stashed in a long wooden cradle near enough that she can rock it with a foot, but she's just letting him cough, all red in the face like a baked apple. And to be sure she can't call on anyone for so much as a poultice.

No one can, in the village, anymore.

"Go on, then," she says to me, giving the cloth a final twist. She's got some arms, has Goody Reverend Green. "Don't you keep him waiting."

If she weren't there, I could sneak away. I feel my heart pressing against my ribs, and the top of my head opening, as if my soul were being ripped from my body by the hair.

A girl in a dirty coif wanders in from the yard, finger in her mouth, her apron splotched with mud. She looks over at me all shy, because she doesn't know me, or perhaps because she's been warned to keep away. She's like a sweet piglet walking on two legs, with those pink cheeks all in mud like that, and I smile at her. She squeaks in terror and runs to hide behind her mother.

"Come now, Ann," the Reverend coaxes me from within his study.

It's cooler in there. It's away from the kitchen fire, with its window over the side yard, facing away from the sun. I'd like to sit. My feet are so tired.

"There's nothing to be afraid of."

But there is.

There is everything to be afraid of.

I swallow the lead ball in my throat that no amount of swallowing can be rid of, and move into the shadows of the Reverend's study. There's a bench between his desk and the fireplace. It's as hard as a church pew. I could swear the back isn't so much straight as curved, to force my head to bow. But it's not the bench that's making me hang my head.

The Reverend gingerly sands his paper, blows it clean, and blots, holding the paper to the light to approve of his work. Satisfied, he turns at last to me.

But when his eyes fall on my face, he recoils, as if I'd moved to strike him.

I've come to Reverend Green to make my confession.

Part 1

JANUARY

YULETIDE

And it was at Jerusalem
the feast of the dedication,
and it was winter.

JOHN 10:22

CHAPTER 1

The truth is, I'm not sure when it started. I don't actually think anybody really knows.

For a while figuring out the very first instance of it seemed really important. They were interviewing all of us because they wanted to find the locus of it, or whatever, I don't really know. They marched us into the office one at a time, and there was this big map of the school up on a wall. It was covered in pins with little flags, each one with a date. It was super complicated. I think they thought that with enough pins and flags and yarn and everything, they'd figure it out, or at least it would look really impressive for the news cameras. And don't get me wrong, it *was* impressive. All those arrows and everything looked wicked complicated. It didn't help them figure anything out, though. I think it just made them feel better.

But I'm getting ahead of myself.

If I was really forced to pick a date, like at gunpoint, I'd have to go with January 11. I'm saying that only because it was just a completely basic Wednesday with nothing much to recommend it.

Exactly the kind of day I shouldn't remember.

We'd been back from winter break only a couple of days, but we'd already gotten into the routine. Senior year. Last semester. We were pretty keyed up. I mean, everybody's always on edge when the semester starts, kind of, except spring semester senior year is like that normal nervousness times a million. Senior year is when it all comes together, all the years of studying and work and projects and sports and campaigns and whatever we're into that we've been working really hard for—it's either about to pay off or everything is about to completely fall apart. And don't even get me started about waiting for college acceptance letters. But even though senior year is massive, is basically the moment that sets up the rest of our entire lives and whether we're going to be successful and get everything we want or whether we're going to die alone in a ditch in the snow, we still have to get up and make it through every day. I still get up and brush my teeth, right?

This Wednesday should have been the most generic Wednesday imaginable, even if it was a Wednesday of the spring semester of our last year at St. Joan's.

"Sit," my mother said.

I was standing by the kitchen sink shoving a cranberry muffin into my mouth.

"What?" I said, plucking at my shirt to shake the crumbs out the bottom.

"Colleen, for God's sake. You won't be able to digest anything. Would you sit down for five minutes?" Mom used the toe of her slipper to brush the crumbs under the edge of the dishwasher.

"Can't. I've got to go," I insisted as Dad came up behind us, rattling the car keys.

"Did you get the problem set done?" Mom asked. She licked her thumb to rub crumbs from the corner of my mouth, and I squirmed away from her.

"Mom! Get over it! Yes, I got the problem set done."

"You want me to look it over real quick?"

"Linda," my dad warned from the front door. He jingled the keys again, and I slung up my backpack and kissed Mom on the cheek.

"It's fine," I said. "I promise."

Could there be a more normal Wednesday morning? It's so normal, I almost want to embellish it, and add something kind of exciting or dramatic or interesting. But I just can't, because nothing like that happened. Dad dropped me off at school, and the upper school hallway was awash like it always was in an ocean of girls in plaid skirts and cardigans and wool tights and Coach handbags from the outlet store. I knew most of them, at least well enough to say hello, though every class adds a lot of new girls freshman year and so the older we got, the more strangers started peppering the hallways.

"Hey, Colleen," said someone in passing, I didn't see who, but I said "Hey" back and nodded to be nice. I stopped by my locker to swap out some books and scroll through a few texts that didn't seem very important. I was just replying to something, I don't remember what, when I heard it.

"Colleeeen, I saw you standing alooooooone, without a dream in my heart . . . without a love of your own. Colleeeeeeeeeeen," a voice hummed from inside my advisory classroom.

I looked up and grinned at the spines of my textbooks. Deena was stuck on "Blue Moon." Again.

Deena's the first one who's important to know about. She came to St. Joan's in sixth grade, and when she got here, she was the tallest one in the class, even taller than me, this string bean girl from Charleston with a shock of baby dreadlocks falling in layers to her shoulders. She had such a thick Southern accent that at first I kind of couldn't tell what she was saying. But she lost the *y'alls* after only a couple of weeks, and then she started dropping her *R*'s. That girl is a total language sponge. The craziest is when she speaks Japanese. I think she gets a special kick out of shocking people with it, especially when she was on her exchange program in Tokyo last summer—a six-foot-tall African American girl speaking near-fluent Japanese after just three months.

"Hey," I said, sliding into my seat.

Deena grinned at me, spread her arms wide, and went for the big finish.

"Collleeeeeeeen! You knew just what I was there for, you heard me saying a prayer for, someone I really could care for!"

"She's already been at this for, like, ten minutes," Emma whispered to me, loudly enough that Deena could hear her.

Emma. Nominally, Emma is my best friend. I don't even remember when I first met her, but we were tiny. Before preschool. She's from Danvers, her parents are from Danvers, her grandparents were all from Danvers, her whole family lives in Danvers. Her brother, Mark, went to Endicott in Beverly because he didn't want to be too far from Danvers. They all look alike, too, all the Blackburns. And they're really clannish. Emma's mom is one of those delicate blondes who is usually shuttered away with a headache, and when that happens, we can't go over to the Blackburns' house. They're all very protective of each other. If somebody mentions, as I made the mistake of doing once, that maybe Emma's mom would feel better if she just went outside once in a while, Emma will cut them dead with a look and say, "She can't."

Emma has always had a quietness to her, which is one of the reasons I like her so much. But it can also make her hard to read. Her reserve is a complete inversion of the chaos of my house. Emma was the last one of us to play with dolls—she was thirteen, which is kind of crazy, and we'd all already gotten our periods and were starting to text boys, but she'd still ask shyly if I wanted to bring my American Girl doll when I came over. They're still out in her room, and I sometimes imagine her whispering to them when the lights go out. She has buttery-blond hair, which in the summers turns almost white in the sun. Her eyebrows are so light and pale, they almost don't exist, and she refuses to wear makeup at all, which gives Emma a naked, otherworldly look.

Once it was clear that I liked Deena, Emma decided she was okay, too. It was Emma who taught Deena to stop saying "milk shake" when she meant "frappe."

Deena's elbow was taking up so much room that Fabiana had to squeeze herself around the desk to sit down next to her. Fabiana, I don't know as well. She came to St. Joan's as a freshman, part of that influx of new people when we got to upper school. She's okay. Kind of annoying. I didn't like to give much of myself away to Fabiana. It's not that I didn't like her, it's just that we were applying a lot of the same places, and we were sort of in competition for grades, even though it was spring semester.

I don't know why I just said "sort of" when I don't mean that at all. Fabiana and I were competing for valedictorian. I know it's not cool to seem like I care that much, and I wasn't really supposed to make it look like I was trying hard to get the grades I was getting, but the truth is, I was having a hard time with it. For all of high school I'd been able to hold everyone else off without any trouble, and keep up the fiction that I didn't have to work hard at it, and I didn't really care. But the truth is, I cared. I cared a lot. And so did Fabiana. She watched me as coolly as I watched her.

Fabiana sat near us, but she wasn't part of our group. We're not supposed to have cliques at St. Joan's, but honestly, good luck with keeping teenage girls from forming cliques. It's not like we all had matching satin bomber jackets with our cutesy nicknames on the back. But Deena, Emma, and I were a clique, and the fourth member was Anjali. So Anjali was there already, too, and she'd been talking the whole time, pausing just long enough to give me a wave hello. I could tell we were all alive and breathing because Anjali was talking about Yale. It was the surest way to start a morning off right.

"Like in that movie, where he's, like, a crew guy?"

"*The Skulls?*" someone asked.

"They are totally not like that at all, though I've heard that the inside is actually really that nice. It's all crazy old, with portraits and everything. I heard that George Bush's family gave them like a million dollars to redo the parlor after he trashed it at some party back in the sixties."

I wasn't sure whom Anjali was talking to. Emma? I glanced at her.

Maybe, on a technicality, but Emma was only half listening. Deena was too involved to care, and anyway this was all old territory.

"Secret societies, you know," Emma explained in a whisper.

So she had been listening. Emma misses nothing.

"I mean, they don't, like, give everybody cars like that. That's totally not true," Anjali continued, not seeming to care if anyone was listening or not.

Sometimes I felt a little sorry for Anjali. She had come to St. Joan's the previous year because her mom got a job at Mass General. They lived a bunch of places before that—Houston, Chicago, I forget where else. Her mom is a big deal medical researcher, and her dad's a lawyer, the kind who wears a gigantic watch and leaves papers all over the dining table so no one can ever eat there. They are really, really intense. Anjali fell in with us right away, because she's completely fun and hilarious and smart, but I've seen her in tears over an A-minus—on a physics problem set, thanks very much, not even a final.

"They give you *cars?*" Fabiana butted in.

"God," Anjali said, rolling her eyes. "*No.* I just said they didn't."

I shared a look with Emma, and Emma smiled out of the side of her mouth.

"It's just for networking, you know? That's basically the whole point. Did you know that if you get into Skull and Bones, you're basically automatically in the CIA?"

"Since when do you want to be in the CIA?" I asked her. "I thought you were going pre-med."

"I *am*," Anjali said. "I'm just saying."

"She could be a doctor for the CIA," Emma reasoned, and Deena laughed.

"She could reprogram enemy agents," Deena said, grinning. "Then send them back behind the lines where they'll be like a sleeper cell ready to activate when they hear the secret password."

"And the secret word would be?" Emma asked.

"*Jason*," I said, sending Emma and Deena into fits of giggles.

"You guys, shut up!" Anjali said, turning around and hitting my arm. "You are so gross."

She was pretending to be upset, but she was smiling. Being the only one of us with a boyfriend came with the assumption that it was her privilege to let us tease her.

"*Jason* is so gross," I clarified as Deena said, "Mmm-hmm," and shot Anjali her *We keep telling you* look. That look is deadly.

The bell rang just as Father Molloy strode in, clapping his hands and saying, "All right, girls, let's take it down a notch."

Father Molloy is the kind of priest that my mother likes to call "Father Oh Well." That's such a Rowley family Irish name joke. Pathetic. Anyway, she says that because she thinks he's cute, and I guess he sort of is except for he's really old, like, forty. He perched with one knee up on the edge of the desk and frowned at the roll sheet. I don't even know why he was bothering, since I don't think we had any new girls this late in the year. We'd already had him for eighth-grade catechism anyway, most of us.

While he was distracted, Anjali pulled her phone out of her sweater pocket and slid it under the lid of her desk. There's a pretty intense "no cell phones in class" policy at St. Joan's, and Anjali is a prime offender. She can text without looking, which she swears is easy, though I've never been able to do it. They had taken at least two phones away from her in the previous semester that I know of, and when they take your phone away, they actually keep it. What I

7

couldn't believe was that Anjali's parents kept buying her new ones. My mother told me that if they ever took my phone away, I'd be buying the next one myself. Which is fine, except I don't have three hundred dollars just kicking around. I now texted during class only in the event of a dire emergency. Anjali, though, she's ridiculous. I peered over her shoulder to see what she was writing.

"You shouldn't text him back right away like that," I whispered.

"What?" Anjali whispered back.

Father Molloy had started down the roll sheet for attendance, and girls were responding when he called their names.

"Emma Blackburn?"

"Here," Emma said.

"Jennifer Crawford?"

"Here," said the girl with pink-streaked hair and heavy eyeliner sitting in the back of the room.

I leaned in closer so Anjali could hear me. "You should at least wait five minutes. Or, heck, wait 'til fifth period. Then he'll appreciate it."

Deena had her eyes fixed straight ahead, but I could tell she was listening.

"What for? I like him. If I text back quickly, I hear from him sooner," Anjali said out of the side of her mouth.

"But, Anj," I said, leaning forward on my elbows hard enough to tip the desk. "You've got to—"

"Critical commentary, Miss Rowley?"

Crap.

"No, Father Molloy."

He dropped the roll sheet on the desk and folded his arms. I'd seen him give other girls that look before, but I didn't think he'd ever given it to me.

"I'm sorry, but I think only half the room caught what you were saying," he said. "Would you mind repeating it?"

"I'm sorry? I wasn't saying anything."

"Fair enough. Perhaps Miss Seaver in speech and debate didn't cover projection. Stand up, if you will."

Double crap.

"Chop chop," said Father Molloy.

I stood up, a whole roomful of girls whispering a decibel above silence, rows of wide-blinking eyes staring at me with pity and, in a few faces, delight. So far this year I was perfect: attendance, lateness, everything going seamlessly. I had two early decision deferrals to think about, and another dozen applications had gone out last week. Plus the thing with Fabiana. I needed to get out of this without it going down in writing. I tried to smile around the room, but the effort made my cheeks hurt.

The priest cast an appraising eye up and down me, with a flicker of mirth in his eyes that let me know we were both in on the joke.

"Perv," I thought I heard Deena mutter.

"Miss Rowley. As this is your senior year, and you've been a student at St. Joan's since the Bush administration, I feel certain you are aware of the dress code?"

I cleared my throat. "The dress code?" I echoed.

"Next year you'll be at whatever university will be fortunate enough to have you, and you will be free to wear as few scraps of handkerchief as you see fit. But at St. Joan's, we still stubbornly insist that our students wear actual clothing. That skirt is—six inches, I believe? Seven?—above the knee. Roll it down, please."

Eight, actually. Okay, maybe more like nine. I reached to my waistband and tugged to bring it back down to regulation length. All around me, girls with rolled waistbands shifted in their seats, some pulling down the ends of their cardigans to cover the evidence. I didn't see why he'd want to call me out on some BS skirt-rolling. Everybody does it. They start doing it in middle school.

"Thank you. Now then," he said. "Would you mind repeating your comment to Miss Gupta just now? The suspense is killing us."

Anjali squeaked and pressed her lips together, since I'm sure she was afraid I'd rat her out about the phone. I opened my mouth to speak, not really clear about what was going to come out, when the door to advisory clicked open and I was momentarily spared while we all dropped everything to watch Clara Rutherford come into class.

The first thing to know about Clara is that I like her. I really do. And she likes me too. We're not *not* friends or anything like that. That was the crazy thing about Clara—pretty much everybody liked her. She was so nice that I kind of wished I could hate her, if for no other reason than that she was definitely nicer than me. But as much as I may have wanted to, I couldn't quite hate her. I don't think I'd ever seen her get mad or lose her temper at anyone. She wasn't friendly, exactly. There were plenty of girls at St. Joan's who thought that being friendly to everyone, even people they hated, would make them popular. Instead they just came off as insincere, and fewer people wound up liking them than if they'd just acted normal.

That wasn't Clara's style. Instead she had this air about her, as though there was always a red velvet carpet rolling out under her feet. She did okay in classes, but not so well that anyone would resent her, or feel like she was so much smarter than them that it was annoying. She played field hockey well enough that everyone wanted to have her on their team, but not so well that anyone would find a reason to high-stick her in the face. She even managed to look cute in the field hockey skirts, which really killed me, because I had a serious complex about my knees. Her hair was just the right length, with just the right amount of wave, and with a reddish-nut hue that glowed. Clara didn't even have to straighten her hair, which I could admit envying about her. Mine springs straight out in dark corkscrews all over my head, so that half my childhood was spent with my mother ripping a hairbrush through thick snarls, saying I looked like the teenage bride of Frankenstein. It wasn't until last year that I finally figured out the stuff to use to get them to fall in spirals.

It was like Clara Rutherford belonged to some other species, one that didn't sweat or smell or have anything go seriously wrong in its life. Her family, as far as I knew, was wealthy, and happy, and healthy, with a chocolate-haired mother who manned booths at school fund-raisers and a squash-playing father who actually came to some of her field hockey games. She had a brother who was in Emma's brother's class, as unblemished and likeable as she was, who played lacrosse and did student council and threw one memorable party after graduation where there may have been some drinking, but no one got in any serious trouble, and everyone just had a good time. Clara had it all figured out.

Of course, not everybody liked Clara. When a girl's on a pedestal, there's nothing some people would like better than to shove her off it, just to know what kind of noise she'd make when she shattered.

Emma's face didn't change when Clara came in. Instead her gray eyes seemed to glimmer, like light on the inside of an oyster shell.

But I saw Deena's smile slip. I thought she was a little jealous of Clara, which I didn't understand, because Deena was so funny and talented and it's not like she wasn't popular too. But she had heard that Clara was also applying to Tufts, and now Deena was paranoid that Clara would take her spot. Most of the colleges we were all looking at had quotas for the kids they'd take from the top private schools. It was going to be a tense three months in advisory if both of them were waiting to hear from Tufts.

And then there was Jennifer Crawford, with the pink hair. When Clara walked in, Jennifer's lip curled like she was looking at a roadkill fox. Disgust and loathing.

Jennifer had issues.

So Clara walked in, and it was like we all paused for a moment of silence to appreciate that she'd decided to join us.

Our eyes tracked Clara as she moved to her seat, followed closely by her two Clara-clones. All three of them were wearing low ponytails tied with thin black ribbon. I could feel us all register this information, could almost hear the click of the data being recorded in every girl's head, and wondered how many low-ribboned ponytails we'd see at assembly after lunch. A lot, I was guessing.

"Miss Rowley?"

I jumped, shaken out of staring at Clara Rutherford, who had settled in the seat at the front of the room nearest the window.

"Your comments to Miss Gupta. We're on the edge of our seats."

I glanced down at Anjali, who was sliding her phone up the inside sleeve of her sweater where it would be safe.

"I'm sorry, Father Molloy," I said, looking straight ahead. "But I wasn't saying anything. I just dropped my pen, and leaned over to pick it up. It probably looked like I was talking."

The priest rolled his eyes heavenward and sighed. We both knew I was full of it. I almost respected him more for knowing how full of it I was.

"Have it your way," he said, waving a dismissive hand.

I dropped into my seat, hunching my shoulders to make myself smaller behind Anjali. I just needed a break from being looked at for one second.

"Okay. I'm afraid we've got some stuff to discuss today, so listen up," Father Molloy said.

Groans of annoyance rumbled through the classroom, and Deena and I shared an irritated look. Her hand twitched on her physics textbook, and my own hands were itching to double-check my calc problem set. Usually advisory was the prime time for cramming for tests or finishing up work from the previous night. I was pretty sure of my work, but I couldn't recheck it too many times. Anyway, there was never any actual advising that took place in advisory.

"I'm sure a lot of you have questions and concerns," he began. "And we're going to do everything that we can to address them. But the important thing at this juncture is for me to emphasize that the school cares about you all. At this time there is no reason for any of you to be worried. No reason whatsoever."

"What is he talking about?" Deena whispered in my ear.

"Hell if I know," I said.

I brought a pencil up and held it between my upper lip and my nose, and spaced out a little. Deena inspected her fingernails. Anjali had edged her phone into her palm and was texting again while pretending to absorb every word Father Molloy was saying.

"St. Joan's prides itself on being a place where the students come first," he droned on. "We know it's unnerving, and so I want to encourage anyone who wants to speak to a teacher in private not to hesitate. You can come talk to me, or if you'd feel more comfortable, maybe with a woman, for instance, we can connect you with someone."

The class was starting to get fidgety, but he wasn't ready to let us off the hook yet. "Are there any questions?" Father Molloy said, folding his arms over his chest and looking at us.

I inclined my head over to Emma, about to ask if she had any idea what he meant, but she didn't seem to be listening. She was staring at the front corner of the room, her cheeks flushed a splotchy pink, and gripping her pen so hard, her knuckles were turning white.

My gaze swiveled, following Emma's stare over the heads of my classmates to the hallowed corner where Clara Rutherford sat, her desk practically bearing a little RESERVED card written in calligraphy.

And that was the first time that I saw Clara Rutherford twitch.

CHAPTER 2

DANVERS, MASSACHUSETTS
WEDNESDAY, JANUARY 11, 2012

T *witch* is not the right word. It's the word the media would start to use when things really got going, when they needed a word that wasn't too sensational, because everyone was afraid that sensationalizing what was happening would just make it worse. But *twitch* does not even begin to describe what happened to Clara Rutherford that morning.

Her face seized up, as though an invisible person standing next to her had hooked his fingers in her mouth, trying to peel the skin from her skull. Her hands clenched closed, flew up to her chest, and vibrated under her chin. By the time Father Molloy got to her, her legs had started shaking so violently that she rattled off her chair and fell to the floor, flopping and gasping like a fish.

"Colleen, get the nurse," Father Molloy commanded, sounding surprisingly calm.

Half the classroom was standing up, staring down at Clara. We couldn't believe it was happening. We wouldn't have been able to believe it anyway, but it was somehow even more wrong that it was happening to Clara. Her feet kicked like someone getting electro-shock. Seeing her perfection split apart like that made us panicky.

"Now, Colleen!" the priest said, raising his voice.

He knelt beside her, cradling her head, with his thumb in her mouth to keep her tongue depressed. The last thing I saw before I fled for the door was Clara's front teeth biting down on Father Molloy's thumb. She was making horrible gagging, gurgling sounds, as though she were drowning.

I sprinted down the upper school hallway, my footfalls echoing on the flagstones, running past the vacant student center, skidding on the rug outside the upper school dean's office, ignoring the administrative assistant who stood up and hollered, "Walk, Colleen!"

I rounded the corner from the upper school hallway to the old wing, my shadow stretching long down the hall, so distorted I felt like I was falling into it. I could feel my heartbeat in my throat as I ran down the corridor that used to house the convent bedrooms, all of them so long locked that the doors were rusted shut. At the very end of the hallway one door stood open, with warm light spilling out. I landed at the nurse's office, panting for breath on the doorjamb. Inside, half behind a white partition, the nurse was pulling a thermometer out of the mouth of a green-faced eighth grader.

The school nurse would be famous within the week, but on this Wednesday I have to confess that I didn't remember her name. She was new, and young—so young, I found it weird to address her with a title. She looked like she could be in my class.

When she saw me, she stood up immediately and said, "What's the matter?"

"You've got to come! Room 709. Hurry!"

By the time we burst back into the classroom, Clara was sitting up, her hair disheveled, breathing heavily and looking around with wide, baffled eyes. Father Molloy stood up when he saw us and pulled the nurse aside. They conferred for an urgent minute by the door while I crouched next to Clara. She looked up at me, her eyes shining with confusion. She moved her mouth, but nothing came out.

"Don't worry," I said, touching her arm. "I brought the nurse. You're going to be okay."

She nodded, wrapping her arms around herself.

"Colleen," the nurse said, placing her hand on my back. "Will you return to your desk, please?"

I hesitated.

"Girls, I know you're all worried, but we need to give her some air. Back to your desks, please," the nurse insisted.

I felt someone helping me to my feet and back to my desk. Slowly I lowered into my seat, still watching Clara. She was looking around on the floor, as if she were afraid she'd dropped something but didn't know what.

"That was crazy!" Anjali whispered.

"Oh my God, do you think she's going to be okay?" Deena said.

None of us could even pretend we weren't staring. The nurse leaned over Clara, shining a penlight into each of her eyes, taking her pulse, listening to her heart.

"Oh, she'll be fine," Emma said with a wave of her hand.

"Does she have epilepsy or something?" I asked. "Does this, like, happen all the time, do you think?"

I couldn't imagine Clara having something seriously wrong with her. We'd all have known about it if she did. St. Joan's was a small school. Everyone knew everyone else's business. We knew who was diabetic, and whose mom drank too much. We knew who had a gluten allergy, and who just said she did to hide her eating disorder. We knew who cut. We knew about everyone's tattoos, and we thought they should probably have gone into Boston to get them instead, 'cause the lines were already blurry. We knew within the week when one of us lost her virginity. Sometimes we knew within the hour.

"I don't think so," Anjali said.

"Maybe epilepsy doesn't come on until you're finished growing," Deena theorized. "What if it's like schizophrenia or something, like one of those things that happen for the first time when you're an adult?"

"You think she has schizophrenia?" I asked. I tried not to sound horrified, but I failed.

"No," Anjali said slowly. "That's not what schizophrenia looks like."

"Whatever," Emma said.

Her nails drummed once, twice, three times on the top of her desk.

Father Molloy hovered at the front of the classroom, with an expression on his face that I couldn't read. When the nurse beckoned to him, he seemed to be shaking a thought off before he could concentrate on what she was saying.

Laurel Hocking, that was the nurse's name. I couldn't believe I'd forgotten, especially considering what happened later.

Clara's two minions, Elizabeth and the Other Jennifer, which is what everyone called her to distinguish her from Jennifer Crawford, were huddled together at their desks behind Clara. They obviously had no idea what was going on. If Clara had seizures, they'd have known about it. Then again, maybe Clara was kind of aloof from her best friends, too. Elizabeth was pretty cool, she did field hockey and debate, but the Other Jennifer didn't have much going on. She was not especially bright, and most people assumed she had gotten into St. Joan's only because both her mother and her grandmother went there. I mean, she was nice and everything, and she was pretty, but she was just kind of blah. Maybe Clara just hung out with them because she could dictate the terms.

Nurse Hocking was stroking Clara's hair, and I heard her say, "We'll just make you an appointment, to be sure."

"It's definitely not schizophrenia," Anjali said, looking at her phone, which was still expertly concealed between her hand and the end of her sweater sleeve. "That's a mental disorder, and has to do with how she perceives reality. It doesn't cause seizures, just weird behavior."

"Huh," Deena said. "I hope she's going to be okay."

The bell rang, drowning out what Emma said, which I think was something like "Faker."

"What?" I said, looking at Emma.

"Huh?" Emma answered.

"What did you say just now?"

"I didn't say anything," Emma said, gathering her books.

She wasn't looking at me.

"Okay, girls," Father Molloy interrupted, addressing the whole room of migrating students. "I want you all to remember what we talked about. And if any of you need to speak with me privately, I'll be in office hours after lunch. You're always welcome to drop by. Mary, Queen of Knowledge, be with you all."

"But we didn't talk about anything," Deena muttered.

I hesitated when we reached the door, looking over my shoulder. Clara was still sitting on the floor, her legs splayed out like a kid. The nurse bent over her, offering a sip of water. Elizabeth and the Other Jennifer huddled nearby, as if they hadn't even heard the bell. Father Molloy stood with his arms folded over his chest, frowning.

"Come on," Emma said, plucking at my sleeve. "Or we'll be late."

"Yeah," I said, allowing Emma to pull me away.

As the door to advisory closed, I caught Clara's eye.

I don't think I'd ever seen anyone look so afraid.

CHAPTER 3

A t that point everything still could have gone back to normal. I mean, we'd have gossiped about Clara for a while, and the senior girls who weren't in our advisory would have wanted to know all the gory details, and it's possible that someone (cough cough Jennifer Crawford, hello) would have posted a picture of Clara convulsing on the floor on Instagram and then everyone would have freaked out about her privacy being violated, but then it would have finally blown over. A month, tops, we'd have talked about it, and probably not even that long, before we all sank into our own end-of-high-school worlds, with college acceptances and parties and the spring formal and GPAs and AP exams and guys and other things to gossip about and distract us. I'd have remembered that Wednesday as Clara Rutherford's first fall from the pedestal, which was without question a remarkable thing, but that's all.

There was only a hall's length between advisory and first period, but a hall's length can be a long time at St. Joan's. Any number of things could happen in the time it took to go from one end of the hall to the other.

We four broke apart within the crush of girls. Anjali was off to physics lab, Deena to Calculus BC. Emma and I usually sat together in AP US History. Our class was a pretty tight-knit group of history kids, as we'd been together in the advanced humanities classes all four years: history, English, French, Latin. Most of us had even taken AP Art History, which was an elective, but we'd be crazy not to take it, 'cause all we did was hang out at the Museum of Fine Arts and stare at pretty paintings. If I played my cards right, I'd leave St. Joan's with nine AP exams, and if I scored well enough, that was almost two semesters of college credit. Plus, AP classes weighted your GPA, which was key for valedictorian. Jennifer Crawford was in AP US, too, and for some reason she was less annoying in history class. She would actually talk to us, for one thing. She could be so standoffish the rest of the time.

Most schools do AP US in junior year, but at St. Joan's they save it for senior year. Getting into AP was a pretty big deal—they limit it to twelve slots, and we took an exam the summer before to place in. Every year a couple of girls flamed out, unable to take the pressure. Some of them even left the school. As if we didn't have enough to worry about.

AP US was a choice class, though, mainly because of Mr. Mitchell. He was much cooler than the other teachers, maybe because he was so young. He ran our class like a college seminar, with our desks in a circle, and he emphasized getting us to be able to argue our positions about what we read. We could tell he really listened to us when we were talking. He looked us in the eye.

Some people thought he was kind of cute, and I guess he was, in a hipster-nerd sort of way. Floppy James Franco hair and skinny 1950s ties. Glasses. He went to Harvard, so sometimes we'd even run into him in the Square on the weekend, and it was like spotting a celebrity. We'd laugh and wave and then run away giggling, wondering who he was with and what he was doing and if he had a girlfriend. Before the AP exam every year he had the whole class over to his apartment to cram, and he'd make weird early American food, like Indian pudding and corn pone and dandelion salad, and then after the exam he'd have everyone over again to show *The Last of the Mohicans* with sarcastic commentary about all the historical inaccuracies. I heard a rumor that he bought beer for last year's post-exam party, but I don't think it's true.

Emma and I were dissecting what had just happened to Clara when Jennifer Crawford leaned over. Up close her pink hair looked dry and fried, sticky, like cotton candy. I didn't know why she'd want to do that to herself. She could've been almost pretty if she'd just tried to look halfway normal.

"That was intense," she said.

"Yeah," I replied. "We were just saying."

"It's all over Facebook already," Jennifer said, flashing us her phone.

"What are people saying about it?" Emma asked, eyeing Jennifer's phone.

Jennifer slipped it into her purse with a quick glance at the class-room door.

"Just that it was totally crazy, and nobody's seen anything like that before."

"Do people know what's happening?" I asked. "Is she going to the hospital or something?"

"Oh, she doesn't need a hospital. She was fine when we left advisory." That was Emma.

"A couple people were saying she's going to the hospital, but the Other Jennifer said her dad's coming to pick her up."

"Dang," I said. "Poor Clara."

"It's Elizabeth and the Other Jennifer you should feel sorry for," Jennifer Crawford said with a curl of her lip. She leaned back, coiling a hank of pink hair around one finger. "What are they going to do with no one telling them where to sit at lunch?"

"Come on, Jennifer," I said. "Can you try to not be a total bitch for, like, five minutes?"

But Emma was silently laughing behind the sleeve of her sweater.

I was eyeing Emma when the door opened to reveal not Mr. Mitchell, but some random woman with huge eyeglasses and an armful of papers that slipped loose while all twelve of us watched. I could feel us all deflate when it wasn't him.

"Oh, dammit," the woman said, pushing the door closed with a hip before bending to pick up each leaf one at a time. "Is this," she spoke to the floor, waddling from paper to paper, "Room 811? AP US History?"

Curious glances crackled around the perimeter of the room, followed by shrugs and more than one surreptitious peek at a cell phone. It took us a minute to realize no one had answered the random woman.

"Well?" she said, standing, the last reclaimed page jutting out from under one arm. She planted her free hand on her hip and looked annoyed. "Is it or isn't it?"

"Ah," someone stammered. "Yeah, this is 811."

The woman gave us the once-over and—upon seeing the North Shore shipwreck map that Mr. Mitchell had hung behind his desk and the poster of the Gilbert Stuart George Washington portrait that they issue to every high school American history teacher at the same time they hand out the Tasers and Valium—decided she must be in the right place.

A hand tugged at my sleeve. Emma.

Where is he? she mouthed.

I shrugged. *Dunno,* I mouthed back. *Maybe he's sick?*

Lame, she said, a line forming between her pale eyebrows.

The random woman stumped up to the front of the room, slapped her papers onto Mr. Mitchell's desk, and hunted around on the desktop, as if she hoped she might discover an instruction manual there. Mr. Mitchell kept his desk as I imagined an intellectual does—chaotic, some of the papers stuck together with rings of coffee. There was even a magnifying glass on it, mounted on a brass stand.

"Okay," she said, more to herself than to us. "Right. Let's get started."

She turned to the board and wrote *Ms. Slater* in cursive handwriting that drooped and melted at such a sharp angle that she had to bend over to finish the *R*.

"I'm Ms. Slater," she said, resettling her glasses on her nose.

We all peered at her, squinting for clues. Our squinting didn't accomplish much—she was still just some random woman in a ponytail and a gray dress. Some non-age, like maybe thirty-five.

"If you'll all just pull out whatever you were supposed to have read for today, we'll see where we are."

"Excuse me, Miss Slater?" a girl in the back said as she raised her hand. Leigh Carruthers. The inevitable Leigh Carruthers.

"Ms.," the random woman corrected her without looking up from the disorderly heap of papers where she was, I guessed, hunting for the roll sheet.

"*Miss* Slater," Leigh said again. "Um, I have to leave early today? For an appointment? So I'm going to have to be going in, like, five minutes?"

The random woman looked up slowly, a wicked smile spreading across her face. When she smiled, she looked younger, and I felt myself smile, too. She had a tiny gap between her front teeth that made her look mischievous.

"Don't like the 'Ms.,' eh, Miss Carruthers?" Ms. Slater said. "We can go with Doctor Slater, if you'd rather. That works for me, too."

Leigh sat back.

"And I'm sure you're aware that student appointments during school hours have to be cleared with the office first. Then they do this thing where they give all the teachers a list of who's going where when, with stuff like your cell phone numbers and e-mail addresses so we know what you guys are up to. Including substitutes like me. You know that, right?"

Leigh. So busted.

"Yes," Leigh said.

"Great," said Ms. Slater. "Now, books out."

Out of the corner of my eye I saw Emma tapping on her phone. She caught me looking, and slid it away quickly.

What are you doing? I mouthed.

Unlike Anjali, Emma wasn't much of a texter. Emma was too laconic for that. She usually waited for the world to come to her.

Nothing, she mouthed back.

I frowned at her, but by then we were all rummaging in our shoulder bags and pulling out the play that we were supposed to be discussing that day. I'd read it. Most of us had, I think. It wasn't bad. There was a pretty sordid love triangle right in the middle, which always helps.

"So, anyone want to fill me in on how this usually goes?" Ms. Slater asked.

While she spoke, she hoisted up the lectern that Mr. Mitchell had banished to the corner at the beginning of the semester, and heaved it to the table at the front of the room. The spectacle of a woman in a fitted dress and kitten heels carrying a huge wooden lectern in her arms should have been hilarious, but it was actually kind of badass.

"Um," Emma hesitated. "Mr. Mitchell was going to hand back our quizzes today, I think."

She looked around at us for confirmation, and we all nodded.

"And then we were going to start talking about the play. That's our whole next unit."

"The play?" Ms. Slater said.

She strode over to my desk and flipped the book faceup.

"*The Crucible,* huh?"

"Yeah," I said. "We're doing the Salem witch trials this month. Quiz next week, then short response paper due sometime after the quiz. That was what Mr. Mitchell said Monday."

"If you're doing the Salem witch trials, what the hell are you doing reading a play about the 1950s?"

We looked around, baffled. Ms. Slater didn't wait for an answer.

"Yeah," she said. "We're not doing that. Put them away and get out your notebooks."

A dull silence hung between us as we gaped at this random woman.

"Notebooks?" she prodded. "You use them to take notes in?"

Mr. Mitchell ran AP US like a seminar. Mostly we just sat around talking in a big group. Sometimes we'd argue for as long as twenty minutes before Mr. Mitchell cut in. Nobody took notes.

"No notebooks?" Ms. Slater said in response to our nonresponse, her other eyebrow creeping up her forehead to join the first one, twin crescent moons floating under her hairline.

"Laptops?"

I cleared my throat.

"St. Joan's doesn't permit laptop use during class time," I said. "We can bring them, but they're for writing papers and stuff in study hall and the library. Otherwise they think we'll just mess around on the Web."

"Well," Ms. Slater said, leaning her elbows on the lectern. "They're probably right. So. Here's what we're going to do. You"—she pointed at Leigh, paused, and then pointed at Jennifer Crawford—"and *you* will take the paper out of *that* printer"—more pointing—"and make sure everyone has three sheets. The rest of you, bust out your pens."

Leigh and Jennifer stood, exchanging uncomfortable smiles.

"*The Crucible,*" Ms. Slater said with her back to us, writing a list of names on the blackboard while she spoke, "is a play from 1953 that is about anti-Communist anxiety in postwar American culture, and about the inscrutable Other lurking behind a seemingly unthreatening facade. And, because it's Arthur Miller, it's also about sex."

When she said that, we all snickered. Ms. Slater pretended she hadn't heard us.

"It's a hugely important work of American literature, and I'm delighted that you've read it. But this is a history class. And in history class, we aren't concerned with what Arthur Miller thinks about sex. In history class, we talk about what really happened."

We all laughed with surprise. Ms. Slater didn't talk like a regular teacher. Leigh raised her hand.

"Question, Miss Carruthers," Ms. Slater said, pointing with her chalk.

"But isn't *The Crucible*, like, about the Salem witch trials?" Leigh asked.

"No," Ms. Slater said. "Its *setting* is the Salem witch trials. Different thing entirely."

"But aren't the characters all, like, real people?" Leigh pressed, looking confused.

"Nope," Ms. Slater said.

She moved to the board and underlined one of the names that she'd written there: *Ann Putnam Jr.* Nobody in the play had that name.

She was at the point of saying something else when she was cut off by a shriek of sirens approaching the quad outside. The classroom full of girls froze, and the half of us by the door stood up en masse and hurried to the window, leaning over each other's shoulders and pressing our cheeks to the leaded glass to see what was happening.

Hot red lights flashed across the window.

"What's going on?" I asked, not expecting anyone to know, but asking just in case the universe felt like telling me.

"It's Clara," Jennifer Crawford breathed.

The other girls burst into a gossipy buzz.

Outside, an ambulance squealed onto the quad and bounced over the curb, squashing a forsythia as it skidded to a stop. A couple of bulky guys in jumpsuits leapt out of the ambulance and pulled out a gurney with automatic unfolding legs. Father Molloy jogged out to meet them, followed closely by the nun who was the upper school dean. There was some hand waving, the dean and Father Molloy pointing to the eastern wing of the high school. The jumpsuit guys hustled off.

The siren stayed on, lights spinning over the trees, the grass, the walkways, the stone walls knotted with winter-dead ivy, and the faces of dozens of uniformed high school girls, all of us pressing our noses to the windows.

For a long minute nothing happened.

Father Molloy and the dean moved out of our sight line, and everyone in AP US History leaned a few inches to the right, trying to improve our angle.

"You guys, they're taking Clara to the hospital," Leigh read from her phone.

"How do you know?" I asked.

"Olivia's in study hall in the classroom next to hers. She just texted me."

"Girls, I really think we should—" Ms. Slater started to say.

"No," Emma interrupted, her eyes staring steadily out into the quad, and all our heads turned to her.

"Excuse me?" Ms. Slater bristled.

"It's not Clara," Emma said, and her voice sounded quiet and flat. "Look."

We all craned our necks to see the jumpsuit guys hustling the gurney back to the ambulance. The dean and Father Molloy scrambled alongside, whispering to whoever was riding on it. Whoever it was, she was covered in a blanket and strapped down, but even at a distance, and through the wavery fishbowl glass of the casement windows, we could all see that the person was shaking. Trembling.

Twitching.

"You're right," I said, pressing my palm to the windowpane. "It's not Clara."

It was the Other Jennifer.

INTERLUDE

I reach my sleeve up to wipe my nose. Reverend Green frowns at me, creasing his fine forehead. He's pleasant to look at, leaning with his elbows on his knees like that, even with the ink staining his teeth. I think of his wife and hiccoughing baby in the hall behind me, their fat housecat gnawing on a chicken bone under the table. I gulp for breath, and start hiccoughing myself.

I am so alone. Even God has turned His face from me.

"Ann," the Reverend says, and he slowly reaches his hand forward.

He hesitates, and then rests it gently on my knee. His touch feels warm, and under all my wool and linen a rich tingling spreads across my skin. As if he can sense the effect his touch has on me, the Reverend pulls his hand away.

No one ever touches me.

"You can tell me," he says, his voice stiff.

The baby's quieted down, and Goody Green is humming. The grubby little girl is babbling to herself, beating on the table with a wooden spoon.

"Whatever it is," Reverend Green says, "all you need do is unburden yourself. Give yourself over to God."

I take a deep breath, but something bursts in me and I groan, slumping over with my forehead on my hands, my mouth open, keening. I cringe, letting the sadness flow out of me, dimly aware of footsteps coming to the door, a low woman's voice asking if I'm ill, should she fix me something warm to drink? And the Reverend saying yes, he thinks that would be best, and then getting up to close the door on the retreating footsteps.

"Ann," he says, shaking my shoulder.

His grip is rougher now.

I shake my head, no, no, no, how can I tell him what a beast I am, what the Devil has got of me? He'll send me away, they all will, and then I'll be bewildered and alone.

"Come now, Ann."

He takes my shoulders in his hands and forces me to sit up, my head lolling back on the bench, my hands beating at him to push him away. He keeps his grip. I feel safer with his hands holding me up.

"I . . . I . . . ," I gasp, choking on my own horror.

My vision starts to cloud. Reverend Green's handsome face swims before my eyes.

Then a sharp burst of white heat, and my head snaps to the side, bumping against the back of the bench. A rain of stars behind my eyes. I bring my hand to my cheek. My eyes open and travel from the floor to the Reverend's face. He frowns when he sees that I'm coming back to myself. He sits back in his armchair, rubbing his palm on his breeches.

"Master yourself, Ann," he says, his eyes sliding from me. "God sees all. We're but miserable creatures in His eyes. You may judge yourself harshly, but your judgment is nothing to God. Now. Tell me what's troubling you, or if you cannot, leave me in peace. I've a sermon to write."

"I want to lie in the dust," I blurt.

Reverend Green brings a finger alongside his temple and narrows his eyes.

"Why?" he asks.

I get to my feet and move with some unsteadiness to the window. Its panes are small, lozenge-shaped, in the old style, like the ones in my parents' house. My house, now. Outside, the sun grows longer, painting the rye field behind the parsonage in deep veins of gold. I've been coming to this parsonage since I was a child. My reflection makes a ghost on the windowpane, and I can see the crimson stripes deepening on my cheek from his blow.

"Is it true, what they say happened to Judge Sewell's house?" I ask.

In the reflected glass, I see Reverend Green shift in his chair to face me.

"What do you mean?" he says carefully.

"Is it true?" I reiterate.

"The Lord works in mysterious ways. What's true to one man, a wonder and a marvel, might not seem so to another, as God didn't intend it for him."

I turn from the window, staring at Reverend Green with desperation.

"Did rocks fall from the sky and pelt Judge Sewell's house or not?" I ask him, my voice shrill.

"I don't live in Judge Sewell's house," the Reverend says. "I can't speak to it."

"But do you believe they did?" I demand. "Has the judge seen signs of God's disfavor? The village is alive with it. I must know. He's a godly man. Has he seen signs that God is turned from him?"

"I've heard," the Reverend says with hesitation, "of an afternoon, that the family praying together, there was heard a great commotion upon the roof, and the judge, being much afraid, ran from the door of his house to behold stones falling from the sky and onto his house."

I wrap my arms about my waist. "And his house only?" I choke. "None other of the houses in his neighborhood, nor his neighbors, were bedeviled with the stones?"

The Reverend clears his throat. "So I'm told. But," he says, pressing his hand flat to the surface of his desk, fastening his gaze on it as if inspecting the movement of the blood under his own skin, "I've not had that from anyone in the Sewell household. It's a story. I'm surprised to hear you repeating it."

"But it's true," I breathe.

The village had been lit up with gossip of it for weeks, and my smallest sister even appeared with a fistful of unearthly pale pebbles, claiming she'd scooped them from the yard of the Sewell house. She rained them all over our hall table, and as each pebble bounced from table to floor, I felt a drop of my soul draining out the soles of my feet.

If a man such as Judge Sewell can read God's intent to punish him so clearly, then I can hide from the truth no longer. For what is he? And what am I?

I'm no one, and I'm nothing.

To my back the Reverend says, "Were they stones sent by God bearing an awful message? Or were they the fevered musings of a man haunted by guilt? It speaks more of hailstones than brimstone to me. If Judge Sewell's subjecting his soul to harsh examination, then I'll wager he'd see falling stones wherever he looked. But—" He hesitates. "I can see that you believe it."

"I do believe it," I say. "And I want to lie in the dust. For my soul is as stained as his, if not more so."

The Reverend frowns.

"Whatever can you mean, Ann?"

"I'm in the twenty-seventh year of my age," I tell him. "In my twentieth year I lost my last parent, and took on the care of my brothers and sisters. I've no husband, nor hope of one. I work hard. I try to please God. But my soul is burdensome to me. My heart is black. I wish to humble myself before God."

Reverend Green's eyes brighten with curiosity, and he leans forward. And then I begin to talk.

CHAPTER 4

C olleen, put it away."
            I made a show of sliding my phone into my jeans pocket
            and said, "Sorry, Mom."

"Honestly, I don't know why you can't just sit with us for five minutes. What's so important? And sit up. You'll grow a hump, slouching
over like that."

"It's just Anjali, asking about the physics problem set."

"I thought you said you were already finished with physics this
weekend."

"I am, Mom. It's just Anjali had a question."

It was Anjali, that part was true, but her text had said:

Harvard sq tonite? Plz!

And I'd texted back:

What time?

"Physics," my father said, reaching across me and my brother,
Michael, for the bowl of wild rice. "I always thought I'd do physics in
college, did you know that?"

"Uh-huh," I said. This was familiar ground, my father's various imaginary alternative careers. Next he'd be telling me about the track scholarship he would have been offered at UMass if it hadn't been for his knee injury. *Men's track and field,* he always called it, saying the full name of the sport to make it sound more impressive, I guess. My pocket vibrated.

J says 9.

Oh, great. Jason.

Who else is coming?

I texted something like that. I can never be totally sure when I'm typing inside my pocket.

"I think you have a really good shot at breaking 750 on the SAT subject, if you can stay focused," my mother remarked. "But you need to stay ahead of the work."

"In fact," my father continued, "if I'd gone to UMass on scholarship, for men's track and field, I promised your grandfather that I'd do electrical engineering, with a minor in physics. Did you know he was something of an amateur scientist himself? Pass me the pepper, please, Louisa. Michael, you're not getting anything else, so you'd better go ahead and eat."

"It's nasty," said my brother, a shrimpy eighth grader whom I occasionally forgot to pay attention to, despite my best intentions.

My baby sister, Wheez, passed the pepper to my father and accepted his nod of thanks with a huge, silent smile.

"I'm glad you decided to go with UMass as your safety," Mom continued. "But I'd still like you to think seriously about a couple of your other choices. Maybe the ones out of state. I really liked Stony-brook, didn't you?"

"I like it a lot," whispered Wheez. No one pays much attention to her as a rule, and this was no exception. She was talking about the rice.

"You'll get no complaints from me, going to UMass," my father said.

"Mike. She needs to be prepared in case UMass doesn't pan out. This is a competitive year. It's not like when we were in high school."

One of my eyes crept down to the edge of my pocket under the dining table to read Anjali's response.

J's friend. Pleeeeease! U have to come.

Oh, terrific. Jason the yo-boy and one of his yo-boy friends. Jason with the magic below-ass-hovering blue jeans. I once asked Anjali how he kept them from falling down completely, and she just gave me this prissy look and didn't say anything. Jason the yo-boy with his *know-what-I'm-sayin's* and his pimp roll, which, by the way, he only just started doing this year, which I happened to know for a fact because Jason was from Pride's Crossing and I'd known him in a roundabout way since we were kids. Whenever they were together, Jason rested his hand on the back of Anjali's neck, with the thumb on one side and the fingers on the other, in this proprietary way that made Anjali all giggly and weird. Then he could steer her closer to him and nudge his nose behind her ear and call her "baby." The idea of Jason putting his hands on my friend made me feel ill.

"Of course, then I'd never have met your mother," my father continued, oblivious.

"Aw," my mother said, plopping more rice onto her plate, and some on mine, too, without asking. "BU in the seventies. Berkeley East. Are you sure you don't want to think about BU? I bet we could sneak an application in, still. You're a legacy."

"Uh-huh," I said, tapping out:

What about Deena? I bet she'd like to come

God willing.

"Dad, may I be excused?" my brother asked, eager to get back to World of Warcraft.

"Sure, go ahead. But don't forget you've got dish duty tonight. You think you might want to study physics, Colleen? It's a great field."

Nah . . . J just invited you

Crap.

"Honey?"

Not listening, I typed out:

9 is kind of late

"Colleen?"

PLEEEEEASE!

"Dammit!"

A fork clattered onto a plate and then my mother was standing behind my chair.

"Give it to me," she said, her hand thrust out.

"Mom," I started to protest, but my father spoke over me.

"Come on, Linda," he said.

"Five minutes! It's all I ask!" My mother's voice rose while she waited for me to surrender my phone.

I was clenching my fingers around it inside my pocket and glaring at her. Inside my palm the phone vibrated again.

My father sighed and rubbed his fingertips over his eyebrows and under his glasses. He spoke from behind his hands.

"Colleen," he said. "Next time, we'll leave the phone in your room, okay?"

"I meant to this time," I lied. "I just forgot."

My mother stalked back into the kitchen, muttering "Forgot!" to the invisible committee to whom she liked to refer my family's crimes. The swinging door *whooshed* closed, and sounds of running water and disapproving dishes let me know in no uncertain terms where I stood this particular Saturday evening.

My father's eyes followed her out of the breakfast nook and then hung out for a while on the kitchen door before making their way back to me. He sighed with world-weary resignation. I could tell we were done talking about physics.

"So," he said. "What've you got on for tonight, Colliewog?"

My father was subject to fits of nostalgia, but he wasn't a fool.

"Anjali wants me to meet her and Jason in Harvard Square," I said. It was hard for me to keep the annoyance out of my voice.

"Jason Rothstein?" my father said. He leaned back in his chair and toyed with his beer bottle, lifting it and setting it down in a different spot to make a lattice of water circles on the tabletop. "They're still an item, eh?"

I laughed. Nobody says "they're an item" except parents.

"They are," I confirmed.

Dad made more bottle-circle prints until the pattern resolved into a flower. He reached over with a meditative thumb and smeared a stem.

"Anyone else going?" he asked.

"Some friend of Jason's. Some yo-boy who thinks saying 'all up in here' is standard speech filler that normal people use in regular every-day conversation."

I thought my father smirked, but he wisely kept any further commentary to himself.

"What time will you be back?"

"I dunno. Not late."

Dad nodded, and picked up his beer bottle. He tipped it to the side, weighing it in his hand, and found it empty. We both sat there for another minute, listening to the water in the kitchen sink shut off with a smack and the tinkle of glassware being taken out of the dishwasher and forcefully put away.

"It's just 'cause she's going to miss you next year," he said without looking too closely at me.

My cheeks flushed pink.

"I know," I said.

My right finger and thumb pulled my napkin through my left finger and thumb, ironing it out in a slowly revolving circle.

Dad crossed his ankle over his knee.

"Well," he said, "have a good time. Call if you need anything. Or if your plans change. Long as we know where you are."

"Okay," I said, getting to my feet. I picked up my plate and made to carry it into the kitchen, but Dad arched an eyebrow at me, looked pointedly at the kitchen door, and then shook his head. I lowered the plate back to the breakfast table and smiled at him. He smiled back.

"Frankly," he said, "I like that you're glued to that goddamn phone. You show me one father who isn't happy to know he can always reach his daughter no matter what."

I grinned, kissed him on the cheek, and scurried back to my room to get ready. I peered at my face, wondering if there was a way to fade freckles and wishing my nose weren't quite so snubby. I stuck my tongue out at myself, drew dark liner on my eyelids, and texted Anjali.

Meet at 9 by the newsstand.

J's friend better be cute.

January in Massachusetts can be peripatetic. That's a two-dollar SAT word, *peripatetic,* meaning either "wandering around" or "a student of the school of Aristotle." This time I meant it in the wandering-around sense, both that the weather comes and goes in unpredictable ways, dumping a foot of snow one day and then simmering it into slush the next, and that there was a restlessness in the air, a sense that something was about to happen. Though standing in Harvard Square maybe had something Aristotelian about it, too. Scholarly. Skeptical. Less famous than Plato.

I stood in my peacoat right at nine, damp with sweat because it was one of those nights that looked cold but wasn't, waiting for Anjali and them to get there. I didn't know why I bothered to be on time—Jason was always late. Then when I got annoyed about it, he'd tell me I "gots to chill," and I'd seriously want to smack him in the teeth.

Harvard Square is always a scene, and this Saturday was no different. Everyone was out soaking up some of the unseasonable warmth. Some gutter punk kids had started a drum circle in the Pit. The same homeless guy was selling *Spare Change News.* Grizzled Cambridge types in army surplus jackets hunched over chessboards, timers ticking. Bands of Harvard girls picked their way along the sidewalk, trying to keep their heels from getting caught in the bricks. I leaned against a lamppost, trying to look preoccupied so no weirdos would bother me. It's tricky, looking indifferent enough to keep weirdos at bay but engaged enough that your friends can find you. I usually go for a mix of busy/preoccupied/mysterious, as if I were a woman freshly arrived off an international flight from Geneva and just here looking for my driver.

"Waiting for someone?" said a voice next to my ear.

I jumped. Not something someone freshly arrived from Geneva would do.

The voice belonged to a fresh-looking guy about my age, the kind of guy who smells like soap. His hands were in his pockets, and he had a 1990s retro haircut, short in the back, sideburns, long on top. Button-down shirt under an open barn jacket. He was lean, and standing with his shoulders rounded forward the way tall guys do when they want to be able to hear what a girl is saying. He had a dimple in his left cheek, and the beginnings of lines around his eyes. I smiled.

"Um, yeah," I said. "Sort of."

"Me too," he said, looking off across the crowd of punk-rock drummers.

One of the gutter punk kids, a skinny boy with long cockleshell dreads and a ripped Minor Threat T-shirt, got up in the center of the Pit and coiled his arms and legs in rhythm. The guy in the button-down shirt watched the punk dancer, smiling as though thinking of a private joke. He shifted his weight, and then somehow we were waiting together.

"They'll be here any minute," I said.

I didn't want him getting any ideas. Not all weirdos look like weirdos at first.

"Oh, yeah, mine too." He nodded.

A long pause while we both pretended to scan the crowd for

familiar faces. The new quiet between us grew awkward, lying there under the sound of the drumming.

"So," he said. "Who-all're you waiting for?"

"Just a friend of mine from school. Her and her boyfriend." I added this second part so he'd know a guy was coming. He got the hint, and shifted an inch or so away from me.

"You go here?" he said, gesturing over his shoulder with his chin.

He meant Harvard. Harvard kids always talked like that.

"Nah," I said. I didn't elaborate.

"BU?" he asked.

"No, no. I'm not in college," I said, feeling foolish, though I didn't know why. I mean, I'd be in college soon enough, right? Maybe even "here."

He ducked his head nearer to my ear and said, "Me neither."

"Oh, yeah?"

I was surprised. I'd thought he was older. Most high school guys don't wear button-down shirts unless they're forced to. He had this casual-dressy way about him, loafers and everything, but it didn't look as pretentious as I'm probably making it sound. He carried himself the way I imagined college guys did, though I knew enough actual college guys to know that they were as likely to be in cargo shorts and flip-flops and backward Red Sox caps as any of the guys at St. Innocent's, our brother school.

"Where do you go?"

"Andover," he said.

He wasn't embarrassed about it, either. Usually when I met kids from Andover, they were all apologetic about it, like they didn't want to make me uncomfortable for being such a plebe. Then I'd tell them I went to St. Joan's, and they'd be okay again. I could actually see the boarding school kids exhale with relief when I said that.

"I just hang out in the Square because I'm so punk rock. Obviously." He smiled an ironic smile over my shoulder.

I grinned. "Obviously."

"Where do you go?"

"St. Joan's," I said.

"Oh, yeah," he said, nodding his comprehension. Yep. Typical. Another inch of space formed between us while I waited for him to ask me if I knew Clara Rutherford, because that was what everyone always asked when I said I went to St. Joan's. But he didn't.

"I don't know how you deal," I said. "Boarding."

"Oh? Why's that?"

"I don't know. It's just—I'd be homesick. Don't you get homesick?"

"I guess I did at first, maybe. But no, not really. My parents live in Belmont. So I come in most weekends anyway."

He paused, and I stole a look at him from under my eyelashes, quickly so he wouldn't notice. He was still smiling, but his dimple was gone. I suspected that maybe he did get homesick after all. With his face soft like that, he looked good. Better. I glanced down at myself, wishing I'd maybe thought to put on a skirt or something instead of running out of the house in jeans and boots like it wasn't Saturday and I wasn't going to the Square.

"Anyway," he added, "it's pretty cool, being on your own. Like college."

"Yeah," I said, my eyes roaming over the faces of the throng. I could easily pick out the college kids. A lot of them looked preoccupied and tired.

"You're a senior, right? You know where you want to go next year?" he ventured.

Talking to him felt deceptively easy. So easy it made me examine him more closely, to see what he really wanted. I tended to assume that people who were too nice were being that way because they wanted something. Maybe because at St. Joan's, that was often the case.

"Um," I demurred, "I'm not really sure. I'm applying, like, a million places."

The trick, when someone asked me where I was applying, was to see if they were sniffing around to find out if I was their competition. Was my list the same? Was it different? How smart was I? Was I smart enough that they should be worried?

"Here?" he asked, gesturing with his lifted chin to the gate behind us leading to Harvard Yard.

"Yeah," I said. A flush crept up my neck and started to wrap itself around my ears.

His smile broadened as he said, "Me too."

He didn't look threatened, or worried. He looked . . . happy.

A gap opened up in the crowd of people pouring out of the mouth of the T station, and in the gap I spotted Anjali, looking older without her school uniform, her fingers threaded through an indifferent hand that was loosely attached to a boy with a skinny beard lining his jaw who was wearing a red tracksuit. Yeah, I said a tracksuit. They were half an hour late, and Jason pimp-rolled his way over to where we were standing with such studied care that it felt like another half an hour before they finally got to the newsstand. I felt the boy in the button-down shirt slide his eyes over to watch me watch them.

"Colleen!" Anjali squealed, rushing up to give me a hug even though we'd just seen each other at school the day before.

"Hi, Anj," I said, embracing her. "Hey, Jason."

"'Sup," said the always-articulate Jason, tilting his head to the side.

I turned to the boy in the button-down, embarrassed, trying to come up with a way to make introductions. But I needn't have bothered.

"Spence. My man," said Jason as he slap-clicked their hands together and then back-pounded him in a bro-hug.

The boy in the button-down gave me a sheepish look.

"So *you're* Colleen," he said.

I blinked in surprise at Jason's decidedly not-yo-boy friend and smiled.

"Guilty," I said.

"You guys, I am starving," Anjali announced, bouncing on her toes with a hand on Jason's sleeve. "I'm dying for waffle fries. Don't you want waffle fries?"

"I also am dying for waffle fries," Spence said with just a little too much formality, gently teasing Anjali but still watching me.

"Do you think we could get into Charlie's? Is it early enough?" Anjali looked from Jason to me and back. "It's totally early enough, right?"

"Yeah, baby," Jason said, resting his hand on the back of her neck, a thumb in her hair, and starting to steer her away from the Pit. "We'll get in, no problem. I know the bouncer."

We moved together, the four of us, weaving our slow way through the Saturday night crowds washing over the Square. I watched Jason's hand resting on Anjali's neck and felt my fists ball up inside my coat pockets. The boy in the button-down shambled along beside me. I could feel him looking at me every so often. Why had I worn a peacoat, for God's sake? I could have borrowed Mom's trench at least.

"*Spence,*" I said after a while, arching an eyebrow. "Seriously?"

He laughed once, his mouth open, and did a funny jump-step in his gait.

"Which is worse," he said, "the fact that my name's really Spence, or the fact that Jason even talks like that at headmaster's tea?"

We were just early enough to get into Charlie's without being carded, but only if we made a beeline for the back stairs and didn't look anyone in the eye. The lobsters in their downstairs tank watched us slink by, and I imagined they were waving their feelers with extra-pathetic desperation as we passed, maybe hoping to hitch a ride to safety. We thumped up the stairs and found a big guy with a shaved head settling in for the long haul on a bar stool at the top, but he waved us in without saying anything.

Jason said "Thanks, dude" in the guy's general direction, but the guy either didn't hear him or didn't care, so I guessed this was Jason showing off for Anjali's benefit.

Of course the upstairs was already full. Not packed, not so tight you'd have to elbow your way to the bar and you'd never get your food, but full. Every booth and chair had someone parked in it, everywhere we turned were faces thrust together, pint glasses of beer and plastic baskets of hamburgers and waffle fries. We hesitated, befuddled, before Jason elbowed past us to establish his bona fides at the bar. I didn't have a lot good to say about Jason, but he knew how not to stand out when the bouncer's just waved everyone in.

"Oh my God, we're never going to get a table," Anjali shouted in my ear.

Already this night was turning into a total bust.

"We could just go for pizza instead," I hollered back.

"All right, we're good. What d'you guys want?" Jason yelled upon his return from the bar. He was holding a pint glass of something dark and amber colored.

"Coke," said Spence, turning to me. "Coke's okay by you, right?"

"Yeah," I said.

I was kind of relieved, actually. It's not that I had a problem with people drinking. Not exactly. Everyone did it, basically. I didn't know why I was so on edge. Something about Jason just brought that out in me.

"Jasoooooooon," Anjali whined. "We're never going to get a table. Do you think we'll ever get a table?"

Just then, I noticed a girl who was sitting at a corner table by herself. It was way too big for one person, the circular kind that's meant for like five people, and she had at least one empty chair next to her. Empty, except for a coat and a handbag heaped in a way that was clearly meant to indicate that someone was sitting there when someone really wasn't. It was a Coach handbag, from the outlet store,

43

just like mine. I recognized it because Emma and I had bought them together.

"Emma?" I called.

It was too loud, though, and she didn't hear me. Emma was looking into a pint glass of her own, something lighter than whatever Jason was drinking, and it was nearly empty. She looked like she'd been sitting there for a while.

"Oh my God, EMMA!" Anjali squealed and rushed over to Emma's table.

Anjali's arms were around her neck before Emma could register what was happening.

"Anjali?" she started to say, and her eyes hunted back through the crowd to settle first on Jason, then on me, and quickly she rearranged her features into a semblance of happiness to see us.

"This is so awesome! I didn't know you were going to be here," Anjali said. "Can we join you?" Jason was already moving Emma's coat and handbag off the chair.

"Hey," I said, settling next to Emma. "What's up?"

She looked sort of nervous. She even pulled out her phone and scrolled through her texts and frowned before putting it away.

"Emma, this is Spence. Spence, Emma. She goes to St. Joan's with Anjali and me."

I gestured to Button-Down Boy, who made like he was toasting Emma with his Coke, said "Madam," and then sat back to give us room to talk.

"Were you waiting for someone?" I asked.

I didn't remember what Emma had told me she was doing that night, but she definitely hadn't said anything about hanging out in the Square.

"Um. Kind of?" she said. "But it's good to see you guys. This is better anyway."

She didn't say whom she'd been waiting for. I thought about asking, but the waitress appeared with menus, and we turned ourselves to the pressing decision of how many orders of waffle fries to get, and did we also want onion rings, and since two of us had beers already, could we get away with ordering three more, which, it turns out, we could, because some Saturdays just work out that way and nobody hassles us even though we're still in high school.

To be honest, I don't really remember what else we talked about that night. I'm pretty sure we didn't talk about Clara Rutherford, because the guys wouldn't have heard about it, and what would be the point? We'd have wanted them asking questions about *us,* not Clara. Two guys and three girls, and all three of us friends, and even if one of the guys was Jason, it was still fun to laugh and tease one another and jockey for attention. I'm willing to bet we didn't talk about Clara Rutherford for one second.

The only reason I even remember that night at all is that I met Spence. And that it was so weird coming across Emma, sitting alone at Charlie's, waiting for someone who never came.

INTERLUDE

SALEM VILLAGE, MASSACHUSETTS
MAY 30, 1706

*J*t was January 10," I say to Reverend Green.

He looks confused. "This last January?"

It's not his fault. He's heard what happened, maybe he's even read the book about it, but he didn't live here then. I have to explain.

"No." I shake my head. "A long time hence. I was thirteen," I say. "January 10, 1691/92, with the old calendar. I was supposed to be home already, but Abby Williams stopped me."

"Oh!" the Reverend says, sitting up straighter in his chair.

Recognition splits open his fine features. His hands twitch for the ruffle of linen at the end of his sleeve, and he glances at the door that hides his wife away. I can feel him wanting to summon her, but I want his attention for myself alone. It's time someone listened to me and heard the truth.

"Come see Betty with me," Abby says.

I'm supposed to be home already, my mother's waiting, but Abby's stopped me, and it's hard to break away when Abby's stopped me. She's smaller than I am, small for eleven, and her work in the parsonage keeps her busy most days, but on the days when Abby sneaks off alone, there's no stopping her, whatever you might wish for yourself.

"Betty?" I say. "I can't. They're waiting for me."

"I've never seen one so amazed. Or so stupid. You have to come. Hurry up!"

Abby takes my hand in hers, her grip rough from work, and hauls me along behind her. I struggle to keep up. My hand in Abby's is a soft thing, like a snail, and I fear she could crush it if she chose. Goody Parris never lets her rest much since Abby was bound out to her. Goody Parris runs a household empty of idleness, and no food for wasters. It's why Abby's so thin.

"But Abby," I protest, hunting for a reason to escape.

It's my fault for dawdling. Mother sent me these two-odd hours ago for some thread, silk if I could get it, and I could, of course, but then it's so rare I get a couple of hours to myself. She usually makes my sister go with me. I loitered by the Common for a time, and then I looked in on Mary Warren, who insisted I come inside because my mittens were crusted with snow. It took much longer to warm the mittens than I'd planned, time pleasantly spent eating corn bread with molasses and talking, and then I was late, and feeling idle and ashamed.

Now I'm being punished. As soon as the thought comes to me, I feel deeper shame. God's not about to punish my idleness with a visit to Abby Williams. I can't help it, though. She makes me uneasy. Mother says I should pity her and show Christian charity and take her for my friend. But I hate to do it.

We burst into the parsonage's door, and Tittibe Indian cries, "Be wiping those feet, now! You! Abby!" because we've trailed in mud, and with the hall door open we're blowing a gale into the house.

Abby ignores her, frowning and pulling me harder by the hand. "She's in the loft," Abby says to me.

We mount the ladder. A chunk of ice loosens from my boot and falls to the floor with a thud and shatters.

"You, Ann Putnam!" Tittibe calls after me, planting her hands on her hips. "Why you want to make trouble for me?"

"I don't want to make trouble for you, Goody Indian," I call down through the hatch.

Abby's face darkens. "Why're you calling her that?" she asks, poking me hard.

I blink at Abby, confused. "Why, what should I call her?"

"Call her nothing," Abby spits. "She vexes me all the time."

I shrink away from Abby, but don't contradict her. Mother says we must be kind and godly to slaves, too, if they're Christians. Tittibe loves Jesus, even though she came from that island where the Reverend lived before he came to us. She's told me stories of the island. How the sun always shines there. How she never saw snow 'til she came to this Massachusetts, and she thought it would be soft to touch, like goose down, which it sometimes is, but she didn't know how cold it would be. Now when I imagine Tittibe's island, I dream of the sun shining, and everyone sitting on clouds like in heaven, and lots of good things to eat, and fruit all year round. But Mother tells me it wasn't like that. When I ask her what it was like, she tells me to be quiet.

"There," Abby interrupts me. "Look at her."

Betty Parris is lying in her trundle, with her eyes closed and her cap on, her hands clasped under her chin like a cherub. It's strange to see her lying in bed so late in the day, and her face in the thin January light looks pinched and white. I breathe out through my mouth, and a cloud of mist billows around my head. The cold in the loft is sharp, and ice has grown thick on the loft window over Betty's head. Abby's frowning down at her.

"Betty," Abby says.

She pokes her. Betty doesn't move.

"What, is she sleeping?" I ask.

Betty's younger than Abigail, about eight or nine, and you can see in the slope of their cheeks and the shape of their noses that they're kin. But Betty's hands are softer than Abigail's. She's the minister's daughter, and one of the elect, most probably.

"She's not sleeping," Abby says. "She's lain so all day. Let me carry in all the snow to melt myself. Whore's daughter. Bedbug. Imp!"

I should be shocked, but Abby's always talking so. Her mouth is something to behold, when it gets going.

"Is she ailing?" I whisper, leaning in closer.

I bring my hand, hesitating, to Betty's forehead, as I do for my younger sisters when they won't be gotten up. I half expect to find her boiling hot, clammy with her own sweat. But the skin is cool. Too cool. I wonder if she has enough blankets, if there's a draught that's taking her.

"She's not AILING," Abby bellows, her mouth close to Betty's ear. The younger girl doesn't stir. "She's a ROGUE."

Abby goes in for a vicious pinch on Betty's side, hard enough to make anyone squeal. Betty doesn't make a sound.

Downstairs, I hear Tittibe Indian holler, "You vexing me, girls! Quiet down!"

"Betty?" I say, grasping her shoulder and shaking her gently.

Her eyes stay closed, and her hands folded under her chin. I place my hands on hers and try to move them, but they won't be moved. She's holding them there, tight, and people don't do that when they're come over feverish or asleep, so now I'm sure she's malingering. To cross Abigail, most likely.

"See?" Abby says, petulant. She sits back on her heels and crosses her arms over her thin chest. "They never beat her, and they beat me all the time. She's a whorechild, and I hate her."

"Abby, please," I say, shaking my head.

Abby steps back and sulks.

"Now, Elizabeth," I whisper to Betty in my most soothing voice. "You know she doesn't mean it. She never did. See?"

49

Not a peep from Betty Parris. I rub my hands up and down her arms, bringing warmth to them.

"It were a cold day today, sure," I murmur. "Who'd want to carry in snow? All those heavy buckets? No one would. Now, God's seen your sin, and He pities you. But God made winter, too, and doing our work well gives Him glory, doesn't it? Wouldn't your papa say so?"

I rub harder.

"Open them eyes, Betty," Abby hisses in her ear.

"Shht," I shush Abby with a sour look. I'm older. I know about the special languor smaller children get in wintertime. "Abby, you fetch a mug of hot cider from Tittibe, that's all we be needing. Isn't that so, Betty?"

Abby gives me a dark look and whispers "I hate her" before stomping down the ladder into the hall.

Downstairs I hear voices, Abby's irritable and Tittibe's aggravated. The clanking of a long spoon in a metal pan. The pop of the fire.

"There, my Betty, she's gone now. It's safe. You can open your eyes."

A tiny flicker of movement on Betty Parris's face. One eye opens and peeks at me, like my baby brother does when he is playing now-you-see-me, now-you-don't. I smile at her, encouraging.

"See?" I whisper. "All'll be well. You tell Abby you're sorry, you'll help with chores tomorrow. Give thanks to Jesus for your keeping and tell him you're sorry, too, and all's right."

The other eye opens. They are wide and watery and blue.

"It's so cold, Annie," her tiny voice whispers from under the blankets.

"I know it is," I reassure her.

"I just . . ."

The eyes blink, and a tear puddles up and rolls down her cheek to her ear. The pale white nose bubbles and starts to turn pink.

"Shh," I say, petting an escaped curl with my thumb. "You can make it right tomorrow, can't you? Sure you can."

More stomping as Abby hoists herself, muttering, up the loft ladder, climbing with her left hand and her right elbow so she can grip

50

a little pewter cup. Her feet keep tangling in her skirts. I spy Tittibe's head, wound in a scarf, coming up the ladder behind Abby's feet. Betty sees them climbing into the loft and shuts her eyes tight with a squeak.

"Here," Abby says, thrusting the cup under Betty's nose.

It's warm enough that I can see the steam, and my mouth waters at the apple-y smell.

"She'd better drink it, after all that, or by God, I will," Abby grumbles.

Tittibe hoists herself through the trapdoor, clambers to her feet with a grunt, and joins me at the bedside, smiling down at the form in the trundle. She's wearing a patched jacket that I remember Goody Parris wearing at meeting last year, the one that was later ruined by a scorch from a firebrand. Now the jacket's dusted with cornmeal, and there's a thin mask of it on Tittibe's face. She has holes in her ears for rings, but she doesn't wear them. Whenever I'm near her, I have trouble not staring at her ears. I wonder if on her island everyone wears jewels like that, in their skin.

"How my Betty be, now?" she asks. "She feeling more herself?"

"I give thanks to God, Goody Indian," I say, prodding Betty's leg through the covers where no one can see. "I think Elizabeth'll be quite well. By tomorrow."

But Betty Parris is squenching her face tight closed, and she hasn't sat up to take the cup yet. We all wait, Abby's face darkening. A long minute passes with us three staring down at the girl in the trundle bed.

Downstairs, a door slams, and a deep man's voice growls, "Here, now. John? I've had to put the mare away myself. Five o'clock, and an empty house! What, am I to be starved, too, on top of everything else?"

The sound shatters the fragile peace in the attic. Without warning the cup strikes my cheek and the cider's burning my eyes and dripping down my face. Betty's flown out of bed and hurled herself into Tittibe's arms, her eyes straining wide, her mouth open, red and wailing.

CHAPTER 5

When Dad dropped me off that next Monday, there was a news van parked on the cul-de-sac leading to the upper school building, and a woman in a bright purple suit and newscaster makeup was conferencing with a guy with a camera on his shoulder. Channel 7, the local ABC affiliate. It was a dull morning, not too cold, and the camera's spotlight lit up the front of the school with a flat white glow.

"Huh," Dad said, leaning forward to squint out the windshield.

"That's weird," I said from behind my travel mug of apple cider. The dregs are the best part, where all the cinnamon collects in the bottom.

"What's going on? You know?"

"No idea."

"Guess we'll find out on the news tonight," Dad said. "You walking home today?"

"Kinda cold. I'll get a ride with Deena."

"Great. See you at six."

I hoisted my backpack into place and waded into the river of girls flowing toward the school doors. The reporter had been joined by

52

Father Molloy, whose face looked gray and tired. The interview was already under way, but I couldn't hear them over the sound of other girls chattering around me, cars pulling up, doors slamming.

When I finally drew near enough, I could make out the reporter saying, "But Father Molloy—"

"I'm sorry, but I really can't say any more, and I can't stress enough how important it is to give these families privacy. Thank you." Father Molloy turned to the cameraman and added, "That's it. We're done," while making a throat-slicing motion with his hand.

The spotlight snapped off, throwing the front of the upper school into Gothic shadow. The gargoyles perched on the corners of the building grinned down at us, tongues lolling. The reporter's microphone drooped like a wilted flower.

"This is a crock," she said to Father Molloy. The girls standing on either side of me giggled, and the priest scowled at us and turned his back.

"Well, I guess I can understand why you'd feel that way, but that's all we're prepared to say at this time," he said, trying to keep out of our earshot.

"I think you're really missing an opportunity here, Father. The community deserves to know what's happening. They want to know that our children are safe."

"Oh, give it a rest, TJ."

TJ Wadsworth did the local morning show and reported for the evening news. She was usually assigned to cover human-interest stories, which in our town could be anything from trends in dog Halloween costumes to domestic violence and murder. Danvers is a funny place that way.

"We both know why you're here," Father Molloy continued. "And it has nothing to do with what the community deserves to know. You're really a vulture, you know that?"

"We're here to talk about the safety of teenage girls, Father Molloy. Or isn't the church concerned with that anymore?"

The priest's eyes flashed, and he took a step nearer to her, his hands in fists at his sides.

"Don't you ever," he hissed, "*ever* question our commitment to our students' safety and well-being. Not while I'm present. Understand?"

TJ Wadsworth started to object, but Father Molloy had turned his back on her.

"Okay, girls." He raised his voice and spun both index fingers in a let's-get-this-show-on-the-road gesture. "Show's over. Let's get in and start our day, what do you say?"

Without waiting for our response, the priest stalked to the ornate double doors of the upper school and flung them open. We moved behind him, a sea of girls in matching uniforms, murmuring among ourselves and casting the occasional look over our shoulders at the reporter and her cameraman. "The kids have a right to be safe, Father! Any of you guys want to talk to us, just call the station!" she called after us.

But then the doors closed. And though they would talk about it, and they would speculate and reconstruct and imagine, no one outside of St. Joan's would see what happened next.

"Colleen is sad and loooooonely, for her I cry, for heeeeeer, dear, onlyyyyyy . . ."

The haunting tune wafted its way down the hall, drifting over the heads of my classmates, echoing on the flagstone floor, resonating in the polished wood of the walls, and I grinned. Deena. This week's song was "Body and Soul." That song would worm its way into my brain, I knew it. Since it was Monday, I suspected she was already sitting in chapel, and maybe even saving me a seat.

The nuns who used to live and pray at St. Joan's back when it was a convent belonged to an order that flickered out of existence sometime early in the twentieth century. We'd see pictures of them here and there in the halls, especially in the disused dormitory wing—framed black-and-white photos of serious girls in wimples all lined up in a row, with rope knotted around their waists, bleached almost white from time. I didn't really know much about them, but Joan of Arc was their patron saint, and I heard that they died out in part because girls were required to join by the time they were fifteen.

The doors into the chapel were made of the same heavy carved oak studded with iron bolts as the front doors of the upper school, but the inside of the chapel was as narrow and light and airy as a medieval Gothic church. The light was flecked with bright colors, gleaming through the stained-glass panels that ringed the back of the ambulatory. In candlelight the whole chapel glowed like a jewel.

All of the stained-glass panels in the chapel showed images of St. Joan's life. My favorite was the one of her on horseback, dressed in armor, her hair streaming behind her. She held the reins in one hand and a spear in the other, and her mouth was open, urging all the troops behind her onward into battle. Both of the horse's front legs were drawn up, as though about to rear, his eyes rolling back in his head. I got shivers whenever I looked at it.

My least favorite was the one of Joan burning at the stake. The flames were made of these long shards of red and orange glass, and there were coils of smoke in black iron tracery all around her. But Joan looked different in that panel—her mouth closed, her hands bound before her, and her eyes looking up at heaven in this beatific way. Instead of her armor she was dressed in a white linen shift with a bow at the neck, like what a little girl would wear to bed. A crowd of people milled around her, their hands clasped in prayer, looking on with these fake sorrowful faces, as if they really wished they could do something but couldn't be bothered. But Joan didn't seem to mind. Her face was smooth and passive.

It pissed me off. I hated seeing Joan look okay with being burned alive.

"What's up?" I whispered to Deena as I slid into the pew next to her. I realized that I'd missed Deena over the weekend. Emma was my best friend, but that was mostly because we had so much history together. I didn't like to admit it to myself, but Deena and I had more in common.

She shuffled her coat and backpack out of the way and smiled at me. She'd changed up her dreads, weaving them into two heavy braids and pinning them behind her head like an Edwardian lady.

"Nothing much," she said with a shrug. "Boring weekend. You?"

"It was okay, I guess."

"How's Jason?" Deena asked, in the mock-sighing way she used to make fun of Anjali.

"Two words sum up my experience of Jason this weekend. And those words are *track*. And *suit*."

Deena threw her head back and laughed, clapping her hands.

"Yes!" she said. "My God, I love that boy."

The sound in the chapel rose as girls filed in, each class pooling in their allotted section of pews, seniors on the front left, juniors front right, sophomores rear left, freshmen rear right, middle school in the upper central gallery, lower school flanking them in the choir gallery on either side.

Emma dropped into her seat next to me, nudging me with an elbow in greeting. I smiled back at her, but it was a habitual smile. She'd seemed pretty miserable on Saturday night. She sucked at pretending to have fun. Even Spence had thought so when we talked about it Sunday, and he didn't even know her.

Anjali came huffing in just behind her, not looking up from her lightning-thumbs on her phone, and dropped into the seat on Emma's other side. The sound of girls grew deafening, each squeal or chatter or footfall magnified by the echo off the glass windows and stone floor.

I didn't see Clara Rutherford. Or the Other Jennifer.

"All right, all right, find your seats," intoned the upper school dean, a gray-faced nun in practical shoes, waving her hands like someone trying to conduct an orchestra that hadn't rehearsed.

Teachers picked their way to seats among the various classes, choosing them seemingly at random, though the careful eye could discern that they chose spots next to known troublemakers. The sound in the chapel lowered to a simmer.

"NOW THEN," the dean said, too close to the mic.

A squeal of feedback whined through the sound system and we all flinched, some of us putting our hands over our ears. *"OW-UH!"* a small girl's voice echoed in the choir loft. Someone else said, *"Shhhhh!"* and she settled down.

"Now then," the upper school dean tried again.

"Mary, pray for us. Amen." A quick cross of herself, and those of us who were Catholic followed suit. "As you can imagine," she continued, resettling her glasses on her nose, "we have some important announcements, so I'd like to get started right away. You all probably noticed the news van at the front of the upper school when you arrived this morning."

She scanned our faces, waiting. No one spoke.

"Well, the first thing is that we urge you to avoid speaking to the press. I know they can seem awfully friendly, and it's very exciting having someone with a camera want to talk to you, but we don't need to be airing any of our private business to them. You are all young ladies of St. Joan's, and one of our school precepts is to behave with honor, both in public and in private. It's part of the pledge you all sign at the beginning of the school year, and this is the kind of situation in which I would ask you to remember what you've promised. There's no need to speak with anyone outside of school and your families. Just ignore them."

Soft murmuring circulated in the pews. Deena and I exchanged a look. Out of the corner of my eye I could see Emma gazing at the chapel ceiling, lost in her own thoughts. Her eyes glimmered in the candlelight.

"Now, because I don't want any of you to be concerned, I've asked

Miss Hocking to say a few words that will clarify the situation and hopefully put your mind at ease. Miss Hocking?"

The school nurse had pulled her hair back into a chignon to make herself look more serious and had procured a white coat. She always used to wear those casual nurse blouses, the ones that come with teddy bears and stuff on them. But now she was straight-up white-coated.

"Good morning, girls," she said.

Part of me thought that though she looked serious, it was an artificial seriousness. It looked like she was trying hard not to enjoy herself.

"I'm sure you've all heard what happened to a couple of our seniors last week. Now, first of all, I want you to know that I've talked with the families of all three of the girls, and they're all doing just fine."

A frisson of excitement thrummed through the pews. Deena and Emma and Anjali and I exchanged quickly mouthed confusion: *Three? I only knew about Clara and the Other Jennifer. Who's the third? Three? What is she talking about?* All around us blue phone screens flipped on, and thumbs started to move.

The thrumming didn't abate until the upper school dean stood up and bellowed, "LADIES. Your attention to Miss Hocking, please!"

Phones slid back into sweater sleeves and voices quieted down.

"As I was saying. They're all doing just fine, and they're expected to be back in school later this week. So I don't want any of you to be concerned. For those of you who were present when your friends fell sick, we know it was scary, and I just want to reiterate this very important fact: they are just fine. There's nothing to be concerned about. If you have any questions about what's happened, now's the time."

We all paused, looking at each other. Then Leigh Carruthers's hand shot up. Of course.

"Miss Carruthers," the upper school dean called on her.

"Yeah, sorry, who's the third one?" Leigh called out, and we all murmured our assent in wanting to know.

The nurse and the dean exchanged a look, and the nurse leaned into the microphone to say, "Unfortunately, I'm not at liberty to say. Confidentiality. Are there any other questions?"

A hand in the center gallery shot up, from the seventh-grade section.

"What do they think caused it?"

"That's a good question," the nurse said. She glanced at the upper school dean, who shook her head.

"As far as we can tell, all three of the girls go to the same pediatrician. At this point we think they may have gotten some vaccinations at about the same time. It's possible that they had a slight allergic reaction to a preservative in the vaccine. It's not a big deal—people have allergic reactions to vaccines all the time. The important thing is, they're going to be fine."

Almost-audible cries started going up among us, cries of "I just went to the pediatrician, like, last week!" and "I totally felt light-headed in biology on Friday."

Another hand shot up, this time from within the junior class.

"Could you tell us what signs to watch out for? I mean, if it's so common. What if more of us have it?"

Another look passed between the dean and the nurse. Miss Hocking cleared her throat.

"Well, first of all, I'd say that there's nothing for any of you guys to worry about. If you feel slightly off in any way, you're always welcome to come see me in the nurse's office."

"But what, exactly? Not all of us were there," the junior pressed, to supportive calls of "Yeah, tell us."

"You should feel free to come see me for anything at all, of course. But, let's see. Definitely come by if you feel faint, if you pass out for any reason, if you experience any unusual discomfort in your limbs, like tingling or twitching, if you have any trouble controlling your mouth or your speech. You should definitely feel free to—"

A scream rang out, and we all spun in our seats to see what was going on. A girl I didn't know, a skinny little thing with thick glasses and a bob haircut, had slumped over on her friends with her arms and legs sticking out at right angles. She was perfectly still for an instant, and then her mouth opened and her tongue stuck out and her entire body started to vibrate.

Cries of "Oh my God!" and "Has she got it, too?" burst from mouths all over the room, bouncing off the walls of the chapel, rising to a cacophony. Miss Hocking leapt out of the pulpit and sprinted down the aisle, wading through the sea of students' legs to reach the spasming girl.

"Everyone stay calm!" the upper school dean commanded into the microphone. "Girls! She's going to be fine! I need you to stay calm!"

Girls were standing up, elbowing each other to get a better look, and some of the little kids had started crying. The nurse held her hands on either side of the bobbed-hair girl's head while the girl's arms and legs shook with terrible force. Her heels beat on the floor, and her mouth issued gagging sounds that sounded primitive and animal-like.

Another scream pierced the rising chaos in the chapel, and we all looked around in increasing frenzy to see where it had come from. A second girl, this one a junior, had collapsed onto her back, arms and legs bicycling in the air, her head thrashing, her mouth spewing nonsense as all her friends looked on in horror. The force of her kicks pushed a pew out of line with a groan of wood scraping over the flagstone floor.

Everyone stood up, moving like bees in a hive. I realized that Emma and I were clutching each other, our fingers digging into each other's upper arms, our shoulders pressed together, and she whispered, "Colleen, we've got to get out of here."

I nodded, struck dumb by what I was seeing. Anjali and Deena had been swallowed by the crowd, and I couldn't see them.

"EVERYONE. I want you to WALK. Single file. Down the aisle.

And report to your advisories. NOW," the upper school dean commanded from the lectern. "Teachers, let's help our girls get organized. I want everyone to stay calm. Stay calm!"

If the dean thought we would obey her, she was mistaken. The girls of St. Joan's surged for the chapel doors, elbowing each other, screaming, some girls tripping and falling, teachers standing waist-deep in a tide of girls, pawing at our heads as we crested past them to keep us from bowling them over as we built up and then spewed in a torrent through the doors.

Over all of us, her eyes turned beatifically to heaven, stood Saint Joan, her body licked in flames.

Part 2

FEBRUARY

CANDLEMAS

Moreover, no operation of witchcraft
has a permanent effect among us.
And this is the proof thereof:
For if it were so, it would be effected
by the operation of demons.
But to maintain that the devil has power
to change human bodies or to do them
permanent harm does not seem in accordance
with the teaching of the Church.
For in this way they could destroy the whole world,
and bring it to utter confusion.

MALLEUS MALEFICARUM, PART 1, QUESTION 1

CHAPTER 6

G ood evening. Tonight, the mysterious illness that has taken over a local private school. What's causing it? And are your children at risk? St. Joan's Academy, an elite private school here in Danvers that's long been a finishing school for the daughters of the North Shore elite," the broadcast began.

I snorted. I mean, it was sort of true, I guess. Except that fully a third of us were on scholarship in one way or another. Even I had a little one, not that I liked to broadcast that to people. But say "private girls' school," and people just assume it's going to be only one way. Plaid skirts and rainbow parties and people with their parents always going out of town. I may wear a plaid skirt, but how often do my parents go out of town? Approximately never, that's how often.

". . . has been shaken by a bizarre illness that has doctors scratching their heads. School officials aren't saying what they think is causing the strange symptoms, which are manifesting as odd tics, twitching, and outbursts of disordered speech, but they are confirming that at least five students, ranging in age from thirteen to seventeen years old, are affected. And parents are worried."

"I just think they know more than they're saying," said a bleached-blond woman whose face was frozen in a stapled-back rictus of imitation youth. Below the close-up of her face a TV news caption read CONCERNED PARENT.

"Kathy Carruthers is a parent of a student at St. Joan's, and she says that she's worried for her daughter's safety," the voice-over explained.

"I mean, so far, no one's been able to give us a straight answer," Leigh's mom continued. "We just want to know how to keep our girls safe. I think it's really time that the school showed some accountability. After all, what're we paying for?"

The picture cut to the school nurse, her makeup expertly done, her white coat pressed.

"We are not at liberty to comment on the medical condition of our students," Nurse Hocking said. She managed to sound serious and concerned at the same time, which I suspected was why she, and not the upper school dean or Father Molloy, who just sounded pissed off whenever he talked to the media, had become the face of Mystery Illness 2012.

"Laurel Hocking is the nurse at St. Joan's, and she says that although she understands that the parents have some concerns, there is nothing going on that should worry them," the newscaster summarized.

"What I can say is that these are nice, wonderful, special girls, and we're all very concerned about their welfare. All five students are being given excellent care, and we're very close to figuring out what's causing the symptoms. We'll be holding a community meeting for students and parents within the next few days, and we really appreciate the community's concern."

I was impressed. She had already mastered the art of not saying much of anything at all.

The picture cut to TJ Wadsworth in her purple skirt suit standing by the Gothic doors of the upper school, a drainpipe gargoyle salivating over her shoulder, the tip of her nose pink with cold. The steps were crusted with ice and salt, and I wondered if she had a parka waiting for her in the news van.

"Harvey, the school isn't commenting on the record further. But right now, it's safe to say that as far as the Mystery Illness goes, we're left with more questions than answers. All we can do, as a community, is ask what's really happening to the girls at St. Joan's. For Channel 7 News, this is TJ Wadsworth, live in Danvers, Massachusetts."

My phone was ringing before I could even press the mute button.

"Did you see it?" I asked without preamble into the phone.

"I was just watching. Did you know it was five now for sure? I can't believe they only talked to Leigh's mom." Emma sounded amused more than anything else.

"I'd heard five, maybe more. I heard they talked to a whole lot of people. But Clara's parents won't speak to anyone."

"I heard Clara's mom's looking into hiring a publicist."

"What?" I said. "You've got to be kidding."

"That's what I heard."

"What for?"

"To handle the media, I guess. I don't know. Damage control?"

"What damage? Her daughter had a bad reaction to a vaccine. What's to control?"

"I'm not saying it's what I would do," Emma said.

"Hang on," I said. "Someone's on the other line." I clicked over. "Hello?"

"Did you see it?" Deena.

"I was just talking about it with Emma."

Deena squealed. "How Botoxed is Leigh's mom's face? Tell Emma I say hi."

"Hang on, I'll conference it," I said.

I frowned down at my cell phone, poking buttons, and then held it up to my ear.

"Hello?" I asked.

"Hello? Hello?" said Deena and Emma, overlapping.

More squeals, cries of greeting.

"Deena, Emma said she heard Clara's mom's hiring a publicist."

"Well, that makes sense," Deena said.

"It's crazy!" I insisted.

"It's not if she wants to make sure the media portrays them okay. I think it's smart, them not talking to anybody yet."

"See?" Emma said, as though that had been her position all along.

"What's with everyone being so paranoid? That report seemed okay to me."

"Kinda," Deena said. "Except for the part where TJ Wadsworth is trying to make it sound like there's some big cover-up going on, when they really just aren't allowed to talk about it. Like, legally."

"Yeah," Emma agreed. "The Rutherfords are kind of a big deal. If I were them, I'd definitely think about it. They're probably worried about news coverage hurting Clara's college chances."

"Oh my God. Do you think it could?"

"I mean, how could it not?"

"I don't know," I ruminated. "I mean, maybe it could help. Make you more interesting, you know? Memorable. My mom is always saying you have to be memorable."

"If she gets in to Tufts and I don't, I swear, I'm going to freak," Deena muttered.

"Deena, you're being crazy. You are so much smarter than her."

"Yeah. But my dad doesn't play as much squash."

"I still think it's weird," I said. "Why wouldn't they just come out and say what it is? People have reactions to shots all the time."

A silence on the three-way call.

"Um," Deena said. "Yeah. I don't know. Unless that's not what's causing it."

"You are so paranoid," Emma pointed out.

"Just because I'm paranoid," Deena countered, "doesn't mean I'm not right. I think they don't actually know what it is."

"What I want to know is, who are they?" I asked.

I'd been combing Facebook and Instagram for days and I couldn't figure it out.

"Clara," Deena counted off.

"The Other Jennifer," Emma added. "And the third one was Elizabeth."

"It was?" I asked, interrupting Deena, who was saying, "How do you know?"

"You didn't know?"

"No!"

"I heard, like, three days ago. I thought you guys knew already."

"Who told you?"

"How should I know? I don't remember. Someone."

"I checked her Facebook, 'cause I wondered. I mean, she hangs out so much with Clara and them. But she posted a status yesterday and it just said something about homework. It didn't say anything about being sick."

"Well, would you want people to know you were twitching and falling all over yourself? I wouldn't. I'd pretend like everything was normal."

"So who are the other two?" Deena wondered.

"Probably the ones who collapsed during chapel."

"Yeah, I guess."

"Yeah."

"I don't know them."

"Me neither."

We paused, worrying.

"Do you think it's contagious?" one of us said in a small voice.

"Nah. They'd have said something," another of us insisted. "They'd close the school. Bring in the CDC or whatever."

"Have you guys tried Googling it?"

"Oh, yeah. But it seems like it could be most anything. Tourette's. Allergic reactions. It's too vague. Web MD can't figure it out."

"Me neither."

"Anyway," I said, eyeing the television screen, where the newscast had moved on to talking about the weaknesses in the Patriots' offensive line. "Did your parents see it?"

"My dad did," Deena said.

"My mom is home, but she won't watch TV," Emma said. "What about Mike and Linda?"

"Not home yet," I said.

"Did you guys hear Mr. Mitchell might be back this week?"

"Um, I'm not in AP US," Deena reminded Emma.

"Sorry, that's my other line again," I said.

"That's okay, I've gotta go anyway. Catch you tomorrow," said Deena.

"Me too. Bye!" Emma rang off.

"Bye, guys," I said.

I clicked over.

"Hello?"

"Did you see it?" asked a young male voice pretending to be a young female voice.

I rolled onto my back on my bed and grinned.

"Yes," I said slowly. "Did you?"

"I did," the young male voice said, back to its normal male self. "The wardens do let us have television here, if I bribe them with cigarettes. So what's the real story, huh? Can you tell me? Is this a secure line?"

"Spence," I sighed. "You should know better than to ask if this is a secure line. Use the code phrase."

He cleared this throat. "Excuse me. This is Charlie's Kitchen. I have an order of . . ." He paused with fake gravity. "*Waffle fries* for delivery. Did anyone there order some . . . *waffle fries?*"

"I believe I did," I said, smiling.

"What the hell is this?" my father asked the mudroom.

When I roamed back into the living room an hour or so after

70

getting off the phone, I found my father frowning down at a paper in his hand, the gutted envelope it had come in bunched in his fist.

"What the hell's what?" asked my mother, coming up behind him.

She read for a minute, frowned, and plucked the paper out of his hands for a closer look.

"Colleen? Do you know anything about this?"

It was a letter, on heavy cream St. Joan's stationery, announcing that there would be a "community meeting" the following night for all parents and students in the upper school. Everyone was to convene in the chapel, and St. Joan's families were kindly requested not to speak to the media. My brother, Michael, was sitting at the breakfast table with my copy of *The Crucible* open for some reason, and earbuds in, plugged into what looked like a new phone. There wasn't any music playing in the earbuds, I suspected. It was a trick I'd taught him. He just wore them because it created a quiet barrier between him and the rest of our family. I knew he was listening to us.

"Yes," I confirmed. "I heard they might be having a meeting."

"A meeting? What for?"

"Is this about drugs?" My mother planted her hands on her hips and gave me a look straight out of a parenting pamphlet from the YMCA.

"What?" I blinked. "No! Jeez."

"Do you think we both have to go?" my father asked my mother. "Someone should stay here with Mikey. He's got a test. And there's Wheez."

This was the way my family usually remembered it had a fifth member, my baby sister, Louisa, who was seven and big on stealth. Sometimes it felt like I went days without seeing her. She could be under my bed for all I knew. I wasn't even sure if she was home right then.

From the tension in my brother's body I knew he was listening very hard. He went to St. Innocent's, our affiliated boys' school, where he was in eighth grade, and for the first time I wondered if there was talk about the Mystery Illness among the boys, too.

"I can go. I guess." My mother didn't sound pleased. "If it's important."

My father rested a paternal hand on my shoulder and looked me in the eye in that "we're really communicating" way that he had, which made me pity him in spite of myself.

"It's not about drugs, Colliewog?"

I sighed. "It's not. I swear. I'll show you."

I herded my parents back to my room, which they both hesitated to enter, each waiting for the other to go through my door first. While they sorted that out, I opened my laptop and booted it up. They stepped around heaps of clothes and made a big show of being careful not to touch any surfaces. My mother avoided looking at my Killers poster in a way that was almost acrobatic. I could hear the forcible restraint of them not commenting on the state of my room.

Both my parents' breaths warmed the back of my neck as I brought up the video of the report. A soft footfall while it was loading let me know that Michael had crept in after them, his headphones draped around his neck like a rosary.

"Nice phone, Mikey," I muttered to him. I'd been lobbying for a new phone for months.

"Oh, this?" he said, pretending to be casual. "Thanks."

"I didn't get to have a phone 'til I was in high school, you know," I remarked as three dark curly heads crowded together around my shoulders.

"I didn't get to have a phone 'til I was thirty," my mom said. "And then I paid for it myself."

My father stifled a laugh.

"Hilarious," I muttered.

I hit play on the news clip. Then, without warning, a fourth head materialized at my elbow. So Wheez had been under my bed after all.

"Hi, Wheez," I said to her.

"Hi, Colleen. Don't worry, I still don't have a phone."

"Oh, God," my mother said to the video screen. "Kathy Carruthers."

"What, Kathy Carruthers?" my father asked.

"Well, I mean. Just look at her."

"Linda, come on."

"Sorry."

They watched the rest of the video in silence. At one point, Michael whispered, "Five!"

When it was over, my parents straightened up and looked at each other.

"Okay," my mother said. "We're both going."

INTERLUDE

*E*lizabeth Parris, you're talking about?" Reverend Green asks me. "Samuel Parris's daughter?"

"The same," I confirm. "We were friends, in a way. She was the same age as one of my sisters. The Parrises would sometimes send her out to us to spare her Abby's haranguing. Betty Parris was always delicate, and Abby had no patience. I liked her. Abby was a beast, but she ran riot with us, too, me and Betty Parris and the other Betty, Betty Hubbard, and Mary Warren and them. Mary was bound out as help for the Procters, but they didn't work her as hard as the Parrises worked Abby. We were always together, doing chores, at the market square, wasting time in the Jacobses' back field, sitting at meeting and trying not to yawn, in and out of the parsonage, in and out of Ingersoll's Ordinary. It was Mary who first explained to me about the—"

I'm about to say "about the monthlies," but I catch myself in time. I'm not about to speak of such things to him, though I would rather like to see what Reverend Green looks like when he blushes. But it's true, I learned about that particular curse from Mary, and not my mother, who never deigned to talk about uncleanness.

Recalling our band of firebrands to him fills me with longing. Those girls are married now, most of them, and the better part have moved away.

But then, it was never the same with us, after.

"Anyhow," I say. "We were friends. But Abby Williams had the strongest will of us all."

"I don't know this Abby Williams," the Reverend says. "I've heard the name, is all. But the girl herself, I don't know. Did she marry?"

"No. She's gone. I don't know where. The Parrises had taken her in for service from some kin at the Eastward, who couldn't afford to keep her, and after everything was over, she vanished."

He frowns. "So this Elizabeth Parris. She was frightened of her father."

"Oh, but she was. We all were. He could freeze us with a look."

"Why would that be, with a man of God?"

The Reverend seems perturbed that a shepherd would instill fear in the weakest members of his flock. A minister can be beloved on occasion, can be loathed as often as not, but isn't often feared.

"Lots of reasons," I say. "When he first started in the village, he'd built a group around him who put a lot of stock in his word, my parents first among them. My mother hosted him very often in our home. But by January things had changed. He'd grown angry, I don't know what about. That winter he'd given over his sermons to warning against Satan and temptations into sin. How even good people can be turned to witches by his wicked promises. Every Sunday that winter without fail, four hours in the morning on the wages of sin for weak and prideful people who don't love God enough, then four hours more in the afternoon shaking his fist at the Devil hiding among us, cursing his myriad faces, saying that only Christ knows how many devils there are. And who they are."

"So it was his preaching that made you afraid?"

"It made us all afraid. We were none of us ever good enough. We never loved Jesus enough. We looked into our souls and saw them for the pits of tar they were. But it weren't only his preaching."

Reverend Green frowns, creases forming around his handsome mouth. I feel a stirring within myself, something I oughtn't feel.

"What was it, then?" he asks, leaning forward with his elbows on his knees.

I swallow. The Reverend's eyes are soft on mine.

"Reverend Parris was a learned man. A gentleman, my mother said," I say.

"That's true."

"He'd been educated at the college. And for a time, he'd had a plantation, on the Barbadoes. He could talk business with my father and make my father feel wise."

"Yes."

"So you wouldn't think he'd be the sort of man . . ." I stop. I'm worried about speaking out of turn.

"What sort of man?" the Reverend asks, lowering his voice to a whisper.

"The sort of man who . . . well . . ."

He rests a hand gently on the back of mine, and I thrill at the touch.

"A . . . bodily sort of man," I falter.

"What does that mean, a bodily sort of man?"

"It means that if his words didn't persuade, he'd use other means."

A brief expression of distaste crosses the Reverend's face.

"And Elizabeth Parris?"

"Betty was his daughter, so she learned soon enough how to be. She made herself delicate, kept herself small and obedient. She made it so she never needed any persuading. And so, when she fell ill, it seemed a natural thing to me."

"But I don't understand. I thought you said she was pretending."

I pause, staring out the window. I put myself back in the loft that icy morning, with Betty bawling into Tittibe's neck, her arms twined around the slave's waist, the stamping of her father's feet up the loft ladder. Abby's hands on her hips, laughing. In my memory I'm standing at the foot of the trundle bed, and I have a decision to make, a decision that I don't entirely understand. I've visited that morning more times than I can count, have pored over what Betty did, what I said, what Abby said, what Tittibe said. What happened next.

I don't know how to answer Reverend Green.

"Ann?" he prods me.

"I thought she was," I say. "At first."

CHAPTER 7

S t. Joan's had disappeared behind a cloud of words. When we got to school the following day, the Channel 7 news van had been joined by two other local affiliates and one from Boston. The reporters stood, forming a gantlet, each bathed in a separate white spotlight. We had to elbow over each other to reach the front door of the school, shouldering past waving microphones and glaring lights. Girls were pointing out TJ Wadsworth to each other, hopping and waving and grinning into the cameras.

"... standing in front of ground zero for the Mystery Illness, and it looks like ..."

"... where some of the North Shore's most pampered daughters have ..."

"... are asking if the HPV vaccine could possibly ..."

"... side effect of an age of oversexualized childhood, when girls are ..."

I paused, frowning, before shoving my way inside.

Nobody had seen Clara or the Other Jennifer or Elizabeth since it happened, and because they weren't back in school, rumors were flying low and thick. One rumor claimed that all three were in the hospital, hooked up to tubes and beeping machines. Another one countered that they were totally fine and would be back in school tomorrow. One tried to claim that Clara had been shipped to some top-secret clinic at Brigham and Women's in Boston. Last night I'd even seen a tweet suggesting that Elizabeth was dead, but it was quickly deleted.

By the time I sat down in advisory, it was like a full day had gone by. The rumors were so intense that it felt like a physical experience, walking through them down the hall. Even Deena looked exhausted.

We nodded our hellos, Emma and Anjali each drifting into the classroom under her own draggy steam, Fabiana coming in with a cursory glare at me that made my jaw tense. Jennifer Crawford looked so tired that she hadn't even bothered to update her hair color.

A squeak of feedback, the upper school dean said, "Mary, Queen of Knowledge, pray for us," over the PA system, and the day began.

"Okay, ladies, let's get to it," said Father Molloy, shutting the door behind him.

Even Father Molloy had purplish shadows under his eyes.

"Your parents should've received a letter yesterday," he began.

Inside my bag, my phone vibrated. I felt it buzzing all the way up the strap until my seat back was vibrating, too. I shifted my eyes left and right. Anjali already had her phone out under her desk, continuing her nonstop digital romance with Jason. Slowly, I inched my hand from my lap to my bag.

"And I hope you're all able to attend our community meeting tonight. With at least one parent each, but if it's at all possible for both of them to come, that would be ideal."

A hand shot up. Father Molloy turned his head to call on whoever it was, and I closed my hand around the vibrating phone.

"Yes?"

"Can siblings come? My mom wants to know."

"Absolutely. We're going for total transparency here. Siblings welcome. What else?"

Another hand went up, and I slid the phone into my lap. It blinked with a text message from an unknown number.

"The newscast said there were five students now. Is that true?"

"I'm not surprised you guys are curious, but unfortunately, I'm just not allowed to talk about it. Which is a shame, because I think secrets can make people more scared than they should be. But that's the school's policy. I may not agree with it, but I have to abide by it. That's all I can say. You guys probably know more on this score than I do, anyway. More questions?"

I clicked on the incoming message.

It was a snapshot of an unfamiliar hand holding a copy of *The Crucible*. No text or subject or anything.

"What the hell?" I said aloud.

"Colleen? You have a question?" Father Molloy asked.

I shoved the phone up my sleeve and said, "Yes. Is it true that they think everyone's just having an allergic reaction to a vaccine? It sounded like that's what the reporters are saying."

Father Molloy sniffed with annoyance at the mention of the reporters.

"I've heard that rumor, too," he said. "I'm not sure. But I know we should have more answers by tonight, for whatever that's worth."

I nodded. When Father Molloy moved on to answer something Fabiana was asking, I slid the phone out again and unlocked the screen.

There the cover of the play sat, making no sense at all.

Keeping my eyes on the front of the classroom, I texted back.

Mikey is this your new number? I'm gonna need that back when you're done.

But there was no answer.

. . .

A hall's length of rumor yawned between advisory and first period, and Emma and I shoved through it with our arms linked, as if our doubled number made us safer. But it didn't.

Did you hear the Other Jennifer's hair fell out? Clara's dad is suing the school. Elizabeth can't even walk, can you believe it? I'm so glad my mom didn't think I should get the HPV vaccine. What, did you get it? You did? Ohmigod, you did?

Clawing our way out of the rumor stream, Emma and I collapsed in our chairs in AP US.

"I can't believe the day just started," I moaned.

"I know."

"You going to the meeting tonight?"

She nodded. "Of course. I'm curious. My mom doesn't think we should go, though. She'd rather we all just stay home. She thinks the rumors just make everything worse."

"Mine thought it was about drugs," I said, and Emma laughed.

"Mike and Linda are adorable."

"Aren't they?"

We sighed in companionable silence, staring at the ceiling.

Ms. Slater elbowed through the door and strode to the front of the classroom, her arms full of ominous-looking papers.

"Hi, gang," she said.

Emma frowned, glanced at me, and frowned deeper.

"Hi, Ms. Slater," a few of us chorused.

I frowned back at Emma, shrugged, and mouthed *What?*

She shook her head and waved me off. Weird. Just when I felt like we were getting back to normal, Emma would do something that I didn't understand.

"So. How's everyone doing?" Ms. Slater asked, leaning on the lectern with her elbows.

Silence as we collectively shrugged.

"Ms. Carruthers? How're you doing?"

Leigh sank a little lower in her chair, hunching her shoulders. "Okay, I guess," she said.

"Your mom's not very opinionated, is she?" Ms. Slater asked.

"Um. What do you mean?" Leigh feigned ignorance in a way that I found particularly grating.

"I don't mean a thing," Ms. Slater said, turning her attention to the papers in her hand, riffling her fingers through them. "Not a god-damn thing."

I smiled before I could help myself, and brought my sweater sleeve up to hide it.

"You all seem pretty wiped, if you want to know the truth," Ms. Slater said. She started to move among our desks, slapping down a paper before each of us.

"All the more reason to shake things up. What lies before you now, and which you are not to touch until I say the word, is a pop quiz."

Universal groans of "Oh, God" and "Oh, come on!" rose to the dark oak rafters of our former convent classroom. A few bolder voices even said things like "Mr. Mitchell never gave pop quizzes. College doesn't have pop quizzes!"

"Oho!" Ms. Slater grinned her gap-toothed grin and crossed her arms. "Who are you who are so wise in the ways of college? Have you been?"

Begrudging silence.

"Didn't think so. First of all, I'm not Mr. Mitchell."

A few of us muttered that we knew *that*, and frankly we wished he'd come back already.

"And second of all, even college occasionally has pop quizzes. And third of all," she said, smiling broadly, "this one's a cinch. If you're caught up on the reading, it's an easy A."

This time we glanced at each other under our eyelashes. The promise of an easy A was intoxicating. Those of us who were deferred from early decision at our preferred colleges were in the habit of calculating our GPAs down to tenths of a point from week to week. Behind a dozen sets of tastefully lined girls' eyes, wheels turned as grade point averages were quickly tallied anew. Eyelashes blinked as tantalizing numbers were arrived at. Wolfish teeth peeked from fruit-glossed mouths as small smiles flickered into being on the faces of AP US History. Many of those smiles were slowly aimed at our substitute teacher.

She eyed us each in turn.

"The honeymoon period had to end sometime," she remarked, reading the calculation in our faces. "I just hope, for your sakes, that you did the reading."

Mine was not one of the smiling faces. My wheels had turned and emitted a dry grinding squeal. A sweat spread across my palms, and one of my thumbs twitched. The reading. What had we been assigned for reading? I shut my eyes, reviewing the previous week. I'd had a short response paper for AP English. I'd had a calculus problem set, which I'd finally gotten through when Deena helped me. I'd had . . . God, I couldn't remember. I usually used advisory to review my history stuff. Was I caught up on the reading?

"Ready?" Ms. Slater asked, her eyes on the clock.

With a nauseating certainty I knew.

I wasn't.

"Begin."

CHAPTER 8

DANVERS, MASSACHUSETTS
THURSDAY, FEBRUARY 2, 2012

Nobody said anything when Michael, earbuds still in his ears, wearing a huge parka that had belonged to Dad, climbed in next to me in the back of our station wagon that night. My brother is a skinny, pale kid, his hair a mushroom of dark curls on top of his head, and his shirt collars never seem to fit him right. Huge feet, though. My father insists he'll be playing for the Celtics by the time he's twenty.

"Where's Wheez?" I asked as my father backed our creaking station wagon out of the driveway, flattening the crust of plowed snow at the edge of the street. The car fishtailed in the slush and then righted itself, as though working from muscle memory.

"She's at a friend's," my mother said. "She'll stay the night."

"On a school night? You'd never've let me sleep over on a school night in a million years," I pointed out.

I liked reminding my parents of the diminishing returns of their parenting as their family expanded. And they liked suggesting that I'd just worn them out.

"They didn't want her to get scared," Michael said to me, in a voice so quiet I almost thought my parents wouldn't be able to hear.

"It's not . . ."

I started to say, "It's not that big a deal," to dismiss whatever they were worried about, to make it sound stupid that Louisa might be scared. Okay, so Clara hadn't been back in school yet, but I'd heard very definite rumors that she would be back tomorrow, and so would her minions. She wasn't even sick, not really. She'd just had a bad reaction to a vaccine. What had been a theory at school in the morning had solidified into fact, at least within my own self. My certainty was aided by the knowledge that I'd had all three of the HPV shots, like, two years ago. No way was any of that going to happen to me.

But as I looked at my brother, streetlights flashing over his face as we trundled through the snow to the St. Joan's campus, I thought better of it. He was scowling, and his arms were knitted over his chest, folding himself deep into the parka.

"You're right, I wouldn't have," my mother agreed from the front seat. "But Louisa isn't you."

"Well, thanks," I said.

"You're welcome."

I leaned my forehead on the window and stared through the night as house after house rolled past, polite clapboarded ones with historical plaques by their front doors, petering out to self-important Victorians, the thick frosting of snow making them look like gingerbread houses built by witches to lure lost children in from the woods.

Incredibly, there wasn't a single news van parked in front of the school. I'd thought someone would have slipped up and talked to them, but apparently not. Or at least I'd thought TJ Wadsworth would have been staking the place out, sleeping in the news van with one eye open. But we made it from the parking lot through the Gothic front doors without incident—no cameras, no shouted questions, just the silent gargoyles rubbing their claws together as we passed. I let myself feel a glimmer of relief. I thought maybe they were calling everyone together to tell us that whatever it was was already over.

Was I ever wrong.

The scene inside the chapel hovered on the knife edge of bedlam. Girls and their parents and their siblings all crammed together, everyone wanting to find seats together and nobody able to do it. We located Emma and her mom right away. We hardly ever saw Mrs. Blackburn. She was like Emma, pale and blond, but she'd grown almost transparent with age, like one of the faded nun photographs hanging forgotten in the darkest wing of the upper school. She didn't go to school events, on account of her migraines, or even leave the house all that much. Emma waved at me but didn't make a move to bring her mom over to say hello.

We spotted Anjali, who had Dr. Gupta with her, but not her dad—he was on a business trip to Jakarta, which is exactly the kind of glamorous thing that he was always doing. Deena was there with her dad, who shook hands with mine and said, "Hey, Mike, long time." Jennifer Crawford scowled from a corner while her mother, an aging debutante type in pearls and a twinset, wrapped a loving arm around her pink-haired daughter's shoulders and whispered in her ear. Fabiana stood off to one side with an intense look on her face, speaking a language I didn't understand with a woman I initially took to be her sister. They moved their hands the same way, and they were exactly the same height. If I hadn't known better, I'd have thought Fabiana's mom was barely twenty years old. Leigh Carruthers hung on her mother in the center of the room while Kathy Carruthers recounted her television appearance to a knot of other listening mothers. Leigh gazed with worshipful eyes into her mother's face, ignored.

". . . better give us some answers," Kathy Carruthers was saying. "I swear, they will if they know what's good for them. If they don't, we're going to take it to the next level, you see if we won't. I've been getting a lot of calls."

When she said that last part, she raised her eyebrows, or at least, I thought that's what she was trying to do. The Botox made it so all she could do was widen her eyes until they bulged.

"A lot. Of calls," she said again.

The women bunched around Mrs. Carruthers all chattered and nodded, a buzzing hive of plotting and scheming and planning to take it to the next level, whatever that meant.

What really surprised me most, though, was the presence of Clara Rutherford.

Yep. Clara.

She floated near the front of the chapel, not far from the lectern, sweetly dressed in a soft pink cardigan and skirt. She was flanked by her parents, each of them holding on to one of her elbows. A void yawned around the three of them. No one crowded in. No one buzzed too close. If it was possible, Clara looked more noble than ever, even though every couple of minutes her head flung itself backward and she let out a sharp cry that sounded like "Tzt tzt tzt HA!"

The Other Jennifer was also there with her parents, and so was Elizabeth. Elizabeth's mom surprised me—I didn't remember ever seeing her before. Elizabeth was pretty athletic, doing field hockey and stuff, and I thought she also rode horses. But her mom was this tiny wisp of a woman, wraithlike, her face drawn with worry. We all feasted on the reason why: Elizabeth was in a wheelchair, her wrists drawn up under her chin, contorted with tension, her mouth flapping open and shut, and her eyes kept drifting up to the chapel ceiling. Elizabeth's mom's hands gripped the wheelchair handles as if she needed them to hold herself up, too.

"Thank you!" the upper school dean blared into the microphone. "Parents! Students! If I might have your attention, please."

Our voices lowered without stopping while family clusters started moving into pews.

"Thank you!" the dean said again. "If you all could find your seats, we promise not to take up too much of your time."

"God, I hope not," my mother muttered. "Michael? Come over here, please."

My brother loitered near my father's shoulder, staring at Elizabeth.

"Mikey, come on," I said, poking him. Usually he was better than that.

"Sorry," he said, looking first at his feet and then at nothing in the exact opposite direction from Elizabeth, Clara, and the Other Jennifer.

"Jeez. Way to stare. What's the matter with you?"

"Nothing. Sorry."

I liked Michael most of the time, but he could be a real pain in the ass. He had the subtle ability to sow discord in our family, in ways that I sometimes didn't figure out until days later. Stuff of mine would disappear, I'd blame Wheez, there'd be a huge door-slamming fight, my mother would yell at me for yelling at Wheez, and a week later my stuff would reappear and Michael would be looking smug at the breakfast table.

My mother grasped his parka sleeve and moved him bodily to stand next to her.

"Come on," she hissed. "Let's sit down."

The pews were filling up, so there wasn't room for all four of us to sit together. My mother parked Michael in a pew with a glare, and my father took my elbow.

"Come on, Colliewog," he said, more gently than I expected. "I've got us some seats over here."

Clara and her parents settled into the seats of honor in the front pew, with the Other Jennifer and Elizabeth flanking them. They were all still wearing the same elegant low ponytails tied with black ribbon. So Clara.

The upper school dean cleared her throat, and started to say, "Mary, Queen of Knowledge, pray for us," but was interrupted by Clara going, "TZT TZT HA!"

An awkward silence settled upon the senior class, and we all looked at our hands in our laps so that we wouldn't stare at her, which is what we wanted to do.

"Now then," the dean said, visibly flustered. "We'd like to thank you all for taking the time to join us this evening. I know a lot of you have concerns about what's been happening to some of our girls, particularly after that unfortunate and inaccurate news report. The administration is meeting privately with the teachers so that everyone is prepared to offer your children the support they most need, on an individual level, as we move past these concerns. As you can see, our three special girls are here this evening, and I, for one, would like to give them a round of applause. We're so glad to have them safely back in the St. Joan's community."

She beamed a thoroughly insupportable smile and started clapping her hands. The noise boomed through the microphone, each clap an explosion with a corona of feedback. We all looked at each other in the pews, and then slowly joined her in a halfhearted clap. Several of the parents sat, staring in disbelief.

After a minute of overly vigorous clapping the dean discovered that we had all stopped, so she stopped, too. A nervous frown fled across her face, and she said, "I've asked the school nurse to say a few words."

Nurse Hocking got up, with her new white coat on, and her tasteful makeup that she never used to wear. I glanced sideways at my dad and saw his eyebrows low over his eyes. In the pew in front of us, I spied Emma's mom hunched forward as though she were in pain, massaging her temples with her fingertips.

"Tzt tzt HA HA HA!" Clara cried. Some of us may have snickered, but if so, we kept it pretty well under wraps, especially when our parents shushed us.

"Good evening, everyone," Nurse Hocking said. "Girls," she addressed herself to the front pew, "it's such a pleasure to see you all looking so well. And I'm delighted to be able to tell your classmates that you'll all be back in school tomorrow."

We gasped, and glances were exchanged. Some of us exclaimed that this was awesome. Others of us wondered under our breaths if that was really safe, since they hadn't told us what was going on yet, not really. What if it was contagious? But the nurse had started clapping again, farther away from the microphone, and so we all joined in, and eventually the applause started to feel genuine, like we all got swept up in a feeling of relief that they were okay, and the proof was that they'd be back in school tomorrow and everything would go back to normal.

When the clapping died down, everyone was smiling and parents were hugging their children to their chests. Nurse Hocking had a huge grin on her face, and gradually we all turned our attention back to her.

"Now, we also wanted to let you parents know that over the next couple of days we'll be talking with every member of the senior class, just so we can make sure that this doesn't happen again."

A hand shot up, and a father called out, "Talking with them about what?"

The nurse nodded and said, "We'll be asking them a few questions for their medical files. Every year we ask you all to share your children's pediatric records so we can keep track of their immunizations and health history. Totally confidential, of course. The administration has decided that we can best protect your daughters if we gather just a little more information. So we'd like to take a minute and talk to everyone. Everything will be held in complete confidence, and it's nothing to be concerned about."

Another hand shot up. Kathy Carruthers. Of course.

"Why haven't you told us what's the matter with them? Is it really that sex vaccine? We have a right to know!"

Nurse Hocking's smile grew tighter, but it didn't budge from her face.

"Thank you. As I've just said, all medical information collected about our students is kept strictly confidential. That means we aren't at liberty to share the specifics of the girls' diagnosis with you. But the important thing is, they're doing just fine, and we're doing everything in our power to keep our students safe. Thank you all so much for coming, and we'll see you at school tomorrow!"

For an agonizing minute the chapel sat frozen in silence.

A few people shifted as if they were going to stand up, but no one wanted to be the first. *Is that it? I guess that's it. We pushed back dinner for this? Ridiculous.*

A shuffling of feet as everyone gradually stood, murmuring, pulling car keys from pockets, climbing into coats.

Dad glanced down at me and said, "Guess you'll be talking to the nurse, then."

"Huh," I said. "I guess." My stomach rolled over uneasily. What could they possibly want to know? Why hadn't they said what was wrong?

I spotted Emma steering her mother to the side door, away from the milling crowd of parents and girls. Mrs. Blackburn looked stricken. I reached forward to pluck at Emma's sleeve, but my hand only grabbed thin air.

I felt Michael's hand clutch my arm through my coat sleeve.

"Why didn't they tell us what's happening, Colleen?" he whispered to me, his eyes wide with panic.

"I don't know, Mikey," I whispered back. I put my arm around his shoulder and pulled him closer. "I just don't know."

CHAPTER 9

I t was a very formal e-mail. Too formal for before breakfast.

> *Dear Ms. Rowley,*
>
> *Greetings. I am the Harvard alumna who has been assigned to conduct your admissions interview. I will be meeting with prospective students in forty-five-minute appointments at the Dado Tea House in Harvard Square this Saturday and Sunday between 2:00 and 5:00. Please inform me which of these blocks of time will be convenient for our interview.*
>
> *It is not necessary to bring a curriculum vitae or transcript, as we have that information already, but you should come dressed appropriately and prepared to discuss your accomplishments at St. Joan's.*
>
> *I may be reached at this address, or through my assistant at the phone number listed below.*
>
> *Cordially,*
> *Judith Pennepacker, H'99*

Crap. As I read the e-mail, I felt my heart rate rise and my palms grow damp.

I stood up.

Then I sat down again.

I lifted my fingers to the laptop keyboard.

Then I put them back in my lap.

If I wrote back right away, would I look too eager? But what if I waited until study hall, or after school? She might think I was making her wait. Judith Pennepacker didn't seem like the kind of woman who would look too kindly on being made to wait.

Curious, I entered her name into Google to see what I could find out. That was a pretty weird last name, so I thought I'd find something.

Sure enough, I found a Facebook page, featuring a formal profile photograph of a woman in a business suit with serious eyeglasses and hair parted in the middle, smiling like she was ready to eat my entire family for a snack and pick her teeth with our toenails. I also found that she happened to share her last name with one of the oldest freshman dorms at Harvard University.

Awesome. Just really, really great. This wasn't intimidating at all.

Dear Ms. Pennepacker, I began. Good start.

Thank you so much for your e-mail. I am so looking forward to meeting you and having the opportunity to learn more about Harvard from an alumna such as yourself.

Such as yourself?

Such as you?

Like you?

Crap.

Backspace, backspace.

Thank you so much for your e-mail. I am so looking forward to meeting you and learning more about Harvard.

Better.

Okay. Now, what time should I ask to go? Did I want to be the first interview, or the last? I bet that if I were the last one, she was going to be tired and grumpy. Right? But if I was the very first, she might talk to someone completely amazing later on that day and then forget all about me. I wanted to be fresh in her mind, right? Right. Okay. So let's say . . . Sunday. Second interview, Sunday. Yes. That should be good.

Would it be possible for me to meet you at 3:00 on Sunday? Sincerely yours, Colleen Rowley

I hunched over the keyboard, staring at the e-mail, thinking. I backspaced again.

Yours truly, Colleen Rowley

No, no. That's stupid. I'm not hers, truly or otherwise. I've never even met her before.

Backspace.

Sincerely, Colleen Rowley

Satisfied, I sat back in my chair, staring at the e-mail for a full five minutes.

"Colleen!" my mother hollered up the stairs, breaking my concentration. "Your dad's ready to leave! Hurry it up!"

"Okay, okay!" I hollered back.

I reread the e-mail one last time. This interview could be life-changing. I'd applied early to Williams and Dartmouth, but they'd both deferred me. That just about ruined Christmas, I'm not going to lie. Reach schools. I mean, I'd had a shot, but they're reaches for everyone. My parents pointed out that a deferral wasn't the same as a rejection, but that was exactly the kind of thing parents were supposed to say. Deferral is just rejection for kids with high self-esteem, I told them. Then they tried a different tack, suggesting that if I'd gotten in early decision, I'd be locked into one place, without having the option to choose.

And now, here was Harvard, in the form of Judith Pennepacker.

And she wanted to interview me.

I just had to send it, right?

So I did. Poof. There it went.

I fled from my e-mail, grabbing my bag, elbowing Michael out of the way in the hall outside the bathroom as he cried, "Colleen, God!" and thumping down the stairs. I landed in the mudroom in a two-footed stomp and said, "Boom! I'm here, I'm ready."

"Jesus!" my mother admonished me, thrusting a lunch bag into my hands. "Take your time next time, why don't you. It's not responsible behavior, making people wait for you, Colleen."

"I had to return an e-mail, Mom," I said, giving her a withering look.

"Oh, an e-mail! That does sound important, doesn't it, Wheez?"

She addressed the underside of the piano bench, where I could hear my little sister giggling.

"Um, it was for my Harvard interview? Okay?" I said. "Is that okay with you?"

"Oh!" My mother stopped short. "Your . . . What?"

"Yeah. Thanks," I said, turning my back.

Dad was already outside warming up the car, and I made for the front door.

My mother's hand squeezed my shoulder on my way out. Neither of us said anything, but I knew she was proud of me.

"We're gonna be late," my father remarked as he backed the station wagon out of our driveway, bouncing over the curb with a jolt.

"I had to write back to my Harvard interviewer, Dad," I said as I fished my phone out of my backpack. I wanted to let Spence know that I was going to be in the Square on Sunday. Maybe he'd be in town, too, and want to . . . I don't know. Hang out?

"Oh really?" my father asked with interest. "You got one, eh? When's it gonna be?"

"Sunday, I think," I said, peering at the phone.

When I went into the text message application, I found I had one already waiting, from a number that said UNKOWN.

Mikey showing off his awesome new phone as payback for me

pushing him at the top of the stairs. I didn't see why he should get a new one when mine had had a huge crack in it since summer. Who was he going to call, anyway?

I clicked on the message, frowning.

Did you read it?

Read *The Crucible*? Well, yeah, everyone did. So what?

Yeah Mikey . . . So what?

"Sunday, huh?" my father continued. "Well, that's damned exciting. You tell your mom?"

"Uh-huh," I said.

The phone vibrated in my hand. A new text.

Spence. My mouth twisted itself into a smile and I opened it.

Hey. Happy Friday

I grinned wider and tapped back, bringing the phone closer to my nose for a better view.

"What'd she say?" my father pressed.

"Dad. Just give me a minute, okay?" I said.

"Oh, excuse me," he said, pronouncing it "ex-kee-yoooze" to make fun of me. "Sure, I'll just wait. Just chauffeuring the car, no big deal. Nothing to see here."

I snorted, tapping my response to Spence.

Hey. Guess what?

"That's a fine thing, a Harvard interview. No reason to be nervous." My father would not be thwarted. "I know your guidance counselor said not to read too much into whether you get one or not, but I can't help but think it's a good sign, don't you?"

"Uh-huh," I said.

The phone vibrated immediately with his reply. I wiggled my feet.

What?

"We'll have to remember to see if your suit's been dry-cleaned. I guess we could get it done tomorrow if we really have to. That place in Marblehead'll do it in twenty-four hours, and I'm pretty sure they deliver. You ever use that place, or do you just go where your mom goes?"

96

"Dad!" It was impossible to concentrate, with him talking so much.

"Sorry, sorry! Just making conversation on a Friday morning with my eldest child."

I wrinkled my nose at him, but then smiled to show I didn't mean it.

I'll be in the Square Sunday. Where are u?

"What're you doing over there?" My dad pretend-craned his neck to get a look at my phone screen.

"Jesus, Dad!" I exclaimed, angling my shoulders so that he couldn't see the screen.

"Is it a booooooooooy?"

The phone vibrated again.

"Dad, honestly, I'll talk in just a sec, I'm just trying to do this one thing, okay?"

I'm not Mikey.

I sat back, confused. Then I realized that in my haste, I'd just opened the newest text without looking. But this one wasn't from Spence.

Who is this??

I tapped back, frowning at the phone.

"Bad news?" my nosy father asked, noticing the change on my face.

"No," I said. "It's . . . No. It's fine."

I waited.

"You sure?" he asked.

The phone vibrated again, and I jumped in my haste to open the next text.

Belmont this wknd. Harvard Sq. sunday pm? No Jasons allowed. ☺

Wait, what?

Oh, Spence! For a second I was disappointed that it wasn't from the mystery texter, but only for a second, because then I realized that I now would be spending Sunday afternoon after my Harvard interview hanging out with Spence in the Square. Alone.

HA!

Grinning like a maniac, I texted him back.

Lol. Meet u at 5 at COOP

"My goodness." My father seemed to be speaking to some invisible person sitting in the backseat of the station wagon. "The emotional ups and downs of this car ride rival some of the great films of Hollywood's Golden Era. Such drama, such pathos, such . . ."

"DAD. Could you just cut me, like, a little bit of slack? Please? Just this once?"

"Who are you texting with, anyway?"

"Just a friend."

"A guy friend?"

I felt my ears grow pink under his interrogation.

"I plead the Fifth," I said.

We rolled up to the front drive of St. Joan's, and my father shifted the car into park and looked at me.

"Have it your way," he said. "You usually do."

I smiled, leaned over, and kissed him on the cheek.

"Bye, Dad. Love you."

"Still with the news vans, huh?"

We both looked out the car window at the wall of white camera lights beaming up into the silent Gothic windows of the upper school. One of the front door gargoyles cast a contorted shadow over the lawn, a beaked demon with wings.

"I guess so. They didn't get the memo about it all going back to normal."

My father sighed and said, "Love you, too, sweetheart. Have a good day."

As I hoisted my bag into place and prepared to face the gantlet of news vans and students streaming toward the front doors, I realized that the mystery texter had never written me back.

"Colleen! The strawberry girl, Colleen!"

I couldn't place the song Deena had chosen to mock me with this week. All around me the girls of St. Joan's were alight with the news of Clara, Elizabeth, the Other Jennifer, and the two underclassmen being back. Everyone had contradictory information, and everyone was certain that her information was unassailably correct. But one thing was for sure—Clara and her minions were back.

Sort of.

I mean, yes, they were present. But they were pretty far from back in any normal sense.

I could spot them in the hall with no problem, because each of them had an orb of space around her, like an invisible force field. People hovered around them in a tight-packed mass, but just out of reach. Maybe it was because we wanted room to stare at them. Maybe it was because we were afraid. None of us wanted to touch them.

I don't know.

But I could scan the entire length of the hall, over the ribboned heads of my classmates—I was tall enough to see over most of the other girls in the upper school—and could easily discern three separate bubbles of space, floating at different paces and trailing different thicknesses of hangers-on. The three bubbles drifted, drifted, drifted, eventually drawing together into one big bubble outside Father Molloy's advisory. Then the big bubble floated through the door, and the built-up mass of followers dispersed, breaking apart into separate individual girls, whispering, worrying, each squirreling away her own private nugget of truth.

I hesitated outside the classroom door, a sickening void opening somewhere deep in my entrails. My relief from the community meeting the previous night was abruptly pushed aside by a nauseating unease. I felt like I'd forgotten something, but I couldn't put my finger on what it was. Nothing was missing from my backpack, I'd done all the reading for that day, I had a ride home with Deena, I'd answered the Harvard e-mail, all of my other apps were already in, everything was where it was supposed to be in my life. But something still felt wrong.

I realized that I was scared of Clara, too.

I put my hand on the classroom door, seeing by the silhouettes in the pebbled glass that most of the other girls in advisory were already there. Deena's song continued, in fits and starts. It had bored its way into my head, but I still didn't recognize it. Father Molloy leaned on his desk at the front of the room, looking haggard.

Clara perched in her usual spot, which no one would dare to touch. The Other Jennifer sat on one side of Clara, with a weird silk scarf wrapped around her head in a turban. Elizabeth was parked on Clara's other side, still in a wheelchair. Every few seconds Clara said, "Tzt tzt tzt HA!" though she seemed better able to keep it quiet instead of crying out at the top of her voice like she had the previous night.

Every single girl in the classroom was pretending not to stare.

Except Jennifer Crawford. She was openly staring.

"Hey," I said, sliding into my desk next to Deena.

"Hi," she said.

Her eyes kept slipping to Clara's corner of the room, but she was clearly trying to keep them from doing it.

"I don't recognize today's song. What is it?"

"Huh? Oh. Yeah. It's 'Christine.' Siouxie and the Banshees."

"It's goth. Like, really old goth," Anjali tossed over her shoulder. "Hey, Colleen."

"Hey, Anj. Goth?"

"Like, really old goth." Anjali smiled.

I shook my head. "Since when do you know really old goth?"

"Since forever. I mean, Taylor Swift is okay, but come on."

"Emma, did you know our friends were so sophisticated?"

She slowly nodded, pulling a long hank of blond hair into a mustache under her nose.

"Wow," I marveled. "All my friends have totally secret lives that I know nothing about."

"You never asked," Emma said, smiling out of the corner of her mouth.

I smiled back and settled into my seat, trying just as hard as everyone else not to stare at Clara. Anjali sighed loudly, and I perked up.

"Hey, Anj, guess what." I leaned forward and prodded her shoulder with a finger.

"What?"

"I got one."

Anjali spun in her seat, eyes bright, grabbed my forearm, and whispered, "Oh my God. You did?"

I nodded, and for the first time actually allowed myself to feel excited. Anjali had grades just about on par with mine, so we were applying to a lot of the same places. There was some competition there, no question, but she was so focused on Yale, and I didn't want to go there, that it wasn't as big a deal as it could have been. Deena wasn't interested in big schools; she was just looking at little liberal arts colleges. She said she wanted to go somewhere where she could actually know everyone, if she felt like it. Which was a relief, because then we could just support each other without any of that weird pretend-supporting, really-resenting stuff that happens. But Emma, well. Her grades were good and everything, I mean, I'm not saying they weren't, but they weren't that great. She was in the humanities AP classes, but not the science ones. And anyway, she was going to stay in Boston for school just like her brother. I was sure of it. She could never leave Danvers. I don't even think she's ever left Massachusetts in her life.

"Yeah!"

"When? When?"

"Sunday."

"What are you guys talking about?" Emma asked.

"Colleen got a Harvard interview!" Anjali burst out.

I hadn't even needed to tell her where, because we'd both been sweating our respective Ivy interviews for weeks now. After I'd gotten deferred from Dartmouth, I hadn't heard anything about an interview one way or the other. My guidance counselor said it didn't matter, but of course it did. Anjali's Yale interview had been lined up since late December, and she'd gotten one for Cornell, too. I didn't remember when they were supposed to be, maybe like a week after mine. I guess Judith Pennepacker didn't feel like she needed to give us any warning. Well, she was right. When Harvard said jump, we jumped. They knew it. We knew it.

"She did?" Emma said in a small voice. She turned to me. "You did?"

"Yeah," I said, uncertain. I couldn't read Emma's face. It looked drawn and masklike, with those oyster-colored eyes.

"When did that happen?" Emma asked.

"Just this morning. I got an e-mail."

"Oh." Emma looked back at her desk. "That's great."

"I'm sure you'll get one," I said, putting a hand on her arm. "It was totally last minute. She's making me meet her on Sunday. So, like, no lead time."

"Yeah," Emma said. She didn't look at me.

"Sunday!" Anjali squealed. "Oh my God, are you excited?"

"Harvard?" Deena broke in. "Colleen, that's so awesome."

"Yeah." I couldn't help myself. I grinned.

I was on the point of saying something else, and to be honest I have no idea what it was, because I was interrupted by a commotion on the other side of the room.

"Would you STOP?"

We spun in our seats to see who had spoken.

The Other Jennifer was twisted around in her seat, a fierce glare aimed right at Jennifer Crawford.

Jennifer Crawford was smiling.

"I'm sorry," she said. "It's just, like, a totally new look for you. I mean, I love it. It's so Elizabeth Taylor."

"SHUT UP."

"Girls." Father Molloy got up from behind his advisory desk, standing at the front of the classroom with a stern expression. "Come on. It's been a long week. Let's not and say we did, okay?"

"What?" Jennifer Crawford said, widening her eyes with false remorse. "I didn't do anything. I was just complimenting her . . . *turban.*"

"You bitch!" the Other Jennifer hissed.

We all inhaled sharply. It was rare to see open aggression at St. Joan's. Oh, it's not like we were innocent lambs who sat around holding hands all day. It's just that most of our methods were more subtle. If we wanted to make someone feel how truly insignificant she was, there were ways and ways of doing it. Backhanded compliments on a Facebook feed. A subtweet or two. A stare just a second too long, followed by a tiny roll of the eyes. Whispering, always whispering. These were the methods of discipline and hierarchy employed in the halls of St. Joan's.

Elizabeth slumped in her wheelchair, caught in the crossfire between the Jennifers, trying to pretend like it wasn't happening. Clara had turned around in her seat, too, and watched with interest. We all waited, wondering what ruling the queen would make.

"Jennifer . . . ," she started to say.

We weren't sure which one she was talking to. She worked her mouth for a minute, as if trying to form the words. Her head twitched with the effort.

"Girls . . . ," Father Molloy tried again. "I really think that—"

But he was cut off when Clara sputtered, "TZT TZT TZT HA," opened her mouth wide, rolled her eyes in her head, recovered herself, and commanded, "Show her."

The Other Jennifer got to her feet. She glared at Jennifer Crawford, reached up, and pulled the scarf off her head.

We gasped, horrified.

The Other Jennifer was completely bald.

INTERLUDE

everend Green leans forward, his face so near to mine that
I can taste his breath.
"You thought," he says.
He means Betty Parris, that I thought she was playing.

"Yes," I say. "That first day, I thought once Reverend Parris came
home, she'd awake to her senses. But she didn't. Tittibe put her
straight back to the trundle, and rustled Abby down from the loft to
get his supper. I'd never heard such things come out of Abby's mouth
as came out of it that day when Betty got put right back in bed."

From the hall outside the closed study door a girl squeals in laughter, quickly shushed. The Reverend smiles and toys with his mustache
in the manner of a young man who has some idea of what foolishness
girls can be gotten up to.

"What happened next?" he asks.

"At first, nothing. Betty stayed abed, Abby got bossed about
the house left and right, Tittibe giving her extra duties now that
Betty weren't well enough to help. The other children, Thomas and

104

Susannah, carried on with nary a complaint, but then Thomas were a bookish sort of boy who never made much fuss, and Susannah just out of babyhood. The Reverend working away on his sermons, grim as ever, his wife flitting about, full of recriminations, pining for Boston. My mother called on her very often. Sometimes my mother'd take me with her, but I was never allowed to linger with them. I'd be sent up to the loft to look to Betty."

I have Reverend Green enthralled. His eyes gleam in the fire-light, and his pretty mouth with its well-formed lower lip is parted, unaware of revealing his black-stained teeth. A shiver travels up my spine and spreads deliciously over the top of my head. To my shame I feel myself basking in his attention. It's more intoxicating even than the cider Bridget Oliver used to serve us at her inn, when we'd laugh and sing late into the night while playing at the shovelboard.

I know it well, this feeling. It's not to be trusted.

"It went on thus," I say. "Two weeks or so without change. And then one day, early February it was, my mother sent me to the parson-age to drop off some things and ask Tittibe after some onions and a pound of rye meal. That was the day I started to understand."

"What, Ann? What did you start to understand?"

I gaze on him, and let my eyes smolder with the knowledge I am about to impart.

"To understand," I say, "what girls are capable of."

By the time I spot the corner of the slatted fence that marks the kitchen garden of the Parris parsonage, I can't feel my feet. They're there on the end of my legs like two stumps of wood, and a new sugaring of snow has been drifting down from the sky since last night, settling on my shoulders, the top of my head, the tip of my nose. I look like I've been rolled in goose down. The snow muffles all sound, swallowing my footsteps, so I can hear only the crunch of my footfalls and my own labored breath. My mother's laden me with a basket of linens she was having our girl mend for Mrs. Parris, as our servant is English and so has a finer touch with a needle than a common Indian woman, or so Mother says.

I stop by the fence corner and drop the basket at my feet, shaking out my arms and flexing the fingers in my mittens to see if I can bring feeling back to them. I stamp my feet but in vain: there's no blood for them to be had. I shake my cloak and skirts, knocking loose the freshest layer of snow. My breath circles my head like a halo and I pause, listening.

Silence.

I like the quiet in winter. Our house is so busy, with Mother's friends, Father and his business interests, always a strange hat on the peg near the door. At least one servant, usually two, though one just served out his indenture and he's left us shorthanded, Mother complains from behind her needlepoint near the fire. And all us children, as many as three to a trundle, which makes for warmer feet in wintertime, but also plenty of wakefulness between the scratching and the snoring and the nightmares of all my younger brothers and sisters.

Usually I linger an extra minute or two on the way to an errand, enjoying the time to myself. But today I'm too cold. I want a hot drink and to rest the soles of my feet near the kitchen hearth, and maybe be asked to stay for supper, even though it would mean enduring Abby's glares.

Abby hates being made to wait on me. I can't prove it, but last time I was pretty sure she spat in my peas.

I'm on the point of taking up my linen basket again when I hear it.

At first, I think it must be a bird. My ears twitch and I listen. The birds have been gone for weeks.

There it is again: a high, distant shriek.

It goes on for a long time.

I take up the basket and hurry. The snow sucks and drags at my feet, and I scramble, floundering under the weight of all my layers of wool, wading off the path into deeper drifts, stumbling, falling, catching myself by sinking my arms in up to the elbows in crusts of ice.

As I make my way nearer the parsonage, the shriek grows louder. My first thought is of Betty. Little Betty's died.

I raise my fist to beat on the door when it swings open and I behold the ashen face of Mrs. Parris.

"Oh, Ann!" she cries.

She gathers me to her bosom, the linen I've brought scattering unheeded to the floor. Inside I spy Susannah hiding under the table in the great hall, her tiny hands pressed over her ears. Tittibe stands rod-straight by the fire, her eyes wide. A man's voice is bellowing something incoherent in the loft overhead. I catch only snippets of words, like "God" and "cast out" and "merciful heaven."

The shriek has been interrupted only long enough for the being generating it to draw breath, and then it continues with renewed force. The sound fills the house, almost shaking the rafters. Little Susannah starts to cry.

"It's been days and days," Mrs. Parris says, her voice catching. "I can't . . . I can't . . . I can't take much more, Ann. I was at the point of sending for your mother."

"Is it Elizabeth?" I ask.

Mrs. Parris just looks at me, her eyes raw from crying. She shakes her head.

In the loft I hear a commotion and beating of feet, and the wail is replaced with high screams of "I'll never sign, no, I never shall, you can't make me! NO! NO, I WILL NOT SIGN!"

Mrs. Parris gasps and brings a hand to her mouth. Heavy footsteps, and we track their progress across the ceiling. Each deliberate footfall knocks loose a puff of dust from between the floorboards. Through the gaps in the boards we can see a shadow move.

The cries have lapsed into a formless screech, and a low male voice rumbles, "May God have mercy. May Christ bring his everlasting mercy on us all."

Then the Reverend Parris mounts the ladder and lowers himself back into the hall with an exhausted grunt.

We stare at him, waiting for him to explain to us what's befallen the creatures upstairs.

"Samuel?" Mrs. Parris whispers.

I've never heard Mrs. Parris use the Reverend's Christian name before.

The Reverend collapses in the armchair at the head of the trestle table and rests his forehead in his hands.

"Tittibe," he says absently to the slave, who has been lingering in the shadows cast by the low-burning hearth fire.

It's cold in the parsonage, colder than at our house, everyone wrapped in shawls and extra woolen stockings. With this snow, they should have brought in more wood than that, is what I think, looking at the pitiful heap next to the hearth. I seem to remember some talk between my parents about firewood and Reverend Parris's living from the parish being cut by some maneuverings by other villagers. Now I see how bad he has it.

He doesn't name his wish, but she guesses it and sets a mug at his elbow. He takes it without a word and drinks. We wait. The screams continue upstairs.

Reverend Parris casts his eyes up to the attic, then brings his gaze to meet his wife's.

"Betty continues much the same," he says. "But Abigail's worse. Much worse."

Abigail! I'd had no idea she was unwell. I'd seen her only a few days earlier at Ingersoll's Ordinary, where she had much to say about the wateriness of the soup.

Mrs. Parris emits a sigh of dismay, and Tittibe murmurs, "Ah, my poor Betty."

"At meeting I'll be calling on the congregation to pray for their delivery," he says, bringing a closed fist to the tabletop. "But I fear the time's come. You've tended them as best you can, and so have I. There're the other children to consider, the burden this is placing on them. The risk. I've decided. A doctor must be called."

"A doctor!" Mrs. Parris exclaims. "But . . ." She's on the point of saying something else, but remembers me with a nervous glance and stops herself.

"Indeed. But," Reverend Parris says, getting to his feet and striding to the window.

His back turned, he says, "Will he even come if I ask him? That's a question. They think they can starve me out. Think I'll be broken. Well, they're wrong. I've faced worse."

He glances at Tittibe, who sees his look and turns her back without a word. She's been with Reverend Parris since before he was Reverend Parris. Since before Mrs. Parris. A dark look passes between them. One of those island looks.

"I just go check the children, then," Tittibe says to the kettle over the fire, not addressing either of the Parrises directly.

"There'll be nothing to pay him with," Mrs. Parris whispers once Tittibe is up the stairs.

I realize that there'll be no onions, nor rye meal either, to spare in this house. The Parrises are proud; they won't want Mother and Father to know. Maybe I'll tell them I forgot to ask. God forgives a well-meaning lie such as that, surely.

"There won't," Reverend Parris agrees. "But one must be found all the same. Someone who might feel it his duty to help. Bill Griggs, maybe. I'll make inquiries straightaway."

The screams have continued throughout this entire conversation, but now they coalesce into a bitter howl of "BEGONE, WITCH! Rogue! I want none of you!"

A crash as an object is hurled across the room overhead and shatters.

Presently Tittibe reappears on the attic ladder, her eyes cast down. Once her foot falls on the floor near us, the screams overhead stop abruptly.

The Reverend and Mrs. Parris exchange a look. The only sound is of little Susannah under the table, quietly weeping, unattended.

"Ann," Mrs. Parris says, touching my arm. "You go up."

"Me, Mrs. Parris?" I say, scarcely able to find my breath.

"Yes, you. They'll be pleased to see you. You'll go up, won't you?"

I can't disobey the minister's wife if she tells me I must go. And so I do.

"Yes, Mrs. Parris," I hear myself say over the sound of blood rushing in my ears.

I mount the ladder, my arms shaking. The feeling has started to come back into my feet, but they're not all there just yet, and I struggle to keep my footing on the narrow steps.

When I achieve the loft, in the thin gray light of windows frosted thick with snow, I find Betty in her trundle, eyes open wide, bedclothes gathered tight up under her chin.

And in another trundle, her hair streaming loose over her shoulders, a warm woolen blanket tucked across her lap, sits Abigail Williams.

Grinning at me.

CHAPTER 10

Everyone in Father Molloy's advisory gasped. And then, slowly, inexorably, it began.

The giggling.

I could tell we were trying to keep it together, I could tell that it was partly out of shock, and fear, and discomfort, but none of that mattered, the giggling was pressing up through our chests and nothing we could do would stop it coming out and filling the entire advisory classroom.

The Other Jennifer was bald. And I don't mean shaved-her-head bald. I mean *bald*. I mean gleaming pinkish-white skin on her scalp, so gleaming it looked polished, marred by one incongruous mole tucked behind one of her ears. The Other Jennifer still had her eyebrows and her eyelashes, so it wasn't like cancer-patient bald, either. It was bizarre, and horrible, and yet it was also hilarious. The laughter came bubbling up in me as much as in anyone else.

"Oh my God," Jennifer Crawford said, bringing her hands up to her mouth, her eyes wide with laughter.

The Other Jennifer stood before us all, her silk Elizabeth Taylor scarf hanging from her hand, her face a twisted mask of humiliation and pain.

"You think this is funny?" she screamed, her voice shrill.

The giggling swirled around her in eddies. Some of us tried to make it stop, and choked with the effort. Others of us didn't try all that hard. The Other Jennifer was popular, but she wasn't well liked in the way that Clara and Elizabeth were. Popularity can be funny that way.

"Oh my God, Jennifer," Jennifer Crawford sputtered from behind her hands. "What happened to your hair?"

"Girls," Father Molloy started to say. "I'm serious, now—"

But it wasn't Father Molloy who commanded our attention.

"Jennifer," Clara said, turning in her seat and addressing Jennifer Crawford.

The sound of her speaking brought us all to heel. Her voice was quiet, almost conversational. And she didn't sputter or say, "Tzt tzt tzt HA."

Instead she simply said, "I don't think that's very cool, do you?"

Clara leveled her gaze at Jennifer Crawford, who shrank before the interrogation of the queen.

"C'mon, I was just—" Jennifer Crawford started to protest.

Without bothering to get out of her seat, Clara rested a hand on the Other Jennifer's arm. The Other Jennifer was vibrating with tension, her hands clenched at her sides, as though she couldn't decide whether to run away or smack Jennifer Crawford in the face. At Clara's touch, the Other Jennifer blinked, and the tension in her body uncoiled by a perceptible degree. She looked down at Clara, who tilted her head to the side in an interrogatory way.

Our giggling died down as we watched. Within a minute the advisory room was silent.

The Other Jennifer turned back to Jennifer Crawford, and held her in a steady glare while she lowered herself into her seat.

"I mean," Clara continued, even more quietly, "they still don't know for sure what's wrong with us, you know? I think you could have, like, a little more respect. Don't you?"

Jennifer Crawford hunched in her chair like a chastened puppy.

"I guess," she said, her voice barely above a whisper.

Clara stared at her for another long minute, and then she swept the classroom with her eyes, implicating all the rest of us in Jennifer Crawford's disobedience. We stared hard at our hands. We had giggled, every last one of us. We were guilty.

When Clara decided that we had been placed on sufficient warning, she resettled herself in her seat, folding her hands on the desk. She nodded at Father Molloy, as though granting him permission to continue with whatever it was that he was about to do.

Father Molloy blustered his way back to the front of the classroom with a lot of "Well, all right then"s, interrupted by the hiss of the antique PA system crackling to life.

"Holy Mary, Queen of Knowledge, pray for us. Amen. Attention, seniors. Would Colleen Rowley please report to the nurse's office? Colleen Rowley to the nurse's office. Thank you." Hiss, pop, click.

All eyes in the room swiveled to me.

"Me?" I asked.

I looked at Emma. She shrugged. Her eyes glimmered with private thoughts.

Then I looked at Deena, who mouthed *It'll be fine*, and at Anjali, who nodded and waved her hand dismissively.

"I guess you're up, Colleen," Father Molloy said to me.

I stood, gathering my belongings, baffled about why I was being called so soon. I mean, I knew they'd be talking to all the seniors. But somehow I'd assumed they'd go in alphabetical order. I thought I'd be going well after Emma and Anjali.

Father Molloy came over and rested a hand on my shoulder.

"You know," he said, "you shouldn't have to do this. It's none of their business."

I was surprised that he would say that. I wondered if it was true, that they really didn't know what was making everyone sick.

"I don't mind," I said.

But his words made me hesitate.

Father Molloy looked hard at me. "None. Of their business," he said again, enunciating every word.

I nodded, but gathered my books to my chest and moved to the classroom door, tracked by a dozen pairs of the eyes of the girls of St. Joan's.

"Colleen," Nurse Hocking said, looking up at me from some papers on her desk. "Thanks for joining us today."

Us?

The school nurse was looking pretty plush these days. Like she was getting her makeup professionally done. She was even wearing heels. I knew that she was in the habit of giving a quote or two to the reporters every morning, fluff about how the girls were doing fine, how no, she was not at liberty to share their diagnosis for reasons of confidentiality, but that she could assure the community that the school was completely blah blah blah blah blah. For a while we'd all made a point of watching every newscast every night, hoping to glean more information. But quickly we'd learned that the only information that was going to show up on the news would be put there by Nurse Hocking. Most of us figured that we could do a better job of gathering information ourselves.

"Have a seat," Nurse Hocking said.

She gestured to the chair on the opposite side of her desk.

The school nurse was accompanied by a woman in a suit whom I'd never seen before. She also held a clipboard, and she was doing her best to blend in with the curtains.

"Hello," I said directly to her.

"Please," Nurse Hocking said, indicating the chair again. "Sit down."

"Um," I said, lowering myself into the chair and watching the woman in the suit. "I didn't know there'd be anyone else here?"

"Oh," Nurse Hocking said with a wave. "Don't worry. She's authorized."

I suppose I could have asked a dozen questions at that point, reasonable stuff like *Authorized by whom?* or even *Who is she?*, but I was nervous and confused. And I still trusted Nurse Hocking— I mean, she was so young and pretty and nice, and she gave me notes to get out of field hockey if my cramps were too bad, and she didn't even try to laugh it off or make me feel like I was faking. Honestly, it felt a little weird having someone else there, okay, but it didn't occur to me to object. How old do I have to be before I start disagreeing with doctors?

There was a floor plan of the upper school pinned to the wall behind Nurse Hocking's desk, and it had seven red push pins in it, each with a Post-it note underneath, and a date. The Post-its were all connected with different colors of yarn.

"Now then," Nurse Hocking said, opening a file folder. "This shouldn't take too long. I apologize for some of the questions we'll be asking you. Some of them might seem pretty personal. But I assure you that everything will be kept completely confidential."

There was that word again, *confidential*. Nurse Hocking had been using that word a lot.

"Okay," I said, with an uneasy look at the woman in the suit. "But I thought everyone was getting better."

"Yes," Nurse Hocking said. But she hesitated over the word just a little too long. "This is just a precaution."

"A precaution," the woman in the suit said with more force.

It was the first time she'd spoken. Her voice was gravelly, like a smoker's.

"Now, Colleen." The nurse was using my name an awful lot. It was weird. "It says here you're up to date on all your immunizations. Diptheria, pertussis, TB, chicken pox—"

"I can't believe they immunize for that now," the suit woman said with a hacky laugh.

"Yeah," I said, eyes moving between them both.

"And have you ever had an adverse reaction to any immunization?"

"I don't think so. You'd have to ask my mom, I don't really remember."

"Never any itching, rash, headaches, fatigue?"

"Um." I tried to remember anything remarkable about getting vaccines, but other than kicking my feet and crying when I was eight and going through a shot-freakout phase, I can't remember a single thing worth mentioning. "No. Not that I'm aware of."

"And have you had the HPV vaccine series?" Nurse Hocking asked, and the woman in the suit looked up from her clipboard with interest.

"Um," I demurred.

"Colleen," the nurse broke in. "Are you sexually active?"

Oh. Oh, great.

How does anyone know how to answer that question? I mean, I guess technically, the answer was no. But it was also not no. It depended on what she meant. I'd had near misses. Freshman year at a student council dance, this guy Clark whom I knew from church youth group pulled me close during a slow song and pressed his lips to mine. They'd been warm and his chin was rough and he tasted like Skittles and I'd kissed back, and then when his tongue moved between my lips, I was seized with such intense waves of desire that I had to break away and run to the ladies' room and throw up.

There'd been other guys, nothing major, hookups at parties and stuff like that. Then there'd been Evan. He was in my same class at St. Innocent's, and we'd hung out pretty steadily last year. Most of our relationship, if you want to call it that, had been over text message. One night we went for coffee at this place in Salem, and when we realized there was a band setting up, we left to roam the streets. Our hands found each other in the dark, our fingers lacing together, and the feeling of his skin against mine caused my knees to shake and that same coil of almost-nausea to wrap around my stomach. It was a warm night, and we sneaked into the cemetery behind the art museum. He kissed me, hard, and when I put my hands in his hair and groaned into his mouth, he lifted me up onto one of the tombs and spread my knees apart and his hands found me in the dark. He moved a finger into me, within me, and he looked into my eyes and the stars around me fell into blackness.

I stole every minute I could with Evan after that. It was so much better than what I . . . Well. It was good. It was really, really good. He'd wanted to. He'd asked me. But I was afraid. I didn't know why. Everyone told me it wasn't that big of a deal. I didn't think my hesitation was why we stopped hanging out—Evan wasn't a bad guy. He just had an internship in D.C. last summer, and we both got busy with other things. I saw on Facebook that he hooked up with some girl he met on his internship, and I spent a night of red-faced sobbing with Emma in my room. But I didn't know why, it's not like he was ever officially my boyfriend or anything. We still messaged each other sometimes. In the end there wasn't any big scene. Maybe I wish that there had been.

And now, Spence.

Sort of.

Maybe.

Had he?

I thought of his ease, his casual slouching posture, his button-down shirts.

Of course he had.

I blushed, worrying that he wouldn't like it if I haven't. Guys are supposed to like it if you haven't, but I don't think they do, really. I think it stresses them out. Now I wished that I'd had the nerve to try with Evan. I'm sure it would've been okay. Maybe better than okay, and then I wouldn't have to be so worried about it now. Spring semester, senior year, and still acting like a little girl.

"Colleen?" the nurse prodded me.

I realized I hadn't answered her.

"No," I said.

"I see." Nurse Hocking jotted something down on a piece of paper in the file.

The suit woman made a note, too.

I shifted in my seat.

"And what about your friends?" the nurse pressed. "Are any of them sexually active?"

A sickening lurch in my stomach told me that this was a completely inappropriate question.

"I'm not sure I should . . . ," I protested.

"It's all right," the suit woman said. "We've got approval."

I watched her warily, and thought about my friends. Anjali, definitely yes. She'd had boyfriends in her other cities before Danvers, and I thought she'd lost it when she was, like, fourteen, which I personally thought was way too young, but then, I was kind of a prude, as Anjali liked to point out. She and Jason were definitely involved that way, not that she gave me any details, because she knew I didn't approve of Jason. I knew she was careful about it. Like, really careful. Pill plus condoms every time. She was far too serious to let a stupid mistake get in the way of Yale.

Deena had confessed to me that there was a guy in Japan when she was on her exchange program last summer. It was really intense for two months, and now she was on kind of a guy hiatus because they'd ended in this incredibly dramatic way that she was still coming back from, mainly having to do with the impossibility of doing long-distance with a guy in Japan. Screaming and crying in airports and stuff like that. He was from America, on the exchange program, too, but I think they still thought it was impossible. So she was in the yes column, too.

I thought about Emma. I realized that I had no idea whether Emma was or not. Wasn't that weird? She was probably my closest friend, certainly my oldest friend, and I had no idea. She hung out with the same loose confederacy of guys from St. Innocent's and other schools like we all did, and I guessed she hooked up with some of them. But Emma was funny that way. No matter how closely I looked, there was always a layer that I couldn't get beneath.

"Um," I said. I was saying a lot of *um* in this interview. "A couple of them, I'm pretty sure. Yes."

"What about Clara Rutherford?"

"Clara?" I echoed.

It wasn't like Clara and I were close enough friends for me to know. I peered at Nurse Hocking. Of course, she might not know if we were close enough friends or not. From the outside, it probably looked like Clara and I were part of the same essential group. Adults sometimes missed subtle gradations of social distinction like that.

"Do you know if Clara is sexually active?" The gravelly suit woman restated the question as if I somehow hadn't understood.

"Well, I'm not . . . Why are you talking to me first, anyway?" I asked, a twist of suspicion tying itself in my throat.

The nurse and the suit woman exchanged a look.

"You were the first one to bring it to our attention," Nurse Hocking said. "You're kind of ground zero for this whole—" She paused, waving her hand in a circle, looking for the right euphemism. She finally decided on "situation" after the suit woman supplied it for her.

"So?"

"So . . ." She drew the words out. "We're trying to reconstruct everything that happened around when Clara and the other girls fell ill. Just so we can be sure it's contained."

"Why wouldn't it be contained?" I asked.

"Oh, it is," the nurse hastened to add.

"We're almost finished," the suit woman said, as if that would make it okay.

"Just one more question, Colleen," Nurse Hocking said, shuffling through the papers in my file. "How many times have you had strep throat?"

INTERLUDE

*G*rinning at you?" Reverend Green asks, his fine brows knitting over his eyes.

"Grinning," I affirm. "Like a dog with a pullet in its mouth."

"But you said she was screaming bloody murder when you arrived at the parsonage."

"So I did."

The Reverend leans back in his chair, a fingertip alongside his temple. "And that Mrs. Parris said she'd been so for some days."

"Yes." I watch him, wondering if he understands.

"I see," he says at length. "Go on."

I'm standing in the parsonage loft, and downstairs I hear Reverend Parris telling his wife that he'll be calling in some worthy gentlemen for their opinions. He lists several names, all men I know, all of them active in the village church. Among the names I hear mentioned, foremost among them is my father's.

An inquiry from Mrs. Parris, the exact nature of which is muffled.

"Tomorrow, if I can," I hear Reverend Parris say in response.

I hear bustling, Tittibe busying herself with midday dinner. Susannah's stopped crying, and Thomas is asking his father a question that I can't hear.

Tomorrow, Abby's bound to be found out.

"Abby, what's all this? What are you about?" I whisper, not wanting the adults to hear me.

She grins wider. Shrugs.

"You can hear them well as me," I say. "Tomorrow the Reverend's bringing some magistrates in, and they're going to look you well over. They'll find you're not sick. You'll be in the pillory. And I won't be sorry to see it."

"I won't," she says.

"They'll throw clods at you, and cabbages, and they'll be frozen. You just think about that. A frozen cabbage hitting your face."

She leans back on the bolster and toys with a length of her hair. She looks clean and combed, and her cheeks are pink with rest. It's snug up in the loft, with the warmth from the downstairs fire and the smells of dinner, tasty things roasting, rich in the steam collected under the roof. The feeling has finally come back to my feet from my long trudge in the snow. I'd like to climb into that trundle myself.

"Look you, Annie," she says. "If Betty's too sick to fetch and carry, why can't I be, too? Perhaps she's given me her vile distemper. Anyway, I'm much tireder than she is all the time. Why should I be a servant and she not be? She's no better than me. I deserve some rest."

Betty Parris is watching us, her eyes as wide as plates. I glance at her for confirmation. She shakes her head quickly but says nothing.

"It's a lie, Abby," I say, my hands knotting under my apron. "It's a vile sin, lying. If they're working you too hard, it's up to you to ask God for His mercy. You can't just take it for yourself."

She sticks out her lower lip in a wicked pout.

"But I am sick!" she whines. "The Reverend says so. I'm being tortured. I'm near torn to pieces. Look!"

She sticks out one skinny arm and pulls the sleeve of her shift up above her elbow. The skin is mottled red, scored with evil-looking marks.

"Why, Abby!" I cry, horrified. It's like the pox, only worse.

I hurry to her, flushed with shame at my suspicions. She smiles in triumph. I perch on the edge of her bed, taking the arm in my hands and turning it nearer the light.

"See?" she says. "Did you ever see such distemper? I need my rest. Everything they do for me only makes it worse. Mrs. Parris and that island witch are at their wits' end to find a cure."

"And what've they tried?" I ask, frowning over the marks.

Upon closer inspection they don't look like pox at all. I'm not sure I've ever seen the like. Except, possibly . . . I hunt back in my mind for the time my brother met a rat in the hayloft, and ran in sobbing, his hands covered in bites.

"Oh, most everything. Poultices of all kinds, a plaster, warm beveridge with sage leaves, purgatives, and lots of rest, of course. I need my sleep." She says this last bit primly, her eyelashes lowered.

I brush a fingertip over the marks. Abby flinches. They're red enough that they could be growing foul with pus, but not quite. They sure do smart, though, from the look of them.

"And there's no improvement?" I ask.

"None. I just cry and cry and scream and scream." She pauses. "And Thomas has to carry in the buckets for me."

I glance into her eyes, which are gleaming with mischief. She regains her arm from my grasp and pulls the sleeve back down.

"Abby," I start to say.

"It's easy," she says. "You want me to show you?"

"Show me?" I echo.

She nods, a strange smile on her face.

"Roll up your sleeve," she commands me.

I shrug off my cloak and push the sleeve up as far as it will go on the tight jacket I'm wearing, exposing a few inches above my wrist.

Abby takes my arm in her hands. Her touch is gentle as she probes my skin with her fingertips. She glances at me, her smile growing wider.

Then she pulls my wrist to her mouth and sinks her teeth into my flesh.

I scream, yanking my arm away, and stare at her with horror.

She's laughing, wiping her mouth with the back of a wrist.

"Abby!" I cry, cradling my arm in my lap. A semicircle of marks on my skin flushes crimson, some of them deep enough that droplets of blood are pushing to the surface.

A commotion stirs downstairs as the Parrises wonder which of us cried out. *Was it Betty? It didn't sound like Betty. And that wasn't Abby's scream. Could it be Ann? What if it's Ann?*

At the foot of the ladder Reverend Parris calls up, "Ann? Are you all right?"

Abby has her arms wrapped around her waist, and she's laughing silently.

"See?" she whispers. "Easy."

I've gotten to my feet, staring down at her with equal parts wonder and horror.

"Ann? Answer me! I'm coming up."

"No!" I find my voice, though it's shaking. "I'm quite well. Thank you, Reverend Parris."

"Who was it cried out just now?"

Abby watches me, waiting to see what I'll say. Betty's watching, too, the blankets brought up before her mouth.

"Ah," I demur. I could say it was Abby. But then she'll have me in a lie. "It was me, Reverend Parris. I cried out. But I'm all right."

Abby has settled back in her bedclothes, arms behind her, cradling her head, sleepy and smiling.

"You'll see," she whispers. "It pays to have a good distemper now and again."

"Ann, I want you to come down this instant. The girls need their rest, and we've got a message for you to take to your father. Come down!"

The ladder rattles with their insistence.

I gather my cloak up to my chest and back away from Abby. Each foot goes down unsteadily, as though a fearsome pit were widening around me.

"Coming," I call, my voice shaking.

"Always have to come when called," Abby whispers. "Fetch and carry, obey everyone. You'll see, Annie. Don't we deserve some sport?"

CHAPTER 11

The school nurse and the mystery suit woman interrogated me for seemingly ever. All sorts of questions about strep throat—have I had it? How many times? Did it ever turn into scarlet fever? What about rheumatic fever? I said I didn't really remember, but wouldn't all that stuff be in my file anyway? They said yes, but they wanted to be sure the file was accurate. Would I please ask my parents? And on and on. The whole time I kept staring at the floor plan spread behind the nurse's desk.

The one with seven pins on it.

By the time I was free, the class period had already changed over and I was due in AP US History. Almost overdue—class was all of ten minutes from being over. At that rate, they'd never talk to every-one in the senior class. Or if they did, they wouldn't finish until we were all in college.

When I skulked into the classroom, Ms. Slater was wrapping up a long lecture about early colonial architecture. She had an overhead projector and was drawing on a transparency of a house floor plan, with lots of little arrows and things. She saw me come in and nodded at me to sit. Emma must have told her where I was.

Emma pulled her coat off the seat she'd been saving for me and whispered, "You were gone for forever. What did they ask you?"

"Weird stuff," I whispered back. "Like about what vaccines I'd had, and if I'd ever had strep throat, and if I was having sex with anybody."

Emma blanched. "Oh my God. That sounds awful."

"Yeah. But that wasn't the weirdest part." I shifted my eyes left and right to make sure no one else would be able to overhear me. Emma leaned closer.

"It's not five," I whispered.

"What do you mean, it's not five?"

"It's seven."

"No way." Emma sat straight up in her seat, her eyes wide with panic, hands planted on her desk to force herself to stay seated. "Seven? They told you that?"

"No. But they've got this floor plan." I gestured to the image Ms. Slater was projecting. "It's of the whole school. And there were seven push pins on it, in different clusters. Like markers. I definitely recognized two in the chapel."

"Seven," Emma repeated, staring at nothing.

I let my eyes drift over the faces of the other girls in AP US, wondering if any of them knew. If any of them were one of the seven. If, maybe, this were only the beginning.

The bell rang, and I was gathering my things to go when Ms. Slater stopped me.

"Colleen? Could you hang back a second?"

"Sure," I said.

We waited while everyone filed out. Emma loitered until she saw that Ms. Slater wanted to talk to me alone. She left, but not before squeezing my arm in good-bye. When the room was empty, I made my way to Ms. Slater's desk.

"What's up?" I asked.

"You tell me," Ms. Slater said, handing me a sheet of paper.

I took it from her, and frowned. For a minute the markings on it didn't make sense. Lots of red Xes and question marks.

"You want to tell me what happened?" Ms. Slater asked, leaning back in her chair and toying with a pen. She clicked it to open the tip, then clicked it closed.

"I'm . . ."

I looked more closely at the paper. There was a 65 written at the top. Sixty-five? Sixty-five what?

Oh my God.

It was my pop quiz.

A deep pit of panic groaned open beneath my feet, and I felt myself plunging into it, down into the darkness, spinning and clawing at the walls and unable to stop myself from falling. The hand holding the pop quiz trembled.

Ms. Slater clicked the pen again, in slow motion, like the rumble of a cannon.

"Sixty-five?" I said, my voice thick.

Click. Boom.

"I know. I thought from your comments in class that you were keeping up with the material. Especially given that you and Fabiana are—"

I knew what she was about to say, and I cut her off, sputtering with rage.

"Sixty-five? This is a crock!" I spat before I could stop myself. I had never gotten such a low grade. Never. Not once in my life. It wasn't possible. She must've made a mistake.

Ms. Slater's face hardened.

"Colleen, I know you're upset, but that language isn't appropriate."

Appropriate! I'll tell her what's appropriate. Me not having a 65, that's what's effing appropriate. My chest constricted, one hand crumpling the quiz in my palm, as the walls of the pit of panic edged closer, closing me in.

"I'm sorry," I said, my throat tight. "But I can't have a sixty-five. That is not possible."

My GPA was blown. Fabiana would get valedictorian. I wouldn't get into a good school. It would be over. All of it. All the years of hard work, the late nights sweating problem sets, the volunteer work, the extra credit, the research papers. None of it would matter, because this one woman—who was she, anyway? What gave her the right to decide? One stupid quiz about one stupid thing that happened three hundred years ago to a bunch of people nobody cared about, that didn't have anything to do with real life.

"It's not only possible, it's probable, if you don't do the reading. That's how it works."

Ms. Slater was watching me, not unsympathetic exactly, but not giving an inch either. I groped blindly for a chair and sat down, hard.

"I can't . . . I can't . . ."

I felt the inside of my nose getting tight and prickly, and I bit down on the inside of my cheek to keep myself from crying. I wasn't about to let some random goddamn substitute teacher see me cry.

"What kills me," Ms. Slater said, laying her pen delicately down on the desk blotter, "is that I'd really designed it to be an easy one for you guys. All you had to do was skim the material to get an A. I figured, y'all are seniors, you've worked hard, the AP is there waiting at the end, right? Why not toss you a softball once in a while? Everyone else did just fine on it. Yours was the only failing grade."

I was too angry to see straight. I was sure I'd faked my way through enough of the short answers to pull off a B. A B and I would have been fine. *Failing grade.* Didn't she see what this one quiz would do to me? It wasn't fair. I'd worked too hard. Ms. Slater swam back and forth before me in a liquid haze of red.

I glared at her with a flash of bitterness and said, "Well, it won't matter anyway, when Mr. Mitchell gets back."

"It won't?"

"No. He'll throw out whatever you had us doing anyway, so what difference does it make."

I wasn't sure if it was true, what I was saying. But I knew I wished it were true. Mr. Mitchell would never judge all our hard work based on some BS pop quiz. He was far too intellectual for that. And who was Ms. Slater anyway? Where the hell had she come from? What did she know?

My life was such a careful balance, a fragile nexus of work and attention and preparation and planning, like the old vaudeville trick of spinning plates on poles all over a stage, running from one to another to another, not letting any of them fall. I'd been so good at it, the running and the spinning. I'd been getting up before dawn and staying late after school and running and spinning the plates for as long as I could remember. I was getting so tired. I didn't want to run and spin anymore. But I didn't know what would happen, I didn't know who I would be, if one of the plates broke.

I hated Mr. Mitchell for getting sick. I hated Ms. Slater and her goddamn *y'all* for thinking pop quizzes were something that it was okay to give us. I hated my friends for doing the reading and acing the quiz. I hated myself for not.

Ms. Slater got to her feet with a heavy sigh and roamed to the blackboard, where she took up an eraser and started wiping the day away, one stroke at a time, her back to me.

"Well, Colleen," she said. "The thing of it is, Mr. Mitchell's not coming back."

My breath caught in my throat.

"What do you mean, he's not coming back?"

She placed the eraser back in the tray and turned, leaning against the blackboard, arms folded over her thin chest, the wickedest of her eyebrows cocked at me. It occurred to me that she would get chalk all over her ass, leaning like that. The thought made me feel marginally better.

"Just that. He's not coming back, and the university job market doesn't start up again until next fall, which means we're stuck with each other for the rest of the year. So we're going to have to come up with a way to move past this. Now, I know you're upset, and I think I've got a pretty good understanding of why, but that doesn't make it okay for you to behave that way. I'd like an apology, please."

Stuck with each other? I looked down at my hands, still chewing the inside of my cheek. I wiped the suggestion of tears away from beneath my eyes and felt shame boiling red on my forehead.

"I'm sorry. I was just—" My voice caught. "I'm pretty upset. I didn't mean to freak out at you."

Ms. Slater's expression softened and she returned to her desk, where she leaned forward on her elbows.

"That's better. Thank you. I accept your apology. Now." She paused. "You want to tell me what's really going on?"

I brought my hands to my forehead and rubbed. My fatigue was deadening. I could have put my head down on the desk and fallen asleep right there.

"I don't know," I said from behind my hands. "It's just . . . I'm just . . ."

She waited. I appreciated that she waited. Teachers at St. Joan's are big finishers of other people's sentences.

"I've been working so hard. And I'm so tired." My voice came out small.

"I know you have," she said.

We sat for a minute in silence.

"So," she said. "How'd the interview with the nurse go? Was it as awful as the faculty meeting made it sound?"

I laughed weakly and dropped my hands.

"Worse," I said, rubbing the corners of my eyes. "God. What I don't understand is, I thought they'd figured out it was just about vaccines. HPV shots, or whatever. But then they were asking me all about . . ." I paused, embarrassed. "Other stuff. Like how many times I'd had strep throat. How random is that?"

"Pretty random," Ms. Slater agreed. "Have you had strep throat?"

"Hasn't everyone had it once or twice? I don't remember."

"Well," she said, "I suppose they have their reasons."

"I guess."

A funny expression crossed Ms. Slater's face. She seemed on the point of saying something else, but then she changed tack and said, "And what's happening for you with colleges? Did you get in early anywhere, or are you still in applications?"

Ms. Slater was looking at me with such warmth and genuine-seeming interest that a tear escaped my cheek-biting and traced down the side of my nose. "I got deferred," I whispered. "Williams and Dartmouth. I don't understand it. I mean, they were both reaches, but still."

I didn't speak any of the secret, tarry resentments I thought, things like *How could Fabiana have gotten in early to Vassar? I mean, I know about her grades, but she's so vacuous* or *I don't understand why Deena's not applying to bigger places, even if I should be glad because it means she's not competition for me like Anjali is.* Or even *Leigh Carruthers should just be packed off to finishing school and call it a day, I mean, don't they still do that sometimes?* We're supposed to be positive. We're not supposed to say this stuff out loud. Especially not about our friends.

"So you're still applying. No wonder you're upset."

I nodded.

She sighed, and said, "Tell you what."

I looked up quickly, my face alight with hope.

"I can't vacate the grade. It's not fair to everyone else." My hopeful expression slipped. "But we can talk about some extra credit if you want."

"Oh my God, yes! Really? I could do that?"

She smiled. "Sure. But you can't half-ass it. There's going to be work involved. You'll have to manage your time very carefully so you don't keep falling behind."

"That's fine, I can totally do that. You should know, Ms. Slater, this is really uncharacteristic of me. I never show up unprepared. Never."

"Yes. Your reputation has preceded you," she said. There was that wicked eyebrow arch again. "And normally I wouldn't be having this conversation, since I tend to be pretty strict in my grading policy. But given everything that's been going on the past couple of weeks, and given your involvement, I think we can make an exception just this once."

My involvement? Was I involved? What did she mean by that? God, who cared, if it meant I could do something about that 65.

"Thank you so much, Ms. Slater. I really can't begin to tell you how—" I started to say in a rush.

She cut me off with a smile and a wave of her hand. "All right, all right. Shut up already."

I smiled back.

Ms. Slater reached into her desk drawer, pulled out a book, and tossed it to me. I snatched it out of the air and looked at the cover.

The Crucible. Which she had told us was a complete waste of time. I opened my mouth to say something, maybe to object.

"Here's what we're going to do," she said, interrupting my thoughts. "You're going to write me a ten-page research paper on someone from the Salem panic who's been either written out or turned into a composite by Mr. Miller here. It's going to have a solid thesis statement, and it's going to rely on primary sources and secondary sources. You're not even going to think about looking at Wikipedia. You're going to get started on it, and then you're going to check in with me, and we're going to decide on a due date together that's not going to get in the way of the rest of your work. Okay?"

I hugged the play to my chest and beamed at her. The walls of the panic pit opened over my head, letting in a tiny bit of sunlight. "Okay. Yes. Thank you!"

"You're welcome." She paused, and then added, "Don't screw up."

I gathered my things together and tucked the play under my arm. She really wasn't that bad. Okay, she was kind of weird, for a teacher. And she was nowhere near as cool as Mr. Mitchell, but still.

Halfway out of the classroom I turned.

"Ms. Slater?"

"Hmm?" She had turned her attention to marking some papers and didn't look up at me.

"What happened to Mr. Mitchell? Did he quit or something? I thought he was out sick."

Now she looked up. A shadow darkened her face. "You really don't know?"

I shook my head.

"Well," Ms. Slater said, "I'm afraid all I can tell you is, you won't be seeing him again. And not to worry about it."

The substitute teacher gave me a long look, as though sending me a telepathic message. But whatever it was, I wasn't getting it.

"Thanks," I said, and slipped out the door.

INTERLUDE

*S*he *bit* you?" Reverend Green exclaims.

"Yes."

"And you think the marks on her arm came from her biting herself."

"Yes. Though maybe she had Betty Parris bite her, too. To make it look better. Abby had a way of making people do things."

"Some people have that way about them," the Reverend says. "As though they compel you from inside your own mind."

"They do," I agree, watching him.

"But you must've gone straight downstairs and told them what had happened."

My right fingertips brush over the skin inside my left wrist. A semicircle of pale white marks still lies there, a memento of Abby Williams that will always scar me.

"I didn't."

I bring my gaze up to meet his. I hate showing him how wretched I am. But that is why I've come. So that at last, someone will know.

• • •

It's some days later, around February 25, when I'm at the table peeling potatoes with one of my sisters. Our only servant at that time, a sullen girl named Mercy, is busy brewing, and my mother squints over her needlework, making a sour line of her mouth when she drops a stitch. My father is looking over his accounts. The previous day my aunt visited, after many weeks of us not seeing her, and there was a dreadful row that I didn't understand. Now my father's spent all day in his books, scribbling figures in the margin. Every so often my mother glances at him with worry in her face. But it's not my place to ask.

I haven't been back to the parsonage, and I've told no one what Abby's done. I've bandaged my welts myself, but they're starting to seep and itch.

If the rumors are true, several worthy gentlemen spent the last many days up in the parsonage attic, gathered about Abby and Betty's bedsides, united in prayer. They've fasted, and Reverend Parris's been heard to claim that Satan is laying siege to Salem Village, and that the village must look into its soul and find what sin we've committed that's brought such misery to bear.

My mother has her theories about which families might be harboring the sin. My father has them, too.

"Coreys, I'll warrant," she's muttered. "And those Procters. He's a godless man. Not been to meeting since I don't know when. And his first wife never kept the house that way. She was a gospel woman, but this one . . ." She shakes her head and tsks over Elizabeth Procter's housekeeping.

The talk of Betty and Abigail is nothing but pity for their suffering Christian souls. They are innocent lambs being punished for the sin that's hidden in the heart of the village, and we should all examine our souls with open eyes to root out the evilness within.

I'm prising the eye out of a potato with a paring knife when the sound of hoofbeats drawing up to the yard outside causes me and my sister to look up. The creak of wagon wheels, and a young girl's voice says, "Thank you, Uncle."

Then a sharp rapping on the door.

"Get it, Mercy," my mother says. She's learned that there's no point waiting for Mercy to know what her duties are without us telling her.

Without ceremony Mercy stalks to the door and pulls it open. A stooping man of middling build and grizzled appearance steps in and hands the servant his hat. He stamps the snow from his boots and looks around. Behind him trails a girl about my age in a cloak too big for her, who beams when she sees me.

"Thomas?" he asks. "Good day to you, Goody Putnam. Girls. Is he in?"

Mother has put her sewing aside and gotten to her feet.

"Dr. Griggs." She comes over to take his hand. "Yes. He's in the best room. I'll take you."

"Sit with the girls, Elizabeth," Dr. Griggs says to the creature behind him with a gesture to us. "Make yourself useful."

Betty Hubbard rushes over and puts her arms around my neck. I return the embrace. She's gotten taller since last I saw her, which doesn't seem that long ago, but it was before the snow, that's sure. Now she's the same height as me.

"Ann!" she cries. "I begged him to let me come."

"Come and sit, Betty," I say, bringing her to the bench.

I hand her a potato so that we may both look busy while we talk. She turns it in her palms. We can hear muffled adult voices in the other room, but we can't hear what they're saying.

"We're on our way to the parsonage," Betty Hubbard informs me in a whisper. "Reverend Parris sent for Uncle special, and I made Mother have him take me. Said I was a friend of Betty Parris's, and it would do her well for her to see me there."

I laugh.

"Scamp, you," I say. "Since when were you a friend of Betty Parris?"

Betty Hubbard, the Other Betty, smiles behind her wrist and says, "Well, I *would* be her friend, if she'd have me. And I do wish her well, hand to heaven I do. She's so little and frail. But how are you, Ann? It's been an age since I saw you. Isn't the cold wretched this winter? I don't hardly go out at all, and you must not either. Mother says it's the worst she can remember, and you know she can remember since before Moses was found in the rushes."

"I'm all right, I guess," I say.

Seeing Betty Hubbard makes me realize how tired I've been. For weeks now I've been coiled tight as a snake under a rock, worn down with worry. Sitting next to Betty makes me uncoil some, and all I want to do is rest. If it were warmer, I could sneak off to the hayloft and lie on my back and count the wasp nests under the eaves until I fell asleep. But it's too cold, and I've too much to do.

I pick up another potato.

"I was going to the parsonage pretty regular," I say. "I can't make heads or tails of Betty Parris. She won't talk. When it's just us, she's well herself, but when the adults are there, she acts like a wooden poppet. But even with just us, she won't speak. She must be sick, but of what?"

"Hmm," Betty Hubbard sniffs. "Why'd you stop going?"

"Oh." My welts throb under my sleeve, invisible and insidious. "No special reason. I had chores."

Betty Hubbard looks at me under her eyelashes. "Not afraid of that Abby?"

I glance at Betty, eyes wide, suddenly fearful. What has she heard?

"I would be," Betty Hubbard whispers.

The door to the best room thumps open and Dr. Griggs reappears, followed by my father and my mother, who flits about the two men like a moth around a lamp.

". . . be getting there as soon as we can," Dr. Griggs is in the middle of saying. "If we go now, Thomas, I warrant we'll be there within the hour, or at least no more than two. Can you?"

"Indeed," my father says, groping for his greatcoat. "Ann, I don't know how long we'll be. Can you have the girl get us a pone?"

He's talking to my mother, who is also Ann. Sometimes he teases me and calls me "Junior," as though I were an eldest son. I'm not, though. And never can be.

"Elizabeth!" Dr. Griggs barks to his niece. "I trust you made yourself a boon to this household in my absence?"

"Oh, yes, Uncle," Betty chirps, placing down the identical unpeeled potato that I handed her upon her arrival.

"But what if there's contagion?" my mother asks from the table near the hearth, where she's wrapping some corn bread in a napkin to give to my father. Mercy's standing by watching, as though she'd never heard of a pone, much less how to wrap one up.

"We'll be taking every precaution," Dr. Griggs assures her. "All will be quite well, Goody Putman."

It's a matter of indifference to most people if our name is Putnam or Putman. I've even seen my father sign our name both ways. Sometimes I wonder if one is righter than another. If I can secretly be two people at once.

"Goody Putnam," Betty pipes up, tying her scarf under her chin in preparation to go. "Couldn't Annie come with us? I'd be so much quieter if she could be there. She loves Betty and Abigail as much as I do."

I'm torn, part of me yearning to flee across the yard to the barn no matter how cold it is and hide in the stall behind our old cow where no one will find me. But I admit to being curious. If Dr. Griggs is called, they must be nearing the end of the praying. I want to know if Abby'll be found out. I look at my mother, trying to arrange my features into a semblance of filial piety.

"Betty's right. Perhaps I ought to go?"

My mother looks between us, worried.

"You're certain there's no danger?" she asks the doctor. "Thomas, you'll watch her, won't you?"

"Of course," my father says. "I'm sure the Parrises'll be only too glad of the extra help. Annie, step lively."

I drop my eyes and hurry to the door, assembling my winter garb with an air of submission and obedience. Out of the corner of my eye I can see Betty Hubbard smiling. She winks at me. A smile twitches my cheek.

"Here." My mother thrusts the wrapped pone into my hands. "It could be a long night. You mind your father. And Mrs. Parris. Make yourself useful."

I nod. "Yes, Mother."

Betty and I follow close on the heels of Dr. Griggs and my father, who are murmuring between themselves about Reverend Parris and what we're likely to find.

Once we're settled in the back of the wagon, Betty takes my hand. As the doctor tells the horse to walk on, Betty whispers, "I can't wait to see them with my own eyes, can you?"

"I can't," I agree. But the gleam in Betty Hubbard's eye is troublingly bright.

I don't know how much time passes. In the parsonage's hall there's nowhere to sit, so Betty Hubbard and I stand, tucked in a corner out of the way by a straw pallet rolled up against the wall. The men are all up in the loft, and the excitement of their voices is almost enough to drown out the occasional cries breaking forth from Abby, and now from Betty Parris, too. We hear pounding and shattering and rumbling of feet, and a man's voice shout, "Grab her! The window!"

The hall is packed with women, some of them pretending to make themselves useful by stirring a pot or folding a cloth, and some there under pretense of errand, baskets clutched on their laps. A few hands busy themselves with darning. But the majority sit and stare, their eyes steady on the ceiling of the hall.

"Ann!" a scream rings out. "Oh, Ann, God in heaven, they want me to sign!"

A commotion overhead as all the eyes in the long hall swivel to me. Betty Hubbard widens her eyes with excitement, and I can tell she's struggling not to smile. She tugs on my hand under our cloaks and whispers, "You get to go up!"

"Ann Putnam?" a male voice calls down the loft ladder. "Would someone send up Ann Putnam?"

"Fetch her," Mrs. Parris says to Tittibe, who's standing close to her husband, John, a blocky Indian used by the Parrises as a man of all work. Tittibe and John exchange a look, and she releases his hand and approaches me with a worried expression.

"Come, my Annie," Tittibe says.

She holds her hand out to me. A sheen of sweat gleams on her forehead.

I take her hand and feel the stares of the village women as Tittibe leads me to the attic stair.

"Ann! Is someone bringing her?" the impatient voice calls, which I now take to belong to Reverend Parris.

"Hurry now," Tittibe says to me.

On trembling arms and legs I hoist myself up.

In the loft, I find Betty Parris and Abigail Williams tucked into a trundle together, though I can scarcely see them through the forest of black-coated men clustered around the bed. They are murmuring their bafflement.

". . . cannot be a brain fever, for her face is cool to the touch . . ."

". . . and what of the marks? Is it a pox of some sort? . . ."

". . . the coolness of the feet and the disordered speech must surely mean . . ."

"Here! It's the girl she's asking for."

A man I don't recognize takes hold of my upper arm and steers me roughly to the bedside. I behold Betty Parris, lying stiff as a board, purple rings circling her eyes. Next to her Abby sits bolt upright, hair streaming back from a sweaty forehead, a finger outstretched, pointing at me.

"There she stands at Ann's shoulder! Do you not see her? She holds the book out to me, but I will not sign!"

"What book?" Dr. Griggs asks, looking curiously between Abby and me. "What does she mean, child?"

"I don't know of any book," I say.

The bite marks under my sleeve are itching something fierce.

"Ann, tell them! Tell them how we've seen their Sabbaths out on the rye field from this very window, where they ate red bread and drank blood like sacramental wine! Tell them how they bade us sign their vile book, but we wouldn't!"

"A book!" Reverend Parris gets to his feet and rushes to me. He takes me by the shoulders and shakes. "What is she speaking of? Who conspires against me? Tell me!"

I feel the force of him, his fingers digging into my upper arms.

"I . . . I . . . ," I stammer, panicking as the many older learned male faces crowd down upon me, all urging me to explain, to tell them, to reveal the truth of what Abby's saying. And the oddest part is, I feel myself wanting to tell them. They are so keen to know, and I want to obey. Of course I know Abby's dissembling, I saw that wicked grin, I know she's reveling in the care that's been lavished on her these past weeks. But now all the eyes are on me, fine men in periwigs, who've been to the college and can read the Word and are accustomed to being harkened to by other men and women and girls like myself. They're all bearing down upon me, and I'm powerless to find the words they want to hear.

"Show them, Annie!" Abby screams. "Show what happens when we don't sign the book!"

Wordlessly I reach down and roll my sleeve, turning my inner arm faceup to catch the yellow lamplight. Reverend Parris releases my upper arms and steps back that he might see. Dr. Griggs peers down at my arm, squinting.

I'm on the point of saying that Abby bit me, that she's a liar and a rogue and they should beat her, but the focused breathing of the roomful of men as they stare at my tender flesh stops my tongue. A silence falls over the company, and even Abby seems to be holding her breath, awaiting the doctor's verdict.

Dr. Griggs looks the marks up and down, takes my arm in his hand, and turns it this way and that in the light. Then he stands upright, pressing his lips together in thought and looking each gentleman in the face.

"Well?" prompts a man whose face I cannot see, obscured as he is by half a dozen others.

"It's as I feared," the doctor says.

An excited murmur circulates among the assembly.

"I'd say these symptoms are beyond what's in the power of natural disease to effect. It's preternatural."

"But what can that mean, Doctor?" Reverend Parris asks, worrying his hands together.

"I fear, Reverend Parris," the doctor says, "that these poor girls are under an evil hand. All of them."

CHAPTER 12

I pulled up the driveway to Emma's house, flipped off the radio, and leaned my head against the headrest. I was early, and I could see by the movement of silhouettes behind the living room curtains that the Blackburns were clearing the dinner table. I counted heads, and guessed that Mark was probably home for the weekend from Endicott. It was pretty weird, him going to college so close to home. But that's how they did it in Emma's family. Her mom liked to keep them all close. Like if she let them get too far out of her sight, something might happen.

I mustered myself, not really feeling in the mood to socialize. But it was set to be a pretty low-key night. Movies with Emma, just hanging out. We hadn't done that in forever. I used to go to Emma's all the time when we were younger, but in the last few years we'd gone out more instead. Partly it was because we were older, and so we could, but if I'm honest, it was also because the Blackburn house was grim. One of those fifties split-levels with cheap siding and a chain-link fence. Thick layers of dust and a greasy smell. Carpet stains.

Out of the car, doorbell, and Mark answered.

"Oh, hey, Colleen," he said.

He was like the male Emma. Blond, slim, with practically no eyebrows, and permanently tanned. I tried to remember if he still played lacrosse. Damn, he looked good. What was he, twenty? If he weren't Emma's brother, seriously.

"Hey, Mark. Sorry I'm early."

"No worries. Come on in."

"Emma!" Mark called to the kitchen. I heard the sound of running water and dishes.

"Hey," Emma said, emerging from the kitchen, wiping her hands on a dish towel.

She had a funny look on her face, and her parents were nowhere to be seen. Which was weird, since I'd just seen them all through the window. I knew they were home.

"Hey," I said, looking between Emma and Mark. The silence between them was hard to quantify. I wondered if I'd interrupted an argument or something.

"So, d'you want to go out for a while?" Emma asked.

Mark disappeared into the living room.

"Um," I hesitated. I was pretty tired, and we'd already talked about staying in and watching movies. I missed lying on my stomach on the floor of Emma's room, like we used to do every weekend in middle school. I'd been looking forward to a night like we used to have. But I guess there weren't going to be any more nights like we used to have. "Sure, I guess. Where do you want to go?"

"I don't know. I just feel like going out. I figure, you've got the car, right?"

Of course, if Emma really wanted to go out, couldn't she just borrow Mark's car? But whatever. Maybe she'd had a fight with her parents, and that's why the atmosphere in their house was so off.

"Sure. Whatever. You want to tell your folks?"

"Nah. Mom's having one of her episodes." Emma enclosed this

last word with ironic air quotes. "She felt a headache coming on. It'd be better if we just left."

"Oh. Okay."

I hadn't even taken off my coat. I was still holding the car keys in my hand. Emma wound a scarf around her neck and said, "Let's go."

"Bye, Mark!" I called.

No answer.

Once we were in the car, Emma started spinning through radio stations and said, "Thank you. This is so much better. Want to drive to the water?"

Emma was a sailor, and I knew that during the winter she pined for the ocean. I liked sitting by the ocean, too—it was one of the nicest things about living where we did, along the water north of Boston. Most of us took the nearness of the ocean for granted. Not me. Definitely not Emma. Maybe that was why the Blackburns liked to stay close to home.

"Sure. Any place special?"

"Nah. Beverly, I guess. Or the Willows?"

The Willows was Salem's old boardwalk, and one of our favorite places to go when we felt down. But Beverly was closer, and there was a park close to the harbor. Without discussion, I started driving us there.

A Florence and the Machine song came on, and Emma sang along. I cracked the windows and we let the cold winter night wash over our faces. Emma leaned back in her seat, her knees drawn up, boots on the dashboard, and smiled at me. But it was a sad smile.

We pulled into the parking lot off the oceanfront park. All the boats had been taken out of the harbor and parked on jacks in the boatyard by the overpass, a spiky forest of masts against the starry sky. Through the cracked windows we could hear waves curling onto the rocks below. The air smelled crisper. Sharper.

"You want to get out?" I asked.

"Nah," she said.

Instead she rummaged in her jacket pocket and pulled out a small baggie. I pretended not to see what she was up to, ignoring the rustling and the flick of the lighter.

"You want?" she asked, trying to pass me something small and burning, with a thick, acrid smell.

I eyed her, my temple resting on my fist.

"Nah," I said. "Thanks, though."

"Suit yourself."

She rolled the window down more and blew a lazy plume of smoke out of the car. She hadn't even asked me if it was okay. I considered the problem of the smell, but decided that could probably be taken care of with some air freshener.

We sat for a while, and Emma let out a long sigh. The atmosphere in the car loosened.

"That's Clara's house, over there," Emma said, gesturing with her free hand.

"Which one?"

"That one, with the one light on upstairs."

Clara lived in one of those wedding cake houses, painted navy blue with crisp white trim, the kind of house that a self-satisfied merchant built himself in 1880 to show that he'd arrived.

"I wonder if they're home."

"Dunno."

We both gazed at the wedding cake house. It had a widow's walk on the roof, with what must have been a killer view over the harbor. I reflected that if that were my house, I'd hang out on the roof all the time. I'd be up on that roof right now, if I could.

"I'm surprised there's not a news van outside."

"Maybe there is. Look."

I squinted, and sure enough there was a dun-colored, unmarked van, barely visible in the shadows cast by the naked trees across the street from Clara's house. And it had a small, unobtrusive satellite dish on its roof.

"Oh my God. Why don't they just leave us alone?"

Emma smiled and said, "The Mystery Illness of 2012. They can't just drop a story that great. Not when it's up to seven now."

"I can't believe that. You don't know who, do you?"

Emma shook her head, rustling in her plastic bag again. I weighed whether or not to comment. Nobody wants a friend who's judgmental. But then . . . I'd just ask. Why not.

"Are you, like, okay?" I asked, trying to keep my voice light.

I knew she dipped into that on occasion—got it from Mark, was my impression—but this seemed kind of uncharacteristic for her. Weed was more of a lazy summertime activity for Emma. Seasonal. Like eggnog.

The lighter flicked once, twice as she tried to get the spark going, splashing her face with snaps of yellow light. She took a long drag, held her breath, coughed, and exhaled out the window. She proffered me the joint again out of habit, and I waved it away.

"Yeah," she said. "I guess I'm just disappointed."

The Harvard interview. A twist of guilt knifed in my gut, followed by one of those unwelcome, secret thoughts: *Well, let's be honest, Em, your grades aren't up to it. I mean, B-plus GPA?* As soon as that thought bloomed in my mind, I pushed it away as disloyal.

"I'm sorry, Emma. They're crazy not to give you one. I probably won't get in anyway."

"Sure you will." She smiled out of the side of her mouth and took another long toke on her joint. "Anyway, those interviews don't even really matter." She said this casually, a reassurance for herself. But also a pinprick for me.

I was trying to come up with something encouraging to say, or barring that, something sufficiently self-deprecating, when I felt the atmosphere in the car plunge in a sudden chill. The air pressure changed, as though the barometer had fallen.

"It's him," Emma said.

"Who?" I asked, following Emma's stare.

"Mr. Mitchell," she said.

Sure enough, the slim figure of our AP US History teacher was loping down the sidewalk, coming from the direction of Clara's house. Mr. Mitchell's hands were thrust in his jacket pockets, and his head was ducked down in thought. He looked different, and I realized it was because he wasn't in a jacket and tie like he wore at school. He wore a motorcycle jacket and jeans. His hair was sloppy.

Emma palmed the joint and slouched down in the passenger seat of my station wagon.

"That's weird," I said, watching him pass. I'd forgotten how cute he was. He looked younger, dressed like that.

"Shh!" Emma hushed me, sinking lower.

"He doesn't look like he's been sick or anything," I remarked.

As I spoke, he paused, looking out over the water, its waves glittering under the starlight, and ran his hand across the back of his neck. Even through the darkness I could see he looked upset about something. Almost like he'd been crying.

"Will you shut up?" Emma hissed, grabbing for my shoulder and dragging me down out of sight lines with the park.

"What? He can't see us. It's *night*," I pointed out, struggling up on one elbow so that I could finish watching him pass by.

He considered the ocean for a long moment, breeze ruffling his hair, before continuing on, his eyes on his feet. Mr. Mitchell never glanced at our car. After a few minutes he was swallowed by shadow and disappeared. I sat all the way back up, staring down the block to the last corner where I'd seen him.

"Why do you suppose he hasn't come back, Em?" I asked, bringing a knuckle up to my mouth for a thoughtful chew.

Emma didn't answer. When I looked over at the passenger seat, I saw Emma sitting with her hands over her face. A wet snuffling sound was coming from behind her hands.

"Okay," I said. "That's it. We're going to the Shanty."

. . .

The Shanty is about the size of my closet, and my closet isn't exactly a walk-in. It's this lobster place on Artists' Row in Salem, and has a vibe about it that I particularly like. I found a spot on Essex Street, got us out of the car, and steered Emma by her elbow. She wiped her face on her sweater sleeves and slurped the snot into the back of her throat. There never was an uglier crier than Emma Blackburn. I'm serious: her whole face just folds in on itself and her eyelids puff up and she looks like a completely different person.

"Hey, Leland," I said to the recalcitrant owner of the Shanty.

He grunted in greeting. We took one of the plate-sized tables in back, close to the lobster tank. I plopped Emma down and stuffed a fistful of paper napkins into her hands, and she buried her nose in them. Two menus were slapped on our table, followed by two sets of silverware in a defensive heap.

"I'm sorry," Emma bubbled. She blew her nose with a honk.

"Shh," I said.

Leland came back with a pad. "Get you girls something?"

"Yeah. Two beers, please. Sam Winter?"

"Hmph," Leland said. "Anything to eat?"

I looked at Emma, who slumped in her chair like a potted plant someone forgot to water.

"Just some sweet-potato chips. Thanks."

Another grunt, and Leland withdrew.

I turned to Emma.

"I think you should lay off that stuff. Seriously. It just makes you paranoid and depressed."

Emma smiled wanly at me and blew her nose again. On the television screen behind the softly bubbling lobster tank, the evening news began. TJ Wadsworth, in a deep violet suit this time, was reporting on a house fire in Peabody the previous night.

"Maybe," she said. "I just hate this. Don't you hate this?"

"Hate what?" I asked.

"I don't know. This. Everything. It's all ending. I don't want it to change. Do you?" Emma's eyes were rimmed in red, and she looked at me, pleading. But the truth was, I didn't understand. I didn't know why she was so afraid.

"Um. I do, actually. Kind of," I said. "Don't you?"

"No!" she cried. "I hate that everyone's going to move away next year. I hate the idea of leaving my parents alone. I wish everything could just stay the same. I like it here. I like things as they are. I don't want it to be different!"

We were interrupted by two pint glasses plunked down in front of us, with a basket of sweet-potato chips dropped in between. I took a sip and grimaced.

Root beer.

Leland smirked at me and said, "You want me to run you a tab?"

I scowled at him, and he went away chuckling.

Emma took a sip of her root beer and piled some sweet-potato chips into her mouth. We chewed in silence while the weatherman pointed out a cold front that would be dropping up to three inches of snow on the Eastern Seaboard, beginning the next day. Emma wiped her mouth and face with more paper napkins and raised raw eyes to the television screen.

"My head's killing me," she remarked.

"You're probably just dehydrated from all that crying," I said. But I wasn't really listening.

Over our heads the news crawl announced that the St. Joan's Academy Mystery Illness, once thought to be an isolated outbreak of sensitivity to a batch of vaccines in a small handful of local pediatricians' offices, had spread.

To eight.

Part 3

MID-FEBRUARY

LUPERCALIA

The magistrate sits in your heart,
that judges you.

ELIZABETH PROCTOR
THE CRUCIBLE, ACT 2

CHAPTER 13

T here," my mother said, plucking a fluff of lint from the front of my sweater. "No, wait." She licked her thumb and then wiped something off my cheek.

"Mom! Come on!" I reached up to dry the streak of her spit on my skin. But I actually felt better.

"Let me look." She stepped back and surveyed me, tugging and adjusting. Mom and I were the same height, and her hair was like a steel-streaked, unraveled version of mine. We had the same green eyes, but her freckles were darker.

Cardigan, wool skirt, tights, ankle boots, peacoat, new scarf, hat with wool flower. Good Coach handbag from the outlet store. Makeup, but not too much of it. Hair with the right stuff in it to make it fall in spirals. If Emma were here, she'd pull one curl and make it bounce.

"Think it's okay?" I asked.

My mother fussed with my curls and smiled proudly at me. "You look darling."

I wasn't sure if I wanted to look darling. I thought I'd rather look collegiate. Intellectual.

"Maybe I should wear my glasses instead of my contacts."

"Nonsense. You look fine. Now, do you have everything? Transcript? Résumé?" Mom hunted in her pockets as though she were the one heading to her college interview instead of me. "What about a copy of your personal essay?"

"She said I didn't need to bring any of that stuff. She doesn't need it."

"Are you positive?" I could tell my mother was worried about me confronting the Harvard interviewer without a portfolio of achievements for us to discuss. But I liked that Judith Pennepacker wanted to meet me, rather than some list of things I'd done.

"We'd better go or you'll miss your train," Dad said as he passed through the kitchen.

Michael slouched at the kitchen table, earbuds in ears, reading a book, head nodding in rhythm. Maybe there was actually music playing in the earbuds this time.

"Where's Wheez?" I asked.

"Oh," my mother said, waving her hand. "Around. Are you really sure you don't need to bring anything? Maybe you should pack a résumé, just in case. So you have it."

She thrust the folded packet of my St. Joan's dossier into my hand, and I accepted it with a roll of my eyes. It was easier to take it than to argue.

"Train, Colleen!" my father called from the mudroom.

"Coming!" I called back.

I cast a look at Michael, and he glanced at me quickly before returning to his book. Under the kitchen table he pulled out his new cell phone and texted something, not meeting my eyes.

On my way out the front door a voice from inside the coats hanging thick and puffy on the pegs in the mudroom said, "Good luck, Colleen! I like your hat. Can I have it?"

"Sure," I said with a smile. "When I get back. Bye, Wheez."

• • •

The day was blistering gray and cold, but even in the grimmest doldrums of February, Harvard Square was ablur with people. I always felt a charge of excitement in the Square, but today the quality of that excitement was subtly different. For the first time I allowed myself to pretend that I might be one of the students I saw hurrying off to class, or one of the glamorous girls out on Friday night, tottering over brick sidewalks in high heels with a tiny coat over an even tinier dress.

I was early, hanging around, gazing into the windows of the Coop. The sign said next month there was going to be some professor from Northeastern there, giving a talk. That would be crazy, having to give a talk in front of people like that. I guessed professors spoke in front of people all the time. But still.

A sharp wind kicked up, tumbling wet leaves and bits of paper down the street, blowing up my legs and under my skirt. I shivered. My knees were getting numb. It was too cold to kill time outside. I still had fifteen minutes before my interview, but I thought I'd go to Dado Tea anyway and loiter. She wouldn't know it was me, anyway, right? No big deal.

I hunched my shoulders to my ears and leaned into the wind, my hands bunched in my pockets, as I made my way to the café. Inside my coat pocket, my phone vibrated with a text received. I pulled the phone out to see what was up. Spence and I had already made a plan to get together about an hour after my interview. Maybe he was writing to wish me luck.

It wasn't from Spence. The number said UNKNOWN.

The play. I'm serious. Look at it.

I frowned.

I'm pretty stressed right now, Whoeveryouare. Stop bothering me.

I stared at the phone, wind tangling my spiral curls into a cloud around my ears. A full minute passed, by the clock on my phone. No response.

Grumbling, I thrust the phone back in my pocket and kept trudging to the café.

It was packed when I got there, warm with bodies, crowded with coats hung over the backs of chairs, and after I ordered my tea at the standing bar, I scanned the room looking for a woman who might resemble Judith Pennepacker's staid Facebook photo. At first I didn't see anyone I recognized. My gaze slid over the faces, lots of teacher types, with piles of papers to grade under their mugs of coffee. I stumbled momentarily over a face that I half recognized, but rejected it as belonging to a stranger. Then I looked again.

The face belonged to a young, clean-cut guy in a sport coat and tie spotted with tiny ducks in flight, sitting at a table with a woman whose back was to me. All I could see of her was a heavy brown French braid, tied with a scrunchie. I frowned, trying to place him. Was he one of the guys in my class at St. Innocent's? No. But he definitely looked . . . Wait . . .

The guy must have sensed me looking at him, because he met my gaze and his face drained of all its color as he recognized me.

Jason Rothstein. Anjali's Andover yo-boy boyfriend. Meeting with Judith Pennepacker for his Harvard interview.

I opened my mouth in a silent laugh, pointed at him to make him feel even more embarrassed, and then turned my back, sipping a bubble tea and waiting my turn at the pillory.

I was slurping the last taro milk from the bottom of my tea glass when I sensed someone standing at my elbow.

"Hi, Jason," I said. "Nice sport coat."

"Hey, Colleen. 'Sup?"

"Don't even try to fist-bump me, okay?"

He snorted and ordered a tea of his own.

"How was Judith Pennepacker? She as tough as she seems?"

"Tougher," he said.

"Terrific."

"Oh, like you have anything to worry about. Jesus. Give it a rest, Colleen. On the real."

I glanced at Jason, surprised. He sounded genuinely irritated.

"What's that supposed to mean?"

"Nothing," he said, turning his profile to me. "It's supposed to mean nothing."

I considered asking him what his problem was. But I didn't particularly want to get into it with him, not when Judith Pennepacker was waiting for me at a table fifteen feet away.

"Okay. Well, I've got to go," I said, tossing some money on the tea bar. "Hope your interview went okay. Tell Anj I said hi."

"Colleen," he said, putting out a hand as though to stop me.

"What?"

"You talk to Anj today?"

"Anjali? No. Not since Friday. Why?"

Jason looked abashed. "She's not returning my texts."

"What do you mean, she's not returning your texts?"

Anjali could have both her arms encased completely in plaster casts and she'd find a way to text Jason every five minutes. She'd text with her toes. I only just thought that, but upon reflection, I bet Anjali totally could text with her toes. I should ask her if she can do that.

Jason's face took on a stricken cast, and I was puzzled. I guess I knew Jason was really into her. Didn't I? Maybe I was too busy being distracted by how much I disapproved of him to see that. My cheeks flushed. I didn't like Jason any more than before, but it occurred to me that maybe he wasn't just a manipulative appendage attached to my friend. I stared at him, seeing for the first time that Jason was actually a person. A nervous boy.

"I been texting her all day, you know, like we do. And she ain't returned a single one. You think she's mad at me? She usually got no trouble letting me know, when she is."

Of course, on the one hand, I'd have liked nothing better than for

Anjali to break up with Jason. But his face looked so wounded-puppy sad, and his grammar kept slipping between Andover and Brooklyn-on-TV. Jason actually seemed upset.

"I'm sure it's nothing," I said. "Did you try calling? Maybe her folks put her on a limited data plan, and she's over the limit already."

Jason's face flooded with relief. "Oh, yeah, that's gotta be it, yo. I didn't even think of that."

"Yeah. There's other ways of communicating with people besides texting, Jason. You could, like, actually pick up the phone. You could *call her*."

He smirked and punched me lightly on the arm.

"Colleen. My shortie."

I shook my head and said, "For Pete's sake. I've got to go."

"Your stuff's tight, yo. Peace out."

"Thank you? I think?"

He laughed and said, "You'll do great. You'll kick my ass. Go on with your bad self."

I smiled at him, collected my almost-empty tea glass, and went to join Judith Pennepacker for the most important interview of my life.

Okay, so she wasn't that bad. I was so keyed up that most of it wound up being kind of a blur. Judith Pennepacker looked younger than her picture, despite the scrunchie, and she asked me some pretty hard-core questions, like why was I only vice president of the debate club and not president (because Mr. Mitchell picked someone else, thanks for bringing that up), and what I thought the point of college athletics was, if any (huh?), and how realistic were my chances at valedictorian.

I hated talking about valedictorian. It was just kind of embarrassing, admitting that I wanted it so badly. I didn't want to jinx it. And it was tricky, because I was within a tenth of a point of Fabiana, and so every tiny assignment mattered. I decided early on that I couldn't think about it too much or I'd psych myself out. Anyone could see why the Mystery Illness was something I couldn't deal with thinking about. I had enough on my mind.

So I wasn't too pleased when Judith Pennepacker asked me about it. I shouldn't have been that surprised. It's pretty typical for college interviewers to ask us about current events and expect us to have some well-formed opinions. But usually the questions are more along the lines of politics or international affairs. Instead Judith Pennepacker said this, and I quote:

"Seems like there's a little hysteria problem at your school. Would you care to comment on that?"

"I beg your pardon?"

"Hysteria. These things are more common than you might realize, though it's been a while since we had one in Massachusetts. What are your thoughts on the St. Joan's Mystery Illness?"

I was torn. There was what the school had told us. There was what I'd heard. And there was what they'd asked me in the meeting with the school nurse and the suit woman. Were those things the same?

"Well," I said, "the general consensus seems to be that everyone's suffering from an allergic reaction to a vaccine."

"Sure. And do you think it's a coincidence that the vaccine in question guards against a sexually transmitted disease?"

Judith Pennepacker clearly had drawn some of her own conclusions about our Mystery Illness.

"There's a long history of adults being anxious about teenage girls' sexuality," I said, sounding like a women's studies major. "And hysteria, as I understand it, is a largely nineteenth-century psychological phenomenon that's also connected to fears of women's bodies and sex. But I have to say, from what I've seen, that what's happening at St. Joan's definitely looks like a real illness. It's not like they're making it up or anything."

"Hmm," Judith Pennepacker said, steepling her fingers in front of her mouth. "And that something has to be outside their bodies? It can't be in their minds?"

I frowned.

"I suppose it could be. But the girls who have it—they're not really that type."

"What—the type with minds?" the interviewer said, smiling.

I was on the point of trying to explain about Clara Rutherford—was there ever a girl less prone to psychological problems?—but Judith Pennepacker looked conspicuously at her watch. It was a large-faced man's watch, heavy and expensive, which looked kind of badass on her, with her skinny wrists.

"I see that we've just about run out of time. Do you have any last questions for me about the undergraduate experience, or Harvard more generally?"

That was my cue. I got to my feet.

"I think you've answered all the questions that I had. I was partic-ularly impressed with everything that you had to say about the house system. I have to say that Harvard seems like a remarkable place to attend college, and I so appreciate your taking the time to share your thoughts on it with me."

I held out my hand and Judith Pennepacker took it. Her hand-shake was as firm as my dad's.

"The pleasure was mine, Colleen. Good luck with the rest of your semester. If you think of any other questions for me, don't hesitate to e-mail."

E-mail! I beamed. That was a good sign. She liked me!

I wound my scarf around my neck. I had an hour to kill before meeting Spence at the Coop. This was shaping up to be an ideal Sun-day. That is, until I scooted my café chair back and rammed my elbow right into Judith Pennepacker's next interviewee.

"Ow, man," said Spence, inhaling through his molars to hide the pain.

"Oh!" I gasped. "It's you!"

"Hey. Yeah. Sorry. I didn't want to freak you out," he said, helping me out of my chair while pretending it didn't hurt.

Judith Pennepacker leaned back in her chair, with an appraising eye on us both.

So he decided to not freak me out by surprising me? Great. Good move, preppy boy.

I covered my consternation with a new, more formal version of my usual smile, and said, "Not at all. Have a great interview. Text me when you're done."

"Thanks, I will. See you."

"See you. Thanks again, Ms. Pennepacker."

Spence took the seat across from the Harvard interviewer, which was probably still warm from my squirming over the past hour. I pulled my winter stuff back on and slunk out of the café.

Well, it figured that he would get an interview, too, right? And it's not like we were in competition. Well, we sort of were. But not exactly. Not like I was with all the girls at St. Joan's. We wouldn't necessarily be in the same quota. Spence would be in closer competition with Jason—Jason! I couldn't believe he got one—than he would with me. But still. Not so many spots in the freshman class at Harvard. Not so many at all.

I trudged back to the Coop, which was really just a big bookstore that also sold sweatshirts and bears and things and had a coffee place where I planned to wait. The sky had started to spit dry, feathery snow, and I squinted against it, white flecks collecting on my eyelashes.

When I got to the bookstore, I roamed the fiction section. My fingers walked the spines of the books on the remainder table, caressing them the way a hungry person might touch ripe apples. Not that I had time to read for fun. I sighed. Between my APs and the battle for valedictorian, I didn't think I'd be able to read something fun until the summer. I wondered if Fabiana had slipped up in any of her classes.

Just a little. An A-minus, maybe. Something that would nudge her down by that crucial tenth. She was already in at Vassar anyway, and it was her top choice. Couldn't she just let things slide? Couldn't she just let me have it?

My fingers lit upon a spine with a familiar title.

The Crucible. That damn play was stalking me.

Okay, I'd read it, but that was weeks ago. And now I had that extra-credit assignment hanging over my head. How the hell was I going to find time to do a huge research paper in between all my other work? Maybe I shouldn't have agreed to it. But then, there was that 65.

At the thought of the 65, I felt sick. Like, almost ready to throw up in the bookstore sick. Of course I was going to do the extra credit. I should be grateful Ms. Slater even offered it to me. I might as well just buy this remaindered copy—it was way cheap—and reread it while I waited for Spence. Then I wouldn't spend the entire time worrying that his interview was going better than mine.

I made my way to the register, feeling cold and conspicuous.

The guy behind the counter took my book and asked for my Coop number.

"I don't have one," I said.

"Want to open an account?"

"No, thanks."

I was checking my phone to see if Spence had texted yet. He hadn't. What if his interview went longer than mine? What would that mean?

"Good choice," the counter guy said as he slid the paperback into a bag.

"Oh. Yeah. I've read it."

"If you're interested in this stuff, you should check out an event we're having in a couple weeks."

He gestured to a poster a little ways off from the register, half hidden behind a display of toy mice wearing plastic galoshes. The mice were kind of cute. I found myself wishing I could have one.

"Oh?"

"Yeah. She's an authority on that stuff. You should come."

It was the talk I'd noticed in the front window. Some professor from Northeastern.

Constance Goodwin. *English Cunning Folk Tradition in a North American Idiom: A Cultural Studies Approach.* I'd never heard of her. Her book looked really boring anyway.

"Yeah. Thanks," I said, fully intending to forget about this conversation the moment it was over. I pulled my phone out again and saw that Spence had texted in the time I'd spent talking to the guy.

There in 10. Whew!

My nausea receded, and a smile pulled at my cheek.

Cool

Jerk, I thought as I slid the phone back into my pocket. *He's totally going to rock his interview and I'll be screwed.*

I spotted myself in the mirror on either side of the beverage cooler in the café. My cheeks looked drawn and tired. Dotted with freckles.

Come on, I said to my reflection. *Maybe he screwed it all up. You don't know.* I paused, waiting for an answer. *You're right,* I replied to myself. *You don't know.*

Now to find a place to sit and try to look all casual while I waited for him.

I settled on a table in the corner, a little ways away from the television, with what I hoped was particularly flattering light. I took my hat off and settled my curls back down and arranged myself in such a way that I hoped looked completely at ease and mysterious. I slicked on a fresh coat of lip gloss.

I flipped open the play and was thumbing through it when I heard a voice say, "Hey."

Spence slid into the seat across from me.

His cheeks were flushed from the cold, and his nose was wet underneath. When he took his hat off, his hair stood up in a mess, and I grinned. He was wearing a sport coat under his parka, with a tie that was also patterned with little ducks. What's with Andover boys and ducks?

"Here," I said, offering him a paper napkin.

He took it, abashed. "Thanks," he said, and blew his nose into it. Then he rolled his head back and exhaled at the ceiling. He hadn't taken off his coat.

"Well, that sucked ass," he said.

I felt simultaneous twinges of relief and dismay, followed immediately by a nice splash of guilt. It's not like I wanted him to do badly. I liked him. And if we both were . . . But I was being ridiculous. I mean, I hardly knew him.

"What happened?"

"I don't know! It's like all she wanted was to talk about stuff I hadn't done, and not stuff I had. Like, why did I quit lacrosse, or why was I only associate editor of the paper, and not editor. Jesus. Was she like that with you?"

"Kind of. I guess? I don't know. I thought she was pretty nice."

"Well, you're lucky," he said, but without malice. "It could be that she'd already made up her mind. I'm a legacy, but I don't have grades like yours."

I blinked. How did he know what kinds of grades I had? It's not like we'd ever talked about it.

"Um," I started to say.

He smiled out of one side of his mouth, as though reading the worry on my face. "Anjali told me. Or, I guess she told Jason, and he told me. She's pretty intimidated by you, you know. In a good way. She was, like, bragging on you."

"Anj? Come on."

"She was."

"Whatever," I muttered. But my cheeks flushed under his compliment.

"Anyway. At least it's over with. I've got one more next week, and then it's just a waiting game. What about you?"

"This is it for me. A lot of my places don't really interview."

"Yeah. Mine either."

He watched me, smiling. I smiled back, and removed my finger from the place it had been holding in the play.

"You look nice today," he said.

My flush deepened until my cheeks felt hot. "Jeez," I said, because I'm really terrific at taking compliments. "I'm . . . this?"

"Yeah."

"Well. Thanks."

"Prep is the new punk. At least in Harvard Square." He smiled more broadly, I think enjoying how awkward he was making me. But then his eyes shifted to something that was over my left shoulder. His smile slipped.

"Did she ask you about that?"

I turned in my chair, following his gaze. A woman in a purple suit filled the television screen. There was a news crawl moving underneath her face.

"Hey, could you turn this up for a second, please?" I called to the girl behind the counter.

She shrugged and reached up to the volume on the television.

". . . reveal the truth behind the cover-up of what's really happening to the girls at St. Joan's. Join us tomorrow morning on *This Is Danvers*, when we'll have an exclusive interview with one of the mothers of the sixteen girls who are now afflicted with strange tics, twitching, and mysterious physical symptoms that doctors have, for some reason, been hesitant to explain."

The picture dissolved from TJ Wadsworth to still pictures of girls I knew, taken from their Facebook accounts or the St. Joan's yearbook. Clara, Elizabeth, the Other Jennifer, some others.

The last face was one I knew all too well.

Anjali.

INTERLUDE

SALEM VILLAGE, MASSACHUSETTS
MAY 30, 1706

*P*reternatural!" Reverend Green exclaims.

I nod.

"In truth," I say, "I think Reverend Parris was happy with the diagnosis. He never thought their—" I pause. And correct myself. "*Our* illness was natural. But he knew an outside opinion would hold more weight. It affirmed what he already thought was true."

"But Ann," the young minister says, urgency in his voice. "Why didn't you say something? Why didn't you tell them right then of Abby's and Betty's deception?"

This is the question, isn't it. I've asked myself this question every day, perhaps hundreds of times a day, for a decade and a half. My entire life, all its tribulations and shortcomings, its solitude and shame, can be boiled down to my failure to answer this question.

I get to my feet and cross the study to the window. I've never gotten used to being in this same parsonage. After the Parrises left, I avoided stopping here. Just looking at the parsonage made me sick. I went to meeting only because I knew what kind of talk there'd be if I didn't.

I'm looking out now over the very rye field where Abby described watching Sabbaths of an unspeakable nature from the attic window, describing women we'd known from childhood standing with their hands linked, braying at the moon like animals. Now the field is dry and baked by the summer. The sun has dropped lower, reddening the field, red as wine. Red as blood.

"Ann?" the handsome Reverend prods me.

I turn to him, struggling to explain.

"Do you know what it's like," I ask him, "to not be listened to?"

"What do you mean?"

I can tell from the look on his face that the Reverend is about to insist to me that of course he knows. And he probably thinks he does. But he doesn't.

Look at him. He's a son, maybe even an eldest son, I don't know. He's educated. His clothes fit. He's got that hearty wife in the hall, with the piglet girl and the hiccoughing baby. A whole churchful of parishioners ready to attend to his opinions, looking to him for guidance. Even me. I'm appealing to him, I'm prostrating myself, showing him my sin, as if it's in his power to absolve me, which it isn't. He's been listened to all his life. He always will be.

"I was an eldest daughter," I begin, hunting for a way to make him understand. "We were people of worth in the village. I wasn't bound out, like Abby. My labors weren't half as hard as hers. But even so, to be a girl of thirteen . . ."

I hunt in his eyes for understanding, and I can see him straining to find it. Silently, I beg him to *see me*.

But I read it on his face plain as day.

He doesn't. He can't.

I bring my hands to my face to hide my shame.

A minute wears by while I wait for Reverend Green to cross the room to comfort me, to put his arms around me and draw me to his chest and tell me it's all right, what's past is past, that Jesus stands ready to fill my soul with cleansing light and welcome me into the Kingdom of Heaven, where I can lay down my weary burdens and rest.

But he only says, "Tell me, Ann. Tell me what happened next."

My arm hurts where the doctor is gripping it. The men cluster and talk amongst themselves, and after the doctor releases my arm, male face after male face, of varying degrees of whisker, thrusts forward to examine the marks on my flesh, to touch and inspect.

"An evil hand!" they repeat one after the other, gathering ranks around Reverend Parris.

"I knew it," he's saying to them. "Thomas, didn't I tell you there was some evil brought among us? Why else would this distemper fall upon my own flesh and blood? It's been in the making these many months. You've all seen it."

Abby, meanwhile, has collapsed, worn out from the excitement of her visions. A young minister, Mr. Hale from Beverly, dabs at her brow with a cloth. Betty Parris lies tucked in next to Abby, her eyes open wide and unblinking as though painted on her face.

"Come," Reverend Parris says. "The children must rest."

"But . . . the window?" a man asks.

The Reverend frowns down at the two girls on the bolster.

"They'll be all right. Reverend Hale can stay. He can pray over them."

The younger man starts to object, but catches a fast look from Reverend Parris.

"Come, let's go down." Reverend Parris ushers the worthy gentlemen of Salem down the stairs. "You too, Ann. I don't want you upsetting them any more."

I flush under the implied rebuke, but don't object. When I regain the ground floor, I find the men folded into the close crowd of women in the parsonage's hall as husbands tell their wives the doctor's verdict.

"Well, I said so right along," one woman insists. "I raised ten children, and ain't none of them ever carried on so. Ain't natural."

"An evil hand!" whispers another, who draws away from me when I pass near her. "But what evil hand?"

Someone else whispers, "And whose? How'll the malefactor be discovered?"

I elbow my way through the crowd to the corner where Betty Hubbard waits for me, her brows arched in inquiry.

"Annie," she whispers. "What's happened? What did the doctor say? Did they catch Abby out?"

I look at her, and shake my head once.

Betty Hubbard claps her hands together in glee.

"Ha!" she trills. "She's a clever one. Bad, but clever. How'd she fix it?"

I'm ashamed to tell Betty Hubbard that it is I who have fixed it.

"Ah," I demur. "The doctor's said he can't find a natural cause for our illness. He's said we're under an evil hand."

"Our?" Betty Hubbard repeats. "What do you mean, our?"

I'm on the point of rolling up my sleeve to show the bite when I'm stayed by a woman's voice announcing, "I know what's to be done."

I recognize the speaker as Goody Sibley. She's got an unpleasant, meddlesome way about her, with puckers around her lips. She's exactly the sort of woman you'd expect to find waiting in the hall of a house where something interesting is happening.

"What's that?" an unseen voice asks.

"Prayer," someone mutters in response. "Prayer shall be our only salvation."

"Yes, prayer, of course. But there's a method we can use. Some simple physick, I've seen it done many times. John?" she addresses herself to Tittibe's Indian husband, who steps forward out of the shadow in the corner where he'd been lingering. Goody Sibley gestures with an impatient flick of her wrist for the slave to come to heel. He does so, but warily.

"Now then," Goody Sibley says, and I wonder where she got so much authority, talking of physick like this. She's no cunning woman, that much I know. There is one, I've heard, but I don't know her. She lives in squalor at the outskirts of the village. Goody Dane, she is. Someone that low wouldn't mix with worthy folk such as we are. Or are supposed to be.

"We'll be needing some rye meal. You know where your master keeps it?"

John doesn't know, as he doesn't work much within the household, and his wife's not there to tell him. He looks at Reverend Parris.

"It's all right, John," the Reverend says.

"That sack, there," Mrs. Parris says, pointing.

John goes to the sack and opens it.

"How much?" he asks in a quiet voice of Goody Sibley.

"Oh, I don't know. Not so much. A fistful. That should do."

John Indian fills his hands with rye meal and sifts it into a shallow dish that one of the other goodwives has passed along for the purpose.

The island woman has reappeared from the attic, her apron full of bits of broken bowl. She goes to the door to the side yard and shakes her apron out into the garden, incurious about what her husband's up to with the bothersome English woman.

"Tituba," Goody Sibley says, raising her voice in command.

The slave's name is hard to say. We all pronounce it differently. I suspect John has an Indian name, too, but none of us know what it is. At the sound of her name, or near enough, she turns and faces the crowd of onlookers in the parsonage hall.

"Ma'am," Tittibe says evenly.

"I want you to take this upstairs and collect the girls' water in it." Goody Sibley thrusts the pan of rye into a surprised Tittibe's hands.

"Their water?" she protests. "But why?"

"Don't argue with me, woman," Goody Sibley says, scowling. "Just do as you're told."

Tittibe glances at Reverend Parris, whose face is white with tension. He issues a curt nod. She then looks at Mrs. Parris, who's frozen in place, unable to make hide nor hair of what's unfolding in her house.

"As you like," Tittibe says with some distaste.

While she's upstairs, we all wait, murmuring amongst ourselves, wondering what Mary Sibley could be up to.

"I've heard tell of this before," another goodwife whispers aside. "There used to be a woman would do it, for pay, in Lynn, the village where I was a girl. Ann Burt was her name. It's for uncharming."

"Do you think it'll work?" Nicholas Noyes asks. Adam's apple like a nervous mouse.

"Might could," the woman from Lynn muses. "It has before."

Upstairs we hear muffled protests and then silence. Presently Tittibe reappears at the head of the attic stairs, making her way down with care, the shallow pan sloshing and full.

"They didn't like to do it," Tittibe remarks to no one in particular. I gather she counts herself among the number of those who didn't like to do it. "Now you, my Annie."

"Me?" I squeak.

"But yes, you. You be ailing, too, it's said. Come on, now."

I look around, my armpits growing damp from nerves and the heat of so many people. Of course I'm used to doing it with my brothers and sisters around, and no one paying any mind. But there must be twenty people here, many of them strangers, and all of them with their eyes on me.

I spot Betty Hubbard still standing in our corner, her hands clapped over her mouth to force herself to keep from laughing aloud. I shoot her a vicious glare.

"Come along, Ann," Reverend Parris encourages me.

Tittibe stoops with a grunt and places the pan at my feet. There's a strong smell, and the water coils around the heap of rye, rolling its grains in little eddies. I wrinkle my nose and look around at the crowd of faces pressing in around me, waiting.

"Best do as they say," Tittibe whispers. Her eyes blink with knowledge that I cannot see, but knowing it's there makes me afraid to disobey.

Swallowing my fear, I hoist my skirts, pulling layers of linen and wool out of the way, and squat, lowering my bareness over the pan. Everyone stares. My body has shifted over the past year, changing, making my joints ache, growing heavier in the hips, and I have a tuft of fur that's new and soft in my most secret parts. Everyone can see it. I'm worried they can smell me, this rich smell I have now. They're all looking. They're all waiting, and they can see my nakedness.

The water won't come.

I have to close my eyes and pretend there's no one there but my baby sister, who watches me all the time, since she's too little to be let alone. There's no onē there but her and my mother and that lazy Marcy. Not even my brothers are there; they're all outside. It's all right. No one's looking.

The pretense works, and I empty myself into the pan. A little splashes on my boots.

"All right," Goody Sibley says. "Now pick it up, Tituba, and knead it into a paste."

I've covered myself quickly, and am avoiding looking at Betty Hubbard, who's in a veritable fit of laughter behind one of the coats on a wall peg. My ears burn.

Tittibe stares at Goody Sibley. She doesn't speak, but the challenge is there in her eyes.

"Do it, woman," Reverend Parris commands.

Tittibe levels her eyes at her master and lets him feel her objection. Slowly, no faster than dripping molasses, she moves to the table with the pan. She rolls her sleeves and lifts her hands before her face. We watch, holding our breath. I'm relieved no one's looking at me anymore. I've let myself be absorbed in the crowd in the hall, watching, too. After a moment, her expression unchanging, Tittibe sinks her hands into the wet rye and starts to knead.

CHAPTER 14

DANVERS, MASSACHUSETTS
MONDAY, FEBRUARY 6, 2012

Who watches TV at 6:00 A.M.? Nobody. Seriously. I would rather be asleep any day. But that Monday, I was up at 5:30, blanket wrapped around my shoulders, slumped on the floor of the living room, my mother on the couch behind me in flannel pajamas, her hair a gray-brown thicket of sleep, her glasses making her look like a tired mole. Though dawn was thinking about getting started outside, inside our house it still felt like night. My father had snapped on a light in the kitchen, the one over the sink, so that he could start the coffee. Even Michael was up, in one of my old band T-shirts. I wasn't sure where Wheez was—still in bed, maybe.

I hadn't been able to get Anjali on the phone since seeing her yearbook smile splashed across the news. I'd tried texting her, I'd tried calling, and it went straight to voice mail. I'd checked her Facebook and Instagram and Twitter, but they hadn't been touched since Saturday. I'd called the Guptas' home phone a half dozen times, and nobody answered. Her dad could still have been out of town, and I felt sure that whatever was happening with Anjali, Dr. Gupta was all over it, so I told myself there was no reason to be worried. But I wanted to hear her voice.

"Here," my father said, thrusting a mug into my mother's inert hand. He settled next to her on the couch with a habitual grunt of relief.

"I don't get any?" I complained from inside my blanket.

"Your legs are broken? I'm so sorry, I didn't know," he replied, eyes wide with innocence.

I stuck out my lower lip at him.

Without saying anything to anyone, Michael unfolded himself from the recliner and shuffled into the kitchen.

"I don't know, Mike," Mom said, rubbing under an eye with her fingertips. "Maybe we should keep her home today."

"Maybe," my father said.

He looked at me.

"What do you think, Colleen?"

It was tempting, from a laziness standpoint. The thought of just turning around and shuffling back to bed was seductive. But it also felt stupid. Immature. Plus, I had that awful tenth of a percent, always floating at the edge of my consciousness. Of course, if I stayed home, I could get started on the extra credit for Ms. Slater, which I totally hadn't started working on yet. But then I'd fall behind in everything else. Too far behind to catch Fabiana.

"Don't be crazy," I said. "It's not even a big deal. If it were a big deal, they'd suspend classes."

"Sixteen, you said?"

"That's what they said on the news."

Michael shuffled back in, bearing two coffee mugs. To my surprise he handed one to me and climbed back into the recliner, cradling the other in his lap. I didn't know he drank coffee. But I slurped mine gratefully anyway. I guessed he could keep my shirt if he really wanted it.

"Look, it's starting. Turn it up."

Someone did, and the chipper opening theme to *This Is Danvers* blared through our living room. The blue glow from the set bathed our tired faces in a flat, cold light.

"Good morning, everyone, and welcome to *This Is Danvers*. I'm TJ Wadsworth, and we're just so happy to see you all today!"

That was her catchphrase. Pretty catchy, right? As if.

"Nice suit," Michael said from behind his coffee mug.

I smirked as my mother shushed him.

"We have a very special edition of our show for you today. The Mystery Illness at St. Joan's Academy. What's really causing it? Is the school doing enough? And what do you need to know to keep your children safe? An investigation by this station has revealed that all is not as it seems at the august private school, and we have some exclusive guests here in the studio today who are going to tell us more. Then later, a visit from Cupid as our correspondent Sasha Dobson tells us some surprising ideas for new places to take your valentine this Valentine's Day. Stick around."

Chipper morning show transitional music, and the screen cut to an ad for floor wax. The woman in the ad looked way too happy about her floor wax.

"Mute it, would you, Mikey? My head's killing me," my mother said softly.

My brother rooted in the cushions of the recliner for the remote and obeyed.

"Maybe you should stay home," my father said, scratching at his stubble. "Just 'til we get a handle on what's going on."

"Dad," I started to object.

"God, all that money. You'd think they could keep something like this from happening," my mother said.

"Linda, come on."

"Seriously. I would've been fine, sending her to the public school. Mikey, too. What's wrong with public school? I went to public school.

You went to public school. We're doing fine. And so far I don't see that guidance counselor making such a big difference in her college options. Nothing like they promised."

"We talked about this."

"Yeah, well, we're going to talk about it again when it's Louisa's turn."

"But I want to go to St. Joan's," my sister whined from next to my father on the couch. No one had seen her come in. Maybe she'd been there the whole time. "Besides, Colleen got to go all twelve years, and I'm only going to get to go for six. It's not fair."

Still without saying anything, Michael unmuted the television. TJ Wadsworth was now sitting, knees crossed, in a dun-colored over-stuffed armchair next to a coffee table scattered with mugs. It could have been any morning show at any station anywhere in America. But it wasn't.

It was Danvers.

My home.

". . . joined in the studio today by Dr. Sharon Strayed, professor of epidemiology at the University of Massachusetts, by Laurel Hocking, nurse at St. Joan's Academy and first responder to the Mystery Illness, and by Kathy Carruthers, mother of one of the afflicted girls, who'll be talking exclusively with us today. Ladies, welcome, and thanks for joining us on *This Is Danvers* this morning."

"Well, of course Kathy Carruthers is on," my mother muttered.

"Did they say they're going to talk to the Carruthers girl?" my father asked the room at large.

Leigh! My first thought was *That wannabe.*

Seriously. TJ Wadsworth couldn't even get an A-list afflicted girl? Where was Clara? Maybe the network had called the Ruther-fords and their publicist had told them not to go on for some reason. Maybe the Other Jennifer didn't want to go on TV with no hair. But surely they could have gotten Elizabeth.

I didn't even know Leigh had gotten sick. She'd been fine when I saw her in class last week. I wondered how many other members of the senior class had sickened, just in the span of a single weekend.

The phone in my sweatshirt front pocket vibrated softly with an incoming text. I pulled it out to peek, my heart doing a few quick hard thuds at the thought that it might be Anjali finally texting me back.

No Anjali.

Spence.

He'd been really cool about yesterday, which made me feel even more guilty about how annoyed I'd been about the interview. Of course after he'd said *legacy* all casual like that, I'd wanted to break my coffee mug in half, which is even worse. But when I couldn't get ahold of Anjali, he saw right away that I was too shaken to hang out. He'd actually ridden with me on the T to the train station. And then he'd waited with me for forty minutes before the next commuter rail like it was no big deal. And before he'd put me on the train, he'd wrapped his arms around me without even asking and whispered into my hair that I shouldn't worry, that he was sure there was some mix-up and that Anjali was just fine.

U watching?

I eyed my mother from my perch on the floor, not wanting to send her over the edge about my texting before we'd even had breakfast. But she was absorbed in the program.

Yeah . . . you?

And back into my sweatshirt pocket.

". . . Hocking, it's such a pleasure having you here. You've become something of a household name these last couple of weeks, with everything that you've done for these girls. That must be such a good feeling, knowing that you're helping them like that."

"Oh, definitely, it is. I'm just glad they're doing okay."

"Can you tell us when you first realized that the symptoms weren't being caused by what the school initially claimed?"

"Definitely, TJ," the school nurse began. She didn't look nursey at all for this interview, but like an impeccably styled talk show host herself. Made up, really nice suit, no nurse jacket or anything. Hair sprayed into place. Deena had told me someone started a Facebook fan page for her, and it had 127 likes already.

"The *school* claimed?" I said, incredulous. "I don't remember the school making the diagnosis. I thought she did."

"Did she?" my mother asked. "I don't remember."

"She did," my brother said quietly.

"I started to have my suspicions right away, to be honest. The initial expression of the symptoms didn't seem to fit with what you'd normally expect to see in an allergic reaction to a vaccine, even a relatively new one like the one for HPV. Of course, many parents had concerns about the HPV vaccine, for a lot of reasons. The initial cluster of patients were known to have all gotten the third shot around the same time, from the same pediatrician, and there was a lot of play about it in the media—"

"And what're you calling this?" my mother said, flinging her hand into the air.

She was a big TV talker. She talked back to movies, too.

"—but I was still skeptical. Then my suspicions were confirmed when we had an unfortunate incident of some students falling ill during a school assembly. I've gotten permission from those families to share that the second wave of students had no direct connection with the first, including their pediatricians. There simply wasn't enough evidence to suggest that a vaccine could be responsible for the cluster of symptoms that we were seeing. Unfortunately it was very difficult getting the school to acknowledge that there might be another underlying problem."

Weird. Laurel Hocking was really laying into the St. Joan's administration. I wondered what the upper school dean was thinking, watching this. And then I wondered how much longer Laurel Hocking was going to be the nurse at St. Joan's.

"Fascinating. So what did you decide to do next?"

"She called me," said Dr. Sharon Strayed, whom I immediately recognized as the mystery suit woman from my interview with the nurse.

"Now, Dr. Strayed, you're a professor of epidemiology at UMass."

"Yes."

"So that means you study how diseases spread through populations, is that right?"

"That's right, TJ. Nurse Hocking and I had a long phone conversation, in which she described the symptoms that she was seeing in the students. I knew right away that it wasn't caused by the HPV vaccine. We asked the parents' permission to interview all the members of the class in which the first afflicted girls were enrolled about their health history, so that we could start looking for patterns."

"Asked?" my mother said. "I don't remember being asked. Do you?"

"Not as such," my father said. He'd folded his arms over his chest and was glaring at the television.

"She was at my interview, Mom. With the nurse."

"Well, she never asked me a goddamn thing." My mother scowled, and my father wrapped an arm around her shoulders.

"And when you started looking for these patterns, as you call it, what did you find?"

"Well," Dr. Strayed said, "I'll tell you, what we found was pretty surprising."

"I'm afraid we have to take a break, but when we come back, more from the school nurse at the exclusive Danvers private school St. Joan's Academy, site of a mysterious illness that has sickened sixteen teenage girls in less than a month. What's really behind their strange symptoms? And what do you need to know to keep your family safe? Stay with us."

Chipper morning show transitional music again, and then a commercial for Jenny Craig.

"Mikey—" my mother began, but my brother had muted the television before she could finish her thought.

"That lady looks weird," said Wheez.

"Which lady, sweetheart?" my father asked.

"The one in the suit."

They were all in suits.

"Uh-huh," my father said, patting her absently on the leg.

"So what all did they ask you, Collie?" my mother said. "Did they tell you what they thought it was?"

"Not really," I said. "They let me think it was still the vaccine. They also didn't say anything about it spreading to anyone else. Though I noticed this floor plan in the office, with push pins on it. I think they knew it was spreading and didn't want to let on. But they did ask me a lot of weird questions."

"About what?"

I purpled with embarrassment, hoping that the color change in my face would be flattened by the blue glow of the television. "Um," I demurred.

I thought I saw my brother smirking from within the recliner.

"Random stuff, about me and my friends. Actually, they asked me if I'd had strep throat. I remember because it seemed weirdly specific for them to ask. I couldn't remember. Have I?"

"Yes," my mother said, exchanging a quick glance with my father. "Twice, actually. When you were small."

"Four?" my father asked her. "And then, what. Six?"

"Whoa," I said. "Twice?"

"Have I had it?" asked Michael.

"Oh, yeah. You caught it from Colleen when she had it the second time. It was no wonder, baby drool all over the house. You were two."

"What about me?" Wheez piped from her corner of the couch. "Have I had it?"

"Um." My father scratched his stubble again. "No, honey, I don't think so."

"Ha!" Wheez trilled at us.

Michael gave her a dark look. "You've had whooping cough,

though," he reminded her under his breath, and Wheez threw a pillow at him.

"But I had strep, like, twelve years ago," I said. "Why would they be asking about that?"

Wordlessly Michael unmuted the television, which none of us had noticed had already gone back to the morning show.

". . . PANDAS," Dr. Strayed was saying to an absorbed-looking TJ Wadsworth.

"You mean, like the bear?" the reporter asked.

Nurse Hocking tossed her hair back and laughed like the reporter had just said something utterly hilarious.

"Not exactly!" Dr. Strayed said, also laughing. "PANDAS is an acronym. It stands for Pediatric Autoimmune Neuropsychiatric Disorders Associated with Streptococcal infections. PANDAS."

"Pediatric . . ." TJ Wadsworth tried to repeat the acronym that Dr. Strayed had just explained, and was at a loss.

"Basically," Nurse Hocking jumped in, thinking that perhaps too much time had been spent on the good epidemiologist, "what it is, is sometimes kids, after getting a strep infection, they'll appear to get completely better, but for reasons we don't fully understand, those same kids can later go on to develop unusual neurological symptoms. In this case, those symptoms would be verbal tics, spastic physical jerking, and anxiety. Though oftentimes the anxiety can be traced to distress caused by the tic behavior."

"That's right, Laurel," the doctor said, elbowing her way back into the discussion. "In some instances, the patient will present with symptoms that in all other respects might be taken for OCD."

"That's obsessive-convulsive disorder," TJ clarified.

The doctor started to agree, but checked herself. "Ah, no, actually. OCD stands for obsessive-*compulsive* disorder."

"Oh! So it does. Excuse me," the reporter said, trying to laugh off her mistake.

In a funny way, though, I could understand why she'd made it. Clara and the others didn't seem to have OCD, not the way I always pictured it. Granted, I'd gotten most of my ideas about OCD from watching movies, and then it seemed mainly to be about wanting to wash your hands a lot.

"Um. Does this seem right to you guys?" I asked.

What did my parents know? They weren't doctors either. I wondered what Dr. Gupta would say when she saw this. I wondered where Anjali was right then.

"I just don't know, Colliewog," my father said.

"Sometimes young people present with uncontrollable physical behaviors—tics, stuttering, and so forth—that will be initially diagnosed as OCD or occasionally as Tourette's. But then upon closer investigation," the doctor was saying, "the timing of the onset of patient symptoms, even subtle ones that don't initially gain enough notice for the patient to be brought in for medical care, can be found to coincide with their recovery from a strep infection. The good news is, these kinds of effects are pretty rare."

"Let's talk about that, Doctor. How common is this? And what can families do to make sure that their children aren't affected?"

"The most important step is prevention," Laurel Hocking said, not to be outdone in the expertise department. "Washing hands, using good hygiene, getting regular checkups—basically the best thing parents can do is take good precautions against their children being exposed to strep throat."

"I see. And what about for those families where the children may already have strep, or have already had it? What do they need to be looking for?"

"Well, the thing that I want to stress here is that despite what you may think about this cluster of cases at St. Joan's, this is a highly unusual autoimmune response. Some children who've had strep infections might experience tics, but the vast majority of kids who've had these infections—and as any parent will tell you, they're very common—will have no adverse effects like this at all," Dr. Strayed said.

"We have another two guests today who have a very personal investment in the development of the Mystery Illness at St. Joan's Academy, and we're going to hear from them, right after this."

Michael muted the TV before we even got to the jingle for cling wrap.

"Well, I can't wait to hear from Kathy Carruthers, I don't know about you guys," my mother remarked. "Mike, could I get a warm-up?"

My dad and my brother were both Michael. Dad is called Mike. My parents called my brother Mikey. He'd been trying to go by Michael since sixth grade, and I was finally able to switch this year. The thing about New England is, we like to keep it simple. Everybody with the same name. Anyway, my dad got up to take my mother's mug to the kitchen. Without a word he collected mine and Mikey's, too. Mikey! I slipped. It happens.

"PANDAS," my mother mused while my father busied himself in the kitchen. "Well, at least they know what it is now. Better than everyone getting hysterical about a harmless booster shot."

"That's a weird name for a sickness," Wheez said. "That's like saying, 'Oh no! I've got a bad case of giraffe!'"

Nobody laughed.

I pulled the blanket more tightly around myself and said, "No way. No way. If it's so rare, why would it all be breaking out at school right now? I don't get it."

"Well," my mother said, rubbing her fingertips under her glasses, "maybe there was a kind of mini epidemic of strep throat at your school last year, sweetie. If a lot of girls got it all at the same time, they could be getting this aftereffect on about the same schedule. The important thing is, they know what it is, and frankly, we know you're going to be okay. You didn't have strep last year."

I hunted back through my mind, trying to remember if people

had seemed to go out sick in greater numbers last winter than usual. I couldn't remember. I mean, people were always out sick. Colds, flu. I guess we could've mistaken strep throat for the flu, if everyone was telling us we probably had the flu.

My father reappeared and passed around mugs. "We need to start thinking about getting ready to go," he said.

"We've got to see the Carruthers first," my mother said.

She patted the couch seat next to her. Now that she was reassured that nothing was going to happen to me, my mother could treat this like spectacle. I'm sure she wasn't thinking about Anjali.

But I was.

"And welcome back to *This Is Danvers*. I'm TJ Wadsworth. We're talking this morning with Laurel Hocking, school nurse and first responder to the infamous Mystery Illness that has sickened a shocking sixteen girls at the exclusive St. Joan's Academy in the past month. We're also joined by Dr. Sharon Strayed, professor of epidemiology at the University of Massachusetts, and by Kathy Carruthers, a parent of one of the students who has been touched by this tragedy. Kathy, welcome."

"Thank you, TJ." Kathy Carruthers was made up like a Vegas showgirl, or at least like what I imagine a Vegas showgirl would look like if she were going on a small local morning talk show. She was clutching a handkerchief. My mother and I rolled our eyes at each other.

"And a very special welcome to you, Leigh." TJ leaned forward and raised her voice a little, the way people sometimes do when speaking to someone they think is slow or who doesn't speak English very well.

"Thanks," Leigh said.

"We just really think it's important that the truth get out. And that's why we're here today." That was Kathy. She hadn't even been asked a question yet.

"Exactly," TJ agreed. "So tell us, Leigh. How *are* you? Really."

The camera zoomed in on Leigh's face, and her lower lip was

quivering. At first I couldn't tell what, beyond a bad case of melo-drama, might be troubling her. But after a minute, I could see it.

Leigh was vibrating.

I didn't know how else to describe it. She wasn't twitching. She wasn't rocking. She wasn't shaking. She was *vibrating*. The camera couldn't really keep her in focus, because while it looked like she was just sitting there completely normal, she was just . . . oscillating. Blurry. She brought a hand up to tuck a hank of hair back behind her ear, and the hand was vibrating.

"How is she doing that?" Michael asked from the recliner.

When Leigh spoke, her voice sounded like she was speaking through the blades of a box fan.

"I have to say, it's just a really, really weird feeling. Like there's something inside of me that's making me do this. I try to control it and, like, tamp it down, but then it builds and builds, and I feel like I have to let it out. It's better if I just let it happen. But once it starts happening, it's like I can't stop it."

"Her father and I want everyone to know that we're holding the school responsible," Kathy said. "We deserve answers, and we deserve to have a plan in place to help our girls feel normal again."

"Well, I can certainly understand that," TJ said. "Laurel, do you have any response for this concerned mom?"

"Of course I do. Kathy and Leigh, as well as all the afflicted girls at St. Joan's, know that we want nothing more than for them to all feel better. Helping them get well is absolutely our first priority. I can't stress enough how everyone at the school only has the girls' best interests at heart."

"We just want to know, you know, why has it been so hard to get a straight answer? I mean, how were we supposed to protect our kids if no one was being honest with us?" Kathy said, not looking at the school nurse. Leigh trained her vibrating eyes on her mother in a worshipful way. Her hand was clutching Kathy's sweater sleeve.

"Well, that also brings us to an important question, I'm sure you'll agree, Kathy, and that is, what's the treatment? How do we help these girls get back to leading normal lives?" TJ directed her question to the doctor.

"That's a completely natural question, and I think one that's on many parents' minds watching this program. But unfortunately there isn't one particular answer. What will be happening in the next few days is that each girl who thinks she's come down with PANDAS symptoms will be meeting with us, and we'll be coming up with a special plan of action tailored for each individual. Everyone's different, and we'll be treating everyone accordingly."

"Kathy? Is that what you wanted to hear?"

"Oh, great," said my mother to the television. "Goad her. Sure. That's a great idea."

"No, that's not what I wanted to hear!" Kathy's voice rose. "If it's some real disease, then there's got to be a real treatment for it, right? Look at my daughter. She can't control herself. She can barely talk. Last week she was a regular, happy kid, and now look! What are you going to do about it? I want to know exactly how you plan to help my daughter!"

The doctor's eyes shifted left and right, and her smile grew fragile. "Well, to be honest, it's a complicated question. Treatment for PANDAS might involve certain medications, and in some instances cognitive behavioral therapy will—"

"Therapy? Are you saying my daughter's crazy? Is that what you're saying?" Kathy got to her feet and starting pointing a finger at the doctor's chest.

My mother laughed.

"Linda, jeez," my father murmured.

"Sorry," my mother said. But she didn't look sorry.

"I'm not trying to suggest that—" Dr. Strayed stammered, instantly seeing her mistake.

"How dare you? My daughter is NOT crazy. She's sick! Look at her! And nobody's doing anything to help! Nobody!"

The camera cut away just as we spotted a burly stagehand begin to approach Kathy Carruthers from behind. We heard scuffling, and the camera zoomed in on TJ Wadsworth's face, whose smiling mouth paired uncomfortably with two worried eyes.

"The Mystery Illness at St. Joan's Academy, now, it seems, with more questions than we have answers. Kathy, Leigh, Dr. Strayed, Nurse Hocking, thanks for joining us today. Up next, has Cupid's arrow struck you yet? Valentine's Day is coming up, and we'll be getting ready by talking to—"

Michael snapped off the television.

CHAPTER 15

You can change your mind," Dad said.

A forest had sprung up overnight on the front steps of St. Joan's. A forest of vans and antennae, klieg lights and sound equipment, cameras and wires, production assistants and monitors, microphones on booms and reporters in trench coats and sprayed hair. I stopped counting past eleven or twelve. Danvers stations, and all the Boston stations, too. One from Providence. A couple from Maine. Framingham. Burlington.

And one from New York.

I tightened my grip on my backpack.

"I'm serious," my father said. "We can just turn around and go home."

I looked at him, and then looked back at the steps of the upper school, which were completely obscured by milling strangers. The microphone booms studding the crowd made it look like a many-legged monster, blistering with metal spikes. I couldn't even see the Gothic front doors, only the snarling mouths of the gargoyles crouching on the drainpipes just out of reach. Over everything loomed the reverse image of the stained-glass window of St. Joan being burned at the stake, its colors dulled by the winter light. Joan's face looked as smooth and beatific as ever.

"What's the point?" I said. "Anyway, I've got stuff to do. I'm this close to catching Fabiana. And I don't see how staying home is going to get everything back to normal any faster."

"Suit yourself," Dad said. "But if you change your mind, you can call me at work, okay? Just this once."

"I'll be fine, Dad." To prove it, I got out of the car, slammed the door, and leaned back into the window, backpack over my shoulder. "Really," I said.

"Well. Okay, then. Have a good day. Enjoy your fifteen minutes."

Was that why I wanted to run the media gantlet to get into school? I asked myself this as I approached. All this attention being lavished on everyone else. Leigh going on television. It's not like I wanted to go on television or anything. At least, I don't think I did. But the things we tell ourselves aren't always the truth.

I spotted a harried-looking Father Molloy on the outer fringes of the camera-toting mob. He was ushering students from the sidewalk to the front doors, herding them like worried sheep. He raised his eyebrows in greeting when he saw me, and took my arm, saying, "Colleen. Here. This way."

And then, before I had time to prepare myself, it started, like a hail of rocks raining down on my head.

"Young lady, young lady! Are you worried about going to school today? Do you think the school is telling the truth?"

"Can we get a quote from her, Father? What's her name?"

"Hey, beautiful! Look this way! Just look over here!"

"Do you think this is just about sex? Have you had the HPV vaccine? If you haven't, are you going to now?"

"Miss, have you had strep throat? Do you think there's something to this PANDAS hypothesis?"

"Are you friends with any of the afflicted girls? Have you talked to any of them?"

Father Molloy kept a gentle hold on my arm and raised his palm between my face and the thrusting glass eyes of the cameras, shielding me from the encroaching boom microphones with his shoulder.

"Just ignore them," he whispered to me. "Don't worry, don't look, you don't have to say anything to anyone, okay?"

"Okay," I said, keeping my eyes on my feet.

"Excuse me, miss, excuse me! Just one question!"

"Aren't you afraid that with twenty students sick, this is just the beginning?"

"What do your parents think of how the school's handling the crisis?"

"Just keep walking," whispered Father Molloy.

I nodded.

"Miss! Miss! Hello, are you deaf?"

"Young lady, just a quick photo!"

"Colleen!"

I froze.

"Colleen Rowley, how's it feel to know you could easily be next?"

I swiveled, hunting the crowd of unfamiliar faces to see who had called my name. Microphones crowded into my face, and a bright spotlight mounted on top of a camera blared into my eyes. The faces blurred in an indistinct haze behind the glare, and I couldn't see who had spoken.

"Just a quote, miss, just a couple of words! Tell us what you think!"

"I'm just trying to get to class," I said, squinting against the lights.

Father Molloy was pulling at my arm.

"Aren't you scared? Do you think it could be something inside the school itself?"

"I . . . Everyone just wants everything to go back to normal. Excuse me."

Camera flashes exploded across my eyes and more questions were shouted, but I couldn't tell them apart. I hunched my shoulders up to my ears, slouching under the protective arms of Father Molloy.

"That's it, that's all, give her some room, please," he bellowed at the press.

We had to force our way through the wall of arms and legs and reporter notebooks and cameras, and when we finally reached the studded front doors, Father Molloy hustled me through them, whispering, "That was okay, you're just fine. Just go to advisory. Okay?"

I nodded, eyes wide, and the door slammed shut.

Inside, the halls were eerily silent.

I turned my back to the door and surveyed the length of the upper school hallway, usually teeming with girls in matching skirts, beehiving our way to our different lockers and classrooms in the complicated dance of early morning in high school. But today I noticed the flagstone floor, a huge expanse of slate darkened with a century of Old English polish. Thin winter light slanted through the pebbled glass of the classroom doors, glowing in the glass transoms overhead. Each transom was engraved with the quote from St. Joan that was our school motto: *Il est bon à savoir.* It is good to know.

Here and there, clusters of girls huddled by wooden lockers, books clutched to their chests. Through the silence we could clearly hear the muffled bray of the press outside, crushing against the doors. Every few minutes the front door cracked open and another St. Joan's student tumbled through, hair disheveled, gasping for breath and looking hunted and afraid.

"Colleen . . . I'm Colleen, and feelin' so loneleeeeeeeeeey! I'm Collleeeeeen, Colleen and feelin' soooooo bluuuuueeee . . ."

I smiled, feeling swept with relief.

Deena.

Deena was here somewhere, and she was making fun of me with a Patsy Cline song. I clung to this life preserver of normalcy, moving quickly down the vacant hallway to our advisory. I could hear each of my footfalls on the flagstone.

When the door swung open, I saw that advisory was two-thirds empty.

Jennifer Crawford was resting with her forehead on her desk in the back of the classroom, her hair a newly applied, deeper shade of shocking pink.

But there was no Anjali.

No Leigh Carruthers.

No Elizabeth.

No Other Jennifer.

No Fabiana.

I tried not to feel a surge of excitement when I noticed that Fabiana wasn't there, but I couldn't help it. Today was the day. I could work hard, and I could scratch a few hundredths of a point closer. I resolved to start my extra-credit paper for Ms. Slater in study hall that afternoon.

Deena was there, and when she saw me, she smiled broadly and waved. I was always happy to see Deena, but today I could have run over and hugged her. So that's what I did.

"Hey, whoa," said Deena, laughing. "What gives? It's just Monday."

"I know. I'm sorry. It's just I still haven't been able to get Anjali on the phone, have you?"

Deena and I had texted fast and furious over the weekend, and neither of us had had any luck raising Anjali.

"No," Deena said. "But look. If your mom were some big medical researcher, and some weird 'Mystery Illness' were breaking out at your school, don't you think your mom would pull you out for a couple of days? Whether you were sick or not?"

"I guess so," I said.

"My dad thinks that a lot of the girls they're saying are sick are really just staying out of school as a precaution. He tried to keep me home today, too."

"So did mine."

"So the fact of the matter is, we don't actually know how many of us are sick. Right? Even some of the ones who've been reported to the school could just be faking to get some time off."

Deena sounded so reasonable. I felt a knot untie itself in my shoulders that I hadn't even known was there.

"You think?" I guessed not everyone cared as much about maintaining her GPA as I did. Maybe not even Fabiana.

"Totally."

I looked around the classroom. The bell had rung, but Father Molloy was still outside ushering students past the reporters.

"Even so," I said, "I'd feel a lot better if she'd just text me back that she was okay. I saw Jason at my Harvard interview."

"Jason!" Deena exclaimed. "Did he wear his grille? I hear Harvard really loves a boy with ice in his teeth."

I smiled. "No grille. A tie with tiny ducks, but no grille. But you know, she hadn't been texting him back, either."

"Huh," Deena said.

Her confidence slipped a fraction, and I didn't like seeing the flicker of doubt in her face.

"Yeah. That's what I thought."

"But there must be a reasonable explanation for it. Maybe she's finally come to her senses and dumped him."

"They didn't have a fight or anything, though."

The door opened and a girl walked in, but Deena and I didn't pay attention until she sat down next to us.

"Tzt tzt tzt HA—ha—ha—hello, girls," said Clara.

I actually jumped in my chair.

Clara Rutherford smiled prettily at me. Her head was twitching, but it wasn't too bad. Her ponytail looked perfect as usual. That's hard to do when your head is always moving.

"Hey, Clara," Deena said. "How're you doing?"

"I'm—tzt tzt tzt—HA—okay, thanks," she said.

She let the verbal tics come, without seeming embarrassed about it or anything. How Clara is that? She can make a Tourette's outbreak seem cool.

"We were just talking about how many people are absent," I said. "It's kind of creepy, you know? It's so quiet in here."

Clara looked around, nodding as though her suspicions were confirmed.

"Well," she said. "It's—tzt tzt tzt—pretty serious, you know? Did you watch *This Is Danvers* this morning?"

Deena and I both nodded mutely.

Clara tapped the side of her nose. Her head jerked, and then she smiled.

I looked from her to Deena and back again, not sure what she meant.

Clara leaned closer. "Just you—tzt tzt tzt tzt—wait," she said.

Clara rose from her chair like Venus stepping out of the scallop shell and drifted over to her usual desk. No one was sitting in that corner of the room, so I wasn't sure why she wouldn't just stay in Fabiana's chair, with us. Deena and I stared after her for a second, and then turned to each other.

"Hey," I said. "Where's Emma?"

There's one part I forgot to mention.

The upper school dean had been fired.

The truth is, I don't remember when I heard that. I don't specifically remember anyone telling me, either in a text or in person. I don't remember if I got it from a teacher or one of my classmates. It was knowledge that I soaked up somewhere along the line that day, knowledge that wasn't there when I arrived at school that Monday, and by the end of the day, I had it. It was fact.

The nun who was upper school dean was gone, and she wasn't coming back. No more blowing into the microphone at upper school assembly. No more sitting in the office for a skirt rolled too high. She was gone.

Knowledge of her departure came with certain theories attached about why she'd been fired, and who was responsible, and what it might mean. Something about the board of trustees, which was a mysterious entity at St. Joan's Academy. Everyone knew they existed, and everyone knew they ruled with an iron fist, but nobody's parents seemed to be one of them. It wasn't clear who they were, actually. Theories had always abounded that the board consisted of prominent families from Danvers, and that getting onto the board was even harder than getting into the Essex Bath and Yacht Club if you were Irish.

The phrase *didn't get out in front of it* was bandied around a lot that day. That didn't sound like a real reason to me, though. It sounded like a PR reason. What, exactly, was the upper school dean supposed to be in front of? A camera? The problem? The illness? The gossip? She was a watery, anxious nun who'd been a teacher before she was an administrator and who'd excelled at enforcing uniform requirements and needling the college guidance office about Ivy League acceptance rates. She wasn't the kind of person to go on *This Is Danvers* and tell the world that the teenage girls at her exclusive private school were twitching and flopping like dying fish.

In any event, after that happened, it became less clear who was in charge. After the dean was gone, the truth grew to be this fat, amorphous, uncontrollable, invisible thing. A monster stalking the halls of St. Joan's, which we all were hunting but couldn't see.

INTERLUDE

*B*ut I don't understand. What did they hope to accomplish with this exercise?" Reverend Green asks me with a curled lip.

"It's a very old method, Reverend Green. I'm surprised you've never heard of it."

"I was brought up to put my faith in God first, and then in science. Not in old superstitions and wives' tales. They lead foolish people away from the truth."

I watch him with an appraising look. It's so easy for him. Judging like that.

"Be that as it may. They had Tittibe bake it into a biscuit, and then Goody Sibley bade John feed it to one of the dogs in the yard."

"A dog?"

"A dog, yes."

"The illogic astonishes me," Reverend Green cries, throwing his hands up to heaven. "Though I don't know why it should."

"The illness had a preternatural cause. The doctor said so! Whyn't they look for a preternatural solution?"

"How on earth could they think feeding a urine cake to a dog would be a solution? You explain to me how such simple minds work, because I'll never understand it otherwise," he challenges me, ramming his fingertip into the top of his desk.

"Well, as I understand it, there were two ways Goody Sibley thought it might work. First, it was thought that perhaps the illness, or charm, or whatever it was, might travel via our water into the body of the dog, and we'd be freed."

"Oh, freed. I see." The Reverend's voice has taken a sarcastic turn. I suppose I can understand why, given all I've said. There was no charm in me to pass away, nor in Betty Parris or Abby Williams either.

"Or," I continue, "the other thinking was that the dog's munching the cake would reflect the charm on whoever had bewitched us. That it would cause the person pain, and so she'd be forced to set us free."

The Reverend watches me, wheels turning behind his eyes. "Now that's interesting," he remarks. "Having a small part stand in for the whole. Not as ignorant as I'd assumed. How did it turn out? Successful, I presume?"

I glare at him.

"We all stood out in the yard shivering, up to our ankles in snow, watching the dog devour the cake. When the dog was licking his chops and the cake was gone, Reverend Parris took hold of me and forced up my sleeve, to see if my arm were healed. But it wasn't. The wound was as red and seeping as it ever was."

"It would be," Reverend Green says.

"Then he sent everyone away. He wanted to pray alone that night. But the word was out in the village. And the word on everyone's lips was *witchcraft*."

Everyone is waiting. I watch people bustle about their business in the village, and to the untrained eye everything looks much the same. Pigs root in the streets, their fur crusted with frost. One day there's a warming, and the snow goes soft and wet, dropping in chunks from the trees. That night, a freeze so deep that when we all awake the next morning, it's like the village has been dipped in glass.

A week or thereabouts has passed since Mary Sibley told Tittibe and John to make the charm, and now everywhere I go I hear whispers. I imagine I feel people's eyes on my back, but the moment I turn, I see nothing. Heads are down, bent to their work. I'm greeted in my comings and goings as usual, but there's some fear underlying the words. Like the normalcy is all just people acting in a play.

A steady stream of gentlemen—ministers and magistrates and doctors and the town fence-viewer—tromp in and out of the parsonage, and if you pass close by, you can hear men's voices in prayer. Women cluster in the parsonage's hall, inventing reasons to be there. The first meeting day after the doctor's failed visit, the minister exhorts us all most grievously. He blames the village. He has sensed the current of our wariness, sees it carrying him and Betty and Abigail further away from our care, and so he tries to swim back into our good graces by presenting us with evidence of our own moral debasement. He stands ready to forgive us on God's behalf, if we'll only repent.

Reverend Parris is scared.

One afternoon I'm in Ingersoll's Ordinary with Betty Hubbard, who's staying on in our house while Dr. Griggs attends to the girls in the parsonage. I've been sent there by my mother for supper with Betty and one of my younger brothers, and we're at a table in the corner near the fire. It's warm in the corner, and I push my coif back from my forehead, which is shining with sweat.

"Let me see it," Betty says.

"No," I say, holding my arm to my waist where it will be safe.

My brother's not listening, as he has told us that he thinks girls are poison, and he won't eat off my plate either, and I can't make him. I've given up arguing with him. At this point, I might secretly agree. Maybe girls are poison.

"Come on, let me see," Betty insists.

I look around to ensure that we're unobserved. The tavern is crowded, bachelor men bent together in one corner, families crowded around tables, babies wailing. I can't see anyone staring. But I have that feeling that people are looking away the minute my eyes land squarely on them.

"No one's looking," Betty Hubbard says, as though she's heard my thoughts.

I lay my arm on the table and pull up the sleeve, grimacing as I do so. The crust of blood on the welts has soaked into the linen of my shift, and pulling it free peels the new skin away. Betty leans in close and sucks on a tooth.

"It's still drawing," she says.

I nod. I dip my fingertips in my cider mug and dab the alcohol on the semicircle of punctures. It stings, and I grimace and pull the sleeve down quickly. My little brother watches with a wrinkled nose.

"That's foul, Annie," he informs me.

"Be still," I hiss at him. "Or I'll send you home without supper, and who d'you think Mother will believe, when you ask her for something to eat?"

He sulks in silence.

"Perhaps you should show it to my uncle," Betty Hubbard muses.

"But he'll think I'm still bewitched."

"Aren't you?" Betty asks, raising her eyebrows. "As ever you were before, I mean."

I grunt and swirl the cider in my mug, staring down into it.

"He's got Abby and Betty to attend to. I don't know why Abby doesn't just confess."

"She's right comfortable up there, that's why," Betty Hubbard says.

Our food comes, roast pork with pickled apple, and we gnaw into it. There's some singing in the Ordinary, and my brother beats time along on the table. We're smiling, mouths greasy. I know my mother's sent us out to get quiet in the house while my father labors over his

201

account books, but I'm happy for it. It feels good to be among the other villagers, to feel safe and another face among many. To be warm while all outside is cold and barren.

The door slams open midsong, and it's my friend Mary Warren, the Procters' girl. A gale blows around her skirts before she can get the door closed, earning her scowling from the table nearest the door and some conspicuous buttoning up of jackets. She spots us and hurries over. Eyes track her movement with curiosity, and I see a few heads lean to whisper in other ears.

"Mary! Have you eaten?" I smile up at her, feeling warm and pleased that we can make a party of us four.

"Yes, yes, they eat early." Mary waves me off and sits on the bench next to Betty Hubbard.

"Why, what's the matter? You look frightened half to death," Betty Hubbard says with concern. And it's true, Mary's face has no color. I feel my meal begin to curdle in my stomach.

"I've just come from them," Mary says. She never likes to name the Procters. She hates waiting on them as much as Abby hates waiting on the Parrises, but Mary's a more godly girl than Abby, and keeps her complaints close. "Goody Procter'd heard a rumor in the town, and I just went to the parsonage to find out after it, and it's true."

"What's true?"

Mary looks at my brother. "Go find Goody Pope's boy, John."

My brother pouts.

"You heard what Mary said to you," I say, flicking him on the back of his wrist with my fingernail. He yelps.

"But he's not here!"

"How d'you know he's not here if you don't bother to look?" Mary says.

My brother gets to his feet, looking confused.

"And don't you come back 'til you've found him," I exhort.

He slinks away, casting a baleful glance at us and at his unfinished rib. When he's out of earshot, Mary leans in over the table, and we lean in, too. I hear chairs and benches creak around us, and conceive that other tavern-goers are also leaning in to listen, but that could just be my imagination.

"Betty Parris's going to tell," Mary whispers.

"Tell?"

"Sure enough, she is. They won't let her alone. All day and all night, for three days, they're after her to say who's bewitching her. They're going to make her tell. I think we should go over."

"You think she'll confess they're just playing?" I ask, panicked.

If they do, I'll be catching hellfire and brimstone rained down from my father. And Reverend Parris will beat Betty Parris and Abby raw.

"What else can she say? Unless Abby thinks of something better. Come on. We should go."

I hunt through the crowded hall to see if I can spot my brother to tell him we've gone, but he's nowhere to be found.

CHAPTER 16

DANVERS, MASSACHUSETTS
TUESDAY, VALENTINE'S DAY, 2012

A week later, and I couldn't stop looking at my phone.

The library at St. Joan's was a deep stone cavern, eerily narrow and tall, with walls of books leaning up into the dimness overhead. The only light came from a distant clerestory of leaded Gothic windows tucked under the wooden beams holding up the roof and the green glass lamps dotting the wooden library tables. As a result, people liked to go in there to sleep.

Deena was bent over her physics textbook at the library table across from me, scratching the part in her baby dreads with the end of her pencil. I arranged my books, including my new copy of *The Crucible*, into a protective wall around my half of the table. Between us, a green-shaded desk lamp buzzed every so often, its brass pull chain hanging exactly where a procrastinating student might most want to play with it, and so I was rolling it between my fingers. The word processing program on my laptop was open to a new document.

The page was blank.

Cursor flashing.

I pulled my phone out again. Nothing. I frowned and stuffed it back in my sweater pocket.

Deena glanced up at me, then looked back down to her physics book as though ready to let it go. She sighed, changed her mind, and kicked me under the table.

"Colleen," she said. "You've got to stop."

"Not even a text?" I said. I was whining, I knew it, but still.

"Come on."

"How long does it take to send a text message? Like, two seconds?"

Deena put down her pencil and crossed her arms. "What are you so upset about?"

"Nothing," I grumbled.

I mean, it wasn't like Spence was my boyfriend or anything.

Reading my mind, Deena said, "What'd you expect, roses? You've only hung out with him, like, once."

"But we text every day, though." I heard myself talking and realized who I was sounding like.

Anjali.

Deena saw the thought cross my mind.

"I just channeled Anjali right then."

"Yeah," she said. "I know."

"I really wish she'd just write us back and tell us what is going on."

"I know. I'm worried, too."

"You haven't heard from her either, have you?"

"Nothing. No selfies on Instagram, even. I guess maybe you were right."

We lapsed into silence. I pulled out my phone again. Deena opened her mouth, but I silenced her with raised eyebrows.

Hey

I tapped.

No, not to Spence. Jeez. I wasn't desperate or anything. It was to

Emma. I knew she was bored, and I wasn't getting anything done anyway.

Hey. How's school?

I smiled. When Emma wasn't in school last week, Deena and I had a momentary panic that all of our friends were dying and no one would tell us. But before second period I established that Deena's theory about nervous parents keeping people out of school for no reason was true, at least as far as the clannish Blackburns were concerned. Emma was on lockdown, getting her homework assignments by e-mail and slowly going crazy. But the good news was, Emma could keep us updated on media reports while we were stuck in class.

Boring. Weird. Nobody's here. How are u?

"Tell her I say hi," whispered Deena.

Good. Got into Endicott!!!

I held up my hands in a silent V-for-Victory, and showed my phone to Deena.

"Oh, like anyone's surprised," Deena said, grinning.

AWESOME!! D says hi too. Any news?

Deena watched me typing, then sank her head back into her physics book, her pencil making notes in a margin.

WBST says up to 25. True?

I frowned and looked around where we were sitting in the library, as if seeing the lack of people would either confirm or deny what Emma had just said. I whistled between my teeth.

Hard to tell . . . nobody here.

Another text came in while I was typing, so I hit send and then opened it.

The play. Don't forget.

"Oh, for Pete's sake," I said out loud.

Deena looked up at me with a quizzical expression.

"Just some jerk," I whispered.

She rolled her eyes and bent back to her work.

DOING IT NOW SHUT UP.

The phone buzzed again.

Come over after? Mom driving me CRAZY.

Emma.

"You want to hit up Emma's after school?" I whispered to Deena, who was my ride home.

"Um." Deena bit her lip and gazed at a point on a distant wall of the library.

I frowned. I'd thought for sure she'd be happy to go see Emma. She'd been out for a week.

"Deena?"

She shifted in her seat. "Well. I mean. I've got kind of a lot of stuff to do at home."

"But I just told her we were coming."

This statement was not, strictly speaking, true. But I was annoyed. Emma was our friend. And she wasn't sick, not really. She just had a hypochondriac for a mom. What was Deena's problem? I considered asking her this while I watched Deena try to come up with a credible excuse.

The phone vibrated again, with the text from UNKNOWN.

"Dammit," I muttered, scrolling to the new text message.

Don't forget.

"Hilarious," I whispered. "Psycho."

Who are you, anyway? Leave me alone I'm WORKING.

I stuffed the phone deep into the recesses of my shoulder bag, irritated with everyone.

"C'mon, Deena," I said. "She's our friend. She's not sick, not really. You know that. And I need you to drive me."

Deena scowled.

"Fine," she said, flipping a page in her physics book with finality.

"I don't see what the big deal is. We won't even stay that late."

"I said it's fine." She flipped another page.

"What?"

"Nothing."

I stared at her for a long moment and then, shaking my head, opened the paperback of the play with unnecessary force, cracking the spine flat. I rustled through the pages of one of my history books, ignoring Deena if she happened to notice my deliberate noise, and settled in to read.

An hour passed. Deena knitted her fingers together and stretched, palms out, and I could hear her knuckles pop. The sound caused Jennifer Crawford, who was napping at the far end of the library table, her head on a pile of Faulkner, to twitch in her sleep.

I flipped a page in the play, frowned, and ran my finger down a list of names in the history book at my elbow. Then I flipped the page back.

"Huh," I said. "That's funny."

"Hmm?" Deena inquired, resting her chin on the backs of her hands and smiling at me. That's one of the things I really like about Deena. We can get annoyed at each other, but it will eventually take care of itself, whatever it is, if we just let it lie for a while.

"This girl in the play. Ruth."

"What play?"

I held *The Crucible* up so she could read the cover.

Deena made a face. "And you all actually compete to be in that class? I mean, Calc BC, okay, I can see competing to get into *that*. Because math is *real*."

I smiled and said, "This is just extra credit."

"Oooooh," Deena said, raising her eyebrows. "Does Fabiana know you've got some extra credit?"

"No," I said, keeping my voice low.

"You're really gunning for her," Deena remarked.

"No, I'm not," I said. But I didn't know why I said that, because it was totally true. I was gunning for her. Why shouldn't I?

"What about her?"

"Who? Fabiana?"

"No, the girl in the play. Ruth."

"Oh!" I flipped back a few pages, and peered at my notes. "That's just it. She doesn't exist."

"What do you mean, she doesn't exist?"

"Look," I said, shoving the history book across the library table. Deena leaned closer so she could see, the green library light casting strange shadows in the hollows under her eyes.

"Um," Deena said. "What am I looking at?"

"Okay, here's the list of names. Right? They're the girls who accused women at Salem like three hundred years ago. And now, look."

I thrust the play across the table. Jennifer Crawford yawned, stretched, and raised her head halfway off her arms, looking at us curiously.

"So?"

"So, these are the characters in the play who are the afflicted girls, and they're all the same as in the history book. Right? Abigail, Betty, Mary, blah blah blah. But. There's a Ruth."

"So he made someone up. Big deal."

I sat back, ruminating.

"Why would he? Everyone else is a real person. It even says here"—I flipped some pages in a different book, one on literary criticism—"that Arthur Miller did research for the play in the real historical records. Like, real trial transcripts and stuff. There's a couple of them in the index here. They're crazy. Like a *Law and Order* episode."

"What are you guys talking about?" Jennifer Crawford asked from her book pillow.

"Some play Colleen's reading," Deena answered.

"Huh?"

I held the cover up for her to see, too.

"Oh, yeah, I had to read that," Jennifer Crawford said, propping her chin on her fist.

"I don't see what the big deal is," Deena said, going back to her science book. "He's a playwright. He can write whatever he wants. It's all made up anyway."

I glared at her.

"That for Mr. Mitchell's class?" Jennifer Crawford asked.

"You mean Ms. Slater's class?" I said. "Yeah. It's just a paper."

"History," Deena snorted. "Who cares? It already happened. Math gets us into space. And music gets us into bed. History's, like, already over."

"But why would he make up only one person out of the whole thing? He could've made up everyone. Or no one."

Jennifer Crawford grinned at me and said, "Maybe he's hiding something!"

"Oh, yeah. He's a Freemason," Deena teased. "It's all code."

"Maybe," I said, sticking the end of my pen in my mouth. I chewed it for a second before realizing that I'd put the business end of the pen in, instead of the cap, which I discovered when a nugget of ink burst under my molar.

"Aw, dammit," I said.

I stood up, wiping my chin and rushing to find a trash can to spit. Ink and drool leaked over my lower lip, onto the back of my hand.

Jennifer Crawford laughed out loud. "Nice one!" she called.

I made my way to the very nunlike washroom in the library, a plain cell of chipped tiles with two antique sinks and a toilet with one of those high boxes and a pull chain to flush. I peeled my lower lip down and inspected my teeth, which were now purply black and rotten looking, like I was wearing a zombie Halloween costume.

"That is basically the sexiest look I've ever come up with," I muttered, running the water in the sink. "Good thing I did it on Valentine's Day. I should send Spence a selfie so he can admire my intoxicating charm."

The door to the washroom opened and Jennifer Crawford came in. She gave me a small smile and offered me a paper towel.

"Thanks," I said.

She shrugged.

"I think it's kind of interesting, actually," Jennifer Crawford said.

"What is?" I dabbed at my lip and teeth, pausing to moisten the paper towel under the sink. Why was she always cool only when no one else was around?

"That he changed only one person's name. But you're right, he must have based her on someone and changed the details. Do you know who she's supposed to be?"

"Not yet," I said. "There were a lot of afflicted girls, turns out. More than you'd think. I'd never heard of a lot of them. Some of them weren't even girls. A lot of them were grown women. And there was one man, did you know that? John Indian. That name sounds totally fake."

"Huh," Jennifer Crawford said.

"I know. It's crazy. Now I kind of wish we'd talked about it in class."

"Me too. Mr. Mitchell would've rocked that."

"Oh, I know."

I watched her in the mirror over my shoulder. She was inspecting the roots of her pink hair and rummaging in her handbag for a lip gloss. Like we were just friends hanging out gossiping in the bathroom.

"Jennifer," I said.

"Mmm?"

"Are you worried?"

"Me? What about?"

"What do you think? About getting sick. About . . ."—I paused, gesturing with my hand in a circle of global consequence—"all of it."

A smile curled up Jennifer Crawford's cheek.

"Nah," she said. "Not really. Why, are you?"

I shook the water from my hands and saw that my efforts had largely been in vain and I was going to spend the foreseeable future with blackened teeth.

"I don't know," I said. "I just don't know."

. . .

I thought the reporters would all be gone when we were finished with sports, because they usually petered out over the course of the day as other newsworthy things happened in other parts of town. But this time the herd of reporters was just as thick at five as it had been that morning. Deena and I peered at them from a crack in the upper school front door.

"Should we just run for it?" she whispered.

"I guess," I said.

"Or we could sneak out the door by the gym and go through that lady's backyard to get to the back fence of the parking lot," Deena suggested.

"Hmm," I said.

I didn't relish a long tromp through someone else's yard after I'd already spent the afternoon running up and down a hockey field. Plus, the last time we did that, the lady had been home and threatened to call the cops on us. That would really put a damper on the afternoon.

"I say we run for it," I said.

"Okay." Deena grinned. "Ready? Set? Go!"

We threw our coats over our heads like we were mob informants running down courthouse steps to a waiting limousine and sprinted together, laughing, to Deena's car. Cameras clicked in rapid succession and questions were shouted at us, each overlapping the other.

"It's up to twenty-five now, you girls know that?"

"Aren't you scared for your safety?"

"D'you think it could be asbestos, or something in the water?"

"Tell us about PANDAS! Are you worried you'll get it, too? Have you had any strange symptoms you want to tell us about?"

"They're thinking of closing the school!"

"What's the administration telling you that it's not telling us, girls?"

"Talk to us!"

We reached the car, Deena fumbling for her keys to get it unlocked, and then we both dove inside, slamming the doors and muffling the cries of the press into a dull throb.

"At least the days are getting longer, finally," Deena said as she gunned the engine.

"Yeah," I said, gasping for breath. I turned to her and grinned. She grinned back.

"To Emma's?" she said.

"Mush!" I agreed.

We flipped on the radio and pulled away, reporters' hands trailing off the trunk of her car, like ghosts clutching at the living.

Deena's car crunched up the driveway to Emma's house a few minutes later, and the curtain over the picture window into Emma's living room twitched. Someone had been watching for us to pull up. Or watching for something, at any rate.

"You go get her," Deena said. "I'll stay here."

"Why?" I asked, giving her a look.

Deena shuddered, her hands on the steering wheel.

"Honestly? Emma's house kind of creeps me out."

"Creeps you out? What's to be creeped out about? It's just a house."

"I know." Deena watched the closed living room curtain carefully. I waited.

"Are you sure?"

"Maybe it's her mom? I don't know. I'd just rather wait here."

"Suit yourself," I said, climbing out of the car and slamming the door behind me.

A long silence wore by after I rang Emma's bell. Long enough for me to turn back to Deena, see her shrug in the car, and for me to shrug back. I rocked on my heels, waiting.

Nobody answered.

I was at the point of pressing the bell again when the front door creaked open, and one pale eye surveyed me from the shadows inside the house. It was almost six, and they still hadn't put any lights on.

"Yes?" said the wraith inside the door.

"Um. Hi, Mrs. Blackburn. Is Emma home?"

"Emma?" The pale eye blinked, as though confused about what I wanted.

"Yeah," I said, my gaze going shifty. "She and I were texting earlier? About me coming over?"

The eye waited.

"And, anyway, I'm here with Deena. We thought we'd take her out for a coffee or something."

"Oh." The door opened a little wider, but the wraith retreated farther out of view. "Colleen. Yes. Were you girls in school today?"

"Yes, Mrs. Blackburn."

"Ah. You weren't afraid to go?"

"No, Mrs. Blackburn."

"Oh. That's good." She had rounded the corner of the hallway into the family room, and I could hardly hear her. "I see. I'll get her."

The house went silent, and I loitered just outside the front door, not sure if I was supposed to step in or not. While I waited, I brought my fingertip to my temple and rubbed in a little circle. It felt nice. I was more tired than I'd realized.

Presently there was thumping on the stairs and Emma materialized out of the gloom, face shining with happiness at getting out of the house.

"Hey!" she chirped, giving me a quick hug. "Oh, good, Deena came. Hi!" she called, waving at the car. Deena gave a half wave back.

"Hey," I said, baffled by the difference in tone between Emma and her mom. "Listen, is your mom okay?"

"Mom? Yeah, sure. Why?"

"I don't know. She just seemed . . ." I paused, hesitating. The Blackburns, as I've mentioned, are ridiculously tight. "I don't know. Off."

214

"Nah." Emma waved me off and started for the car. "That's just Mom being Mom. Hey, Deena!"

Emma hopped into the backseat, grinning under a cute wool beret, her blond hair in two long ponytails over her shoulders.

"Hey," Deena said. She still seemed hesitant to me, but that could have just been because I was watching so closely. "How's vacation?"

"Oh my God, you guys. I am so. Bored. So bored. I was getting desperate."

Deena backed the car down the driveway and Emma practically bounced on the backseat, she was so excited.

"I thought we'd go to the café, just hang out for a while," I said, watching Deena's face to make sure this plan met with her approval. After all, it was her car.

"Perfect!" Emma cried. "And I have a great idea for what we can do after that."

"I dunno, y'all," Deena said. When she was stressed, her Southern accent slipped back out. "I've got kind of a lot of work to do tonight. I've got a BC problem set, and a book review for Japanese."

Emma leaned forward, thrusting her head between us.

"I know. But trust me. It won't take long. And you're going to love it."

Deena shot me a glance that gave me to understand I was responsible for getting her into this mess, and I would also be responsible for getting her out.

"We'll see," she said as we pulled away.

In the rearview mirror, as Emma's house retreated behind us in the encroaching night, I definitely saw the living room curtain twitch.

INTERLUDE

everend Green is like a boy being told a fairy story before bed. The day's wearing on, and I hear pans and chopping in the hall on the other side of the door, and his chubby baby, finally free of its hiccoughs, babbling to the cat. He pays them no attention.

It's comfortable, here in the parsonage. More comfortable than my own house. My house has most of my younger siblings in it still, but there's a coldness at the center. No happy babies beating on the kitchen table. No husband grumbling over a desk in the best room.

I'm not finished with my story, and I can tell I've seduced the Reverend so that he won't let me go 'til I'm done. His lips are parted. He wants for me to keep talking. I bask in this feeling. I hoard his attention for myself, soaking it up, filling every pore with it, knowing that soon it will be snatched away.

Mary Warren and Betty Hubbard and I leave Ingersoll's Ordinary at a trot, Betty struggling with the laces of her cloak under her chin, me pulling on my mittens in a rush, dropping one and having to run back and fetch it.

"Annie, hurry," Mary urges me, and I flounder through the snow to keep up.

The ice crunches under our boots, and our breath puffs out in steady clouds. Mary's brought a lamp, which smokes for want of cleaning.

It's not often I go abroad at night. Father says it's not safe, that though I walk with Jesus, I'm better off walking with him in the house. Some girls I know, who came down from the Eastward, know too well what kinds of devilish evil lurks in the dark. Godless men, their bodies smeared in grease, draped in the ragged skins of animals, demons who spring forth out of nothingness and burn your house to a cinder and drag your soul screaming down to hell.

I huddle closer to Betty Hubbard, who seems unconcerned. I'm glad Mary's with us; she's older, more sure of herself. Tree branches creak in an invisible night breeze, and in the far distance, a creature— dog or wolf or devil—howls, long and mournful. When we finally spy the black silhouette of the meetinghouse hulking up into the sky from the surrounding trees, I realize that I've been holding my breath.

Inside the parsonage, a terrible racket shakes the rafters, and many heads move in shadow against the narrow windows. We three cluster together, linking our arms. A girl's scream pierces the night, and the sound startles a bird from sleep. It takes off from a nearby tree with a sudden flapping of wings.

"Perhaps we should wait?" I whisper.

"No, Annie. You want the Reverend to beat them? We've got to keep Betty from saying anything. I just hope we're not already too late," Mary admonishes me.

"And anyway," Betty Hubbard says, "aren't you dying to know why she's screaming so?" I can tell from the sound of her voice that Betty's smiling.

"All right," I say, but my voice is small. I don't have my friends' boldness, not at all. I wish that I did.

We creep to the door, and ease it open without knocking.

Inside the parsonage's hall we find a goodly number of villagers, goodwives sitting in knots of two and three, several of them arrayed around Mrs. Parris. Upstairs, screams and rumbling men's voices yelling. Tittibe Indian stands by the wall, her face ashen. Her husband is nowhere to be seen. Heads swivel to us as we appear in the doorway.

"Good God in heaven," someone whispers. "It's the other ones. They've come."

"Why, so they have. You were right."

"Were they summoned? Or are they in their fits?"

"Just when the little one's on the point of naming her tormentor, they arrive? What say you to that, I ask you?"

The women shrink from us, watching with a steady stare as we move deeper into the room. I suppose I should feel afraid, but I don't. Instead I feel powerful. Usually no one shrinks from me for anything. I'm lucky if anyone takes notice of me at all. But now every eye in the room rests on me and Mary and Betty Hubbard, and those eyes all shine with fear and awe. A rill of wicked excitement fills me, and without meaning to, I smile.

Out of the corner of my eye, I see similar expressions on Betty Hubbard and Mary Warren's faces. So they're feeling it too.

"We're going up," Mary announces.

She doesn't ask Mrs. Parris for permission. She doesn't apologize. She doesn't even wait to be given leave. She does as she wills.

We advance to the attic ladder, and no one objects. No one speaks to us at all; they only whisper.

As we three mount the ladder one after the other, I hear Betty Hubbard giggling.

Up in the loft, we arrive to a baffling scene. At first none of the gentlemen upstairs even notice we're there, so absorbed are they in the goings-on of the afflicted.

There's the Reverend crouching next to the trundle, his hands fastened around his little daughter's skinny upper arms. Betty Parris is bawling, her mouth open, face beet red, tears squeezing out the corners of her eyes. Her fists are in her lap, and a string of wet trickles from her nose to her chin. She wails and gasps like a baby.

Abby, meanwhile, is straining at the window, her cheek pressed to the glass, her eyes open wide, dark hair flowing back from her forehead in long snarls. Her hands clutch at the sill, and she's pressing so hard, I can see the sinews in her throat.

"I'd fly!" she cries out. "They'd have me fly away! I'd fly well away from here, even if it meant going to one of their hideous Sabbaths, if only they'd leave me in peace! I'll fly!"

Young Reverend Hale kneels on the floor, his arms squeezed around her waist, and another man whose name I don't know stands behind Reverend Hale, feet braced against Abby's struggling, gripping her shoulders hard. She thrashes and fights like a drowning cat.

"Tell me!" Reverend Parris bellows, his voice ragged from weeks of praying and speechifying and exhortation. "You tell me right now, Betty! Tell me who's bewitching you!"

Betty Parris takes a long gulp of air, and screeches it back out. The Reverend shakes her, and her head wobbles on her shoulders.

"I'll never sign, they can't make me!" Abby screams. "They send their shapes in at the window in the night, and they sit on my chest until my breath is squeezed out of me and tell me I've got to join them!"

"Tell! You'll tell, by God!" Reverend Parris's voice rises.

"Tell, Betty Parris!" Mary Warren cries out. "You tell them what vile witch bedevils us!"

I look at Mary sharply. Betty Hubbard's eyes glitter with excitement.

Betty Parris stares at us, dumbfounded. Reverend Parris glares over his shoulder, and then thrusts his face inches away from his daughter's.

"Tell," he hisses.

"I . . . ," Betty Parris starts to say, eyes peeping open between puffy red lids. She inhales a long sob and stammers, "I . . . I see her come in at the window."

"Yes?" her father urges. The other men are rapt. Even Reverend Hale turns to stare over his shoulder at the little girl who's gone so long without speaking.

"I see her!" Abby screams in ecstasy. "Yes, Betty, I see her, too!"

Betty Hubbard's hands clasp under her chin at the sound of her name, even though Abby's speaking to the other Betty, Betty Parris. My heart lurches in my chest, and I wipe my wrist over my mouth because I fear I'm going to be sick.

"Who? Who do you see?" one of the periwigged magistrates worries, looking about himself as if the witch's specter might be standing nearby, if only he had the power to see.

Downstairs, I hear shuffling and voices, and someone issuing orders to someone else.

"She sends her shape out to torment us!" Mary Warren cries, her eyes wide.

I gaze on her with horror, for Mary knows as well as I do it's all a lie. But the look on her face says otherwise. She holds her hands palms out at her side, her face lifted to the heavens as though awaiting a divine message.

"Yes! She comes to me also, in the night, and I'm sore afraid! She shows me where their names are written in blood!"

I turn on my heel, stunned, for this exclamation comes from none other than Betty Hubbard.

"What, you, Elizabeth?" Dr. Griggs steps out from within the knot of black-coated men and moves to inspect his niece. He places his hands gently on her shoulders and looks down at her with concern.

"Since we come to stay at the Putnams," she whispers, refusing to look at me. "A shape comes and troubles me in the night, and I don't hardly know where I am or what I'm saying, and betimes I awaken and find I've wandered into some other room entirely, with no wrap and freezing with cold."

"What shape? Why didn't you say something sooner?"

"I was afraid, Uncle. I knew not what sort of shape it might be, but it sometimes had a yellow bird with it, and no matter how much I cried, it wouldn't leave me in peace."

Betty Hubbard's been sharing a pallet with me and my sister these past two weeks, in the loft where I sleep. And while it's true there was one night she awoke from a dream in tears and I held her 'til she was quiet, and another night she awoke needing the chamber pot and couldn't find it in the dark in a strange room, and I came upon her weeping in a corner and trembling with cold until I helped her, I never heard any talk of any shape coming in at the window. We've had no nighttime visitors intent on blood except bedbugs.

Now all eyes travel to me. After all, I'm afflicted, too. I've got the marks to prove it.

"Is this true, Ann?"

Mary Warren rests a beatific hand on my shoulder. "It's all right, Annie," she says gravely. "You can say. They only want to help." Her eyes are deep pools of cunning. Abby, at the window, has ceased her struggling and smiles.

"Oh, Annie, tell them how we suffer!" Abigail beseeches me.

"I . . . I . . ." I stumble over my words, terrified. If I continue the lie, I'm sinning in the eyes of God. A vile, hell-sending sin. If I speak the truth, I'll be beaten sure, and all the other girls will, too. My mouth goes dry, and bile rises in my throat.

At length, I whisper, "I cannot say whose shape it is."

"There!" one of the gentlemen exclaims. "She sees it, too!"

Reverend Parris turns his attention back to his daughter, rattling her against the wall. "Girl! You tell us who's tormenting you right now! Say the name!"

Betty Parris's mouth hangs open and her eyes are panicked. She's gurgling, speechless, helpless, even more afraid than I am.

Someone is grunting her way up the attic ladder and fiddling with the trapdoor latch, which we'd closed behind us when we came up.

The trap opens with a slam, and to a man and girl we all jump, Abby letting out a blood-chilling scream.

The cloth-wrapped head of Tittibe appears in the hatch. She's not looking at anyone, but carries some dishes of roast pork with gravy.

"It was she!" Betty Parris screams, breaking free of her father's grasp and pointing with a trembling finger.

"What?" Reverend Parris looks with confusion at the slave who's just climbed into the attic. The woman he's known since the days on the island no one speaks of.

"Aye, it was she! Tittibe! She sent her shape in at the window to torment me! It's she!"

"Yes!" Abby joins in. "I see her, too! She has that yellow bird perched on her shoulder even now, ready to tear out my eyes!"

Tittibe looks stricken, the plate of food shaking in her hands.

"But . . . ," she says. "Betty, you know me. You've always known me."

Reverend Parris has gotten to his feet, nostrils flaring, his hands curling slowly into fists. His breath comes fast. Seeing the change in the minister, the younger one, Reverend Hale, untangles himself from Abby's skirts and scrambles to his feet, maneuvering between the elder man and the Indian woman.

"Wait, Reverend," Reverend Hale says, his hands outstretched.

Mary Warren and Betty Hubbard fall into each other's arms, weeping, and Mary's arm shoots out and enfolds me, bringing us into a tight tangle of trembling, frightened girls.

"You!" Reverend Parris growls at Tittibe, whose terror deepens.

"That must be why the water charm didn't work," one man whispers to another. "Why, she must've fouled it somehow, to avoid detection!"

"You!" Reverend Parris bellows again, his voice rising an octave, and he struggles to fling himself at the woman, with only Reverend Hale's hands holding him back.

With a cry Tittibe drops to her knees, the food falling from her grasp and splattering across the floor, the plate splintering in two. She covers her face with her hands and begins to sob.

"No, no!" she moans, rocking to and fro. "No, it cannot be, it cannot be. Not I, it's never I, not I."

"Are you the witch who's tormenting my child? My child whom you've known from a babe in arms? Is it you?" The Reverend's voice cracks with grief, and we can hear our commotion drawing the crowd to the foot of the ladder, gathering and murmuring, a pond of faces staring up with horror and disbelief.

She only wails, "No, no, it were never me, I'm no witch, I not be hurting my Betty!"

The Reverend turns away in anguish, wiping his face with his hands. When he turns back, his entire countenance is warped with rage.

"They're all against me, Tittibe!" he screams. "All of them! And now you! You bring this evil witchcraft into my house? Onto my child? You'll confess, by God! You'll confess if I have to beat it out of you with my own hands!"

CHAPTER 17

Emma beat time on her lap to the music we had going in the car, bobbing her head and grinning out the window. We found a spot without too much trouble and tumbled out of the car in a tangle of coats and scarves, and I was feeling relieved to be out with Emma and Deena like it was any other basic Tuesday night. It was almost enough to make up for Spence not texting me to wish me happy Valentine's Day.

Almost.

Jerk.

Emma promised we wouldn't stay at the café too long, because she had some top-secret location that she wanted us to go to afterward. No matter how much Deena and I wheedled, she wouldn't even give us a hint.

"Nope," she said. "It's too good. You guys just have to wait. Does this place have frappes?"

"No frappes," I said, smiling. With her pot smoking I'd started to wonder when Emma had gotten older than me all of a sudden. But wanting a frappe when everyone else was having coffee was vintage Emma. "There's tea, though, if you don't want coffee."

The three of us milled around, craning our necks to read the menu blackboard and drooling over the chocolate chip muffins and brownies and cookies.

"Oh, I'm so getting one of those," Deena said, indicating a Rice Krispies treat. When I ordered chamomile tea, Emma let out a sharp laugh.

"Oh my God. What happened?"

"What?"

"Your teeth!" Emma reached a fingertip forward, as though she were going to stick it into my mouth.

"Oh, this?" I laughed, ducking her finger. "You know. Just trench mouth. Nothing serious."

"What did you *do*?"

"Don't worry, it's not contagious. Unless I BITE YOU." I lunged, making like I was going to bite her.

Emma squealed, fending me off with both hands, and I chased her in a zombie shamble around Deena, who held her coffee high overhead where it would be safe. Emma and I collapsed on each other, laughing, with Emma trying to stick her finger in my mouth and me grasping her wrist and holding her off.

"You guys!" Deena chastised us as she found a table and started shedding her winter layers.

"BIIIIITE YOUUUUU!" I moaned in zombie voice, 'til I noticed something odd on Emma's hand. I stopped zombieing around and took Emma's hand more gently.

"Dude," I said. "What's this?"

She had a growth of some kind on her knuckle. It was pink and tender looking, wettish, and the skin around it was red and irritated.

"What. Oh, that?"

Emma reclaimed her hand from my grasp, looked at it briefly, and then thrust it into her pocket.

"It's nothing. A wart."

"Gross," I said.

"Gee, thanks, Trench Mouth," Emma said.

She was joking, but I thought she looked halfway irritated.

"Bite youuuuuu!" I zombie-moaned again as we all settled around our café table with drinks and sticky baked goods.

We were getting situated in our chairs and stuffing our scarves into our jacket sleeves when something across the room caught Emma's eye. As I watched, the remnants of her smile melted off her face like running candle wax.

"What is it?" I asked, resting a hand on her arm.

Emma kept staring and didn't answer.

Deena and I turned in our seats, following Emma's gaze.

On the other side of the café, close to the back door, was a small table under a low-hanging red lamp, with a guy and a girl sitting at it. The girl was a tweedy college type in a blazer and knee-high boots who had a laptop open and wore heavy-framed hipster glasses. The guy she was sitting with was angled partway away from us, about the same age as the girl, maybe early twenties, slim, and had mussed hair and a black T-shirt that had been washed to a perfect, weathered dark gray. He cradled an open book, one hand holding his head up by an ear. For a second I couldn't figure out why Emma would be bothering to look at them. They were probably just a couple of Salem State students on a study date or something.

"Oh my God," Deena said.

Then I saw it.

The cute young guy was Mr. Mitchell.

"Oh, hey!" I said, my eyes brightening. "Wow, that's crazy. You guys want to go say hi?"

"Eh," said Deena. "You go ahead. I didn't have him, remember?"

"Come on," I said to Emma, plucking at her sleeve. "Don't you want to say hi?"

Emma looked up at me with wide gray eyes.

"Sure," she said. But her voice sounded funny.

We made our way over, hesitant, and I would have been giggling the way I would if I were about to accost James Franco, except that Emma wasn't giggling with me. We arrived next to their table and stood there, close together, waiting to be noticed.

The girl saw us first, looking up with her glasses reflecting the blue-white light of her laptop screen.

"Tad," she said.

Mr. Mitchell looked like he was trying to collapse in on himself, shrinking smaller the closer we drew. But at the sound of the girl's voice, he glanced up, first at her and then at us.

"Oh!" he exclaimed.

I caught a lightning flash of panic zigzag across his face, but he covered it quickly with a professional-seeming smile.

"Colleen. Emma. Hi."

"Hey!" I said.

Emma didn't say anything, so I poked her.

"Hi," she said, voice flat.

Mr. Mitchell's eyes moved between us uneasily, like he couldn't decide where to look. He swallowed, pulling nervously on his earlobe.

"So," he managed to say. "How's it going?"

"Good," I said. "We're good."

"That's good. I'm glad to hear that." His eyes settled on Emma with rapid blinks.

There was a long, deadly pause. I waited for him to introduce Laptop Girl to us, but after a certain expanse of time I realized that wasn't going to happen, and that in fact maybe he wasn't all that happy we were there.

"How've you been?" I asked.

"I've been well, thanks for asking, Colleen," he said, too formally. "How're college apps going?"

"Okay," I said. "I got deferred early decision by Dartmouth and Williams, which totally sucked, but Emma just found out she got into Endicott, so at least she knows she's all set next year no matter what happens."

Mr. Mitchell's eyes settled on Emma with a shine.

"Endicott. That's great." I'd never heard a guy sound more neutral.

"Not that we were surprised, I mean, you know how good her grades are," I continued.

"Yes."

Emma still didn't say anything. The skin on the back of my neck started to feel warm.

"Um." I groped for something else to say. "You should really come back. We've got a substitute for AP US, and she's okay, but she's, like, a little weird. Like, I think she wants to teach college or something, and that she thinks teaching high school is, like, a waste of time."

"Ah," he said. "Yeah, well." A pause. "Crazy stuff happening at St. Joan's, huh."

"Crazy," I agreed.

We all stood around nodding about how crazy it was.

"Well." He gave us a tight smile, and a harder tug on his earlobe. "Nice to see you guys."

I looked at Emma, who was staring at him. Her eyes had that oyster-shell look that they get sometimes. Hipster Glasses Girl stared at her laptop as if we weren't there.

"Okay," I said, a little uncertain. "Well. Nice to see you."

"You too. Good luck with everything."

"Thanks."

I took Emma's arm and dragged her back to the other end of the café, eager to pretend like that hadn't just happened.

"If anyone needs me, I'll be under the table," I muttered. "You can page me when he's gone."

Deena laughed from inside her coffee cup.

"Oh my God, Deena, that was so weird. Wasn't he acting so weird?" I said to Emma.

"Yeah," she said.

"And he didn't look like he'd been sick at all. I mean, what the hell?"

Emma hadn't looked away from them. Mr. Mitchell and the

laptop girl were leaning over their table, having an intense-looking conversation. I caught their eyes sliding over to us, and the conversation grew more animated. The three of us watched their conversation unfold, unable to hear anything, until we realized that we were staring, largely because Hipster Glasses looked directly at us and then all three of us gasped and blushed and stared fiercely at our muffins.

Never have I been more interested in a muffin.

Deena was trying to suppress a snicker, and failing.

"Are they still looking at us?" Emma whispered after a minute of forcible, concerted ignoring them.

I peeked behind a hand, and they seemed to have gone back to their respective projects.

"I don't think so."

We sighed with relief and began to peel the paper wrapping off our muffins in meditative silence.

"Maybe he just, like, quit," Deena ventured after a while.

"He looks so different without the tie. Doesn't he look different?"

"Yeah," Emma said. She'd gone back to staring.

"Why do you think he wasn't excited to see us, Em? I'd think he'd be kind of excited to see us."

"I don't know."

"He wasn't excited to see you?" Deena asked. "It looked like you talked for long enough."

"Kind of. I guess."

"What did you talk about?"

"College, mostly."

"Not about the Mystery Illness? You'd think he'd want to talk about that."

I could hear the words capitalized when Deena said that. That's what they'd taken to calling it on the news. We'd started calling it that ironically, but at some point over the last week it had stopped being funny.

"No, not really. Not as such."

"PANDAS. That doesn't sound like much of an illness." Deena slurped her coffee. "It sounds made up, if you ask me."

"Did you ever get called in to talk to Nurse Hocking and Dr. Strayed?" I asked.

Deena nodded. "Couple days ago. It was weird. Did they ask you all kinds of personal questions?"

"What kind of personal questions?" Emma asked.

I was surprised, as she hadn't seemed to be paying attention to our conversation, so absorbed was she in watching Mr. Mitchell (*Tad*) and Glasses Girl at work.

"Ah," Deena said. "Sex questions, mostly."

Emma's eyes slid from Mr. Mitchell's table and settled on her hands, which were folded around her mug of tea. A finger crept over and played with her new wart.

"Did you tell them about Japan Boy?"

"Colleen!" Deena smacked me on the arm. "No."

Emma smirked.

"Yeah," I said. "They asked me all kinds of stuff like that. Not just about me either."

"About who else?"

"I don't know. People."

"What people?" Emma asked.

"Clara, actually. Which is weird, 'cause it's not like I'd know, you know?"

Emma's ears flushed scarlet.

"Did they ask you about strep throat?" Deena asked.

"Yeah. They seem pretty certain it's PANDAS," I said.

"That's one stupid-ass name for a disease, if you ask me," Deena said, popping a morsel of Rice Krispies treat into her mouth. "But I'll tell you one thing, it made my dad feel a lot better about me still going to school."

"Why's that?"

"'Cause I had strep when I was little. And that stuff, all that weird twitching and whatnot, starts happening, like, a few months after you have it. And I definitely didn't have it last year."

"Me neither," I said.

"Yeah," Emma said.

"So why are you out of school, if you can't get PANDAS?"

"Well," Emma demurred, rolling a muffin crumb between her finger and thumb. "You know."

"Her mom," I explained to Deena. She hadn't grown up with us. She didn't know Mrs. Blackburn as well. Not that I *knew her* knew her. We just didn't ask, when it came to Emma's mom.

"What's your mom's deal?"

Emma shrugged.

"I don't know. She worries."

"Still and all," I said. "It's pretty weird. They said on TV that it was really rare. Why do you think so many would have it at St. Joan's, and no place else? And why would it just be showing up now, and never before?"

We all stared at the center of our café table, and by *we all* I mean Deena and me, because Emma was still staring at Mr. Mitchell.

"Maybe," Deena said, "there was an outbreak last year. Of, like, a special kind of strep throat. One that's more likely to cause PANDAS. Maybe it was just at our school. Like a mutation or something? Why isn't anyone talking about it if there's a mutation?"

She was on the point of saying something else when, without warning, Emma got to her feet and started across the café back to Mr. Mitchell's table.

"Where are you going?" I asked, waylaying Emma with a hand on her arm.

"Um," Emma said, frowning down at me. "I forgot. He offered to write me a rec letter. For college? I have to ask him about it."

"A rec letter?" I echoed, confused.

"Yeah." Emma shook herself free of my hand and gave me a forced smile. "It'll just take a second."

Deena and I watched as Emma marched across the café, coming to a stop by Mr. Mitchell's table. Emma talked, him trying to get a word in edgewise, while Glasses Girl glared at her. Then Mr. Mitchell got up, frowning, and he and Emma hurried through the back screen door of the café. They stood in the alley just outside, their shadows long in the streetlight. I couldn't see them very well, but Emma definitely had her arms crossed, and then Mr. Mitchell's shadow moved over her body and we couldn't see her.

"Did you know his first name is Tad?" I remarked to Deena.

"Huh. I didn't know that. I didn't have him, remember?"

"Yeah."

We both stared at the screen door. Emma's silhouette reappeared, close to his ear.

"Tad," I repeated. "Taaaaaaaaaad."

The name made me think of tadpoles. Tad bits. Small things.

"What's that short for, anyway? Theodore?" Deena wondered.

"No idea."

Another pause, almost unbearably long.

"Maybe he just didn't like teaching, you know?" Deena tried again. "Maybe he just got sick of high school."

"I wouldn't blame him. I'm sick of high school."

Deena turned back and looked at me with surprise. "You are?"

"Definitely. I hate it."

I didn't think I'd ever said that aloud to anyone, but it was true. I hated obsessing about my grades. Hated keeping a weather eye on Fabiana all the time. Hated having my parents track my every move, like they didn't trust me, even though I'd never done anything really wrong. Hated Wheez and Michael always stealing my stuff, having no respect for my space. Hated not having a car, so my dad had to drop me off at school every day and I had to get a ride home from

Deena, never getting to decide where I wanted to go and when. I hated wearing a uniform, God. So dehumanizing. Hated worrying if my zits would come back, hated being so tall that I stuck out in a hallway full of nothing but girls. Hated my ugly freckles. Hated my perennially snarled curly hair.

And I hated how most of us had grown up together, so that we never had a chance to really change. We could try, but people just kept seeing an earlier version of us. We each had our own narrative, our own character we were required to perform in the daily play that was "St. Joan's Academy for Girls," the best school in Danvers, the proving ground for the rich and the smart. Now that I thought about it, I was pretty tired of being in that play. I wanted to appear in something new.

I was on the point of trying to explain this to Deena when the front door of the café squeaked open and a girl came in. She was in ripped black jeans and combat boots and super-heavy goth makeup, and she had pink hair.

And the reason she had pink hair was because she was Jennifer Crawford. Of course. I mean, I basically never saw her outside of school, where I was used to seeing her in a plaid skirt just like mine. She looked completely different. She looked confident. She looked badass, actually.

She didn't seem to be looking for anyone, but when she spotted Deena and me, she grinned anyway.

"Hi, guys!" Jennifer Crawford said, plopping down in our fourth chair. "What's up?"

"Not much. Just hanging out."

"Where's Emma?" Jennifer Crawford knew we tended to move in a pack.

"Outside, asking Mr. Mitchell about a rec letter he owes her for someplace."

"Mr. Mitchell?" Her face brightened under its layers of eye makeup.

"That's wild. Does that mean he's not sick anymore? Maybe he'll be back next week. D'you talk to him?"

"Kind of," I said.

"Colleen said he was acting weird."

"Huh," Jennifer Crawford said, sliding Emma's muffin on its flowered-open paper wrapper nearer to her and picking a corner off of it. "Did he say when he was coming back? I'm getting really sick of that Ms. Slater. She's a bitch."

"Um." I glanced back to the rear screen door. Mr. Mitchell's and Emma's shadows moved over the screen, joining together and breaking apart, making their hands and arms look grotesque. Worry bloomed in my stomach. "No. I guess he didn't."

Jennifer Crawford chewed Emma's muffin and followed my gaze. "Weird," she said. "He say why he left?"

The shadows of Emma and Tad blended together into one shape, and in that moment I saw with perfect clarity why he had left. God, I was such an idiot. How could I not have seen it? I gripped the seat of my chair and stared at the screen door, swallowing my panic.

"No," I said, trying to keep my face neutral. "He didn't say."

"Hmm," Jennifer Crawford mused. She peeled most of the muffin top off and said in an aside to Deena, "I just eat the tops. They're really the best part, don't you think?"

Deena smiled. "Definitely."

"So, I just heard something crazy," Jennifer Crawford continued, apparently finished with the question of our missing history teacher and licking muffin scum from a thumb.

"What's that?" Deena asked.

I pushed my own muffin away. What were they doing outside? Were they fighting? Or were they . . . ? It was disgusting. It was even worse than thinking about Jason Rothstein with his hand on the back of Anjali's neck. He was an adult! I mean, he wasn't old like Father Molloy, but God. He was out of college. He was . . . I felt dizzy. I didn't want Deena to see what I was thinking. I dug my nails into my thighs, hard.

"Well," Jennifer Crawford said, leaning forward in the manner of someone about to impart sensitive information. Deena leaned in nearer. "I have it on good authority"—she dropped her voice to a confidential whisper—"that Clara might be going on *Good Day, USA.*"

"Get out!" Deena cried, smacking Jennifer Crawford playfully on the shoulder.

"Whoa," I said. I reached a shaking hand for my mug to rinse the distaste from my mouth. "Really? When?"

"Don't know," Jennifer Crawford said. "Next week maybe? But I heard she and her mom have been talking to one of their producers."

"Who told you?" Deena asked, leaning forward on her elbows.

"Yeah," I said. "How do you know?"

"The Other Jennifer told me," she said, shrugging. "She was there when Clara and her mom were on a conference call with the TV people."

"No way," I said, leaning back with my arms wrapped over my belly. "No way are they going on *Good Day, USA.*"

"It's true. The Other Jennifer might get to go on, too, she said."

"Why would she even be telling you this? You guys had a huge fight! You don't even talk to her!"

Jennifer Crawford pursed her lips. "You don't know everything, Colleen. We talk sometimes. Like you and I do. I talk to a lot of people."

I flushed, ashamed of myself. It was true, Jennifer Crawford and I talked more in AP US than anywhere else. I'd be more likely to talk with her outside of school than in advisory. I didn't know why that was, but I could admit that it was true. Guess I wasn't the only hypocrite at St. Joan's Academy.

"That's wild," Deena said. "*Good Day, USA.* My mom watches that every morning."

"This can't be happening," I moaned, leaning forward and resting my cheek on the table. I closed my eyes. "I just want it all to go away."

"Come on." Jennifer Crawford laughed. "It's awesome. Maybe they'll come to the school to film and we'll all get famous."

"I don't want to get famous," I groaned into the tabletop. "I want everything to go back to normal."

"Me too," said Emma. "Hey, Jennifer."

"Hey." Jennifer Crawford nodded hello as Emma sat back down.

I hadn't heard her come back. My head shot up from the table and I stared at her. She seemed flushed, but okay. Glassy. Like one of her dolls. She kept her eyes on the table, slipping her knuckle wart absently into her mouth.

"You get your rec letter?" I asked. I tried to keep my voice careful.

"What?" Emma said, pulling the knuckle out of her mouth without looking at me. "Oh, yeah. Sure. He said he was sorry it was taking so long."

"Huh."

"What do you mean, you don't want to be famous?" Jennifer Crawford asked, not noticing my careful examination of Emma. "Everyone wants to be famous."

"Not me," Emma said. Her eyes kept darting to Mr. Mitchell's table, and when they landed there, her flush deepened.

"I don't think I'd mind," Deena mused, also oblivious to what had just happened outside. "I think I'd be pretty good at being famous."

"Would you still hang out with us little people?" I smiled at her.

"You? Oh, yeah. You guys could be in my entourage. I'd let you carry my luggage."

"Oooooh!" Emma grinned. Her eyelids fluttered, and it occurred to me that maybe they hadn't had an argument after all. "Aren't we lucky?"

"I won't carry your luggage," I said, resting my cheek back down on the table, watching Emma's face from my vantage point on the tabletop. There was beard burn along her chin. "I'll only be in the entourage if I get to carry your goldfish bowl everywhere. Like in the limo. Like you won't do any appearances without your goldfish."

"Of course," Deena agreed. "The goldfish is nonnegotiable. And he only gets fresh, organic fish food."

"I'm definitely going to be famous," Jennifer Crawford remarked. "No question."

"For what?"

"I don't know. I have to figure it out. That's why it would be awesome if *Good Day, USA* came to St. Joan's. It'd be, like, a shortcut. I'd get discovered."

"Ha," I said. "Clara'd get discovered, you mean."

"Clara's not so special," Jennifer Crawford said airily. "Once this all blows over, she'll disappear. You'll see."

Emma reached for her beret. She kicked me under the table with a foot and smiled.

"Maybe," I said, also starting to pull on my winter stuff.

Deena saw us getting ready to go with a look of relief. Maybe she really was worried about her problem set.

"Well," Emma said, getting to her feet. "We've got to get going. Deena has to get home."

"Okay," Jennifer Crawford said, covering her disappointment with breezy acceptance. "See you guys tomorrow."

"Not me," Emma corrected her. "Them, though."

"Bye, Jennifer," Deena and I said. Deena gave her a quick hug and I waved.

She waved back, and turned her attention to Emma's castoff muffin paper. She did a good job of seeming not to care that we were leaving.

We piled back into Deena's car, boots and scarves and jackets in a heap and our breath puffing out in clouds of vapor around our heads, steaming up the inside of the car windows.

"Home?" Deena asked as she started to back out of her parking spot.

"Nope," Emma said. Her cheeks were glowing, and she had the tiniest, most mysterious Mona Lisa of smiles on her face. "We've got one stop to make first."

"Emma," Deena said in a warning tone.

"You'll love it. I promise. Turn left up here."

Emma had taken the front seat, with me in the back, and I enjoyed feeling warm inside my coat, not having to give directions or know where we were going. I was thinking about Jennifer Crawford's plans for fame, and about Emma and Mr. Mitchell.

Tad.

How did that start, I wondered.

How does it ever?

CHAPTER 18

We rolled to a stop in a large parking lot by an undistinguished building that I'd passed every day for most of my life—a complex of medical offices and dentists and physical therapists all collected under the impossible name of Our Lady of the Inquisitor Medical and Ambulatory Care Center.

Emma was tapping quickly on her phone.

"Okay," she said. "Come on, we don't have a ton of time."

Deena and I exchanged a look in the rearview mirror.

"What's going on, Emma?" Deena asked.

"Yeah," I said. "What are we doing here?"

"Trust me," Emma said, and her Mona Lisa smile opened up and spread over her whole face, causing her pale eyes to sparkle strangely. "Come on. Hurry up!"

Emma hustled us out of Deena's car and across the parking lot and through a set of sliding glass doors. The lobby of Our Lady of the Inquisitor smelled antiseptic and creepy, and there was this dead ficus in the corner that looked really twisted, like a malformed skeleton.

Emma had her eyes glued to her phone, and Deena and I drew together out of instinctive discomfort, linking our arms as if beasts were going to leap out of the shadows and tear us apart.

"I don't like this," Deena whispered to me out of Emma's earshot. "She's acting weird."

"It's fine," I whispered back. "You just hate surprises."

"I do hate surprises." Deena frowned. "Like, a lot."

We crept forward together, following Emma, who seemed to know exactly where she was going. There was a lone security guard at the reception desk who glanced at us as we passed. Nobody was waiting in the lobby. We started down a long institutional corridor, the only movement besides us coming from a sagging silver Mylar balloon with a ragged string, tacking listlessly against an air vent near the ceiling. GET WELL SOON was printed on its side.

We rounded another corner and spotted a white-coated woman at the far end of the hallway, leaning against the back of a waiting room chair and also looking at her cell phone. At the sound of our footsteps the doctor glanced up and beamed a huge smile.

"Girls!" Dr. Gupta cried, folding us into a hug much bigger than I would expect from a woman as petite as she is. She had a musical British Indian accent that I secretly tried to imitate when I was home by myself. I'd never been able to get it right.

"I didn't tell them," Emma said from inside Dr. Gupta's ponytail. "They have no idea."

Dr. Gupta stood back, one hand on my shoulder and one on Deena's.

"Perfect, that's perfect," she said. "Anjali will be so surprised. She hasn't seen anyone but Jason in days. Come! I'll take you."

Deena and I exchanged one of our instantaneous, communicative looks. *Jason?* We didn't have time to go any further than that, because Dr. Gupta took us in to see Anjali.

She was sitting up in bed in a private room, decorated with flowers and some stuffed bears and a balloon bouquet that might have been short one silver Mylar member. Anjali looked like her usual self.

She even had on her pajamas covered in cartoon manatees, which I remembered from a sleepover we'd had last year.

"Hi hi!" she said from the bed, waving in jazz-hands excitement.

Deena and I squealed and went in for a hug. Emma stood off to the side looking pleased with herself.

"Oh my God! Anjali!" I said, but I may have shouted, because Dr. Gupta put a gentle fingertip to her lips.

"Are you okay?" Deena spoke at the same time as me. "Why didn't you text us back? We've been so worried! Tell her how worried we've been."

"We've been worried," I confirmed.

"I know, you guys, I know. I'm sorry. I didn't mean to freak you out. It's just that my mom took my phone"—she shot Dr. Gupta a dirty look, but Anjali's mom just laughed—"'cause she said it was most important that I get lots of rest and not excite myself. She only let me text Jason once and that was it."

"Dumbass," I muttered under my breath.

"Colleen!" Emma whispered.

"Sorry," I said. "But I mean, he could've, like, called us. We've been freaking out!"

"But how did Emma know where you were?" Deena asked.

"I ran into Jason yesterday," Emma said. "At the café with some people. He's really not that bad, you know."

"I guess," I said.

Okay, maybe he wasn't that bad. For a yo-boy.

"So are you okay? What happened?" I asked, climbing into bed next to Anjali as Deena and Emma piled onto her feet.

"I'll let you girls catch up," Dr. Gupta said. "I'll be back in a few minutes. But Anjali—"

"Yes?"

"Don't overtire yourself. You need your rest. The girls can stay for only fifteen minutes or so, and then they'll have to go so you can sleep."

"Okay."

Dr. Gupta gave Anjali the universal *I-mean-it* look that all mothers give their daughters, and then slipped out. The door clicked closed behind her.

"ANJALI!" I hollered. "What happened?"

"Oh my God. You guys. It was crazy."

"Do you have the Mystery Illness?" Deena asked. "Or something else?"

"Umm . . ." Anjali thought. "I don't really know. My mom's running some tests."

"Like what kind of tests?" we demanded.

"Blood tests? I don't know. For, like, poison, I think? I'm not sure."

"Poison! Like, cyanide or something?"

"No, no, nothing like that. She's not sure yet."

"But you haven't told us what happened."

"Okay, so, I was at home," Anjali said. "Just like normal."

"When?" we wanted to know.

"I don't know. Couple weeks ago."

"Okay."

"So I was working on a problem set for physics, and I was almost done, and then I was going to revise my paper for AP English when I started getting this really weird headache."

"Like a migraine?" we asked.

"No. I mean, I don't know, I've never had a migraine, so I'm not sure. Just like really intense, like it was drilling into my brain, right in the center of my forehead, like into my third eye."

"Crazy," we breathed.

"So I lay down for a while, thinking, Okay, maybe I'm just really tense, I've been working really hard, waiting on colleges and everything."

"Sure," we all agreed.

"And then, I started to cough. I rolled onto my side and I just hacked like you wouldn't believe. That's when my mom came in. I was coughing so loud, Mom could hear me all the way downstairs. Then there was this really intense coughing fit, and some stuff came up. It was really nasty."

"Stuff?" we asked. "What kind of stuff?"

"Um." Anjali took a hank of her hair and coiled it around a finger. "I'd rather not say. It was really disgusting."

"What was it, like, blood or something?"

"Um." Anjali frowned. "No. No, nothing like that. It was weird."

"We don't understand," we protested. "Was it bile? Did you vomit?"

Anjali drew up her knees. "Um. It wasn't . . . liquid. Exactly. That was the weirdest part. That was when my mom took me to the hospital."

"What, did you have, like, a hairball or something?" we teased.

But she didn't laugh.

"No. It actually looked kind of . . . sharp. It was like this little wet lump of stuff. Like fish bones, but all caught up in a ball. And kind of metallic, almost. Like fish bones, but different."

"Ew," we said, grimacing at the thought. "Did it hurt?"

"Yeah," Anjali said. "It hurt a lot. And after it came up, I was bleeding and stuff, like it had raked my trachea on the way up. It was really awful. I was super-scared. My mom bundled me up and drove me straight here. It was the closest hospital, and she's got privileges here, so that's where we came. And I've been here ever since. But I think I can go home pretty soon."

"Have you been twitching, like Clara and them?"

"No. I don't think so. I just get this awful headache, and then the coughing."

"You mean the fish bones keep coming up?" we asked, aghast.

"Yeah," Anjali said. "About once a day. I'll hack and hack and hack, and then I'll spit out this weird fish-bony ball. It's definitely not bones, though. You know how I hate fish."

"It could still be the Mystery Illness," I said. "Look at the Other Jennifer. She lost all her hair. That hasn't happened to anyone else."

"That's true," Deena said. "When you come right down to it, everyone we know has different symptoms. They don't even look like the same thing at all, actually."

"Yeah," I said. "Clara's the only one who really can't talk, right? Elizabeth pretty much only has it in her legs. Jennifer lost her hair."

"Leigh is *vibrating*," Deena added. "Did you see her on television? That was crazy."

"What?" Anjali asked. "I haven't heard any of this. Leigh Carruthers?"

"Oh, yeah. She and her mom went on TV. *This Is Danvers*."

"You're kidding."

"You should see the school. Every day we have to fight through reporters."

"Holy cow."

"And now Jennifer Crawford says that Clara might be going on *Good Day, USA*," I added.

"That's crazy."

"Twenty-seven people," Emma said from her perch near Anjali's feet. "That's the last number I heard."

"Does your mom think it's PANDAS, too?"

"PANDAS? What's that?"

"Um. It's an acronym. Pediatric . . . Autoimmune . . ."

"Neurological Disorder And Stuff," Deena finished for me. We laughed.

"But what does it mean?"

"Basically," I said, "some kids, after they have strep throat, a few months later go on to develop weird tics and things. Like OCD. A lot like what Clara has. Nurse Hocking and this infectious disease doctor went on TV and said that's what it was."

"It's not PANDAS," Dr. Gupta said from the doorway.

We jumped. We hadn't heard her come back.

"It's not?" we asked.

"Definitely not, no. It was very irresponsible of Dr. Strayed to say it was."

"But how do you know?" we asked Anjali's mom. She pulled up a rolling hospital chair next to her daughter's bed and smoothed Anjali's hair away from her forehead.

"Couldn't it just be, like, a mutation?" Deena asked. "Some variety of strep they haven't seen before?"

"No, Deena. I don't think so. For one thing, PANDAS isn't exactly a disease, you know. Not the way you're talking about it. It's more of a catchall term used to describe a constellation of symptoms that can't be explained any other way. It's a little like saying that the universe is made up of puppies, ice cream, and everything else. That's true, technically, but putting it that way puts too much importance on puppies and ice cream, and it doesn't actually clarify much about the universe."

Dr. Gupta checked to see if we were following, but she saw that we weren't really.

"PANDAS doesn't appear in the *DSM,* the diagnostic manual all doctors use to identify diseases," she explained. "Some doctors aren't comfortable even using the term, as the causal relationship between a streptococcus infection and the tic behaviors hasn't been proven. It's not a disease at all, in the classical sense. It's just a hypothesis. A fancy set of words."

"That's weird," we said. "Dr. Strayed sounded so confident."

"Well, that's what happens when the school nurse consults a specialist without even checking with the board of trustees. But there's another reason I'm certain that it's not PANDAS."

"What's that?" we asked.

Dr. Gupta smiled down at her daughter and took her hand. "My Anjali has never had a strep infection."

"Never?"

"No, never."

"But if that's true . . . then what is it?" one of us asked in a small voice.

Anjali coughed. We looked at her sharply. She smiled a reassuring smile at us.

"I'm consulting with some colleagues to figure it out. But the most important thing is for you girls not to worry."

Anjali coughed again.

"Could it be something in the environment?" I asked.

"Perhaps. That's an outside possibility. We just don't know."

Anjali leaned forward and hacked.

"Are you all right, my dear? Do you need some water?" Dr. Gupta said, patting her daughter's back.

Anjali kept hacking, a deep and rattling sound, like her lungs were full of mucus. She shook her head and sat up.

"No, thanks. I'm okay."

"We need to get you up and walking around," her mother mused. Then she continued, "I will tell you girls this much. It's certainly not PANDAS. And although I don't want you to be afraid, I do want you to be careful. Take good care of yourselves and your health. Talk to your parents if you feel anything the least bit out of the ordinary."

Anjali let out a deep hacking cough, along with an agonizing groan. Her face contorted with the effort of it. We recoiled, Emma jumping off her bed and flattening herself against the wall.

"There, sweetheart," Dr. Gupta said, producing a small plastic bin and holding it under Anjali's chin. She pounded her daughter's back while the horrible hacking and gasping continued.

"Anjali?" I asked.

She shook her head, the sound flowing out of her as she strained, in pain, gasping for breath between coughs.

"Just relax," her mother soothed. "Let it come. Don't try to fight it."

"What should we do? Can we do something?" I was afraid I was panicking, but I didn't know what else to do.

"It'll be over in a moment," Dr. Gupta said.

Anjali started convulsing. Waves of spasm bent her forward and back, each forward bend marked by a cough so loud, it was almost a bark. The hacks got closer together, and Anjali's hands gripped the rails on either side of her hospital bed. She leaned forward and with a groan so loud it was almost a scream, spat something wet into the plastic bin her mother was holding.

"There, there. All over," her mother soothed, stroking her hair.

Anjali wiped her lip with a wrist and looked at us with frightened eyes. When she reached for the cup of water at her bedside, her hand was shaking.

Dr. Gupta frowned into the bin, then held it out for us to see.

"Does that look like PANDAS to you?" she asked. "You don't have to go to Oxford to see that's not what it is."

We leaned forward, equal parts baffled, worried, curious, and afraid.

Inside the dish was what looked like a ball, maybe an inch in diameter, made of fine metallic threads, with sharp points at the end of each thread. It almost looked like . . .

"Pins," breathed Emma.

We left Anjali lying on her side, pale, her arms wrapped around a large teddy bear with comforting teddy bear eyes, and with promises to come see her at home as soon as she was out. Her mother saw us to the door of her hospital room.

"Try not to worry," Dr. Gupta said. "Anjali is going to be fine. When we're ready to talk about it with more certainty, I'll let you girls know. And if your parents have any questions, they can call me."

We thanked her and walked silently down the empty corridors of Our Lady of the Inquisitor Medical and Ambulatory Care Center, our footfalls echoing on the linoleum tiles. We crossed through the sliding glass doors, their *whoosh* sounding unnaturally loud in the absence of any other noise.

We crunched across the parking lot, climbing wordlessly into Deena's car, sorting out our bulky winter coats, buckling ourselves in. Deena put the keys in the ignition, but didn't turn them.

We sat there, Deena and me in front, Emma in back. Our breath started to collect on the inside of the windows, blurring the outside world until it was just us three inside the car, alone with our thoughts.

"Y'all, what's going on?" Deena asked at length. "I mean, what the fuck is going on?"

I was startled. Deena hardly ever swears.

"I don't know," I said, gazing steadily at the moisture beading on the inside of the windshield.

Emma didn't say anything. In the rearview mirror I could see her staring out the side window, her knuckle in her mouth. The one with the wart on it.

Deena shook her head, started the car, and pulled out of the parking lot to drive first Emma, then me, back home.

As she put on her turn signal even though it was later than we thought and the street was completely empty, I felt my phone vibrating inside my pocket. A text message. I pulled my phone out and scrolled through my inbox until I found the new one.

Happy VDay! Was at bball tourney. Call me?

Spence. It was only after I read the text that I began, silently, to cry.

INTERLUDE

SALEM VILLAGE, MASSACHUSETTS
MAY 30, 1706

*A*fter that," I say, "things started to happen. They started to happen quickly."

Reverend Green is staring at me, aghast.

"Ann," he says, rubbing a hand over his face. "How could you stand by? How could you let Betty Parris blame the slave like that?"

I get to my feet and pace in the Reverend's study. I can almost hear the screams in my ears, as though they still vibrated in the rafters of the parsonage. It's a wonder we didn't tear the parsonage down after it was all over. The meetinghouse is barely standing as it is. Can the soul of a building be stained, the way the soul of a woman can be? It's ungodly to think so, but yes, I would say it could.

"But it weren't only Tittibe we blamed," I say. "The gentlemen didn't believe a slave like her, an Indian woman, would have the will to become a witch on her own. They thought there must be English witches among us, who'd led her into evil. That night Abby named Sarah Good, which were easy enough. She'd been absent from meeting for so long, none of us could remember the last time she were there. She was shabby, and she kept her daughter dirty. They stank, the Goods, they had no place to live, and went from farm to farm begging for room and board. She'd ask for alms from anyone, even those struggling themselves. Goodwives would close the shutter if they heard her coming. Reverend Parris was ready to believe she carried the Devil in her heart."

Reverend Green grows sad in his eyes. "And yet, consider how Jesus would've treated the likes of Sarah Good," he remarks. "He'd have fed her without thought, and washed her feet with his own hands. The true Christian doesn't hesitate to make himself humble."

"That might be true," I say, frowning. "But Jesus didn't have eight children in the house and an uncommon cold winter to contend with."

My confessor doesn't look too kindly on my position. But it's easy to point fingers from a position of comfort, and nothing he or Jesus says will change that.

"When Abby accused Sarah Good, everyone reacted like they'd just been waiting for someone to say it. And the other that we named was Sarah Osburn. She'd been absent from meeting, too. And she was talked about."

"And why would she be the subject of gossip in the village?"

I give him a wry smile.

"Why, for her husband," I say.

"What of him?"

"He was quite a bit younger than she. And he'd worked for her. It was said there'd been an understanding between them before they bothered to sanctify it."

"I see," Reverend Green says, a finger alongside his temple.

"My father joined some other gentlemen in swearing out a complaint," I continue, "and within a week the three witches were called before the magistrates to be questioned. All us girls were there, sitting together in the front of the meetinghouse. Everyone in the village turned up to feast on the spectacle. And throughout the hubbub, wherever Abby Williams, Betty Hubbard, Mary Warren, Betty Parris, and I walked, the villagers would step aside. I'd never felt like that before."

"Like what, Ann?"

"Like . . . someone."

I'm pressed on a hard bench between Abby and Betty Hubbard, with Betty Parris and Mary Warren and a few others who've started to suffer fits akin to ours. The noise inside the meetinghouse is terrific, a roar of voices and bodies surging against each other, and though it's the first of March, and still bitterly cold outside, the crowd is so thick that the air inside feels heavy and close. The windows in the meeting-house, none too big to begin with, are fogged with moisture from our breath, and the lamps are smoking. I can feel my hair sticking to my neck. I wonder when was the last time Abby washed, for next to me she smells like dirty hair.

On the dais near the pulpit several periwigged gentlemen perch behind a long library table, white linen neckerchiefs crisp against black buttoned coats, the most distinguished of them being Judge Hathorne lording over the very center. He's a wrinkled eminence with hawk's eyes and a long nose under shaggy brows. He's in conversation with the others while Mr. Cheever perches off to the side behind a sheaf of blank paper, clutching a quill with an air of officiousness that makes me dislike him for reasons I can't name.

Betty Hubbard's holding my hand tight, and Abby's so excited that her knees are trembling under her dress, her feet thumping the floor like a rabbit. Betty Parris sits staring straight ahead, still, like a thing amazed. She's barely talking even now. Mary Warren holds Betty Parris's hand in her lap, petting it.

A commotion approaches outside and the crowd at the back rushes the doors, flinging them open with a slam. From behind a screen of adults' limbs I see Reverend Parris and another man I don't know leading Tittibe Indian roughly by her elbow. Her hands are bound before her with rope that's biting into her skin, and her eyes are rimmed with red.

"Make way!" a man's voice booms over the chaos. "Stand back! Make way!"

At length a path parts in the mob, only enough space for Tittibe to be dragged sideways up to the bar that's been hastily erected at the front of the room. Tittibe's hands are fastened there, and she stands shaking before the assembly. Her lips tremble. Her eyes hunt over her shoulder in the crowd, and when they land on Betty Parris, they turn beseeching.

"Now then!" Judge Hathorne bellows, rapping on the table to command everyone's attention. The crowd simmers down, and Betty Hubbard's grip around my hand tightens.

Tittibe tears her eyes away from us and faces the panel of men who will decide whether the accusations against her merit a trial.

Judge Hathorne exchanges a few private words with the gentleman on his right, whose name I think is Saltonstall. Then he nods to Mr. Cheever, who picks up his pen.

"Tituba," he says, "we'll begin. You know who I am, and you know why you've been brought here today. These children suffer gravely, and are under an evil hand. We're here to root that evil out. You desire to help us with this holy task, do you not?"

Tittibe sobs, "Yes! I come to root the evil out."

"Good. Now then. What evil spirit have you familiarity with?"

She licks her lips and says, "None."

The judge leans forward, pointing a long finger at us. We quiver as all eyes in the assembly fall upon our shoulders.

"Then why do you hurt these children?"

"I do not hurt them, sir. I do not."

"Who is it hurts them, then?"

"I know not! It could be the Devil for aught I know, Mr. Hathorne. It must surely be he."

"I see. The Devil, you say."

The gentlemen on the dais all nod sagely. Mr. Cheever scribbles at a furious clip, stopping often to dip his quill anew.

"And did you ever see the Devil when he came to hurt them?"

"See him?"

"Yes. He comes to the house and hurts the children, you just said so. Has he come to you as well? Do you see the Devil when he comes to hurt the children?"

Tittibe shifts on her feet as though she would run away, but the ropes at her wrist hold her fast. "I . . ." She hesitates.

"Did the Devil come to you, Tituba?" Mr. Hathorne prompts her.

The miserable woman sees what the magistrate wishes for her to say, and accedes. "Aye. The Devil came to me and bid me serve him, as you say."

"He did. Good. Now tell us. Who have you seen with the Devil?"

Tittibe looks around herself crazily, and blurts, "Four women sometimes come with the Devil when he hurt the children."

"And who were they?"

The island woman raises her voice and cries, "Goody Osburn and Sarah Good and I don't know who the other were! Sarah Good and Sarah Osburn would have me hurt the children, but I wouldn't do it. And also there was a tall man of Boston that I did see, he come with them, too, and I did see them all together with the Devil."

"A tall man? And when did you see them, Tituba?"

"I saw them last night at Boston."

"Let me understand this properly. They said you should hurt the children? And did you?"

"No!" she cries. "There's four women and one man. They hurt the children and then lay all upon me, and they tell me if I will not hurt the children, they'll hurt me."

The assembly gasps at this revelation, and next to me Abby Williams trembles so much that I'm afraid she might fall from our pew.

"But did you not hurt them also?" Mr. Hathorne says, chastising her.

Tittibe's eyes are wild in her head. "Yes," she sputters. "Yes, but I'll hurt them no more."

"Aren't you sorry for hurting them?"

"Oh, yes. I'm very sorry."

"Then why did you agree to do it? Why obey the four women and the tall man from Boston?"

"They say I must hurt children or they'll do worse to me," Tittibe chokes through sobs.

"Have you seen a man come to you and command you to serve him?"

"Yes," Tittibe gasps, because she's been serving a man all her life. She's been serving a man since she was a girl in the Barbadoes, and she'll serve a man 'til she falls down dead.

"What service did the man require from you?"

"He said I must hurt the children, though I liked not to do it. Last night an appearance come to me and said I should kill the children, and if I wouldn't go on hurting the children, they'd do worse to me." Her voice breaks, and the crowd is growing rowdy.

The judge leans forward with keen interest. "What is this appearance you've seen?" he asks. "Describe it for us. Is it like a man?"

"Sometimes," the island woman says, "it is like a hog, and sometimes like a great dog, the appearance is. I did see it four times altogether."

"And what did it say to you?"

"The black dog said, 'Serve me,' but I said I'm afraid. He said if I did not, he would do worse to me."

"And what did you say to it after that?"

"I didn't like to hurt the children anymore, so I said, 'I will serve you no longer.' Then all of a sudden he looks like a man and threatens to hurt me. When he was like a man, he had a yellow bird he kept with him, and he told me he had more pretty things that he would give me if I would serve him."

The gentlemen all nod and confer, for this is just the sort of silver-tongued lie the Devil might tell to entice a poor woman into trading him her soul.

"And what were these pretty things the man promised you?"

"I know not—he didn't show me them."

"What else have you seen?"

She speaks quickly, without thinking, and I wonder about the realms that unfold in the woman's mind, if we ever bothered to ask. "I saw two cats, a red cat and a black cat."

"What did these cats say to you?"

"They said, 'Serve me.'"

Judge Hathorne leans back in his turkey-work chair and stares at Tittibe for a long moment while the packed crowd gossips amongst themselves.

"Cats!" Betty Hubbard whispers. "And they spoke to her! Whose spirit might they be, do you think?"

"Goody Good and Goody Osburn, no doubt," Abby spits. "Them witches vex me all the time. They come to me in the night and pinch me 'til I bleed."

The judge raps on the table and bellows, "Did you not pinch Elizabeth Hubbard this morning?"

Betty Hubbard collapses against me, moaning. "I was pinched, it was Tittibe that pinched me, I knew it!"

Panicking, Tittibe Indian protests, "The man brought her to me and made me pinch her!"

"Why did you go to Thomas Putnam's last night and hurt this child?"

He's pointing at Betty Hubbard, who's still bunking with me at our house. And it's true, last night she woke up in a fit of screaming. I feel it. We've begun to believe. We've been performing so well, we're fooling ourselves. We've been pulled into our own play.

"They pull and haul me and make me go!"

"And what would he have you do? Kill her with a knife?"

My father is standing with Reverend Parris off to one side, watching the proceedings, and interrupts. "When the child saw the apparitions and was tormented by them last night, she did complain of a knife. She cried that they would have her cut her head off with a knife."

It's true, Betty's nightmare had her screaming she was afraid her head would be cut off. She'd been listening to some of Mercy's stories from her Eastward days. I don't like to listen to those stories. They trouble my sleep, too.

"How did you go to the Putnams' house so late at night? Did you ride?"

Eager to embellish her story, Tittibe cries, "We ride upon sticks and are there presently."

The entire assembly buzzes with interest, imagining Tittibe's invisible spirit streaking through the night sky with a broomstick between her thighs, and Goody Good and Goody Osburn close behind her, their skirts flapping in the wind.

Judge Hathorne is as entranced by this idea as any of us. "Do you go through the trees, or over them?"

"Neither. We see nothing but are there presently."

"Why did you not tell your master, Reverend Parris, when this man came to you bidding you do these horrible things?"

Tittibe's eyes slide to Samuel Parris, who fixes her with a murderous glare. She trembles where she stands, and says, "I was afraid. They said they'd cut off my head if I told him."

"I see," the magistrate says, stroking his chin in thought as he stares down at the shaken woman. "Tell us more, Tituba. What attendants hath Sarah Good when she is with the Devil?"

Tittibe's gaze floats up to the ceiling of the meetinghouse, as though hoping to find the answer scrawled there. When she brings her eyes back to rest on the judge, she says, her voice clear and true, "A yellow bird. And she would have given me one."

I think how pleasant it would be for a tame goldfinch to sit on my shoulder or my lap, and accept tidbits from my fingers. Tittibe must dream of such delicate things, too, on those rare days when she's idle enough to dream. The Devil promises her fine things, and I wish she would tell us more about them.

"A yellow bird, you say? And what meat did she give it?"

"Why, it did suck her between her fingers."

"Did it!" He glances with great meaning at one of the other gentlemen, who makes a note down to himself. "And what hath Sarah Osburn for a familiar spirit?"

"When I saw her yesterday, she had a horrible thing with a head like a woman with two legs and wings."

Abby starts up from her seat next to me and cries, "Yes! I did see that same creature yesterday as I walked outside the parsonage, and as I watched, it changed to the shape of Goody Osburn!"

"Very interesting!" the judge says as Mr. Cheever scribbles on his sheets of paper. "Tituba, did you not see Sarah Good also upon Elizabeth Hubbard last Saturday?"

Next to me on the bench Betty Hubbard nods fiercely.

"Yes," Betty adds, though no one's addressed her. "Sarah Good fell on me, and said she would cut off my head if I told."

Tittibe watches Betty Hubbard out of the corner of her eye and readily agrees. "Yes, I did see Sarah Good set a wolf upon Betty Hubbard to afflict her."

"Yes!" I cry, seized with the drama of it. "Betty did complain of a wolf, she did!"

Everyone beams at me, the periwigged gentlemen and the island woman and my friend Betty Hubbard and my father, the villagers all praising how brave I am for speaking the truth. I glow under their praise, so much that I forget what I've done. I've given them all what they want. I feel pleased. Worthy.

"Tituba," the judge says kindly. "What clothes does the man go about in? How does he look?"

Tittibe stares hard at Reverend Parris. Slowly, she says, "He goes in black clothes. He's a tall man with white hair, I think."

Reverend Parris's hair has been the color of dirty snow for as long as I've ever known him, and he stands over six feet tall. In the pew next to me, Betty Parris starts to bawl.

"Very good. And how doth the woman go? What sorts of clothes does she wear?"

Still gazing on her master, Tittibe says, "The woman, she go in a white hood, and the other in a black hood with a topknot."

She's described Mrs. Parris's usual mode of dress, though many of the women in the village wear the old-style black hood with a topknot. Betty Parris's bawling rises in timbre, and soon enough Abby Williams is shaking in her seat, screeching at the top of her lungs and coughing with great commotion. Betty Hubbard's eyes roll to the back of her skull, and she slumps over, senseless. I'm beginning to panic, and I want to get up and run away and hide in the barn behind our house, but everyone is there and everyone is watching me, and my father is there and I have to stay strong and do what they want me to, and so I stay where I am, making myself small on the pew, and soon enough the tears are springing from my eyes, too.

Judge Hathorne says, "Do you see who it is that torments these children now?"

Tittibe turns and looks over her shoulder. Her dark eye roams over us, taking in our wailing and carrying on. "Yes," she says with resolve. "I see. It is Sarah Good. She hurts them in her own shape."

Abby stands on the pew and turns to look over her shoulder at nothing and screams, "Leave us! Leave us be, Goody Good! We want none of you! Stop sending your shape to torment us!"

"And so she goes," Tittibe says quietly, her eye tracking an invisible thing along the aisle where she herself was dragged, and out the door.

Our screams intensify, Mary Warren's eyes lifting to heaven, Betty Hubbard burying her head in my lap and weeping into my apron. Abby coughs and coughs and presents her open hands full of pins, beaming with triumph, a droplet of blood on her lip. I'm helpless to know what I must do, so I do nothing.

"But they're still vexed, Tituba. Tell us. Who is it that hurts them now?"

The slave leans her head back on her shoulders and closes her eyes.

"I am blind now," she says quietly. "I cannot see. I cannot see what's real."

Part 4

MARCH

MATRONALIA

That Witches may and doe worke wonders,
is euidently proued; howbeit
not by an omnipotent power,
(as they gainsefayer hath vnlearnedly
and improperly termed it)
but by the affiftance of Satan there Prince,
who is a powerfull Spirit,
but yet a Creature, as well as they.

WILLIAM PERKINS
A DISCOURSE OF THE DAMNED ART OF WITCHCRAFT
THE EPISTLE DEDICATORIE, 1603

CHAPTER 19

A nn Putnam Junior. That was her name," I said, tossing a book onto the desk with a thud.

Ms. Slater put down her red pen and glanced up at me.

"Oh?" she said.

"Yes. Look. Arthur Miller called her Ruth. But her name was actually Ann, like her mother."

I pushed the book across Ms. Slater's desk and pointed at a long excerpt of trial testimony, with this one little girl right in the middle of it, talking about yellow birds and all kinds of craziness. Ms. Slater applied her reading glasses to her nose and peered at the transcript.

"Right you are," Ms. Slater said. "So? Maybe he just didn't want people to confuse her with her mother."

"Oh, come on," I said. "Everyone in New England uses the same names over and over again. It's not that complicated. Look at my brother and my dad."

The substitute teacher smirked at me.

"All right. And?"

"And I've figured out he changed a bunch of other stuff, too."

I shuffled through my notes. Ms. Slater leaned back in her desk chair and arched one of her wicked eyebrows at me.

"For instance," I said, pointing my pen at a note. "In the play Ruth Putnam is an only child, because all the other Putnam kids died, and that's why Ann, her mother, is so paranoid and sad and wants to accuse other women of being witches. But the real Ann Putnam—the kid one—had, like, seven brothers and sisters."

"It's a play," Ms. Slater said, shrugging. "Maybe he just didn't want the stage to get crowded. You have any idea how expensive it is, using that many Equity actors?"

She was teasing me, but I didn't care. I wrinkled my nose at her.

"The other thing is, in the play he makes it sound like Ruth—Ann Junior—and Abigail Williams and them start the accusations because Reverend Parris catches them casting spells in the woods, and they don't want to get in trouble. I can't find a mention of that anywhere."

"That's because it didn't happen."

I glanced up at her, confused.

"It didn't?"

"No, of course not." Ms. Slater waved her pen dismissively. "The whole *they were casting spells in the woods* thing comes from one little footnote by one of the girls recollecting it, like, twenty years after the fact. It's totally unsubstantiated. Abigail Williams wasn't having an affair with John Procter, either, for the record. She wasn't seventeen, and he wasn't forty. She was eleven, and he was in his sixties. It wasn't about sex. And it wasn't about magic."

I pressed my fingertips to my forehead. Underneath one of Deena's songs that had burrowed into my mind, an ache was there, I could tell. It wasn't all the way happening yet, but it was coming.

"So what was it about?" I asked, dropping my hands to my desk and staring helplessly at the ceiling.

Ms. Slater sat back and slid the end of her pen into her mouth.

She gave it a meditative chew while she considered me. Then she carefully put the pen down on the desk and pressed her fingertips together in front of her lips.

"What else have you learned so far, about Ann Putnam?" she asked me.

"Well," I said, shuffling through my notes again. "In the play Ruth is kind of marginal. But it looks like in the real thing, she was right in the middle of everything. She was actually kind of a big deal."

"How so?" Ms. Slater watched me.

"Um"—I hunted for the note I was looking for—"it looks like she was"—I flipped to another page—"responsible for accusing everyone who was actually hanged. Like, she wound up accusing even more people than Abigail Williams. And her father, Thomas, swore out most of the complaints. That's crazy! Why would Arthur Miller write her out?"

Ms. Slater looked at me for a long minute. Then she shrugged. "Why indeed?"

I slumped back in my chair and stared at the ceiling, thinking.

"It wasn't about magic. And it wasn't about sex," I repeated.

"No."

I coiled one of my corkscrew curls around a finger, pulled it out straight in front of me, and let it go with a *spoing*.

"I'm beginning to see why you didn't want us to read this play in history class," I said.

She half smiled and said, "Is that a fact?"

"So, what was it really about, then? What was the deal with this Ann Putnam girl, who nobody talks about? Why wasn't Winona Ryder playing Ann Putnam instead of Abigail Williams? And how old was she when she made that movie, anyway, like thirty?"

Ms. Slater muffled a snort of laughter behind a professional exterior. The snort morphed into a cough, and she reached for a sip from her coffee mug. After a swallow of coffee she cleared her throat.

"Sometimes, Colleen," she said, gazing out the window at the gray Danvers sky, "it can be hard to tell, in history. There's the dominant narrative. And there are parts of the story that are overlooked. Maybe because they don't fit with what the people in charge have to say. Arthur Miller isn't interested in Ann Putnam Junior. He's interested in sex and conspiracy and evils hidden within good people. He's basically interested, like a lot of men, in himself. The question is, what are *you* interested in?"

I stared at her, waiting.

She turned her eyes to me and seemed on the point of saying something. Then she stopped herself and tried again.

"It can be worthwhile, for a researcher," she said, placing each word before me with care, "to look beyond the dominant narrative. Sometimes, the people in charge"—she stared at me, hard—"all come to one explanation, and once that happens, they will do whatever they can to cling to it. They've staked their reputations on it being right. You know what I mean? But an attentive researcher—like you— might be able to see something that all the experts can't see. She might be able to rewrite the narrative. If she asks the right questions."

"You mean, maybe Ann Putnam's important, but nobody talks about her because she messes up what the experts think really happened?"

"Maybe," Ms. Slater said. "Yes. That's partly what I mean. Also, maybe the experts have their own agenda. Maybe what's true for one group of people isn't necessarily true if looked at from another group's point of view."

"So . . ." I paused, wanting her to explain more. "You think I should keep going on this for my extra-credit paper?"

"Definitely," Ms. Slater said. She walked her pen between her fingers. "I think you could uncover a lot if you pursue this avenue of inquiry."

"Okay," I said. "Thanks." Something was eating away at the back of my brain. Girls. Dominant narratives. Sex. Death. Arthur Miller.

Ann Putnam sitting invisible right in the middle of history. I began to gather my books and notes together and load them into my backpack. Ms. Slater watched me do so.

"See you tomorrow," I said, making my way to the door.

"Yep," she said, lowering her eyes to the papers, pen in hand.

When I reached the door of her classroom, I paused, my hand on the doorknob.

"Ms. Slater?"

"Mmm?"

"Um. This is a weird question, but have you, like, been sending me text messages the last couple of weeks?"

She laid her pen down. Her face didn't change.

"What do you mean?"

"Nothing. Not really. I mean, they're not weird text messages or anything. Just encouraging me to read the play."

"I think sending anonymous text messages would be kind of inappropriate. Don't you think we've had enough American history teachers leave for inappropriate behavior this semester?"

We stared at each other. Mr. Mitchell. *Tad.* She knew about him and Emma. The entire school would have been instantly alive with that rumor if he hadn't disappeared the same day that Clara Rutherford started to twitch. One day he was there, and the next he was gone, and we were too busy thinking about ourselves to care why.

"Yes," I said. "I guess one's just about enough."

She nodded slowly.

"One is too many. But I'll say one thing," Ms. Slater said.

"What's that?"

"Whoever sent you those text messages? They'd be pretty psyched about your research, don't you think? They'd really want you to write your own narrative."

A broad smile broke across my face, and it felt like the first time I'd smiled in days.

"You think so?"

"Oh, definitely."

She returned the smile briefly, and then took up her pen as if she hadn't just told me the truth without saying a word.

"Thanks, Ms. Slater."

"Go on, scram. I've got lives to ruin."

I grinned and slipped out the classroom door.

The Gothic wood and flagstone floor of the entire upper school hallway of St. Joan's was swathed in plastic sheeting, and had been for two weeks. The sheeting had an odd smell to it, like wet Band-Aids, and our shoes squeaked over it as we shuffled from classroom to classroom. I say *we*, but attendance was down to about a third of our usual numbers. We remaining students were like bacteria in a petri dish, wriggling under bright lights, in an environment we couldn't possibly understand.

Since the upper school dean had been fired, we hadn't had a single chapel or assembly. Official-looking e-mail blasts were issued from the board of trustees, usually authored by Laurel Hocking and Dr. Strayed, and presented with such a chipper tone that we couldn't help but disbelieve them immediately. Father Molloy occasionally gave us terse updates in advisory, but even he didn't seem sure of his information. One day, the plastic sheeting appeared. No one knew where it had come from. No one bothered to explain why it was there.

I came upon Deena standing at her open locker, her forehead pressed to the shelf inside.

"Hey," I said. "What's up?"

When she looked up, her eyes were yellow with fatigue, and she held out a paper for me to read.

"Did you get one of these?" she asked.

I took the paper from her and skimmed it. It was from the Massachusetts Department of Public Health. Something about a schoolwide assembly on Friday. There was no signature.

"Department of Health," I said.

"It was on my locker," Deena said. "Colleen, this is getting crazy. I'm thinking of staying home tomorrow."

I put my hand on her shoulder and said, "I know. But if the Health Department is involved, don't you think that means they're finally getting on top of it?"

"On top of it?" she echoed, slamming her locker shut. "It should never have gotten this out of hand. Every time they tell us something new, it looks like they're lying. I don't know which is worse—that they know what's really going on but don't want to tell us, or that they have no freaking clue at all."

I wasn't used to seeing Deena so freaked out. Usually she was unflappable.

"Deena," I said, looking into her eyes so she would know I was serious. "We're okay. Everyone's going to be okay. It'll all blow over soon. I promise."

But Deena wasn't buying it. "I'm sorry, Colleen, but that's a load, and you know it. Look around." She gestured to the plastic sheeting, which had turned the upper school hallway into a tunnel from outer space. "Does this look like things are getting better to you?"

I didn't know what to say, because the truth was, it looked worse. Much, much worse.

Deena stared at me, waiting for me to say something. Then she turned on her heel and stalked off.

I stood alone in the upper school hallway, my books clutched to my chest. There were thirty minutes to go before last period. I leaned my head on Deena's locker and stared down the vacant expanse of the upper school hall for what seemed like forever. The hall telescoped in a sickening way. My headache was getting worse. All I wanted was to go home and lie on the couch and hear Mikey arguing with Wheez about whose turn it was to hold the remote. All I wanted was not to have to deal with this anymore.

"Colleen?"

"Huh?"

Father Molloy had a hand resting on my shoulder, and was looking down at me with concern.

"Are you feeling all right?"

I blinked and shook myself alert. "I'm sorry, what did you say?"

"Are you okay? Do you need to go see Nurse Hocking?"

"No, no. I'm fine. Thanks."

Father Molloy didn't believe me.

"Why don't you go into the student center and take a break."

"I've got AP French now."

"That's all right. I'll have a word with Mme. Fletcher."

"But . . . Fabiana . . ." I closed my eyes. The words felt thick in my mouth.

"One French class won't make any difference. Not with two-thirds of the school missing. Please. Go sit down. Cut yourself some slack."

I pried my eyelids open again and found the priest looking down at me kindly. He nodded, encouraging, and squeezed my shoulder.

"Go on. It's okay."

"Okay," I said.

I started to move off down the hallway to the student center, and Father Molloy called, "Tell Anjali she's in my prayers."

I looked over my shoulder at him. He gave me a resigned smile and turned away.

The student center at St. Joan's was usually empty, and that day was no exception. I didn't know why, but nobody ever hung out in there. Back when the school was a convent, the room was used as a kind of community room. But because the nuns liked to have pretty decorations only when they were praying, the room was a bare plaster cell, with leaded lozenge-shaped windows that never got any light. One wooden crucifix stood bolted to the wall in the center, the kind with a grotesque plaster Jesus nailed to it, his eyes rolling back in his head and blood trickling down his face. A faux-old tapestry depicting Joan of Arc leading her forces into battle in pigtails (that's how we could tell it was a 1960s pretend-old tapestry) hung on one wall, behind a couple of stained and sagging sofas. Institutional wood coffee tables and some tall brass lamps, and that's it. The room smelled damp and sad. They used to let students smoke in here as late as the 1990s if we had a note from our parents, and sometimes on rainy days it still smelled smoky and stale, haunted by the ghosts of St. Joan's girls past.

I collapsed on one of the couches with a long sigh, sliding down until my head was propped on the back of the seat, my chin on my chest. I pulled out my phone.

Wish u were in town today ☹

I tapped.

I stared at the screen, waiting. Spence was usually wicked fast. A good trait to have in a guy. He didn't make me wait. When he did, it was because he had a reason. He wasn't just messing with my head.

My missive was received. The phone vibrated with a text returned.

Awwwww. Will be soon. Fri. You ok?

A delicious zing of electricity rocketed around in my chest, and I smiled.

I'm ok. Just tired. Dept. Public Health is coming.

Another minute passed, and then his answer.

Weird . . . don't freak out tho, it could be nothing.

The zing came again, but this time it felt more tender. For a second I was worried I might cry. But then it passed.

Yeah you're prob right. Can't wait to see you Friday

I heard the door open softly behind me and lifted my chin to look up over the couch to see who'd come in. It was Jennifer Crawford, her back to me, rummaging in her bag. She hadn't noticed that I was there. She pulled out a pack of cigarettes, shook one out, and lit it.

She took a long drag and then exhaled the smoke up to the ceiling with a relieved sigh.

"No wonder it still smells smoky in here," I said, sliding my phone back into my bag, and she jumped.

"Oh my God," she said, laughing uncomfortably. "You scared the crap out of me."

"Sorry," I said, smiling. I didn't get up.

Jennifer Crawford wandered over and flopped onto the couch across from mine.

"You want?" she asked, offering me the pack.

I hesitated. I didn't smoke.

"Screw it," I said, taking one.

She passed me the lighter and watched, smiling, while I tried and failed to light one. When I gave up, swearing under my breath, she laughed and said, "It's okay. You don't want to start."

"Probably not," I agreed, rolling my head on the back of the couch.

"You get the note from the Department of Public Health?"

"I saw it." I hadn't actually been back to my locker yet.

"Turns out they don't think it's PANDAS after all," Jennifer Crawford said.

"How do you know?"

She shrugged. "I heard."

"Yeah," I said. "Anjali's mom already told me."

"She's, like, super-important at Mass General, right?"

"Yeah."

"She say what it really is?"

I shook my head slowly from side to side. "She's trying to figure it out. She just told us not to worry."

"Not to worry," Jennifer Crawford said around another plume of smoke. "They always say that, don't they."

"They do," I agreed. "They lie and they lie, and they tell us not to worry."

"Well," Jennifer Crawford said, grinding out the nub of her cigarette on the sole of her shoe and then tucking it into her sock, "guess we'll find out on Wednesday."

"I thought the assembly was Friday."

"It is." She got up, sliding her hands into the kangaroo pockets of the hoodie she was wearing over her uniform. The dress code had gotten, shall we say, a little lax over the past few weeks. I had even seen one of the sophomores wearing pajama pants under her plaid skirt. "But Clara Rutherford and them are going on *Good Day, USA* on Wednesday."

"Shut up. It's really happening?" That was enough to get me to sit up.

"Mmm-hmm. They're meeting the nation. I heard she and her mom left today to go down to New York. They're putting them up in a sweet hotel. Driver and everything."

"Really?"

"Mmm-hmm. Leigh Carruthers, too."

"They're all going?"

"That's what I heard. And I heard that what they've got to say will blow your mind."

CHAPTER 20

I feel like we should make popcorn," Dad said as we arrayed ourselves around the TV.

Wheez was up first and had staked a claim on the good recliner, and no amount of wheedling from me, or threatening from Michael, would get her to budge.

"Oh, Mike, shut up," Mom said as she shuffled in from the kitchen, a mug of cold coffee clutched in her hand.

My brother and I exchanged a look. It wasn't often that we saw our parents snipe at each other.

"Shut up, the lady commands," my father said to no one in particular, and he turned up the television.

I settled on the floor in front of the recliner, and Wheez dangled her feet over my shoulders so that she could thread her toes through my curls.

"Quit it, Wheez," I said, swatting her feet away.

"Yeesh," Wheez said, giving me a kick in the back of the head to register her displeasure.

"Louisa," my mother warned.

It was a cranky morning in the Rowley house.

The familiar music began. *Good Day, USA* cycled through the introductions that we have all memorized in the thirty years it's been on the air.

"Nigel Roberts, with weather! And America's most trusted news-woman, Bebe Appleton, bringing you the news you need to get your day going. It's a *Good Day, USA*!"

"I've never understood how people can watch TV in the morning like this," my mother muttered into her coffee mug. "That much chip-perness first thing just makes me want to punch someone in the face."

My father caught my eye, rolled his eyes, and pantomimed inch-ing away from my mother on the couch.

"Good day, USA! We're all so pleased you could join us today. This morning, in our first hour, we're going to spend some time with some very special teenage girls. In January, a Mystery Illness descended on the sleepy suburban town of Danvers, Massachusetts—an illness that no one was quite able to explain. Well, we think we have the answer that's going to help these girls get better, and we can't wait to share it with them. Then in our second hour, the Houston Youth Symphony will be stopping by to celebrate the coming of spring with some Vivaldi. You love the Houston Youth Symphony, don't you, Nigel?"

"She just doesn't age," my mother marveled. "It's like they dipped her face in wax and replace it with a new one every couple of years."

My father snorted.

"Ha ha ha! I sure do, Bebe," the long-suffering weatherman answered, laughing.

"So do I. We'll also pay a visit to Chef Al's kitchen to learn how to make a fresh turnip risotto, and discover the best upstate New York wines to pair with watercress salad. All that and more, 'cause it's a good day, USA! Join us, won't you?"

Everyone in the audience chanted along when Bebe said, "Good day, USA."

"How do they know when she's going to say it?" I asked the room at large.

"There's probably a teleprompter that tells them," Michael mused.

"I can't believe they're putting Clara and them on *Good Day, USA*," I said for probably the twentieth time that morning.

"I can't believe Charlaine agreed to let Clara go on," my mother grumbled. "I'd never subject any of you kids to that kind of attention. No way."

"They're probably getting paid," Michael said. "Cream, yo! Cash rules everything around me!" My brother had started getting into rap lately.

We all looked at him in surprise.

"Well, sure," he said. "They do that. Pay for interviews and stuff. She's probably making bank." He paused. "Nobody likes Wu-Tang?"

"I like nothing and no one at this hour," said my mother.

"Well, if they're making *bank*," my father joked, and my mother swatted him on the thigh.

"And welcome back," Bebe said, smiling. She was sitting in a plush polyester armchair. It looked just like the armchair TJ Wadsworth sat in on *This Is Danvers*. I wondered if there was, like, an armchair supply store that only provided furniture to morning talk shows.

"Our guests this first hour are the brave girls from the exclusive private school St. Joan's Academy in beautiful Danvers, Massachusetts. They're here with their parents and the school nurse who first identified this terrible, mysterious disease. We're going to talk to them about their experiences, and then we have a special guest who we think is going to shed some surprising light on the infamous Danvers Mystery Illness of 2012. Girls, welcome."

The shot widened to encompass a very long, very plush couch full of my classmates. Clara was sitting nearest Bebe Appleton—of course—flanked by her mother. Then Leigh Carruthers, which was weird, because it's not like Leigh was part of their core clique. Her mom, Kathy, was next to her, looking ready to disco. Then there was the Other Jennifer, still wearing her Elizabeth Taylor turban, and a nondescript woman who must've been her mom. Then Elizabeth's reedy twinsetted mother, with Elizabeth parked on the end in a wheelchair.

Clara looked amazing. She was the perfect picture of a well-groomed and well-behaved girl. That always was the weirdest part about Clara—she embodied her Claraness in an utterly unironic way. Not unaware, though. She knew what she was doing. But knowing what she was doing was part of the ineffable being of Clara.

That was why when Bebe Appleton said, "Girls, welcome," it was Clara who responded, "Thank you, Bebe. We're all so happy to be here," and she said it like it was the most normal thing in the world and they were just two people talking about whatever, instead of a high school girl and the most famous morning show host in the country having a conversation in front of a huge picture window that faced Times Square in New York City and was being beamed live to millions of people all over the world.

"How does she do that?" I whispered. My palms were sweaty just thinking about having to go on TV like that.

"That's a good question, Collie," my mother said. She brought a nail to her mouth and gave it a tentative chew. "Also, why can't she control it that well at school?"

"What?" I said. My mom thought I meant how was Clara able to speak so clearly. Not how could she go on TV without freaking out.

"Maybe they drugged her," Michael wondered.

It was true. They all seemed pretty normal-acting, except for Jennifer's turban.

"So, Clara," Bebe was saying, her hands folded on her knee in that concerned talk show host posture. "Why don't you tell us how it started."

"It was a few weeks ago," Kathy Carruthers trampled over Clara before she could get a word out. "A Wednesday. We think the school's just been terribly irresponsible."

"We'll come to that in a moment," said Bebe, not about to let a rube like Kathy Carruthers take over her big interview. "I'd like to hear from Clara first. Clara, you were the first of the girls to experience something unusual, am I right? Would you like to tell our viewers a little about your experience?"

Clara fluttered her eyelashes in a fetching way and nodded.

"It was a Wednesday, like Mrs. Carruthers said. I had just gotten to school and was talking with my friends Jennifer and Elizabeth." She gestured to them, and they both lifted their chins for ease of identification. Of course, so did Leigh Carruthers, so it didn't make much of a difference.

"When did you first realize something was wrong?" Bebe asked.

"I started feeling funny right after we got to advisory," Clara said.

"Advisory, that's another word for homeroom. I see. Feeling funny how, exactly?"

"It was the strangest feeling," Clara said. "As soon as I walked into the room, I almost felt like there was some other thing inside me. Almost like a force field. Like it came into me when I entered the classroom and started moving around inside me, taking me over. It started to change the shape of my face."

"What!" my mother exclaimed, and Michael started to laugh but thought better of it.

Bebe Appleton was clearly not expecting this genteel girl in her ribboned ponytail to start insinuating that she was possessed when she showed up at her respectable Catholic day school. I was kind of impressed, actually, that this reporter who had interviewed philandering presidents and embezzling CEOs would be thrown for a loop by Clara Rutherford from Beverly, Massachusetts.

"That's . . ." Bebe Appleton was groping for a follow-up question that wouldn't send this entire interview into the X-Files. "That sounds like a really worrisome thing to have happen."

"It was," Clara said with gravity. "The force field inside me pulled my mouth to the side, and then I started to shake, and I fell out of my chair and onto the floor. Everyone thought I was having a seizure."

"My goodness. How terrifying. And your friends also started experiencing the strange illness shortly afterward?"

"Good transition," I said aloud. "Otherwise Clara sounds like crazytown."

"Maybe Clara *is* crazytown," my father remarked.

But I wasn't so sure.

"Have you noticed she hasn't had any trouble talking so far?" I asked.

"Yes," my mother said. "I have."

"Yes," the Other Jennifer was saying. "I was in bio lab the next period, and all of a sudden my hair all fell out."

"It fell out, all at once?" Bebe sounded incredulous. "Just like that? *Foomp?*"

"Yes," the Other Jennifer said. "It fell out all at once, and then I started shaking and fell down, too. They took me away in an ambulance. It was really scary."

"It sounds terrible," Bebe agreed. "And what about you girls?" she asked Leigh and Elizabeth.

"I was at field hockey practice after school," Elizabeth said from her wheelchair. "I was running down the field doing a wind sprint when it suddenly felt like my legs had turned to water. Like some force field had come into my body—like Clara said—and pulled the bones right out of my legs. I fell down and started shaking, and I couldn't get up."

Leigh looked like she was about to chime in, but Bebe talked over her. "How devastating. Because your mother tells us that you're quite the athlete, Elizabeth, isn't that right?"

"I was," Elizabeth said, looking down at her lap.

"Now, the school offered several different explanations, didn't they. Nurse Hocking, why don't we hear from you?"

The school nurse wasn't looking quite as sleek as she had the last time I'd seen her, a couple of days before. Her cheeks looked hollowed out, like she hadn't been getting much sleep.

She cleared her throat and said, "Yes, well, of course the challenge that the school faced first and foremost was ensuring the safety of all our girls."

"Well, you didn't do a very good job of that, from what I can see. How many students are said to be suffering from the Mystery Illness as of right now?"

"Well, you know, I couldn't really say."

"Our sources tell us it's more than thirty," Bebe said, and my mother gasped along with the studio audience.

"I can neither confirm nor deny that," said Nurse Hocking, who was looking very much like she didn't want to be there.

"Isn't it true that the students were first told that this was a rare response to the third shot in the series of vaccinations given to prevent human papillomavirus?"

"That was an early hypothesis, yes. We looked into it. Reactions to that vaccine have been reported in some communities."

"Some communities," Bebe repeated. "Just not Danvers, isn't that correct?"

All the mothers aligned on the couch on *Good Day, USA* were watching Nurse Hocking with accusing eyes.

"That's correct," Nurse Hocking said in a strangled-sounding voice.

"So eventually you called in a so-called expert epidemiologist to help you go hunting through your students' private medical files because you thought the illness might be caused by . . . what?"

"PANDAS," Nurse Hocking said.

"That's a lie and you know it!" cried Kathy Carruthers, but Clara Rutherford's mom placed a hand on her arm and quieted her down.

"And what is PANDAS?"

"It stands for Pediatric Autoimmune Neuropsychiatric Disorders Associated with Streptococcal infections. We had a very strong suspicion that—"

"That proved to be wrong, didn't it?"

Bebe Appleton! Going for the jugular.

"This is better than watching the Pats game," my father remarked.

"Definitely better offense," Mom agreed.

"Well, I think that's overstating it somewhat. The thing with PANDAS is—"

"Isn't it true that this so-called PANDAS isn't even a real diagnosis?"

"I knew it!" Kathy Carruthers spat. After that, her lips kept moving, but her microphone had been cut.

"No, well, technically, yes. In a way, but—"

"And isn't it true that you and your ostensible expert leapt to this conclusion without sufficient evidence, even though there are no examples anywhere of PANDAS causing a girl's hair to fall out, like poor Jennifer's did?"

"But—"

Nurse Hocking gripped the arms of her chair and looked like she was on the point of sprinting off the stage to go hide. I didn't blame her. I mean, I thought she was nice. She really had been trying to help. And it's not like she was the only one who was totally wrong.

"Tell me, Nurse Hocking. At what point during the spread of the Mystery Illness were you approached to write a book about your experiences?"

"What?" my mother and father gasped, and Michael said, "Ooh, snap."

"A book? Laurel Hocking's writing a book?" my father exclaimed.

"The hell she is," said my mother. "Look at Kathy Carruthers. I think her head's about to explode."

"I don't see how that's any of your—" the nurse sputtered.

"Weren't you approached right after it became clear that the illness couldn't possibly have been caused by the HPV vaccine?"

"I can't really—"

"And isn't it true that you were given to understand that there'd be a lot more money coming your way if many more girls fell sick before the solution was found?"

"That's preposterous!"

"We at *Good Day, USA* think it isn't," Bebe Appleton remarked, having been passed a sheaf of papers by someone standing off camera.

"This is crazy," I breathed.

"In fact"—America's most trusted newswoman smiled a shark-like smile at Laurel Hocking—"weren't you told in this e-mail dated February 21, 2012, that if more than twenty girls fell sick before you were able to solve the mystery, your advance for a tell-all book would increase . . . by a factor of ten?"

"This is ridiculous!" Laurel Hocking shouted as she fumbled for the microphone pinned to her lapel. She was about to go stalking off, probably into an eternity of obscurity.

"That's harsh," Michael said. "She just let people keep getting sick? To, like, get more publicity?"

"That's insane," I said, crossing my arms. "I can't believe she'd do that. That can't be right."

"Fortunately," Bebe Appleton said, beaming, "our next guest is here to tell us once and for all what's really happening to the girls at St. Joan's, when we come back, right after this. Stay with us."

Chipper, jazzy morning show transitional music while everyone on the couch pretended to talk to each other.

"Well. Guess you won't be seeing her at your assembly Friday," my mother said. "Mike?" She waved her coffee mug at my father, who obediently took it into the kitchen.

"But that's crazy!" I exclaimed again. "I just can't believe she'd do that. Let people get sick on purpose? It doesn't make any sense."

"Well, Collie," my mother sighed, "when you're older, you'll realize that even nice people can sometimes do bad things."

I scowled at my mother. What, did she think I didn't know people could really suck when I least expected it?

"Cream!" Dad cried, handing my mother more coffee and twerking his way back to the couch. "Cash rules my life, too, Mikey."

"Welcome back," interrupted the television. "If you're just joining us, we're here talking to the brave girls from St. Joan's Academy in Danvers, Massachusetts, who for the past eight weeks have been suffering from a bizarre Mystery Illness. An investigation by this station has just revealed that the school nurse, Laurel Hocking, has allegedly stood in the way of getting the students the help that they needed in order to put herself at the center of the publicity. So what's really hurting these girls? And what can be done about it? Joining us now—you know her from her best-selling book *Mouthful of Poison: My Story* and the hit movie of the same title—is environmental activist Bethany Witherspoon. Bethany, welcome."

The studio audience went berserk. Well, of course they would, I mean, it's Bethany Witherspoon. Everybody's heard of Bethany Witherspoon. Especially after that movie came out, the one where she took on some huge hydrofracking company with a toddler on her hip and a bad dye job and emerged triumphant.

"I don't believe this," my mother said, shaking her head.

"Wow. She's held up," my father said.

"I can't believe Clara's just sitting there talking to Bethany Witherspoon. Bethany Witherspoon and Bebe Appleton, together, at the same time!" I hugged my knees to my chest, half envious and half appalled.

"Yeah, well," my mother said. "Wait and see what they say before you get all impressed."

"Thank you, Bebe. It's great seeing you again. You look so tan!" Bethany and Bebe were obviously old friends.

Bebe laughed, shaking her hair. "Well, thanks! Now, Bethany. You have a theory about what's really going on in Danvers, isn't that right?"

"That's right. And I'll tell you first and foremost that no school nurse or epidemiologist would have gotten this. No strep infection I ever heard of caused a girl's hair to just fall out, am I right?"

She patted the Other Jennifer on a knee and everyone nodded.

Laurel Hocking, meanwhile, had either left or been ejected from *Good Day, USA*.

"Now I've got a question for you all. Did you know when you enrolled at that fancy private school that it was basically right on top of a Superfund site?"

The mothers on the couch all looked dumbfounded.

"A Superfund site!" Bebe Appleton exclaimed, because none of the mothers seemed able to respond appropriately.

"That's right, Bebe. Way back in 1969 a paint factory in Danvers had a tremendous explosion, causing what we think is tricoethylene to seep into the groundwater for the past forty-plus years. And it's just been lying there this whole time. They cordoned off the site and did some preliminary cleanup back in the eighties, but it is still officially on the list as eligible for federal funding, and as far as we can tell, no one's made any move to clean it up for good."

"So you're basically saying there's a lake of . . . what? Chemicals? And it's under the school."

"Toxic chemicals. Yes. A number of the girls reported first falling sick after having contact with the athletic fields, and it's also possible that exposure is cumulative, building up over time. That's our theory. And it would explain why the numbers of sick girls just keep going up. It's a classic example of something we call 'sick building syndrome.' I'll be going to Danvers with my team of scientists to check things out at the end of this week. But tricoethylene exposure through groundwater, or concentrations in an HVAC system, or even dirt, like you have on a playing field, can have a number of very serious side effects, especially for growing girls. Taken in isolation, it's easy to confuse those side effects with something like a vaccine reaction or an autoimmune disease, when what we're really dealing with is a failure of corporate ethics vis-à-vis the environment, and an unwillingness by the government to step up and take responsibility for their actions."

"Do you think the school would've been able to figure this out on their own?" Bebe asked, frowning with concern.

"Well, you know, probably not. Though we were contacted by a group of concerned parents—"

"Kathy Carruthers," I said. I turned to my mother. "At the meeting, remember? She said they were going to take steps."

"I guess that's what they did," my mother agreed.

"—who told us they'd noticed a strange glow coming from the athletic fields at certain times of night. They felt that the school wasn't asking enough questions, and frankly, we agreed with them."

"What glow?" I cried. "There's no glow on the athletic field. Are they hallucinating?"

"And it's a good thing you did. What do you say, girls? Are you ready for Bethany Witherspoon to come to Danvers and figure out how to get you all well again?" Bebe asked the couchful of my classmates.

"Absolutely," said Clara Rutherford, our spokesperson.

"It's what we've all been hoping for," said Leigh Carruthers, who, I should mention, didn't even look like she was vibrating anymore.

"Honestly, Bebe, all we really want is to know how to keep our kids safe. Is that too much to ask?" Kathy Carruthers, with her mic back on, was having her moment.

"It sure isn't." Bebe smiled, patting Kathy on her knee.

"I'll say it isn't," Bethany Witherspoon agreed.

"Bethany Witherspoon, coming to the rescue of some truly brave young women at St. Joan's Academy in Danvers, Massachusetts. Bethany? Keep us informed."

"You know I will, Bebe." Bethany Witherspoon grinned straight into the camera, her eye glinting with certainty.

"Holy cow," I said as my phone vibrated in my sweatshirt pocket. I pulled it out.

Anjali.

They're wrong.

I frowned and tapped back.

But who's right?

INTERLUDE

*S*arah Good and Sarah Osburn were examined that day as well," I tell Reverend Green. "When they were finished, they all three were taken to the jail in chains. Goody Good's daughter, Dorothy, hurled a rock at the man who was dragging away her mother. The rock struck him on the cheek and drew blood, and Dorothy screamed at me that it was my fault they were taking her mother away."

The baby's screams—for she was a little thing, Dorothy Good, and even now is small for her age, and insensible like a child—echo in my ears to this day. "Mama! Mama!" She'd clutched her mother's filthy skirts until some women stepped forward to pry her free.

Reverend Green is thinking horrible things of me. I can see it in his face. Yet I revel in it. I want him to see my debasement. I want him to see everything about me.

"And the examinations," he says. "They continued the next day?"

There's a book, I've heard, that a famous divine wrote, in which one can read everything that happened to us then. I've been shown a copy, but little good it did me. I've never learned my letters. To sign my name I draw a curl, the shape of the lock of hair on my baby sister's forehead. I can never encounter the Word of God myself. I always need a man to bring it to me.

"They did," I say. "But something else happened first."

That night, March 1, I'm walking Abby and Betty Parris back to the parsonage with my parents and some others. We've been in the meetinghouse all day, and my back aches from the pew, my eyes are red from crying, and my throat is raw. Reverend Parris walks with his head down, his wife following close on his heels, in her hood with the topknot.

"I don't understand," he murmurs to himself. "Of course the Devil could tempt the likes of Sarah Good, and Sarah Osburn, too. I'd have guessed them above anyone. But how could she not tell me? Right here, in my own house!"

With Tittibe gone, there's no one to offer us anything warm to drink when we return but her husband, John, who's slumped in a corner. When he observes our entry into the house, he gets up without a word and leaves. No one remarks on his departure. Mrs. Parris busies herself to tend to us while my mother looks on with disapproval.

"I never trusted that Indian," my mother remarks to no one in particular. "She had a way about her I didn't like. It's no wonder, if you ask me. She were never a proper Christian."

"But Mama," I say, rubbing my tired eyes with my fists. "You said she loved Jesus as well as anyone."

"Annie! I never said that. Anyone who sends her spirit out in the night to torment innocent children is no Christian."

Mr. Parris sits in his great chair with his head in his hands.

"Thomas," he says at length to my father, "I'm lost. Will you pray with me?"

"Of course," Papa says, and he sits near the Reverend. They fold their hands together and bend their heads.

"Betty, Abby," Mrs. Parris says. "You girls go on up to bed."

Abby wraps an arm around Betty Parris and steers her to the attic. The other Betty, Betty Hubbard, and I huddle together on the bench along the wall with my mother. Mary Warren had to go back to the Procters, who'll be wondering why she shirked her duties that day. I wish Betty Hubbard and I could go up to bed, too. I've never felt so tired. My arms and legs are made of wet oak.

The men pray quietly together, and sleepiness overwhelms me. I lean my cheek against my mother's shoulder, but she pushes me off and snaps, "Sit up, Annie."

A knock comes on the door, and someone opens it to a man standing in the dark with snow on his shoulders. He's carrying a package under his arm, wrapped in cloth.

"Mrs. Parris," he says, removing his hat.

"Oh, Deacon," she cries, getting to her feet. "How good of you to come."

"Word's all over Boston," the man says. "My congregation's been praying for your delivery. Satan may try to pull down the house of God, but he's bound to fail. For that, I came to help. I want him to see this." He indicates the praying Reverend Parris with a nod of his head.

The Reverend concludes his prayer with my father and gets to his feet, shaking hands with the Boston deacon whose name I don't know.

"The Devil will use his wiles," Reverend Parris says. "But we'll be sober and vigilant. He'll not prevail. I won't give in, no matter how they push me."

"Look here, Samuel," the deacon says, unwrapping his package.

It's a book, bound in rich burgundy leather. Everyone leans in for a look. My father has a few books, and he's careful of them and doesn't let my brothers read them. My mother and I cannot read, but more than once I've wished they had some pretty pictures for me to look at. When I see that this one doesn't promise to have any pictures either, I lean back against the wall and close my eyes.

"Ah! William Perkins. *A Discourse of the Damned Art of Witchcraft.*

I've preached from his discourse on the Lord's Prayer, but I haven't read this," Reverend Parris says, running his hands over the pages in appreciation.

"My gift to you. There's a passage I'd like very much for you to see."

The men riffle through the pages, looking for what they want.

"Annie," my mother says. "Get up and fetch me some cider."

Mrs. Parris has come to sit next to her, and they want to talk together. Betty Hubbard has slumped to her side and fallen asleep on the bench, her mouth open in a snore. Sulking, I haul myself to my feet and busy myself at the other end of the room.

"You see?" the deacon from Boston says.

Reverend Parris's eyes are alight.

"Why, John, this could reveal them all. They'd be forced into the light. If she names them, they've no choice but to prosecute."

"Exactly."

"What is it, Samuel?" Mrs. Parris asks in a fragile voice.

My mother takes Mrs. Parris's hands in her lap and squeezes them.

The Reverend has gotten to his feet and is pacing the parsonage's hall. My father watches him, his own eyes glittering with comprehension.

"For months now, we've known there was an alliance against me," Mr. Parris says. "A secret world within our world. They've stopped our firewood, they've spoken against me in town. They've denied us sure ownership of our home. They've done all they can to tear down God's work in this wilderness, and me as his agent. Most of them have been too cowardly to do so in the open. They've enlisted the Devil's help. They've brought their scheming into my own home, against defenseless children. But now there's a way for us to root them out."

The deacon from Boston taps the book twice with his index finger and smiles.

"But what is it?" my mother asks. "What does it say?"

"William Perkins was a Puritan divine in England, one of the worthiest," the deacon explains. "We read him at college. Among other things he was an authority on the prosecution of witches."

"The witch's work is invisible, except to those she torments," the Reverend explains. He stops by the fire near me and kindles a pipe to steady his hands.

"Hard to prove," my father adds. "You can bring an accusation well enough, but the evidence . . ." He trails off. "It's harder to prove than murder."

"And more evil," the deacon finishes.

"But Perkins says there's sure proof, for catching out a witch. Proof unassailable in court. First, if she bears the Devil's mark upon her body."

"Yes, I've heard that," Mrs. Parris says. "Though I know not what the Devil's mark might be."

"A midwife can tell it well enough. They know what's natural in women and what isn't," the Deacon insists. "Second, if witnesses can swear that a witch's ill words are followed closely by accidents or ill-nesses otherwise unexplained."

"That's the surest, I'd think," my mother remarks. "That Sarah Good leaves nothing but vice and foulness in her wake. No sooner does she get turned away without alms than something goes awry in the house."

"Then, there's testimony like today, when the girls so bravely named the shapes of the witches that tormented them. They see them clear as day! They need only be brave enough to say so. Annie?" he says.

I freeze where I stand, a ladle half brought to fill a mug for my mother. I don't know that Reverend Parris has ever spoken directly to me before today.

"Yes, Reverend Parris?"

"You did the Lord's work in court today," he says, his gaze weighing heavy on me. "It takes a pure soul to stand tall in the face of the Devil's torments. I know how they torture you. And you're right to be afraid. But if you stand with Jesus, you may find you're one of the elect."

My hand is shaking as I bring the ladle down, for fear of slopping cider all over the floor.

"Thank you, Reverend Parris," I answer him.

My voice is small and weak. Like my soul.

"But," the deacon says. "The problem with witches is how to find them out. They hide their wickedness, pretending to be the godly people we've always known. And that's where Perkins guides us."

"Goody Sibley tried some method she knew," Mrs. Parris says. "But it didn't seem very Christian to me."

Reverend Parris hurries across the room and takes her hands in his. "The surest way to uncover a witch who's working in secret is by the sworn testimony of another confessed witch."

Mrs. Parris's eyes go wide. She stares into the middle distance of her hall, and I see us all fall away from her as she realizes what her husband has just said.

Slowly, the minister's wife rises from her seat.

"Tittibe," she breathes.

Reverend Parris nods.

"She must be made to tell." Her voice now is run through with iron.

The minister nods again.

"She must be made to tell tomorrow. If she names the witches responsible, they can be tried. They can be convicted and we'll all be free. You must go the jail, Samuel. Take Goodman Putnam and the deacon if you must. Go speak to her. Speak to her now."

Reverend Parris stares into his wife's eyes for a long moment, and a message seems to pass between them that none of the rest of us can see. He hurries to the door and begins to pull on his greatcoat and hat. My father follows close on his heels, and the deacon from Boston, too.

"She'll confess. And she'll name her confederates." Reverend Parris surveys the room with a black gleam in his eye. "I promise."

CHAPTER 21

DANVERS, MASSACHUSETTS

FRIDAY, MARCH 9, 2012

That Friday. Oh my God. How can I even describe what it was like that Friday?

First off, I couldn't even see the school for all the media who were gathered outside. The board of trustees sent an e-mail to everyone the night before, warning us to expect a more intense than usual media presence. That's how they put it—"more intense than usual." Which is a pretty intense understatement, if you ask me. Anyway, we didn't even see the e-mail until early that morning, and by then Wheez was already in the car because my dad was going to drop her after dropping me.

St. Joan's Academy was a mob scene. And not just from all the news vans and the cameras and the cables and microphones and wires and satellite dishes and reporters, all the regional stations and the ones from western Massachusetts and CNN and MSNBC and Fox and all the New York stations and everything. Crowds of random people, strangers, just showed up to mill around and stare at the front of the school. A lot of them were there to see Bethany Witherspoon, since she's that famous. But there were a bunch of people holding signs, too. Protesters.

Those wackos who always crash soldiers' funerals were there, screaming that the Mystery Illness was a punishment from God because the government allowed gays in the military. Or I guessed that was what they were saying. Who the hell knew? Their signs said stuff like SATAN IS COME TO DANVERS and PRAY FOR OUR DELIVERY and GOD HATES SLUTS and CATHOLIC WHORES OF THE DEVIL.

On the other side of the parking lot huddled a small group of Congregationalists in practical sweaters and a van from the meetinghouse here in town. Their signs read stuff like TOLERANCE and REASON and LISTEN: GOD IS STILL SPEAKING. I'm Catholic, I mean, of course I am, 'cause I'm Irish, but they're pretty cool as Protestants go. I didn't mind them. The most puzzling banner they held was DON'T FORGET THE LESSONS OF THE PAST.

"Whoa," Wheez said, pressing her nose to the window of the station wagon. "Daddy, can we stay until Bethany Witherspoon gets here?"

My father shook his head. "We've got to get you to school, Louisa. And we don't know what time she's coming."

But we needn't have worried, because while Wheez was wheedling my dad, a huge bus pulled up, the kind with dark windows that rock bands use to travel around the country. The bus didn't have any markings on it, but somehow everyone there knew immediately who it was. The news station spotlights spun away from the facade of St. Joan's, and cameras and reporters all rushed the bus. The onlookers had already crowded around the bus's door, pressed together by the two sets of protesters, their signs acting like a barrier crushing everyone into one big mass.

"That's her!" Wheez cried. So we three by silent common agreement sat in the car and watched the star arrive.

The bus door slid open and camera flashes popped in a blinding blizzard of light, and by the time I'd rubbed the spots from my eyes, Bethany Witherspoon was halfway to the upper school front door, wearing gigantic sunglasses and waving and stopping to sign autographs for people. A few nondescript men and women followed behind her in matching windbreakers, some of them carrying official-looking equipment. To our surprise, the next people to climb off the bus were Clara Rutherford, the Other Jennifer, Elizabeth, and Leigh Carruthers. Again the waves of flashbulbs popped like firecrackers, and all four of them smiled and waved and started making their way through the crowd of media and well-wishers, stopping to give hugs and take pictures and shake hands.

"Wow," I said. "Elizabeth is walking just fine."

"Hmm," my father said. "So she is."

Even the Other Jennifer had shed her Elizabeth Taylor turban and was sporting a cute baby-fuzz pixie haircut.

"Maybe they've gotten better?" Wheez asked.

The crowd followed my afflicted classmates to the front doors, where Father Molloy stood waiting, his arms folded over his chest. The drainpipe gargoyles snarled over the priest's shoulder, their tongues lolling.

I was too far away to hear, but it looked like Bethany Witherspoon held an impromptu press conference on the school steps, situating herself between Father Molloy and the four girls. Half a dozen microphones were thrust in front of their mouths. Reporters waved notebooks, trying to catch their attention. More popping flashbulbs and stark camera lights threw flickering black shadows over the Gothic doors. Over all their heads loomed the inverse image of St. Joan in stained glass, flames licking up her sides as she stared at the heavens.

Bethany Witherspoon waved merrily at the crowd and then started to head into the school. Father Molloy waylaid her in the open doorway, and a focused argument took place. Father Molloy, unsurprisingly, lost. Into the upper school marched Bethany Witherspoon and her team, followed by half a dozen of the reporters. The priest was able to fend off everyone else, including the random onlookers and the protesters, who gradually drifted back to their opposing sides of the parking lot.

"Well," my father said to me, "looks like it's going to be quite a Friday."

"I want to see what happens!" Wheez whined from the backseat. "Can I go to school with Colleen?"

"Can it, Louisa," my father said. To me, he said, "You feel okay? You ready to go in?"

"Does it matter?" I asked, giving him a wan smile.

"Not really, no," he agreed. "Good luck."

As I climbed out of the car and readied to face whatever bedlam I would find inside, another nondescript van pulled up. Written on the side in bland script was MASSACHUSETTS DEPARTMENT OF PUBLIC HEALTH MOBILE UNIT. Two people climbed out of the van. The press ignored them.

I found Deena in advisory right away, following her hum of "Body and Soul," and to my surprise discovered both Emma and Anjali there, too, everyone in her seat like it was a regular Friday. Anjali looked like she'd lost some weight. She was still coughing weird fish-bone pins up at least once a day, and her throat and mouth were raw from it. The skin at the corners of her mouth was red and peeling. But she wasn't about to miss Bethany Witherspoon riding to our rescue. Neither was Emma, who acted like it was totally normal that she was back, just like it was totally normal that she'd been missing school even though there wasn't anything wrong with her. In fact, just about everyone was back in advisory that morning. The only sign that St. Joan's had been in the grip of the Mystery Illness for two months was the plastic sheeting all over the hallways, and the roving bands of news cameras.

Father Molloy looked like death warmed over. I swear, if I were him, I'd have quit by now. I guess that's the problem with being a man of God. There's no quitting. Unless you're the pope.

"Okay, girls, listen up," he said, rubbing a hand over his face.

He was interrupted by the door opening and Clara Rutherford appearing in the doorway, bathed in a halo of light. This halo emanated not from heaven, however, but from the shoulder-mounted portable television camera a guy was carrying behind her.

"It's okay if they come in with me, right?" Clara asked, but not really, because she was already halfway to her allotted desk and the camera guy had captured it all on film. The Other Jennifer and Elizabeth, back in a wheelchair for some reason, trailed in behind her. The camera guy got footage of them, too, presumably for B-roll.

"Oh no, I don't think so," Father Molloy said, waving his hands in the camera's lens. "This is not happening. You'll have to wait outside, I'm sorry."

The camera guy looked to Clara for confirmation. She shrugged.

"No problem," said the camera guy, possibly because the classroom door's pebbled-glass window meant he could get some atmospheric and creepy shots from outside. The priest hustled them out of the classroom and shut the door with a decisive click. Immediately the glass window glowed with camera light.

"Well," said Father Molloy once we'd settled down as much as anyone could, which wasn't much. "First off, it's good to see you all back. Jennifer, Elizabeth. Clara. Anjali. Emma. Fabiana. It's been mighty quiet around here without you. And I want you to know that we've had candles burning in the chapel for each and every one of you. I think you'll agree with me that the best thing for all of us will be to let this run its course so that we can get back to the matter at hand, which is learning."

Yeah. He actually said that. Sure, I wanted everything to go back to normal, too. But that wasn't about to happen with Bethany Witherspoon clacking up and down the halls in her stilettos (okay, the plastic sort of muffled the clacking) and the assembly coming up that afternoon.

"I guess I know why you all chose today to come back. And I don't have to expend any energy urging you to attend the assembly this afternoon. We'll be hearing from the Massachusetts Department of Public Health, who are on campus today to make sure that none of your symptoms have an environmental cause. Now. Who's got questions?"

A forest of girls' hands shot up.

"Did you see us on TV?" one of the afflicted girls chirped. "How'd we do?"

"Yes," said Father Molloy in a leaden voice. "I saw. Other questions?"

"Is Nurse Hocking back today?" one of us asked, and the entire room tittered.

"I don't believe she is. And I'm told Dr. Strayed has gone back to UMass."

"They are so getting sued," someone whispered to someone else.

"Do you think we'll be hearing from Bethany Witherspoon at assembly?" one of us wanted to know.

"I should hope not," said the priest. "She's not affiliated with the school, and she hasn't been invited here. So, no."

"She was so invited here, by our parents," said another of the afflicted girls. "We think she should be allowed to talk."

"That'll be up to the board of trustees," Father Molloy said, a little sharply. "Now, does anyone have a real question?"

"Do you think the Mystery Illness is really caused by pollution?" I asked, gazing levelly at him.

"No," he said, gazing just as levelly back. "I don't."

"Oh, like you're a scientist," one of the afflicted girls scoffed. I wasn't used to hearing them talk to Father Molloy like that. I saw that it made him angry, but he didn't say anything to stop them.

"Neither is Bethany Witherspoon," he said. "Now take out your books. We've got fifteen minutes before first period, and I want to see some reading."

If I thought the steps of the school were bad, I was totally unprepared for the scene in chapel. Two security guys flanked the chapel doors, guarding against a stampede. At least, I think that's what they were doing there. Maybe they were worried about the protesters. And they should have been; Emma and I were waiting in a thick knot of girls to get through the doors when we saw a heavyset guy in a security uniform muscling out a woman in a sandwich board who was screaming, "Sluts of the Devil! Apostates! Whorechildren!"

"Whoa," Emma whispered. "She's pretty upset, huh?"

"I know," I whispered back. "Those insults are seriously old school."

Inside the chapel was so dense with bodies, there wasn't a question of finding a place to sit. Girls packed into every square inch, sitting on the backs of pews, piled together on the floor, pressed up against the walls. Camera lights blared against the stained-glass windows, throwing the images of Joan's life into white opacity. Nobody was at the pulpit. The room was so crammed with girls and reporters and random people and protesters that nobody could move. I felt sweat beading on my hairline, and a deep ache beginning to bore itself into my forehead. I couldn't find Anjali or Deena. Anjali had just texted me that they were near the front, having sneaked out early from Calc BC, but there was no way we were going to find them.

Father Molloy stood off to one side, hands planted on his hips, glaring at some of the protesters who had sneaked in with anti-Catholic placards. Some of the other teachers were there, too, but no one seemed to be in charge. Through the surging mass of bodies I spotted a familiar wicked eyebrow, which belonged to Ms. Slater. She held my gaze for a split second, only long enough for me to see her shake her head once, and then the crowd boiled her away from us.

Emma and I wedged ourselves into a rear corner by the bank of candles, which someone had wisely thought to extinguish before herding us all in there.

"Is it weird to be back?" I asked her.

"Not really," she said. "It's kind of nice, actually. I was getting really bored. People had stopped remembering to e-mail my assignments. God knows how far behind I've gotten. Good thing I'm into college already so it basically doesn't matter."

"Yeah." I shuffled my feet, thinking about Emma getting into college. Emma, and her fake rec letter from Mr. Mitchell. *Tad.* "Emma? I've been wanting to talk to you about something," I said slowly.

"Oh?" She didn't meet my eyes, instead craning her neck like a seabird to look over the ribboned heads of our classmates. "Hey, look! There she is."

Some of the girls in the front started screaming with excitement, and flashbulbs popped, roiling the mob into a bubbling stew, hot enough to simmer us all alive. Bethany Witherspoon appeared at the pulpit, flanked by some of her people in the matching shirts. They positioned themselves more like bodyguards or henchmen than a science team. Then again, I guess I'd never seen a celebrity science team. Someone else in a white windbreaker was standing off to the side, looking unimpressed.

"So much for what Father Molloy said," I muttered, but Emma wasn't listening. Her pale eyes widened with excitement; she was as much a part of the mob as all of us.

One of the science-team henchmen passed the star a megaphone. She flashed a brilliant smile and cried, "Good afternoon, girls!" Her words echoed off the chapel walls, filling our ears with sound and authority.

The screams rose in pitch. Girls in plaid skirts elbowed each other out of the way, trying to get closer. Camera lights beamed at Bethany Witherspoon from several directions, throwing her into a weird flat light, with freaky shadows under her eyes.

"We've spent the entire day on your beautiful campus!" she boomed through the megaphone. "We've taken samples from the basement, the gym, the classrooms, the HVAC, the athletic fields, and everywhere in between!"

More screaming.

"And we're here to tell you that we're going to get to the bottom of this problem! We're not going to be fooled by any school nurse, or any fancy epidemiologist!"

Everyone was clapping and screaming with their hands pressed to their cheeks. Some of us were reaching for her at the pulpit, clawing to get closer. Girls' arms thrust for Bethany Witherspoon's ankles, as if she alone could drag them out of hell.

"Do you want to have tricoethylene poisoning your air and your water?"

"No!" we screamed.

"Do you think it's okay for them to just dump chemicals right next to a school and not tell anybody?"

"No!!" we chorused in delirium.

"We're going to hold the government accountable for what's happened here! We're going to find the answer! And we're not going to let anyone cover it up, are we?"

"NO!" the entire chapel thundered.

"ARE WE?"

"NO!!" we bellowed louder, many of us beating on the pews with our hands and feet.

"Are you going to sit there and let the Massachusetts Department of Public Health tell you you're not really sick?" Bethany Witherspoon pointed at the nondescript person in the white jacket frowning off to one side of the pulpit.

"NO!!" we bellowed at the top of our lungs.

"We're here to uncover the truth, and we're not going to let anyone stand in our way! Now, who's with me?"

Everyone in the chapel erupted in a formless frenzy, girls and protesters and reporters rushing the pulpit as Bethany Witherspoon passed the megaphone into the waiting hands of an underling and started gathering girls to her, hugging them and waving at the cameras.

The crazy part was, I felt it, too. I wanted to run to her, to surrender to her the responsibility for what was happening. I wanted to let the pressure out of me, the years and years of anxiety and terror and fear, let it all come screaming out of my mouth. And when I looked at Emma next to me, her eyes almost glowing with desire, I knew I wasn't the only one.

INTERLUDE

*T*here's a soft knock on the door, and Goody Green pokes her gentle nose into the Reverend's study.

"Do excuse me," she says. "But the girls're getting hungry. It's suppertime."

I scowl at her with a sudden heated flame of hate.

"Thank you, my dear," Reverend Green says, and perhaps it's my imagination that he looks guilty around the edges.

He'd rather hear the rest of my story. I smile slowly at the minister's wife.

"Well," she says to him, and then her eyes slide to me, and when she sees my possessive smile, she recoils, unable to hide her dislike.

"We won't be long."

"Of course," she says through her lowered eyebrows. "If you and Ann still have things to discuss. I'll be right out here."

The door closes. I'm sure she will be right out there. Maybe she'll go so far as to listen in at the door. I would, if I were her.

"What happened the next day, Ann?" the Reverend says, leaning deeper into my thrall.

. . .

On March 2 my mother shakes me awake before light and tells me I'd better dress myself, and hurry.

"Why, Mama? What's happened?" I ask through squinting eyes.

Betty Hubbard's lost in sleep next to me, one of her skinny arms around my neck, and I'm loath to leave our warm pallet. I rub my eye with a fist and look up at my mother's pinched face. She's wearing a fresh linen liner in her hood, and its crisp white lace makes her face look milky in the early spring morning.

"Your father's been at the jail all night. With Reverend Parris. We're to meet them at the meetinghouse this morning."

I lift myself on an elbow and say, "They were talking to Tittibe?"

A shadow crosses through my mother's eyes that I don't understand.

"Yes, Annie. Talking to her. They expect she'll name the Reverend's enemies today. It'll be a great day for the village. We'll be whole again."

A deep and sickening fear grips my entrails, and I swallow thickly to keep from being sick all over the linens. Then I'd have to wash them while everyone else goes to the meetinghouse to see what happens.

"Come along. Don't lie abed like a lug. And get Betty up."

At the sound of her name, Betty Hubbard stirs, rolling onto her side and murmuring, "Go away."

"Insolent girl." My mother scowls. "Be dressed before I can blink twice, or your hide'll regret it."

"Betty," I say, shaking her shoulder.

"What?" she moans. "Leave me be. I'm bewitched. It makes me tired."

"You wake up right now!" I dig my nails into her shoulder flesh and shake like a dog on a squirrel.

"What?" Betty whines, opening an eye and looking at me. "I want to go home. I'm going to tell my uncle today he'd better take me."

"That's all well and good, but today we're expected back at the meetinghouse," I say. "Now get up."

"What for? They already talked to Tittibe. And those other two.

Sarah Good scares me." She draws the bedclothes up under her chin and pouts.

"My father's been with the Reverend at the jail all night. Your uncle, too, I wager. Talking to Tittibe Indian. Mother says today Tittibe's going to name the people who've been hounding Reverend Parris. Trying to undermine his ministry."

"His ministry?" She sits up now, also confused. "But . . . Abby said . . ."

"What do they care what Abby Williams says? She's eleven."

I've known for a while that most of the adults in town only pretend to get along well with each other. They always tell us we must behave, we must be kind to children whom we hate. They tell us that God can see into our souls and knows our blackest thoughts. They tell us to do and say only the purest things, or we'll never gain the kingdom of heaven.

But they're hypocrites, every last one. We're beginning to understand that our game has been wrestled away from us. That in a way we cannot fully understand, it's nothing to do with us at all.

"Get up," I say. "It's about to be over."

The crowd at the meetinghouse is even bigger and more boisterous than the day before. My mother has to fight our way to the doors. In the throng I spot a girl I half know, Mercy Dane, alone in the crowd, and her icy pale eyes look on me with a hate so burning white, it sears my soul. I look away, and hot tears spring to my eyes. I feel like I've been slapped in the face.

By the time we achieve the meetinghouse aisle, foul and wild-eyed Sarah Good and that libertine crone Sarah Osburn already cower at the front, hunched together, their wrists linked with heavy rope.

My mother elbows her way through the throng, pulling me and Betty Hubbard along by our arms, crying, "Out of the way! Move out of the way!"

The magistrates stand in a black-coated knot off to one side, having a discussion involving much waving of hands and seeming concern about the time.

At the front of the meetinghouse a bench awaits, and I'm surprised to find it occupied only by Mary Warren and Goody Pope. My mother steers us to the bench and pushes us roughly to our seats, then shoves herself into a space on the bench just behind, earning frowns and muttering from those who arrived early to watch the play unfold.

No sooner have we been seated than a hue and cry breaks out at the back of the assembly and the doors are thrown open to the sharp spring air. There stands Reverend Parris, with the sallow face of a man long without rest, flanked by my father, by the old doctor, by a few other men I don't know, by Abigail Williams, and by his daughter Betty Parris. His hand is clenched around the upper arm of Tittibe Indian, who holds her head up high and meets no one's gaze.

When I see Tittibe, I cry out and then quickly cover my mouth.

One of her eyes is empurpled and swollen shut. Her lip is split and cracked with dried blood. As they advance forward, she limps and must be held up by the Reverend on one side and by the warden who guides her other arm. Her skirt, already patched with wear, is torn and ragged at the ends. As she passes by our bench, she does not look at us.

"Unconscionable," spits a male voice a pew behind me. "Look, you, how they've treated her. Didn't I tell you? There's nothing of witchcraft to any of this."

"Hush, Goodman Calef," someone else says.

Abby and Betty Parris slip in next to me, their small faces pointed and serious.

"What is this?" I hiss to them.

Abby levels a prim look at me. "She'll name them all now," she whispers.

Next to her, little Betty Parris, who was brought up by Tittibe, nods. "She'll name all the witches now, Annie. You see if she won't."

The judge begins with no preamble. We all know why we're here.

"You spoke of a man yesterday, Tituba. What covenant did you make with that man who came to you? What did he tell you?" asks Judge Hathorne.

Tittibe speaks in a near monotone, and the pulp of her lip makes her voice thick and hard to discern.

"He tell me that he God, and I must believe him and serve him six years, and he would give me many fine things."

"How long ago was this?"

"About six weeks and a little more. Friday night before Abigail was ill."

"Did you promise to serve him when he spoke to you then? What did you answer him?"

"I told him I could not believe him God. I told him I'd have to ask my master, and I would've gone up to ask Reverend Parris, but the black man stopped me."

"What did you promise him?"

"The first time I believe him God and he was glad of it. Then he tell me they must meet together."

"With the other witches? When did he say you must meet together?"

"He tell me Wednesday next at my master's house, and then they all meet together and that night I saw them all stand in the corner, all four of them, and the man stand behind me and take hold of me to make me stand still in the hall."

"Where was your master then?" the judge asks, glancing at Reverend Parris, who is making notes at the same table with Goodman Cheever.

Tittibe stares at Samuel Parris. She waits a very long moment before she answers. All us girls begin, very quietly, to tremble.

"He were in the other room."

"What time of night was this?"

"A little before prayer time."

"What did this man say to you when he took hold of you?"

"He say go and do hurt to them and pinch them. And then I went in, and would not hurt them a good while, I would not hurt Betty, I loved Betty, but they make me pinch Betty and next Abigail."

Abigail and Betty Parris choose this moment to cry out and rub their hands over their pinch marks, which must vex them terribly, if their consciences do not.

"Did the other witches pinch the girls, too?"

"No, but they all looked on and see me pinch them."

"Did you go into that room in your current form? And did the other witches, too, or did they send their spirits?"

"They went in their natural forms and my master didn't see us, for they wouldn't let my master see. Their magic blinded him."

"When the other witches left the parsonage, did you go with the company?"

"No, I stayed. And the Devil stayed with me."

The entire meetinghouse gasps in horror. The Devil lingered in the Reverend's house. The Devil himself! He may have even sat at the minister's table. Reverend Parris's cheek twitches, and he looks hard at the paper before him.

"What did the Devil then do to you?"

"He tell me my master would go to prayer and Reverend Parris he read in the good book and Reverend Parris he'd ask me what I remember from the Scripture, but the Devil tell me don't you remember nothing."

"And what happened the next time you saw the Devil?"

"He ask me again that I serve him six years. Then he show me a book."

"When did he come the next time?"

"The next Friday in the daytime, betimes in the morning."

"What book did he bring? A great or little book?"

"I don't know. He didn't show it to me, but had it in his pocket."

"Didn't he make you write your name in the book?"

"No, not yet, for my mistress called me into the other room."

"When you came back, what did he say you must do in that book?"

"He said I must write and set my name to it."

"Did you do as he said?" the judge asks.

Tittibe pauses, knowing what horror she's about to admit. She clears her throat, and we all lean forward, our lips parted, as though ready to drink the lie from her bloodied mouth.

"Yes," she says, and we all groan in horrified satisfaction. "Once. I make a mark in the book. I make it with red blood."

Judge Hathorne peers at her with a frown. "Did the Devil get the blood out of your body?"

"He said he must get it out the next time he come."

"Did you see any other marks in his book?"

"Yes, a great many. Some marks red, some yellow." Tittibe pauses, her eye roving over the crowd. "He open his book and I see a great many marks in it." She pauses again. "Belonging to a great many people."

The judge steeples his fingertips before his mouth.

"Tituba," he intones. "Did the Devil tell you the names of the other witches?"

The murmuring in the meetinghouse freezes to silence. The room is so quiet, I can hear Betty Hubbard and Abby Williams breathing on either side of me.

The slave is aware of her abrupt command of us all. Her voice rises with new authority.

"Yes."

The room buzzes with certainty, and I hear many names being whispered of likely witch confederates. The Devil has been loosed in Salem, and we're about to learn who's been serving him in secret, masquerading as good Christians.

"Of two," Tittibe hastens to add. "Not more. Good and Osburn. The Devil say they make their marks in that book, he showed them to me."

Beneath my fear, I marvel at Tittibe Indian. When my father beats me, I'm quick to say whatever will make him stop. She could have named anyone, anyone at all, along with the women we've already long suspected, and we would have believed her.

The judge, however, is bound to find out more. "How many marks do you think there were, in the Devil's book?"

Tittibe shifts her eyes to Reverend Parris, who gives her a curt nod. "Nine," she says. "I counted nine."

"Did they all write their names, too?"

"They make marks. Goody Good tell me she make her mark, but Goody Osburn wouldn't tell. She was cross to me."

Goody Osburn, the strumpet crone, as my mother's called her, spits on the floor between her feet and says nothing.

"When did Goody Good tell you she set her hand to the book?" Judge Hathorne wants to know.

"The same day I came hither to prison," she replies. They were all three put in prison together, Tittibe and the Sarahs. I wonder what they said to each other in that prison cell at night.

"I see. Did you see the Devil that morning in prison?"

"Yes, a little in the morning. He tell me the magistrates were coming up to examine me. He say I must tell nothing, that if I did, he would cut my head off."

"Tell us how many women used to come when you witches rid abroad on sticks."

"Four of them. These two"—she points at Sarah Good, whose eyes won't focus and who seems much amazed, and Sarah Osburn, who seems angry enough to set the meetinghouse on fire with a look— "and two strangers."

The judge, we can all see, thinks he's about to get to the bottom of this. "You say that there were nine witches in total. Did he tell you who they were?"

The assembly behind us all nods, urging her to reveal the witches' names. Some even go so far as to offer suggestions.

Tittibe's voice wavers with panic. "No," she cries. "He not let me see. He tell me I should see them the next time at our Sabbath."

"But didn't he tell you the names of the others?" The judge's lips are pressed together in frustration, and Samuel Parris wears a look of murderous rage.

"No sir," says Tittibe.

"Did he at least tell you where the nine lived?" the judge booms at the frightened slave, who is sagging against the bar, unable to hold up her weight any longer. Tears have begun to stream from her blackened eye. "Speak, woman! You saw their faces! You saw their marks in the Devil's book! You know that they numbered nine in the coven! You will tell us where they live, by God, you will, or you'll suffer the consequences!"

The island woman lets out a desperate scream of anguish and fear. We girls clutch each other, shaking, Betty Parris gasping out tears, and someone moans in misery and despair.

"Yes!" Tittibe screams. "Yes! The Devil tell me where the witches live! Some of them live in Boston and ride here in the night upon sticks! And some are right here in this town among us, but he wouldn't tell me who they were. I tell you, the Devil he a liar, and he wouldn't tell me who they were!"

She collapses to her knees, sinking over to the side in a faint, her head lolling back on her shoulders, her hands still tied to the bar, the ropes biting into her skin. All the adults around me are screaming, "Here? They're here? Who else are they? How do we find them?"

Deep and miserable moaning fills my ears, ripping through my mind, and I cry out for it to stop, stop! Stop your moaning, I can't listen anymore! I can't! I can't!

Until I realize the moaning is coming from me.

CHAPTER 22

was in study hall. I can't believe I kept just going to class and doing my homework like everything was normal. After Friday's assembly, what little remained of protocol at St. Joan's Academy for Girls pretty much flew out the window. Dress code was observed haphazardly, or not at all. Teachers let class out early, or just had us read aloud from textbooks.

Girls stopped showing up.

Some of them never came back.

When Clara and the others moved down the hallway, everyone whispered and pointed and fell back in awe, even teachers. They'd fallen sick, and when the school refused to help them, they'd brought in Bethany Witherspoon to find the solution. They radiated a kind of power that I found as baffling as it was irresistible. I fell back from them, too, in the halls. Even the fringe girls, the second-tier afflicted like Leigh and Anjali, had this aura about them. A sheen of specialness caused the air around them to shimmer. I felt it when I stood next to Anjali. She wasn't acting any different, exactly, except for the coughing and the pins, but the difference was there. She had an authority that she'd never had before. She spoke in more declarative sentences. People listened.

Emma wasn't in, and I hadn't heard anything from her all morning. Part of me wondered if she was sick, too, since rumor had it that the number had passed forty. Like the assembly had almost made it worse, somehow. Nobody could keep track of who had the Mystery Illness and who didn't. But Clara's verbal tics were back, and Jennifer's scalp was once again hidden under a silk turban.

I didn't know what I was supposed to be doing, so I decided I should just pretend like everything was okay. So that's why I found myself in the library, alone except for a sleeping Jennifer Crawford, while everyone else was—where? Where were they? I didn't know. Deena wasn't in school that day either.

Periodically a searchlight spun through the library clerestory windows, making me squint and causing Jennifer Crawford to snort in her sleep. The spotlight belonged to Bethany Witherspoon's team doing God knows what. I didn't know what a searchlight had to do with testing the groundwater for spilled chemicals. But they kept poking around with weird equipment, pausing every couple of hours to update the media on the front steps of the school.

The Department of Public Health van still idled out front. None of us had heard from them, though. As far as we could tell, they weren't doing anything except for rolling up all the plastic sheeting when we got to school that morning.

So I was in the library, alone, working on my extra-credit paper, reading more of the Salem transcripts in the index of my history book, when it clicked.

"Oh my God," I said aloud.

Nobody was there to hear me, and Jennifer Crawford didn't wake up. I gathered all my books and papers and shoved them into my bag and sprinted out of the library, pulling out my phone as I ran.

I was stunned when Spence actually answered, because he really hated talking on the phone. He thought it was weird, not being able to see the other person's face.

"What's up?" he said.

"Spence!" I cried, skidding to a halt before I plunged through the front doors of the school and into the waiting phalanx of reporters. Damn. I couldn't go out that way.

I dove through the doors of the student center to keep myself alone.

"Colleen? Are you okay?" he said. In the background I heard a door click shut and then a deadness in the background that told me he had sequestered himself in his closet, which was where he went when he didn't want his roommate to interrupt us.

"I figured it out," I whispered to him, looking over my shoulder through the student center doors and into the hall. No one spotted me.

"Figured what out? Why are you panting?"

"I figured out why Ann Putnam Junior got edited out of *The Crucible*."

"You called to tell me about your extra-credit history paper? Really?" His voice mingled disbelief and disappointment.

"Spence! Listen to me. It's because she was faking! In 1706 she gets up in front of everyone and basically says they were faking! She was in the middle of the whole trial thing, and she's the only one who ever apologized, and it wasn't 'til years later, but she did. She said she was sorry, and they were wrong, and they were totally faking everyone out."

A long pause unfolded on the end of the phone. Then I heard Spence draw a sharp intake of breath as he figured it out, too.

"They're all faking," he said.

"They've got to be."

"Oh my God."

"I know!"

"Damn, Colleen. That's crazy. Why would they do it?"

"I don't know. Attention?"

"But all forty of them? That doesn't seem possible. How are they keeping organized?"

"They wouldn't have to. Clara could get Elizabeth and the Other Jennifer to play along, no problem. And everyone else just wants to be like them."

"Huh," Spence ruminated. "You know, I bet it makes you a pretty interesting prospect to a college, if you're one of the Danvers Mystery Illness girls. Nobody had any idea who any of them were until this started to get splashed all over the television. Right?"

"Maybe." I slid to the floor, my books between my feet, and leaned my head against the student center door. "Maybe."

"What are you going to do?"

"I don't know. I have to tell someone. Who do I tell?"

Spence paused, considering. "Is there someone at school?"

"I don't know. I don't know. The nurse is gone."

"What about your parents?"

"Yeah," I said. Then a thought stopped me short. "But won't they all get in trouble?"

"I mean, yeah. Of course they will. With everything that's happened? People have lost their jobs over this, Colleen. And think of how they'll get treated in the press, if it comes out. Bebe Appleton? Are you kidding me? She'll tear out their souls on national television. She'll mess up their lives so bad, they won't ever come back. And good-bye, college. That's, like, massive plagiarism scandal times a million. No school in their right mind would want them. Especially not if it's got an honor code, and a lot of them do."

"Christ."

"I know."

We paused, breathing together while I sifted through my brain looking for the right thing to do. I knew it had to be in there somewhere. But I wasn't finding it.

"Spence," I moaned, closing my eyes and leaning my head against the student center door.

"Colleen," he said. I could hear his voice smiling.

"God." I opened my eyes and stared across the room to the bleeding

315

plaster Jesus crucified against the student center wall. With my knees drawn up like that I was totally flashing Jesus, which seemed kind of wrong. But his eyes gazed beatifically at the fluorescent lights in the ceiling, unembarrassed.

"So what are you going to do?"

"I don't know," I confessed. "I don't know. I have to think about it."

"Sleep on it," he suggested. "It's not like one day is going to make any difference. Right?"

"I guess not," I said.

The searchlight peered through the dim windows of the student center, tracing across the fake-old tapestry of St. Joan in pigtails and bringing a glint of life to the plaster Jesus's eyes. I dropped my knees down.

"You want me to see if I can come in this weekend?" Spence asked, sounding manful in his offer of protection. It was pretty hot, to be honest.

"Yeah," I said. "I'd actually really like that. Do you think you can?"

"They're always happy to have me at Belmont," said Spence, and I laughed, because he was imitating his mother's haughty, detached way of expressing affection for her son at boarding school.

"That would be seriously awesome," I confessed. "I mean, if you were going to come home anyway."

He snorted at my half-assed attempt to sound casual. "You could come over and watch a movie or something. Get your mind off things."

A goofy smile plastered itself on my face, and I hoped he wouldn't be able to hear it in my voice.

"Oh really? You think I'm ready for the grand introduction?"

"Piffle. They're always happy to have my friends visit at Belmont." It was his haughty-mom voice again, and we both cracked up.

When I got off the phone, I'd decided what I needed to do.

For one thing, I had to talk to Anjali.

But first, I wanted to talk to Emma.

• • •

I had to walk, since Deena wasn't in school that day and my dad couldn't pick me up until six. I could have begged a ride off someone else, but it was starting to warm up. The first crocuses had peeked up through the snow; they always looked odd and vulnerable when their purple noses poked through all that white. Anyway, Emma's house was only, like, a twenty-minute walk from school. I still had two class periods to go, and I hesitated for about five seconds before I said "Screw it" aloud to the empty hallway and just left.

The parking lot still overflowed with protesters, and the lunatic Whores of Satan people screamed at me when I walked by about how much of a Catholic slut I was, but most of the press clustered off on the athletic field filming Bethany Witherspoon as she did some kind of chemistry experiment with one of her team. She was going to be pretty pissed when she figured out there wasn't anything wrong with the groundwater. What if she realized they'd been fooling her on purpose? Forget TJ Wadsworth and her trashed local news career. Bethany would ruin them even worse than Bebe Appleton would. I saw the Massachusetts Department of Public Health van parked in its usual spot, but I didn't see anyone inside.

The one I couldn't figure out was Anjali. Why would she fake being sick? She was totally getting into Yale without any weird publicity stunt to boost her chances. I didn't get it. Sure, she liked attention. I mean, look at how much she craved all those texts from Jason. It wasn't a mystery to me that Anjali would want more attention. It was a mystery to me how she'd be able to fool her mom.

I trudged up the sidewalk to Emma's front door, sidestepping a puddle of slush in the cracked pavement at the bottom of her stoop. I leaned on the buzzer and waited.

The house looked empty at first, but I saw Emma's mom's car in the driveway. Her mom never went out anyway. Someone had to be home.

"Emma?" I called out. "Hello?"

I banged on the door, and it rattled in its frame.

"Mrs. Blackburn? Are you home?"

I cupped my hands around my eyes and pressed my face to the picture window next to the front door. There weren't any lights on, but I saw a flicker of movement deep in the shadows of the living room.

"Hello?" I called again.

The door creaked open and Mrs. Blackburn materialized behind the screen.

"Colleen?" she said in her wispy voice. I'd known Mrs. Blackburn since I was tiny, but she always wore this vague lack of recognition in her face when she looked at me. I always felt like I had to reintroduce myself to her.

"Yes," I said. "It's me, Mrs. Blackburn. Colleen. Is Emma home?"

"Emma?" she said. Sometimes she had to work to remember her daughter's name, too.

"Yeah. I really need to talk to her. Can I come in?"

"Um." Mrs. Blackburn was still in her dressing gown, and her pale blond hair had grown wintry over the years, giving her a ghostly aspect that I found unnerving. Of course, it didn't help that she never went outside. "I'm not sure now's the best time."

"Please," I said, stepping up and pressing my hands to the screen door. "It's really important. I won't stay long."

Mrs. Blackburn gave me a long, vague look.

"It would be better, I think, if you didn't," she said simply.

"I have to," I said, pulling open the screen door and pushing past Emma's mom. "I'm sorry, but I have to. Emma?" I called.

"Well. It's your decision," Mrs. Blackburn said, drifting back into the shadows of the living room.

Emma's room was off the second-floor landing. It was dark up there, only a thin line of light showing under her bedroom door, but I knew the way as well as I knew the way to my own. I thumped up the stairs into the darkness overhead, coming to a stop with my hand on the doorknob.

Inside, I heard sounds of muffled weeping.

"Emma?" I whispered, gently creaking the door open.

She sprawled on her stomach on the bed, head buried in a pillow that I remembered from our sleepovers when we were little—threadbare Powerpuff Girls pillowcase, with bits of feather leaking out the end. Her arms wrapped tight around her American Girl doll, the one in the funny Puritan hat. The doll's hair was askew, and it smiled with glassy eyes up at the ceiling. Emma's whole body trembled, the force of her crying ripping through her in waves.

"Emma," I said again, tiptoeing into her bedroom. Dozens of dolls gazed down on us from shelves all over the narrow room.

I lowered myself onto the edge of her bed and hovered my hand over her back.

"He—he—he—he doesn't l—l—l—love me anymore!" she sobbed.

"Oh, Emma," I whispered. I wanted to pet her pale hair, but the pure power of her misery made me afraid.

"Wh—wh—why doesn't he love me anymore?" she wailed, gasping for breath in the pillow. "We d—d—dated for months. I th—th—th—thought I was s—s—s—special!"

"What did he say?" I asked as gently as I could.

I mean, what I wanted to say was *He's an adult and you're a kid and that's disgusting and I hate him and I really wish I didn't know this had happened.* But I couldn't say that.

"He s—s—s—said I should m—m—m—meet him at Salem W—W—Willows to talk to—n—n—night, but that it would be the l—l—l—last time."

I brought my hand slowly down onto Emma's back, trying to soothe her. She shuddered at my touch, lifted herself onto her elbows, and stared at me.

My friend's face was puffy and red from weeping. Her pale, almost invisible eyebrows and eyelashes made her look fragile and vulnerable even when everything was fine, and now, when everything had fallen apart, she looked as desperate and tender as a snail pulled out of its shell. Emma's eyes were so bloodshot, they seemed to have changed color, from pale oyster shell to dark red.

I started to say something, but as Emma's eyes bored into me with the full force of her pain and despair, my long-simmering migraine bloomed into being. I felt the dull corkscrew of pain that had been lingering behind my forehead all day twist into my brain. I gasped from the suddenness of it. The pain split my skull in two between my eyebrows. Inside my brain, the pain radiated out in branches, reaching to the back of my eyes, the roots of my tongue, even the roots of my hair.

Emma's eyes flared redder, and my awareness of her room fell away, the dusty dolls with their glassy eyes receded; the twin bed and the Powerpuff Girls pillow drifted away behind a red mist of pain. All I knew were Emma's weeping, angry eyes and the flames of pain filling my skull, wrapping around my head like a halo of fire. I don't know how long it lasted. It felt like forever. My eyes rolled into the back of my head, and with a scream of anguish Emma flung herself facedown on her bed, wracked with sobs.

I must have passed out, but only for a second, because the next thing I was aware of was the *thwack* of my face against the floor. I opened my eyes with a groan to see the edge of the dust ruffle on Emma's twin bed and Emma's foot sticking off the bed right over my head. Next I became aware of someone—Emma—weeping, and another sound. A sound of groaning, but I couldn't tell where it was coming from. When I closed my mouth, the groaning changed timbre. I realized that the groaning was pouring out of me. I sat up, slowly, my thumb pressed between my eyes, my breath ragged from pain.

Emma wept, her whole body shaking with sobs. She didn't even know I was there.

"Emma," I said. The word came out like a pebble in my mouth. I crawled, first one hand, then another, knees sliding across the carpet from the floor onto her bed. She didn't look up.

320

"Emma," I repeated, reaching for her.

She gulped for air, sobbing, her face rooting in the pillow.

"Time." The word was impossible to make, like trying to tie a cherry stem in a knot with my tongue. Also it wasn't the word I'd planned to start with.

"You . . . are . . . time . . . what?" I fumbled, the words tangling together around my teeth.

Emma peeked over her arm, a frightened pale eye staring at me.

I frowned, and tried again.

"Him . . . meeting," I managed to say. Barely.

"What did you say?" Emma asked from inside her pillow, her unnerving pale eye watching.

"Tad," I struggled to say. "Tonight?" I scowled with effort, trying to put the words in the right order in my head. Then I spat out in a rush, "Willows Salem at him meeting you're time what?"

Something was very, very wrong. I sounded like a rewound tape.

Emma lifted her head fully and stared at me.

"How did you know it was Tad?" she asked in a tiny voice, not noticing that something was wrong. With me. Something was desperately wrong. Emma was so deep in her pain that it radiated out, it filled the room, taking over everything, taking over me, forcing its way into my body and rearranging my brain. Like a . . .

As I stared at her, gaping, certainty hit me.

No one was faking.

It was Emma.

It had been Emma the whole time.

Part 5

MID-MARCH

QUINQUATRIA

Aristotle said to Alexander,
that a mind well furnished was more beautiful
than a body richly arrayed.
What can be more odious to man,
and offensive to God, than ignorance.

REGINALD SCOTT
A DISCOVERIE OF WITCHCRAFT, 1654

CHAPTER 23

DANVERS, MASSACHUSETTS
MONDAY, MARCH 12, 2012

W hat do you mean, it's been Emma this whole time?" the
woman from the Massachusetts Department of Public
Health asked me, putting down her pen.

"Don't you see?" I was getting agitated. "Of course it's been her!"

"Colleen," the woman said in her most let's-be-reasonable-now
voice. "You're not making any sense."

"I don't care that it doesn't make sense. It's not my job to make
sense! I'm telling you, it's her. It's Emma. Causing it. She is," I insisted.

"All right. Let's think this through. How exactly would you say
she's been doing . . . whatever it is you think she's been doing?"

"What do you mean, how?" My hands worked over my kneecaps,
digging my nails into my shins.

"What's the mechanism? How does it work? The causality, Colleen. The vector for the disease. What is it?" The woman eyed me
carefully, waiting.

I didn't think she was messing with me, because her face looked
reasonably plain and serious, but honestly, wasn't she supposed to be
the expert? Weren't weird diseases, like, her specialty?

"How should I know what the vector is? All I know is, it's totally got to be her. Just look at what's happened."

"But I thought you just said that all the girls were faking. You were to the point of challenging Anjali about it. You were going to tell your parents. Isn't that what you think happened?"

The woman, one of the two people in white windbreakers standing around doing nothing while Bethany Witherspoon was publicity-whoring it up all over school, hadn't picked up her pen. She'd looked really interested when I'd banged on the van door an hour ago. And she'd been really, really interested when some of my words came out in the wrong order at first. I got a handle on it, though. It wasn't that bad. My head still ached, but the words were basically back to normal.

That's how I knew for sure.

I'd stood up, woozy like I was drunk, and stumbled out of Emma's room. She didn't try to stop me, she just said, "Colleen?" like she was confused, waking up from a trance. Almost like she hadn't understood that I was there, behind her own pain. I stumbled down the stairs, clutching the handrail for support. The pain lessened with each step I took farther away from Emma. Her mom was nowhere to be found.

"Colleen?" Emma called down the stairs, her voice on the edge of panic. "What's wrong?"

I couldn't say anything. I was afraid to talk.

"Later!" I called up to her. "Sorry."

If I said only one word, it couldn't come out backward.

I half ran, half shambled toward school. I had my phone, and I texted Spence. I was relieved to see that I could text in the right order.

Weird stuff happening . . . Can you come? At St. Js.

A minute later my phone vibrated with his response. I'd been clutching it in my hand, waiting. My palms were sweating.

Coming.

That one word was enough. When I got back to campus, I marched up to the Department of Public Health Mobile Unit van and banged until someone opened the door.

But this conversation wasn't going as I'd planned.

"Yeah, that's what I thought happened. I was doing my research project on *The Crucible,* and I found out that Ann Putnam said all the girls were faking. It just seemed so obvious once I saw it spelled out like that. I didn't know why nobody had figured that out sooner. But I was afraid of getting them all in trouble, so . . . But they're not faking! *I'm* not faking! I was looking right at Emma, and it was like something came out of her and went into me and it made me talk backward!"

I was getting shrill, and she'd stopped listening. Never get shrill, that's what my mother tells me. People stop listening to women the minute they get shrill. I took a deep breath, trying to calm myself down. I had to make her understand.

The Public Health woman looked at me with what she probably thought was a kindly expression.

"Colleen," she said gently. "I don't think you're faking. And I can see how upset this is making you. Have you ever heard of a logical principle called Occam's Razor?"

"What?" I squealed.

Okay, still shrill. Keep it together, Rowley. You will not get anywhere by punching a Public Health official in the face.

"No. I don't think so," I said, pretending to be calm. "It's what?"

"Occam's Razor," she lectured, "basically says that the simplest explanation to a problem is the one most likely to be true."

"Okay," I said. "So what?"

"Do you think the suggestion that your friend Emma Blackburn is somehow responsible for the widespread incidence of serious symptoms among fifty-five teenage girls, using a power that is inexplicable, invisible, and heretofore never documented, is the simplest explanation for the Mystery Illness?"

"Um."

"Is it?" she pressed.

"No," I said, glowering. "I guess not."

Okay. She was right. When she put it like that, it sounded crazy. But just because it sounded crazy didn't mean I wasn't right. Did it?

"Okay," the health department woman said. "Now, what would be a simpler explanation?"

"Probably what I thought before, that everyone's faking," I admitted. "Except that can't be right, because it happened to me, and *I am not faking.*"

She looked at me with real-seeming sympathy and squeezed my upper arm. Like she had learned "comforting a hysterical teenager" techniques at a weekend seminar and was just waiting for a chance to try them out.

"I know you're not," she said with gravity. "So if that's not the simplest solution, let's think of some other, simpler ones."

"Tricoethylene pollution," I suggested. "You think Bethany Witherspoon could be right?"

"Well, let's look at that. The parents are pretty persuaded, and you can't blame them, because if there were just one cause, then the solution would be pretty easy. And it would be nice to think there was one easy solution for these girls. So we have an unfortunate spill more than forty years ago, a few miles away from this school, of a chemical with unconfirmed physical effects on those exposed, and symptoms only just appearing in a cluster now. What do you think Occam would say about that?"

"It sounds far-fetched, actually." I frowned.

"It does, doesn't it."

"So, what then? Why can't it be Emma? I'm telling you, I know what happened to me. *It happened.* It happened *like I said.*" I beat my fist on the armrest of the van seat with a pathetic thump.

The health department woman gazed at me. "Colleen. What grade are you in?"

"What difference does that make? Senior." Shrill, Rowley. Come on.

"And what grade were the first group of girls to get sick? They were seniors, too, weren't they?"

"Everyone knows that! So what?" My fingers plucked at my skirt.

"St. Joan's is a pretty competitive school, isn't it?"

"Of course it is!" I shouted.

I couldn't believe she was wasting my time with stupid rhetorical questions when Emma obviously needed help. I didn't know what kind of help, but wasn't that Public Health Lady's job? How could she ignore what was right in front of her?

"And the first girls to get sick, would you say they were popular? Spazzes? Dorks? Jocks?" she pressed.

What was this, some eighties teen movie? Who said *spazzes*?

"They're popular. Everyone likes them. Looks up to them, I mean. You already know that, too."

"Okay. So, a group of girls in the most high-pressure year"—she ticked each point off on a finger—"of a super-high-pressure school career, and they're in the highest-pressure social position. Right? What do you think Occam would say about their situation? About *your* situation?"

"What do I care what Occam would say?" I protested.

As I watched her face, I knew with a sinking certainty what she was suggesting. She just didn't want to come right out and say it.

"You think we're crazy," I whispered, searching her eyes for confirmation.

"No, no. Crazy is not a useful category in this instance." She glanced away from me, and I knew I was right.

"What the hell is that supposed to mean? Admit it. You think we're all completely crazy."

"There's a condition," she said, keeping her voice calm and gentle, just like they'd probably told her to do in the seminar. "It's real, okay? It's a real illness. Nobody thinks you and your friends are faking. Everyone believes you are really suffering the symptoms you're suffering from, okay?"

"What condition?" I asked, waiting to hear some PR doublespeak. I glared at her, suspicious. For one thing, I knew I wasn't crazy. I certainly didn't think Clara was crazy. Some of the others, maybe. Anjali was definitely wound pretty tight.

But I. Was not. Crazy.

"It's called conversion disorder," said Public Health Lady.

"Conversion disorder? What do you mean, like, religious conversion?" My eyebrows knitted together over my nose so hard, it hurt.

Through the tinted van windows I saw the two sets of protesters still camped out in the school parking lot. The Whores of Satan people shouted at the Congregationalists, trying to provoke them. The Congregationalists pointed to their signs that said RESPECT and TOLERANCE and DON'T FORGET THE LESSONS OF THE PAST and smiled beatifically. One of them strummed a guitar to lead a sing-along of "He's Got the Whole World in His Hands." In the great spiritual face-off in the St. Joan's parking lot, I had a pretty good idea who was winning.

Was Public Health Lady trying to tell me I was in the grip of religious mania? I reflected that my parents would be pretty surprised, given how much I complained about going through confirmation a million years ago.

"It sounds like that," she said. "But it's actually something very different."

"So what is it, then?"

"Conversion disorder," she explained, "happens when you are experiencing really serious, really unusual stress in your life. And your body doesn't know how to handle being under so much stress, so it 'converts' it"—here she did the finger air quotes thing on either side of her head—"into physical symptoms."

I gave her a dubious look. It sounded fake. It sounded like a polite way of saying they didn't actually understand what was happening.

"I think that's a crock," I announced, and from the rapid blinking

I got in response, I could tell she wasn't exactly prepared for me to be that hostile. "That sounds like as much of a nonexplanation as PANDAS, which doesn't even exist. It sounds like a trumped-up way of saying we're crazy, and you don't really understand why. Like we can't help how pathetic we are, but we just can't hack it."

"I can see why you'd feel judged, with a diagnosis like that," said Public Health Lady, leaning over to pat me on the knee. "But I assure you, this is real. The symptoms of converted stress can vary widely and be extremely debilitating. Verbal tics, hair falling out, muscle weakness, fatigue. It's a real disorder. It can devastate otherwise perfectly normal, healthy people."

"That doesn't make any sense at all," I insisted. "I'm not that stressed out. And even if I were, how would that make me talk backward? How would it make my friend vomit pins?"

"Oh, really. You're not?" she said mildly. "A high-pressure school environment. College admissions on the horizon. Graduation, lots of life changes. Sexuality, dating. Your friends falling sick all around you. A media firestorm. And aren't you in contention for valedictorian, and on the brink of missing it? I'd say you're under quite a lot of stress, wouldn't you?"

"Who told you that?" I shouted, struggling to my feet, nearly hitting my head on the roof of the van. "Who told you I was missing it by a tenth?"

"It doesn't matter," Public Health Lady said reasonably. "The point is, I think you're being too hard on yourself, Colleen. Conversion disorder is nothing to be ashamed of. And it's relatively easy to treat."

"Oh, yeah? If it's so easy, how come nobody's treating it?" I stood with my neck bent over, hands pressed to the van roof.

"We've only just settled on the diagnosis this afternoon. We wanted to run some tests first to rule out tricoethylene poisoning so that the parents would trust our opinion. People haven't been willing to hear us out just yet. But we're working on sending Bethany

Witherspoon and her 'team'"—again with the air quotes—"back where they came from. Then we can start to make some real progress. I've already had a meeting with the board of trustees. We're confident that this is the correct diagnosis. And the solution is a special kind of talk therapy, and in some cases, antidepressants. Cognitive behavioral therapy. Which is just a fancy way of learning to observe and modify your own behavior. It's easy, and you don't even have to lie on a couch. You'll see, Colleen. In a few months this will all be over."

My certainty wavered. She sounded so sure of herself. If conversion disorder was real, then it wasn't our fault. Who's to say we couldn't be crazy and not know it? Maybe that was all being crazy was—not knowing we were crazy.

But deep inside me, where I stored all the secret truths that I didn't like to admit even to myself, where I kept my competition with my friends and my feelings about my body and the things I wanted to do to Spence and the things I dreamt of saying to my parents when I was angry at them and the arm-twisting I sometimes wanted to give Michael and Wheez, when I looked inside that secret box and tried to tell myself that Public Health Lady was right, and I'd just lost my grip along with everyone else, when I opened the lid and peered inside that secret box, I saw Emma's weirdly red, glowing eyes staring back at me.

I picked up my bag and flattened my mouth into a stern line.

"You're forgetting one thing," I said to her.

"Oh? What's that?" Public Health Lady said to me.

"Look at where we are," I replied.

"What do you mean?" she asked. "St. Joan's? It was a convent."

"No," I said. "Look at what town we're in."

"Danvers?" The Public Health Lady looked perturbed, like maybe I was more off my rocker than she thought.

"Exactly," I said, sliding open the van door and stepping out into the damp spring afternoon.

"What's so special about Danvers?" she asked, sticking her head out the van door after me.

I turned and gave her a withering look. "You don't know?"

"No," she said.

"Danvers," I said, "changed its name in 1752. From Salem Village."

INTERLUDE

SALEM VILLAGE, MASSACHUSETTS
MAY 30, 1706

*Y*ou think Mr. Parris forced Tituba to confess," Reverend
Green says, clearly doubting me.

I shrug, looking down at my hands. "I know he'd been
gravely vexed. In want of money. He felt there were forces aligned
against him in the village. And it was true."

Reverend Green runs a hand through his hair, and it falls hand-
somely over his eye. He knew what sort of contentious community he
took over, at least I think he did. But the proof is stark.

The smell of supper comes drifting under the door, and my mouth
waters. My hearth at home is cold, unless my sister's kept it going. I
banked the cinders before I left. It'll be cold salted meat for our supper tonight, and some forage, and maybe pone I baked yesterday. The
table's been thin since my parents died.

"If she, a confessed witch, named the others, then he'd have a
means to prosecute them. He'd have proof," I insist.

Reverend Green eyes me warily. He sees that the adults had taken
over our game. But he also sees that we did nothing to take it back.

334

A week and some passes, with the village talking of nothing but who the other six witches might be. Visitors come streaming into town, some who'd lived here and moved away, like our old minister Mr. Lawson, and some who venture in from nearby towns hoping to catch a glimpse of us girls. Wherever I walk now, I feel eyes follow me. The attention makes me squirm, but it enthralls me, too. Abby flowers under so many watching eyes. Betty Parris gets smaller and paler, but Betty Hubbard's gotten more beautiful.

Tittibe has confirmed our accusations of Sarah Good and Sarah Osburn, and they've been locked away at Boston jail. Some of us thought that with the witches removed from the village, our torments would lessen. But Abby and Betty Parris and Betty Hubbard and I continue to be vexed by invisible shapes in the night. Even Mercy Lewis, who's been bound out to my parents in service, fell down screaming one morning near the fire. If anything, once the known witches were taken away, our torments worsened.

"The Devil knows we've found him out," my father muses one evening, on March 19 or thereabouts. My mother is on her feet, pacing. "He must advance his game if he's to keep ahold of the village. I hope Mr. Parris is prepared."

"Oh," my mother cries, wringing her hands. "But I can't stand it. Thomas, I can't. Two from Boston, Tittibe said. All right. And then the three we know. But that leaves four. Four, here among us! I can't stand to think. I can barely look anyone in the face for fear of seeing the Devil."

"It goes far to explain the envy, doesn't it," my father muses.

He's moneyed. My mother's clothes are well made and new. It's a sin to be proud, she tells us over and over, but when Mrs. Parris inquires after her hood and topknot, I see my mother's cheeks grow pink with pleasure. She talked once, and with covetous wonder, of a woman she met at Boston who wore pearls in her ears. That image haunts me still. I think sometimes of the holes in Tittibe's earlobes and wonder if everyone on the Barbadoes wore pearls, too.

"Oh, but it would. God has blessed us, and yet we're made to feel we should be ashamed of His favor. I try to pity them, I do, but it's hard."

"There's no shortage of pride in the village," my father growls. "You're right about that. Annie?" He holds his mug out for me to fill.

"Let Mercy do it," I complain, my head bent over my dinner.

"I asked you," he says with a chill in his voice. "Mercy's busy already."

Grumbling, I get up and take the mug to the hearth. Mercy sticks her tongue out at me, and kicks my shin in passing.

"Oh, but you're right," my mother says. She's been bouncing one of my sisters on her knee, and now sets her down to toddle away. "That Lady Martha, for one."

"What, Goodman Corey's wife?"

"The same."

"He's a rough one. You'd never know it now, but years ago . . ."

"Thomas. The children."

"Oh, I think they deserve to know. Mercy, did you know Goodman Corey once beat one of his servants to death?"

Our servant Mercy Lewis doesn't look at my father while she clears his plate.

"I did, sir," she says, in a low voice.

"He was fined. Undue force. But even so. And his wife, well."

"Didn't she pass hard words at Annie at meeting last year? She did, didn't she?" my mother asks me when I reappear with my father's ale.

"Yes, Mama," I say. "I cut in front of her, and she boxed my ears. Called me a vile imp."

Mercy Lewis laughs through her nose, but a look from my mother silences her.

"And she's always reading in strange books," my mother continues. "I've no use for women who read."

"It can start you down a wrong path, sure," my father says into his drink.

My mother is ruminating, a fingernail between her teeth.

"Why, Thomas," she says, staring hard at a memory and laying a hand on my father's sleeve. "I don't know why I didn't see it."

"What?" my father asks, lowering his mug.

"Last year. The children's boils. Remember?"

"Boils?"

It's true. Last year sometime I grew a hideous boil on my neck. The doctor had to lance it, and we were afraid it would fester. My brothers got them also. Mercy said it came from want of washing, that folks got them at the Eastward all the time. At the time, that's what my mother thought, too.

"Ann. Are you certain?" my father asks my mother.

"Why, nearly so."

"We should ask the doctor if he remembers. Annie, fetch Betty Hubbard down from the loft. We're going to speak to her uncle."

Within an hour my mother, my father, Betty Hubbard, and I have arrived at Ingersoll's Ordinary down the street, where the doctor's been staying, within sight of the parsonage. The tavern's a busy place all hours, and that late afternoon's no different. We enter a hall packed with people gathered around tables or sitting on benches against the wall, many of them strangers, all of them there to gossip and stare. We find Dr. Griggs at his supper, and he wipes his lips and bids my parents sit. They lean close together while Betty Hubbard and I drift off to the side to be nearer the fire.

"There's Mr. Lawson," Betty Hubbard whispers, pointing at our former minister.

"I heard he's to preach on Sunday," I whisper back. "That Reverend Parris's too distracted with Betty and them."

"No small wonder," Betty Hubbard says. "If Satan were trying to tear down my ministry, why, I'd be distracted, too."

Betty Hubbard, it seems to me, has forgotten how our ailments began. When she talks, I hear the force of conviction in her words.

I know that she believes the adults. She believes them so fully that I almost believe them, too.

The door opens, and another girl about our age appears, her face looking pale and pinched.

"Who's that?" Betty pokes me.

"Oh! It's Mary Walcott," I say.

Betty frowns, confused.

"You know Mary Walcott. Her father's a captain?" I prod her.

Betty peers at Mary, squinting to remember her, but before she's left the doorway, Mary opens her mouth in a wretched scream. Betty and I jump, clutching each other, and the room plunges to instant silence as everyone turns to stare.

"My wrist!" she wails. "My wrist! It burns!"

Some women hurry to her, clucking and soothing. One of them brings a candle. They pull her sleeve up, and underneath they find a perfect red semicircle of teeth marks, oozing blood. A crimson drop falls on the floor of the tavern.

"God in heaven, her, too!" someone cries, and Reverend Lawson leaps to his feet, rushing to Mary Walcott's aid.

"Did you see whose shape did it?" Betty Hubbard asks me, her fingers digging into my upper arm.

"What?" I sputter. The room is roiling in confusion, people shoving past us to get a look at Mary's wound.

"Why, it looks just like yours, Annie!" Betty Hubbard cries, and before I can say anything, my parents and Dr. Griggs have appeared from the throng, taking my arm.

"I was right," my mother whispers to me. "Those boils came right after Goody Corey boxed your ears last year. And now her shape's gone out to bite poor Mary Walcott, as she did you!"

"But Mama," I start to protest.

"We're going to the parsonage," my father informs us. "We've got to let Reverend Parris know Martha Corey's one of the nine."

A half dozen people flow out into the street with us, Martha

Corey's name on all their lips. Her grandness, her elderly but violent husband, her books. Reverend Lawson's among our number, with Mary Walcott tucked under his arm in tears, holding her wrist, blood oozing between her fingers. In a trice we're at the parsonage, banging on the door, and Mrs. Parris opens it, her face already white with tension. Screams pour from inside.

Our mob crowds into the hall, and when we behold the scene unfolding inside, we flatten ourselves against the walls in terror.

There's Abigail Williams, lit horribly from below by the flames in the hearth, her body twisted into fits. She's hurrying with violence to and fro across the room like a trapped animal. Lieutenant Ingersoll steps forward and tries to catch her, but Abby stretches up her arms and flies out of his grasp.

"*Whish! Whish! Whish!*" she cries at the top of her lungs. She flaps her arms like a bird, caroming around the room with her hair streaming behind her. All at once she stops short.

"Oh, no," Abby moans in horror, staring at an empty space on the floor.

"Who is it?" someone from our mob calls out. "Is it Goody Corey?"

"Goody Nurse!" Abby screams, pointing a shaking finger at nothing.

"Where?" someone else cries.

"Do you not see her? Why, there she stands!" Abby trembles.

We're shocked. Rebecca Nurse is of very good name. I've never heard aught said against her, and I've heard things said about most everyone.

Abby shakes her head in a panic, holding up her hands as if to fend something off.

"No!" she screams. "I won't, I won't, I won't take it!"

"Take what, girl?" Reverend Lawson beseeches Abby. "What's Goody Nurse giving you?"

"A book, a book." Abby squenches her eyes closed tight and shakes her head.

"What book?" Reverend Lawson presses her.

"I don't know, I don't know what book it is. I'm sure it's none of God's book, it's the Devil's book for aught I know!"

Abby breaks away from invisible hands, running in circles as though she were going to go up the chimney. Then, eyes alight as with a fever, she falls to her knees at the hearth, thrusts her hands into the fire, and pulls firebrands from within, shrieking and cackling, the sparks falling around her like rain.

CHAPTER 24

The reporters once again stalked the upper school entrance, though half of them were following Bethany Witherspoon across the field hockey field, looking for the rumored glowing toxic waste. I reached the outer edge of the wall of reporters and started elbowing my way to the door.

"Excuse me," I muttered, shoving aside someone in an ill-fitting pantsuit.

A light snapped on and beamed into my eyes.

"Young lady!" some guy hollered close to my ear. "What do you think of Bethany Witherspoon? Are you excited she's here?"

"Excited?" I said. "No."

Microphones surged toward my mouth.

"Don't you think she'll finally get the attention from the world that the Mystery Illness deserves?" someone else shouted.

"I'm not convinced it deserves any more attention. Excuse me," I said, keeping my eyes down.

"Miss! Miss! Are you friends with any of the afflicted girls?" cried one voice.

"Do you think the church should try an exorcism? Could the illness be spiritual in nature?" bellowed another.

"Would you go away? Jesus!" I put my hand over the CNN guy's camera lens and gave it a solid push. Then all at once I was through the doors and safe in the deserted upper school hallway. I paused, realizing I had been holding my breath.

The pain in my head was loosening. It wasn't totally gone, but the corkscrew felt like it had twisted out partway. And when I yelled at the news guy, my words came out in the right order.

I set my jaw and hurried to Ms. Slater's room.

Fifth period dragged on for five more minutes, and I had to wait while she finished with her freshmen. I peered through the pebbled glass of the classroom door, seeing the blurred outline of my substitute history teacher pointing to something written on the chalkboard. The classroom was less than half full.

My mind roamed to Mr. Mitchell.

Tad.

Tad and Emma. How did that even happen? I couldn't get my head around it. Who started it? Was it just a matter of stolen glances over pop quizzes? Did a hand one day brush against another hand?

Did she really love him?

Did he love her?

I pictured Mr. Mitchell tipping Emma's face up by her chin and bringing his mouth to hers, them leaning into each other. I thought about their mingled shadows in the alley behind the coffee shop. Maybe I was naïve. I mean, I knew I was. I wondered if her parents knew. I wondered if that was the real reason they'd been keeping her home.

The bell rang, and a dribble of freshman girls filed out of the history classroom, their heads hanging, whispering among themselves. A couple of them glanced at me and quickly looked away. God, there were only like eight of them.

"Colleen?" Ms. Slater called, spotting me loitering outside the door. "Are you waiting to talk to me? Is everything okay?"

I looked over my shoulder, nervous, and hurried in, closing the door behind me.

"No," I said. "No, it's not. I have to talk to you."

It took only a couple of minutes to tell her what had happened with Emma. I watched Ms. Slater's face as I talked. Ms. Slater was an outsider, and she was smart. She had that weird academic vibe that for some reason made me trust her. She'd understand. Maybe she even suspected it herself, but couldn't prove it.

Instead she sat down, heavily, behind Mr. Mitchell's abandoned desk.

"Um," she said. She brought a hand to her forehead.

"It's Emma, right?" I said, leaning my hands on the desk. "It has to be. Maybe she doesn't even know she's doing it. But it's got to be her, right?"

"That's . . ." Ms. Slater trailed off. She blinked once, twice. Then she leveled her gaze at me. "That's not what I expected you to tell me. At all."

"But you must have thought something like that. Why else would you have pushed me to work on Ann Putnam for my extra credit?" My voice sounded fragile.

"Honestly? Because I thought you needed extra credit." She rubbed her forehead with a wary eye on me.

"Oh, come on!" I picked up a piece of chalk from her desk and chucked it across the room.

"What do you want me to say, Colleen?" Ms. Slater got to her feet and stalked over to the lectern at the front of the classroom, gripping it with white knuckles and leaning her head down between her arms.

"But Ms. Slater," I started to protest.

"Christ, Colleen. I thought you'd figure out that they were all faking. Okay? That's what I thought was going on." Ms. Slater's voice rose. "I thought for sure you'd see it, too. I thought you'd learn about Ann Putnam's apology, and you'd figure out that all the girls were doing this for attention and to get out of working, just like they did in 1692, in this same goddamn town. Frankly, I thought you were smart enough and popular enough and had been at the school long enough and knew the girls well enough to get the administration to listen to you. I thought the only way to get this under control would be if an insider, like you, made an objection. And then this ridiculous outbreak would come to an end without anyone else getting fired, or sued, or sick, or any of that crap. That's what I thought, okay? That's why I steered you to look at Ann Putnam. That's why I pushed you, and pushed you, and sent you text messages to keep after you about it. Okay?" Her voice broke, and her fist rammed down onto the lectern.

"But I'm just a kid!" I protested, my voice rising. "Nobody's going to listen to me! You're a teacher! If you thought they were faking from the beginning, why didn't you say something? Why didn't you go to the board of trustees? Or the media?"

"Oh, yeah," she said with a bitterness that shocked me. "Sure. That'll fly. 'Hey, rich and powerful private school board of trustees, I'm an unemployed adjunct professor with thirty thousand dollars of credit card debt and six figures of student loans who's taken a substitute high school job 'cause I'm desperate, and guess what? I think all your daughters are full of it.' Yeah. That would totally have worked."

"But . . ." I didn't know what to say. It never occurred to me that they wouldn't have respected her.

"'Hey, I'm the sub who's been hired at the last minute with no secondary teaching experience because your last history teacher was basically a statutory rapist, and guess what? I have some negative opinions about how your school is run.'" She threw her hands up in the air in hopeless rage.

"Why would they all get better when they were on television in

New York, then?" I demanded. "You saw them. Clara wasn't stuttering at all. It's like the farther away from Emma they got, the better they were. Like me today."

"Oh, hell, I don't know," she sighed. "Maybe it's site-specific. Maybe it's being here, in this context, among their classmates and parents and everything. How should I know? But it doesn't prove Emma's responsible. Only that it's only a problem while they're here."

"But Ms. Slater," I said, fear making the words come out shaky and wet. "I'm not faking. It really happened. It happened to me, too."

She looked up at me with tired eyes, and I realized that Ms. Slater was probably not all that much older than me. I was fooled by the glasses and the serious dresses and the kitten heels. But right then she looked like an overwhelmed girl wearing a woman costume, as afraid as I was.

"I know it did, Colleen. I believe you. And I couldn't be sorrier for you, I really couldn't. But I've already talked to the Department of Public Health people."

"You did?" My certainty crumbled.

She wasn't going to believe me.

"Yes. Have you heard what they think?" She eyed me carefully, as though she were nervous that I was going to freak out.

"Yes," I whispered.

I lowered myself into one of the desks near the front of the classroom.

"It happens, sometimes. This conversion disorder stuff. I checked." Her words sounded gentle. Not judgmental, like the Public Health Lady's.

"It sounds made up." I couldn't meet her eyes.

"It's not. It actually happens pretty frequently, and all over the world. Most commonly to adolescent girls. Girls who are under intense amounts of pressure and stress."

There was that word again. *Stress.*

"But why would it happen to so many of us? If it's just that we're all so stressed out and our bodies can't take it, why would it look so much like a disease?"

"Speaking frankly? Mental illness can sometimes spread among people like that. It's weird, but it happens. *Folie a deux* is one term for it. But there's another that we don't use as much anymore."

I stared at her with horror. "You think I'm hysterical. You actually think I have hysteria. What is this, 1896?"

"No, Colleen," Ms. Slater said, leaning an elbow on the lectern and her cheek on her fist. "I think you guys are all just really, really stressed out. And I think the school has done a terrible job of helping you. That's all. I think as soon as we can get rid of these reporters and this Bethany Witherspoon person, and once everybody gets their college choices squared away, and spring finally comes and you realize that high school is about to be behind you forever, and only getting further away the longer you live, this will all become a weird, distant memory. Then one day, it will be a funny anecdote. And then eventually, it'll feel like it happened to someone else. Someone you used to know."

I rested my head in my hands. I trusted her. I trusted Ms. Slater more than the Public Health woman. Maybe they knew better. I wavered, torn between what they were telling me and what I was telling myself.

I rose to my feet, bringing my bag to my shoulder.

"All right," I said, doing my best to make my face look resigned.

She watched me, to see if it was sinking in.

"I'm sorry," she said. "I should have trusted you more. Pulled you aside at the beginning and told you my doubts about Clara. But they're quick to fire people around here, as you've probably noticed. And I'm totally new here. I need to pay my rent like everyone else."

I realized I was disappointed in Ms. Slater. I wanted her to be better than that.

"It's okay. I understand," I said. "I would've done the same thing, probably. But there's one thing I'd really like someone to explain to me."

"Anything," Ms. Slater said.

I gave her my steeliest stare.

"How is hysteria making Anjali vomit actual pins?"

Ms. Slater's mouth opened to object, but no words came out. I frowned at her, but I didn't wait for a response. While I was talking, my phone had vibrated with an incoming text. Spence was waiting.

"You know, it's pretty weird to go to boarding school only a forty-minute drive from your parents' house," I remarked as I slid in next to him.

"Colleen!" he breathed, pulling me to his chest, his fingers in my curls, and knocking me into the steering wheel as he did so. "I was worried."

"Ow," I muttered into his shirt.

"What's going on? Are you okay? What happened?" Spence pulled away just far enough to look into my eyes and smooth a curl off my forehead, touching my face with his fingertips as though to make sure I were really there, and safe.

"I'm okay," I whispered.

His fingertips brushed down my cheek, lingering at the corner of my mouth, and his eyes searched into mine for a long minute. I swallowed.

"Colleen," he started to say, but before he could get anything else out, I took his face in my own hands and pulled his mouth to mine.

He resisted for a second—surprised, I guess—but then his resistance fell away and he kissed back, hungrily. He moved a hand to the small of my back and the other threaded into my hair. He leaned into me, pulling me to him, my knee knocking into the gearshift, and my hands moved to his waist, fumbling under his shirt until they found his skin.

He tasted perfect.

Salty and sweet and male and perfect.

It took real effort on my part to remember that we were sitting in an illegally parked car in my high school parking lot, the self-same parking lot that had been taken over by dueling protesters and a good percentage of the national news media. Shouts from a protester erupted from the steps of the school, and a guy with a camera on his shoulder jogged past the car, followed by a reporter in an overcoat. I broke away from Spence, smiling. I wiped my lips with the back of my wrist.

"Thanks for picking me up," I said.

Spence looked short of breath, and his eyes were blinking rapidly. "I had to skip basketball. What's going on?"

"I'll tell you on the way."

"Okay." He fumbled to start the car, collecting himself. "Where are we going?"

"Anjali's house."

"Anjali's house," he repeated. "I'm AWOL, just so you know. If I'm not back for check-in at ten, I'm getting written up."

"Okay," I said.

"I'm serious. Two more write-ups and I get suspended."

"Okay, okay."

Anjali lived in a sprawling mansion in Pride's Crossing, which looked kind of out of place in New England because it was made of stucco and had these Spanish tiles on the roof and, like, a five-car garage. I always forgot how to get there, and had to use the GPS on my phone. We spent fifteen minutes lost in downtown Beverly before I finally got everything squared away and pointed us in the right direction.

While that was happening, Spence tried to come up with a gentle way to tell me that he thought I was losing my mind.

"It's not that I don't believe you," he insisted, turning down a side street for the second time that carried us past a graveyard full of leaning death's head tombstones. I looked away. Sometimes, I'm superstitious.

"You don't," I countered. "I can tell."

"Colleen. Listen. I do. Okay? It's just . . . I don't know. Leaving aside the question of whether it's even possible for a second, why would Emma do that? I thought she got along great with everybody."

"Maybe she can't help it," I said, peering at my GPS. "Turn left."

"Here? Wait, here?"

"No, we missed it."

Spence rolled his eyes and did a quick illegal U-turn.

"Look," he said. "There's no physical way anyone would be able to hurt people that way. Right? And she wouldn't have any reason to do it. So doesn't it make more sense, what the Public Health Department lady said?"

I flung my phone into my lap and stared hard at him.

"You think I'm crazy?"

"That's not what I—"

"Do you? Just say it."

"But—"

"Because if you don't believe me, I'll just get out of the car and you can go back and not get written up. Okay? That's fine with me." I put my hand on the door handle to show him I was serious.

Spence glanced at me, worried. "Come on, Colleen," he said. "That's not what I meant."

"Okay, then."

"It's just, I don't see how that would work. You know?"

"What. Emma?"

"Yes, Emma."

I gazed out the window as Beverly's modest downtown slowly morphed into stately residences, most hidden behind hedges, with gates and keypads and combinations. Stables in the back. Broad, lush lawns, tipped with frost. Lights winking on ahead of the advancing dusk. Pride's Crossing wasn't much like our neighborhood in Danvers, that was for sure.

I caught sight of my own reflection in the passenger-side window, and was startled by how much older I looked. My cheeks had lost their roundness, leaving hollows under the cheekbones. I turned my face away to hide from myself.

"I don't know either. I don't blame you for thinking it sounds crazy. But if there's one thing I do know, it's that hysteria is all in our heads. And hysteria doesn't explain Anjali barfing up actual pins. Does it?"

I stared at him hard in the dark, watching his profile for signs of agreement. Instead, he kept his face carefully neutral. Spence tossed the flop of hair off his forehead and cast a quick look at me before turning his attention back to the road. Instead of answering, he said, "What's her house number again? Sixteen forty-five?" and put on his turn signal.

We crept up Anjali's driveway, this long gravel road that crunched on for a quarter of a mile. She once told me her dad had to pay someone to rake it.

All the windows in the house glowed orange, like a jack-o'-lantern, and I recognized Anjali's mom's Mercedes parked outside.

My breath puffed from my mouth like smoke when I stepped out of Spence's car.

"Should I wait?" he asked. "I've only met her, like, twice." The light from Anjali's windows threw his face half into shadow.

"You're friends with Jason. She probably knows more about you than I do."

A smile flashed across his face, deepening the dimple in his cheek. As he joined me under the front door light, waiting for someone to answer the bell, he whispered, "I frankly doubt that."

Inside we heard laughter and footsteps, and then Anjali's mom opened the door.

"Colleen!" she exclaimed in her gorgeous British accent, sweeping me up in a hug. "My goodness! Come in, come in. But I wish I'd known you were coming, I'd have made more *poori*. Who's this?" She looked Spence up and down with a polite smile.

"Hello, Dr. Gupta, I'm Spencer," Spence said, sticking his hand out like I imagined he'd been doing since he was four years old and dressed in a miniature navy sport coat with brass buttons. "I go to school with Jason."

"Ah! Spencer, yes. Anjali mentioned you," Dr. Gupta said, clasping and releasing his hand with a sidelong look at me under her eyelashes. "Everyone's in the kitchen. Come."

We trailed after her down a long marble hallway, into a kitchen warm and bright with cooking. At the sound of our approach, a guy sitting at the granite breakfast bar turned to look over his shoulder and grinned. Speak of the Devil, and I'll find Jason Rothstein at the breakfast bar with *pani poori* all over his chin.

"Dude!" he said, getting up and clapping Spence on the back in a bro-hug. "Wassup?"

"Colleen!" Anjali squealed, hug-ambushing me from behind.

"Hey, Anj," I said. Everyone seemed so normal. Except for Anjali's raspy voice and the scabs around the corners of her mouth, I'd never know anything was amiss.

"Can you stay for dinner? We totally have enough. We do, don't we, Mom?"

"I'll see," said Dr. Gupta. She sounded doubtful.

"Um," I demurred. "Yeah. That would be great. But Anj, listen. I have to talk to you."

She could see on my face that something was amiss.

"Sure," she said, eyebrows rising in concern. "Come on, let's go in here."

The boys settled at the breakfast bar, bantering about being AWOL from their dorm and whose ass was going to get kicked which way from Sunday, while Anjali led me by the hand into the family room off the kitchen. The lights were off in there. Anjali had one of those houses where they routinely forgot to go in certain rooms for weeks at a time. The family room felt like that. All overstuffed chintz armchairs that no one sat in.

"Anj," I whispered to her.

"What is it, Colleen? God, you look half dead. Have you been sleeping?" Anjali's voice drifted to me through the dimness of the family room. I saw her shape moving in the shadows.

"Look, you're going to think I'm crazy for asking. But the first time your thing happened. With the pins. Were you with Emma?"

"Emma?" she asked, the contours of her face forming a frown in the dark. "Um, maybe. Yes, actually. I'd just been having coffee with her, now that you mention it. I got home, and it happened like ten minutes later. Why?"

My fingers dug into the deep upholstery of a chintz armchair. "I was at her house today," I whispered. "She was really, really upset."

"About Tad," Anjali said, nodding sagely and drifting by the bookcase at the far side of the room. She was pacing—slowly, but pacing. "Yeah, I know."

"You *knew*?"

"God, Colleen. I thought everyone knew."

"I didn't!" I exclaimed, equally stunned and hurt that Emma would have kept something so huge from me. We were best friends, after all. Nominally. I mean, I guessed I could see why Emma would want to talk boys with Anjali instead of me. Anjali had one, to begin with. He was right there in the kitchen, AWOL from his dorm, joking around with her mom. But now I sort of did, too. Didn't I? Mine was in the kitchen, too.

"Yeah, well." Anjali shrugged, not looking at me.

"What's that supposed to mean?"

"Nothing. You've been working really hard. We understand." She said these words easily enough that I could tell she was saying what she was supposed to say. Not the truth. I couldn't see her at all where she stood in the shadow by the bookcase. Anjali's voice whispered to me from nowhere. I doubled over, my hands on my knees, her words forcing the air out of me as surely as if she'd punched me in the stomach.

"But I didn't . . . I don't . . ."

My closest friend couldn't confide in me about the most devastating thing that had ever happened to her. I'd been too wrapped up in myself to see her pain.

"It's pretty intense stuff," Anjali remarked. She stepped back out of the shadows so that I could see the outline of her hair against the kitchen light. "I mean, they had their whole thing, right, which is crazy enough, because, you know, she's basically never had a boyfriend before. Much less one who was a teacher. Then her mom found out, and he up and quit without telling her, and now he won't see her. She's wrecked."

"God. Poor Emma." I felt ill.

"And then you've got college apps on top of everything. He was supposed to be writing her recs, and she says he won't do it now. Says it wouldn't be *right*." She snorted on this last word with derision. "You know he's probably why she didn't get a Harvard interview, right? He went there and everything."

"What a dick." A rush of protective vengeance flooded me, and I trembled, wanting to run to Emma and shield her. But just as quickly, my protectiveness subsided into shame. I hadn't been there for her. Where had I been?

"Yeah," said Anjali, crossing her arms over her chest.

We stared at each other for a long minute in the dark, the kitchen light falling between us. It was warm and friendly in there, full of food and boys and everything good in life. What were we doing here, sitting in the dark?

"Anj," I said. "While I was with her today, something weird happened."

"Like, what weird?"

"She was crying. Bawling. End-of-the-world crying. I don't remember ever having seen her so upset."

"Okay."

"And when she looked up at me . . ." I struggled to find a way to explain the sensation that I'd felt when Emma looked at me. That digging corkscrew pain. Her eyes going red.

"What?" Anjali prodded me.

"It was like . . . there was this spike of pain, in my forehead. Like, imagine the worst pain you've ever experienced, and then make it one level worse. It felt almost like it came from outside me. Like a spike being driven into my brain. It was so intense, I, like, fainted or something, and when I came to, I was talking backward."

"Are you serious?" Anjali stepped nearer to me, dropping her voice to a dead whisper. "Backward?"

"Backward. Totally."

"Do you think you've got the Mystery Illness?"

My eyes shifted left and right, mindful of how insane I'd sound if anyone overheard me. "Yes," I whispered. "And more than that, I think Emma's somehow responsible."

"Oh, come on!" Anjali's voice rose, and I shushed her.

"I don't know how else to explain it," I hissed. "Everyone who's gotten sick got sick right after coming into contact with her. Right? Clara in advisory. The Other Jennifer in bio lab. Elizabeth at field hockey. Those girls at the assembly. You."

"It's a coincidence. What you're talking about, it's not even possible." Anjali brought her face close to mine, and her eyes bored into me, as if she were trying to read my mind.

"Anjali, I felt it happening." I reached out and grasped her arm, desperate for her to believe me. "She was so upset, she almost didn't know I was there. It was like this feeling was coming out of her. It went into me. I couldn't stop it. All I could do was run away. And after I ran away, I started feeling better. Like, immediately."

"You ran away?" Her face contorted in dismay. "She's lying there upset after going through some of the worst crap of her entire life, and you just ran away? What's the matter with you, Colleen? You never used to be like this."

My hand fell from her arm and I stared at Anjali, shocked.

"What do you mean?"

"Look, I know you're all gung ho about valedictorian and everything, and I think we've all been pretty cool about it, but you need to seriously reevaluate your priorities. Emma's your friend. She's really, really upset. Tad has completely messed with her head, and maybe even ruined her life. And now you're trying to blame the whole school getting sick on her? Seriously, what's the matter with you?"

"That's not what I—" I took an involuntary step back, reeling from what Anjali was saying.

"And anyway, my mom talked to the Department of Public Health, like, two days ago. They already know what it is."

"I talked to them, too," I said with rising urgency. "They called it something like conversion disorder. But Anj, that's, like, a reaction to stress. It doesn't explain why you'd be barfing up pins!"

"No," said Dr. Gupta, silhouetted in the doorway from the kitchen. I started, unsure how long she'd been standing there, or what she'd heard me say. She moved over and put an arm around her daughter. "It doesn't. But that's because Anjali doesn't have conversion disorder. She doesn't have the Mystery Illness."

"What do you mean?" I was baffled.

Dr. Gupta looked kindly at Anjali, who glanced with worry up into her mother's eyes.

"Do you want to tell her?" Dr. Gupta asked. "You don't have to if you don't want to."

Anjali swallowed, and looked levelly at me.

"I have pica," she said.

"Pica?" I repeated, looking between her and her mother. "I don't know what that is."

"Pica," Dr. Gupta explained, "is a brain disorder wherein sometimes people eat things that aren't food. Like dirt, or sometimes pins."

I took another wobbly step backward, my hand groping in space for something to hold on to. I felt like I was floating up into the night air, with nothing tethering me to the ground.

"You do?" I asked.

Anjali nodded. "Sometimes," she said, "it's caused by a nutritional deficiency. Like iron. Like your body makes you eat weird stuff because it's missing important nutrients. But your stomach can't always handle it, and so sometimes, things get vomited up."

"You've been eating pins *on purpose*?" My mouth contorted with unconscious distaste. "Since when?"

"Um"—Anjali looked to her mom for confirmation—"I don't know. I don't remember eating pins. But my mom says that's not so unusual, for people with pica not to remember the eating part. Like I've blocked it out."

"The important thing is," Dr. Gupta said, "we know what the problem is. And we know how to treat it. Anjali is going to be just fine. So are all the other girls. And so are you, Colleen."

"I am," I repeated. I couldn't tell if I was asking or agreeing. I wanted to find Spence. I could hear him in the kitchen, letting Jason call him a douche bag.

"Yes." Dr. Gupta came over and put her hands on my shoulders. My muscles were so tight, it felt like my shoulders were right under my ears. "Look at you. You're such a bright girl. You're working so hard. There's no need. I think the thing for you to do is to go home and have a nice, long talk with your parents. They can make an appointment for you with your pediatrician. There's nothing for you to be ashamed of. Conversion disorder is unusual, but it happens, more often than we realize, especially to young women like you. Your parents love you very much, and they only want you to be happy."

I hesitated. Dr. Gupta was famous. She was my friend's mom. She cared about me. And she was telling me I had conversion disorder.

Everyone thought I had conversion disorder but me.

"Okay," I said. I felt dizzy.

"Come." Dr. Gupta threaded an arm through mine and steered me back to the safety of the kitchen. "I think Anjali's right. I think we have enough if you and Spence want to stay for dinner. Do you?"

I caught Spence's eye, and he mouthed *Suspended* and glanced meaningfully at the door.

"Um, thanks," I said. "But I think you're right. I think I should get Spence to take me home. They're probably wondering why I'm not back already."

"All right," Dr. Gupta said, a reassuring hand on my back. "Next time." She started walking back down the marble hallway, and Spence and I fell in step behind her.

Anjali followed us to the front door. She struggled to hide her disappointment in me, but failed.

"Listen," she said flatly. "It's fine, okay? Emma knows you love her."

"I'm worried she doesn't," I said in a low voice.

"Maybe talk to her about it," Anjali suggested. "She'll understand. She's just having a really rough time right now."

I could feel tears welling behind my eyes, in danger of squeezing out. Anjali knew they were there, I could tell, so instead of saying anything else, she drew me into a long hug. Some of her hair got into my mouth, but I didn't care. I hugged her back.

"Let's do something fun this weekend," she whispered in my ear. "And no more crazy Emma talk. Okay?"

I nodded. "Okay."

Spence was already outside, unlocking the car.

"Bye, Spencer," she trilled.

"Bye, Anjali," he said. "Don't let Rothstein give you any trouble."

"Oh, he's going to give me just the exact right amount of trouble," she said, grinning.

I slunk into the passenger seat, staring straight ahead.

"Well?" Spence said, climbing behind the wheel. "Are you convinced?"

Everyone was right. I was mentally ill. I had to be. Right? Occam's Razor. The simplest answer is the one most likely to be true. And the simplest answer was that I had cracked under the stress of my life at St. Joan's. Lost it. Been torn to pieces by my life.

But I didn't feel like I'd lost it. I felt the same as I always did.

"No," I said to Spence with new resolve. "Can you drive me to Salem Willows? I've got to talk to Emma."

INTERLUDE

$\mathcal{T}$he next day was a Sunday," I say. "March 20. Meeting day." Reverend Green is twisting his shirt cuffs in his hands. "So in that time, two more witches were named," he says.

"Martha Corey," I confirm. "And Rebecca Nurse."

"Ah, yes." Reverend Green looks pitying around his eyes. "I've heard tell of Goody Nurse. Her sisters, too."

"Yes," I say, looking down at my hands. "My mother'd complained of Goody Corey for years. Goodman Corey was quarrelsome with my father. And Goody Corey, his third wife, was well born. My mother felt it keenly."

"How did Mary Walcott get a bite on her wrist?" he asks.

"I don't know," I say. "Perhaps she heard about mine. She could have done it herself. She saw how people were treating us, and so she did it. Or perhaps the Devil sent someone's shape to bite her."

A shadow crosses Reverend Green's face. "Is that what you think?" he asks me.

"I don't know," I admit. "I just don't know."

. . .

We file into the meetinghouse on Sunday, as solemn a procession as I ever saw. The aisle parts before us as Abby Williams, Betty Parris, Betty Hubbard, Mercy Lewis, Mary Walcott, and I, joined by my mother and Goody Pope, process in and take our ceremonial seats at the front of the meetinghouse. I can't hear my own thoughts over the whispering. Goody Corey's there with her husband, sitting on one of the benches off to the side, and there's a strange dead space around them, as though no one wants to sit too close. Goody Nurse is absent, which is strange of itself. She never missed a Sunday meeting.

Reverend Parris sits with his wife, deep circles under his eyes, scanning the face of every congregant who comes through the meetinghouse door. Three more witches, still unknown to him, and they must be in the crowd. Old women, young matrons, worthy gentlemen, laborers, youths, children, frown and smile and whisper in each other's ears, all gathered to come hear the word of God, some of them to receive the sacraments, and three of them devils.

The hymn is named and we stand to sing, lifting our voices to the heavens. I close my eyes, letting the music fill me. I think of Tittibe locked in Boston jail with Sarah Good and her sucking babe, and Sarah Osburn, too. I wonder if they're praying to God. I wonder if the Devil is visiting them that very moment and telling them to be quiet, else he cut off their heads.

Or perhaps the Devil is here. The thought makes me shudder, and I open my eyes, surveying the singing faces all around me, eyes lifted to the heavens or on some faces closed in concentration, forming the hymn's words. I think I catch a glimpse of a shadow ducking behind someone's shoulder, and I whimper, clutching for Betty Hubbard's arm.

"Shh, Annie," she soothes me, but I'm beginning to tremble. I want to run away, I want to flee the meetinghouse and run to our barn, where I can hide in the hayloft and no one can find me.

Betty Hubbard grips my hand hard and pulls me down next to her as Reverend Lawson mounts the pulpit with the big Bible, opening it for the reading of the Word. He recites a Psalm, but I'm deaf to it. Everywhere I look, I see people staring at me. As soon as I catch them, they look away. Out of the corners of my eyes I keep seeing faint shapes moving, like mice scuttling in the shadows. My grip on Betty's hand tightens.

Abby Williams is restless, too, in her seat. She doesn't want to be at meeting any more than I do. Not for eight hours, when it's starting to be spring outside. She keeps snuffling and shifting about on the pew, elbowing Betty Parris, scratching at her clothes and rearranging her skirts around her feet. Mary Walcott pokes her in the ribs to keep her quiet. All at once Abby lets out the loudest, rudest sigh I've ever heard. She stands, and stamps her foot.

"Name your text!" she hollers to Reverend Lawson, who is so shocked he can hardly speak.

The congregation gasps, and falls into appalled silence. Nobody has ever challenged a minister like this. No one. And certainly not a little nothing of a servant girl. It's impossible. But it's just happened.

"I beg your pardon, child?" intones the visiting minister, peering down at her from over the pulpit edge.

"Name your text!" she cries again.

He does so, but I can't hear him over the whispering of the congregation. "Did you ever see such impudence? It's the Devil's doing, surely. She's in her fits, so she is."

Abby hears him, though, and rolls her eyes with drama and despair. "Ugh!" she sighs. "It's a long text."

"Sit down, you!" Reverend Parris shouts from his seat next to his wife, and Mary Walcott drags Abby back to her seat. "You'll hear the Reverend's doctrine."

"I know no doctrine he had, and if he did name one, I've forgotten it," Abby grouses, folding her arms over her chest and stamping her foot.

The villagers gathered in the meetinghouse can't contain their shock and interest; conversation starts to rise among them. Reverend Lawson sees he's lost our attention, so he clears his throat, beginning a long and meandering disquisition on the Bible passage he's chosen to elucidate for us today. I can't sift meaning from his words, so thick is the whispering from the villagers around me. All I hear is my own name, and Abby's, and the other girls', and talk of our marks, and the names in the Devil's book, those that have been named and those that haven't.

Across the room Goody Corey gazes steadily upon us, looking down her grand imperious nose, and then she rests her hand on her elderly husband's arm and he inclines his ear to her. I see her mouth moving and she's staring at us, but I can't hear what she says over the whispering. My head is growing light. I'm swaying in my seat, and Betty Hubbard has to wrap her arm about my waist to keep me sitting upright. Abby notices my panic and follows my stare across the buzzing congregation. She spots Goody Corey talking of us to her husband, her fine brows drawn down over her eyes.

"Look!" Abby shouts, interrupting the interminable sermon.

She points into midair at nothing.

"What? Where?" voices around us cry out in baffling, overlapping waves.

"Look where Goody Corey sits on the beam, sucking her yellow bird betwixt her fingers!"

Goody Corey screams aloud and claps her hands over her mouth as the congregation bursts into angry speculation. "Where? There? She's sent her spirit up to sit upon the rafters!"

Everyone sitting near the Coreys edges away as quickly as they can, and the imperious woman looks about her with a rising sense of panic and indignation.

"What? No. I'm here!" she cries, pointing a finger at her chest.

My vision is crowded with whispers and movement and strange shapes narrowing in. I feel my heart thudding in my chest, the sweat flowing freely in my hair, under my arms.

"I . . ." I'm stammering. My breath won't come.

Betty Hubbard looks sharply at me and says, "Annie? Annie, what is it?"

Something inside me breaks. I close my eyes and open my mouth, and a piercing scream tears out of me. The scream relieves the pressure in my head, and it feels so good that I scream again.

"It's there!" I jabber, lurching in my seat. "I see it there! Goody Corey's yellow bird sits on Reverend Lawson's hat! I see it plain as day, the Devil's yellow bird sits on the Reverend's hat!"

Hands are clapped over my mouth and wrap around my waist as I thrash, trying to hold me back, but I will not be held back. My words are loose.

"It's Goody Corey for certain," the village around me is saying. "Goody Corey's one of the nine. Ann Putnam said so. She sees it. Goody Corey's bewitched Ann Putnam!"

CHAPTER 25

SALEM WILLOWS, SALEM, MASSACHUSETTS

MONDAY, MARCH 12, 2012

Almost seven. I didn't remember what time Emma said she was meeting Tad at the Willows, but I knew I'd find her there.

The Salem Willows was a park, kind of. It was an amusement arcade on this peninsula that stuck out in the water between Salem and Beverly Harbors. It had been there since forever, at least the nineteenth century, and it was kind of the place where people went when they wanted to feel comfortable. Guys fished off the pier. Skee-Ball and saltwater taffy and spooky fortune-telling machines that described the man we'd marry for a dime. A carousel with these horses with bared teeth and their eyes rolling back in their heads that played organ music and had brass rings for us to grab as we went whirling by. We'd try to chuck them into a clown mouth, and if we hit it, bulbs lit up and bells went off and everyone got an extra spin. The carousel was from the 1860s and had been worn thin by generations of Salem kids sliding on and off the backs of the horses.

Salem Willows took its name from the willow trees that dotted the lawn, drooping their branches in curtains around the gazebo. They were two hundred years old. When the wind kicked up over the harbor, curling the waves into white ripples and rushing through the willow branches, it sounded like whispering. In the wind we could almost hear the echoes of old ragtime bands, and children laughing, and Nathaniel Hawthorne's scratching pen.

Emma and I loved to go there when we were feeling down. It reminded us of when we were kids, and Emma and I would wrap ourselves in the willow branches, coiling them around our bodies and hanging from them, dangling our feet. My mom would drop us off with five dollars each and come back two hours later to find us both sticky and exhausted, ice cream down the fronts of our shirts, with fistfuls of arcade tickets that we wanted to trade for Pixy Stix and rubber spider rings. Emma's mom didn't really drive, so it was usually mine who ferried us to and from the Willows in our station wagon, the one that was now speckled with rust in our driveway.

Spence and I rolled past the gate, squinting for a parking space. The evening sky was pale over the water, and the arcade lights had come on, fat glass bulbs flashing on the outside, interior lit by dull fluorescent lights. I think it was probably prettier in the nineteenth century.

"You know she's meeting him here?" Spence asked. "You're sure?"

"Yeah," I said. "How come?"

Spence wrinkled his nose. "I don't know. It seems kind of . . . seedy."

I frowned out the window, not answering.

We climbed out of the car, and a breeze from off the water wrapped around me, peeling away my warmth and making me shiver. Spence pulled me to him in an embrace while the wind lifted my hair, tangling my curls into a thicket around my head.

"I can't believe I ran away," I whispered into his chest. "Do you think she'll ever forgive me?"

"Come on," he whispered. "Let's go find her."

The arcade stretched along a sort of midway, with rolling doors open to the outside forming a pavilion, and we peered into the succession of gaming rooms, dodging kids who chased each other around the whack-a-mole, stepping over an errant rolling Skee-Ball. Emma wasn't there. I checked the old dancing monkeys game—it wasn't really a game, we just put a dime in and these grinning stuffed monkeys beat castanets together while a Dixieland jazz bit played for a few minutes. When we were kids and I lost her, I could always find Emma by the dancing monkeys. But she wasn't there either.

"Gazebo?" Spence asked from a position of safety near the door. His hands were in his pockets, like he was afraid he'd get tetanus if he touched anything. I shot him an irritated look. I didn't want him to be a fancy boy all the time. He ought to be able to be just a normal person sometimes, instead of an Andover kid in a button-down.

The monkey castanets were deafening, and everywhere I turned, lightbulbs flashed on and off, leaving blue-red afterimages behind my eyelids. The fluorescents bathed everything in a sick green haze. I brought my hand to my forehead, pressing my thumb between my eyebrows in an effort to push away the ache that was burrowing in there. I heard a scream and I jumped, my heart in my throat, but it was just a kid running past me with a balloon in her hands. I reached for the corner of a pinball machine to get my balance.

"Colleen?" said a voice by my ear.

"What?" I was confused. It was Spence. God, my head was killing me.

"You okay?"

"Um . . . ," I said. "She's . . ."

Spence frowned, taking me by the elbow. "She's not here. Come on. Let's go outside."

He steered me through the walls of pinball machines, edging warily around a big guy in a sleeveless metal band T-shirt who was swigging a beer and looking disinclined to make room for us to pass.

366

"Hey," said Beer Bottle Guy, folding his arms to make himself bigger. "Watch it."

"Dude," Spence said, running his fingers through his flop of hair. "It's my girlfriend. She's kind of faint. Okay?"

Beer Bottle Guy took one step forward, and for a second I thought things were about to get really, really ugly. "Emma," I said weakly. "Here. She's . . ."

Beer Bottle Guy looked me up and down, and then without saying a word stepped aside for us to pass. I must've looked pretty bad. But then a little girl said, "Daddy," and held her arms up to Beer Bottle Guy, who hoisted her to his hip and turned his back on us with a glare.

"Come on," Spence said, his jaw tight. He propelled me outside to the gazebo, away from the cloying stench of cotton candy and ice cream and boiled peanuts. The wind was stronger out there, and the willow branches brushed together around us as I wrapped my arms around myself against the cold.

"Feeling better?" he asked, looking into my face, smoothing a curl from my forehead.

The corkscrew of pain was back. I shook my head.

"Are you sure she was going to meet him here?" Spence asked. "I think we should go. You can talk to her tomorrow."

"Here," I said. "Definitely." I craned my neck, scanning the faces of people strolling past the game rooms, moving in and out of the carousel, pausing to sift through tickets to see if there were enough for a ride on the kiddie elephant train. My eyes settled on each face, measuring, hunting. Emma, I'd see immediately. Her hair was so pale, it almost glowed at night. But Mr. Mitchell wouldn't look like Mr. Mitchell. No tie and button-down on him tonight. At Salem Willows, meeting his former student lover, he'd look like Tad. And I'd only seen Tad twice.

"Colleen," Spence said. His hand hunted along my hip, and it felt warm and dry as it found and closed around mine. Solid. Reassuring.

"Come on. You're exhausted. And I've got to get back. Please let me take you home."

"Wait," I said.

I spotted a rangy young man hip-deep in a crowd of children, silhouetted against a backlit sign advertising FRESH SEAFOOD LOBSTER ROLLS SCALLOPS FRIED TO ORDER. A familiar slouch, a mess of hair that I recognized. He was just there for a second, his shadow sliding over the wall. Then he was gone.

"There. Tad," I said. I pulled on Spence's hand, whispering, "Hurry!"

He started to protest, but I shushed him, steering him with me into the stream of people shuffling along the midway, making our way through the confusion of noise and lights. I caught a glimpse of the back of Tad's head before he disappeared behind a group of twentyish guys, one of whom spotted me and let out a low whistle.

"I'd hit that," he said straight to me as we passed.

I ignored him. It happened so fast that Spence missed it, not that he would have been able to do anything anyway.

The crowd thinned as we neared the end of the midway, and sure enough, there he was. Tad walked with his head down, shoulders up, hands in his pockets. Washed-black band T-shirt. No jacket. Today looked warmer than it was, and he was probably freezing. New England fools us that way sometimes.

I touched Spence's shoulder to get him to hang back.

"But—" Spence objected as I put a finger to my lips and indicated that we should watch where Tad was going. I hadn't seen Emma yet. But the corkscrew dug in deeper. The pain in my head made the lights brighter, surrounded by coronas of glare.

I knew she had to be there.

Tad paused, backlit by the funnel-cake stand, pulled a cell phone from his pocket, and stared down at it for a second. He texted something, and shoved the phone back into his pocket. He looked around, spotted what he was looking for, and continued on. He was heading for a dark corner of the park, past the reach of the bulbs and lights and music. Over by the water.

When I guessed he was far enough ahead of us, I tugged on Spence's hand, and we followed. The lights fell away behind us. As we moved closer to the water, I felt the wind chill cut deeper into me. I huddled closer to Spence, who whispered, "Even if that is him, I think we should go."

"No," I said. "Soon. Promise."

Presently I saw that we were heading for the older of the two fishing piers, the one out over the rockier water. This one wasn't as good for the stripers, so hardly anyone went on it, mostly just teenaged kids like us who wanted a private place to make out away from prying adult eyes. But the ocean breeze was too cold that night, and only one figure stood on the very end of the pier, her back to us, pale blond hair almost glowing in the dark.

Emma.

I was about to call out to her, but the pain twisting in my head made it hard for me to focus, and I realized from his gait that Spence was practically holding me up.

"Emma," Tad shouted. The wind carried his voice to where Spence and I were hidden by the darkness.

"Wait," Spence whispered, pulling me with him into the sheltering branches of the willow nearest the water.

The pain in my forehead blistered so hot that all I could manage to say was "Okay."

From inside the sheltering willow branches, I saw Emma turn, her face a twisted mask of anguish, her features smeared by grief. The wind coming in off the water gathered her hair and blew it up the back of her head, standing it straight on end, a white-blond halo on an angel of death.

"Tad," she choked, bringing her hands to her cheeks. Emma was weeping. She started to run to him, but his hands stayed thrust deep in his pockets and she stopped short, her arms wrapping around herself in the embrace that she wanted to find in him.

"Emma, listen—" he began, approaching her slowly, one hand extended.

"Why?" The word tore out of her, the sound of a soul ripped asunder, and the pain forced itself deeper into my forehead. I gasped and sagged against Spence, willow branches blowing against my cheeks.

"Why would you leave me for HER?"

With a guttural scream Emma hurled herself at Tad, a screaming banshee of rage and despair. He tried to fend her off, raising his hands to protect his face, cowering, backing away down the pier.

"Emma," he cried, his voice breaking. "You don't understand!"

"She has EVERYTHING," Emma screamed, scrabbling at him. "Why? Why her?"

Blows tumbled down on Tad's head, and he was sputtering, choking back tears of his own, his handsome face contorted in pain. His hands flailed for her wrists, but the wet sea breeze made her slippery, and they couldn't get ahold of each other. Their shadows struggled together against the stars, Emma wailing in anguish, Tad grunting with the effort of fighting her off. Tad took another step nearer the edge of the pier.

"Clara," I moaned. "Oh, no."

"She thinks he threw her over for Clara Rutherford?" Spence said.

I nodded miserably, my hands on my cheeks, tears streaming down my face, and dropped to my knees in the mud.

"I loved you!" Emma screamed. "I would've done anything for you! Do you understand? Anything! Why did you leave me for her? Why? I don't understand!"

"Emma!" he cried. "Emma, please!"

Through her tears and the willow branches and the wind between us, I could somehow feel Emma's eyes burning red. She shoved Tad in the chest with both hands, and he took another step backward.

And then another.

"I—I didn't—" Tad stammered, and he couldn't get a grip on her hands to stop her. The wind kicked up stronger, drenching them with spray torn off the tops of the waves, and he took another step, cringing away from the enraged girl in front of him.

He stumbled one more step back, but there was no more pier.

He lurched.

His heel slipped over the edge.

For a long, sickening moment, Tad's body swayed in space, one hand grasping Emma's wrist, the other cartwheeling in the dark, silhouetted against the starry harbor night. Below the pier, whitecapped waves curled and broke across jagged tips of granite.

"He's going to fall!" Spence shouted.

"EMMA!" I screamed. "DON'T!"

Emma spun around to see who was yelling, and when she moved, she pulled Tad along with her. His weight shifted forward, and Tad flung his free arm around her waist, hurling himself into Emma. They tumbled away from the pier edge and he got a better grip on Emma, dragging her screaming, spitting, fighting from the end of the pier and wrestling her to the grass in front of the willow.

"Is that what you think?" Tad shouted, tears streaking his face, straddling Emma with her wrists in his hands, pinning her to the ground like a wriggling fish. Her head thrashed back and forth, her feet churning in the mud. "You really think this is about someone else?"

Emma sobbed, gasping, "I loved you, I loved you, I've never loved anyone but you."

Tad leaned over, placing his hands on her cheeks and forcing her to look him in the eye.

"Emma," he said, his voice breaking. "Listen. Listen to me. I love you. *I love you.* There isn't anyone else. There's only you. There only ever was you."

I clutched Spence, who'd wrapped his arms around me. I felt the corkscrew of pain moving in my mind, like a living thing, burrowing in. Black mist started creeping into the corners of my vision.

"But—" Emma sobbed. "Clara! You dumped me for Clara!"

"What are you talking about?" Tad shouted. "I broke up with you because I'm your *teacher*. I'm twenty-three, Emma! Do you understand? Twenty-three! I'm not allowed to love you the way I want to. Do you understand?"

Her chest heaved, her face red with weeping. "But—I saw you! You were at her house! I watched you leave! Colleen was there, we saw you with her!"

Tad glanced at Spence and me cowering in the willow branches, and shouted, "No, you didn't. My apartment is in Beverly, Emma. Her house is between my apartment and the park. Remember?"

"But—"

"For God's sake, you've been there! Why do you think we had to drive up from the other direction? You think I wanted to drive right past my student's house? With you in the car?"

Emma gasped a ragged breath and started to keen. Her entire body trembled, her mouth pulled back in a rictus of pain, tears pouring from her eyes and into her hair.

"Emma," Tad murmured, smoothing her hair away from her forehead, cradling her. He placed a soft kiss on her pale eyebrow. "Emma."

Something burst. I couldn't explain it. One minute I was there, watching my friend's lover lean forward and press his lips to her, kissing her eyelids and cupping her cheek and smoothing her tears into her hair, and the next all I could see was red, and fireworks exploded in my brain and I was surrounded by sparks raining down from the sky, as if all the stars were falling around us, lighting up the willow and raining sparklers everywhere, flaming up into a deep red glow, and then, there was nothing.

"Colleen?"

I groaned and rolled onto my side. There was grass in my mouth.

"Hey," someone said. A guy. He rested his hand on my cheek.

I blinked once, twice, and turned my head in the direction of the voice.

A face swam into focus. It had a funny flop of hair on top, and sideburns, and pleasant smile lines around the mouth. The face was frowning down at me with concern, lit up with garish carnival lights. I could hear children screaming, and the music of the carousel. I broke into a smile.

"Spence," I sighed.

"Can you sit up?"

"Huh?" I groped around myself, feeling the damp mud underneath me. I pressed my hands against the ground, testing to see if it would give. It didn't, and I maneuvered myself into a sitting position with care so as not to dislodge any of the rattling pieces inside my head.

"Are you okay?" He was picking willow leaves out of my tangled curls and brushing dirt off my shoulders. His eyes looked worried.

"I'm—" I looked around myself, as if maybe the answer had fallen out of my pockets. Then I remembered, and my eyes widened. "Emma!"

"Shh," Spence shushed me, placing a finger on my lips. He glanced over his shoulder, and I followed his look.

My friend was sitting cross-legged on the ground, her limbs tangled together with my disgraced AP US History teacher. His fingers were in her hair, and he was kissing her pale eyebrows, murmuring, "I'm so sorry, Emma. I'm sorry."

She was crying, softly, but her face was smooth, her eyes closed, her hands twisted in his T-shirt, soaking him in.

I looked back at Spence, who mouthed, *We should go.*

I nodded, wordlessly, and he helped me to my feet. My knees felt watery. Spence wrapped an arm around my waist and we tiptoed away, leaving Emma and Mr. Mitchell—Tad—alone together, in the shadows, unobserved, the only place where they were allowed to be.

INTERLUDE

Y ou started to believe?" Reverend Green whispers. He's edged nearer to me in my telling. His handsome face is inches from mine. I can smell his breath, the sharpness of cider and ink.

I study his face. His teeth and lower lip are still darkened from licking the tip of his quill. The whiskers on his face are growing in from a long day listening to me. It's nearly dark, and I'll be sent home soon. But then again, we both know how it ends. We both know the root of my infamy. Why even bother to finish?

Without making a conscious decision about what I'm going to do, I take the Reverend's cheeks in my hands and pull his face to mine. His skin feels like satin under his rough whiskers, and I have just enough time to know the warmth and salt of his lip as I take it between mine. It's soft and delectable, and my tongue edges forward, wanting to touch him, wanting to taste him, wanting to take him into my mouth. Our kiss lasts only an instant before his hands close over my wrists and he pushes me away from him in horror.

"Ann!" he hisses with a panicked look at the door.

We struggle, his fists gripping my wrists and forcing me apart from him.

I laugh, pulling my wrists free and wiping my mouth on the back of my sleeve. I wonder if my own lip is stained with ink now. The look of tension in his face suggests that yes, it is.

"Don't worry, Reverend Green. It's almost over," I whisper to him.

The next day, a Monday, the village reassembles in the meetinghouse to witness Martha Corey's examination. We girls are there, and the crowd in the meetinghouse is even denser than it was yesterday, with more of them milling about outside, craning their necks to hear reports repeated by listeners stationed at the door. They lead her in, her imperiousness dampened by the binding around her wrists, and she's brought, glaring, up to the front of the room while Goodman Noyes begins with a prayer. Goody Corey looks appalled that she must listen to prayer while her hands are bound at her waist.

"Goody Corey. You're here to answer to the charges brought against you," Judge Hathorne bellows so that everyone can hear.

The woman who once boxed my ears after I trod upon her foot lifts her chin and says quietly, "I should like to go to prayer."

"Very well."

We all wait, obedient to the judge's mandate, while she closes her eyes in silence.

Finally, unable to keep the assembly waiting any longer, Judge Hathorne interrupts her silence. Pointing to us, he says, "Why do you afflict these children, Goody Corey?"

On cue, we girls begin to tremble and shake.

"Afflict them? I do not," she says with a toss of her head.

"Who does, then?" Judge Hathorne asks, looking down his long nose at her.

"I don't know. How should I know?"

Our numbers have grown. In addition to me, the two Bettys, Abby, Mary Walcott, and Mercy Lewis, there's my mother sitting with us, as well as Goody Pope, Goody Vibber, and Goody Goodall. At a look from Goody Corey the women around me shriek. My mother's hands fly to her throat, as though she were choking. Some of us scream of being bitten and pinched.

"I see her likeness coming!" one of us screams. "She's bringing a book! She'd have us sign it!"

Onlookers shout encouragements, urging us to look away, urging us not to sign.

Goody Corey frowns at us and holds her bound hands up. "I have no book."

"She has a yellow bird!" I cry, half out of my mind, unsure where the words are bubbling up from. "It used to suck betwixt her fingers!"

"Do you have any familiar spirit that attends to you?" Judge Hathorne asks the prisoner at the bar.

"I have no familiarity with any such thing. I'm a gospel woman," Goody Corey insists.

"Ah! She's a gospel witch!" I scream.

The judge turns his attention to me.

"Tell us, child. You have proof of this?"

"Yes," I say, scarcely aware of what I'm saying or what part of my fevered mind invents it. "One day when Lieutenant Fuller was at prayer at my father's house, I saw the shape of Goody Corey and someone else, I think it was Goody Nurse, praying at the same time to the Devil. I'm sure it was the shape of Goody Corey."

Goody Corey looks on me with a mixture of pity and distaste. Her face says that she's always thought I was a rogue, and that now she's finally been proven right.

"They are poor, distracted children," she says, keeping her voice measured and sane. "And you'd do well to give no heed to what they say."

"On the contrary," Judge Hathorne says, his voice mild and

instructive. "It is the judgment of all who are present that these children are bewitched. It is only you, Goody Corey, who claims they are distracted."

Uncertainty pulls at Goody Corey's cheek. For the first time I think Goody Corey sees the danger. While she weighs how to answer this charge, how to face those powerful men who are aligned against her, she bites her lip.

Abby screams, and we all join in, a pleasurable and horrible echoing in the meetinghouse, and it feels so good, the screaming, letting out all the fear and recrimination and frustration we carry around day to day.

"Look!" Abby wails, producing my arm with the infected bite. "See how Goody Corey afflicts us!" Mary Walcott holds out her bitten arm, too.

Next to me I spy Betty Hubbard digging into the flesh of her inner arm with her fingernails, clawing into herself deep enough to draw blood, and she holds up her arm and shrieks, "And I, too, Goody Corey sends her shape to bite and bedevil me!"

Around me all we girls are screaming, producing bite marks on our arms and wrists, and the magistrates and spectators crane their necks like pecking chickens to get a better look at our ripped skin, our bleeding flesh, the evidence of our bewitchment.

Goody Corey's face drains of blood, and she slips as though she cannot stand. She leans forward against the bar, pressing her breast to it, and more screams burst forth from our mouths as we hold our hands to our breasts as though our breath is being crushed out of us. I hold my hands there, too, and I can almost feel it, I am screaming, the air is being crushed out of me as I watch, and I am helpless to stop it.

"You foul creature!" Goody Pope screams, doubling over with her hands on her belly. "You're tearing my bowels out!"

Goody Corey turns half of her face to us, and Goody Pope is so overcome with rage that she throws her muff at Goody Corey's head.

The throw goes awry, glancing off Goody Corey's shoulder, though she winces as though she's been slapped, more from surprise and shame than from pain. With a guttural screech Goody Pope tears the shoe off her foot and hurls it at Goody Corey's proud, wincing face. The shoe hits its mark with a *thwack* and Goody Corey cries out, bringing a hand to her cheek where a fresh gash has begun to ooze dark red blood.

Goody Corey's feet shuffle, as though she is fighting the urge to run away, and I feel my own feet move, and all of the girls arrayed about me stamp their feet in a thundering chorus as though powered by something wholly diabolical.

Judge Hathorne glances between us and the pitiful woman at the bar, whose eyes well with tears. Blood trickles down her face between her fingers, fanning a dark red stain across her linen collar. At the sight of the blood Abby rises to her feet, teeth bared like a wolf set to tear out the throat of a wounded calf.

"Why did you not go to the company of witches who were mustering before the meetinghouse?" Abby screams, pointing a servant's finger at the cowering, lordly Goody Corey. "Didn't you hear the drumbeat? You have familiarity with the Devil! He's a black man whispering in her ear, her yellow bird sucks betwixt her fingers in the assembly!"

"What yellow bird?" Judge Hathorne says. "You, check her hands."

A bailiff approaches Martha Corey and says, "You hold your hands out like the judge asks."

Shaking so that she can barely obey, Goody Corey extends her bound fists out for his inspection. The bailiff peers between each finger, holding her hands gently in his. Abby catches my eye and tries to get me to understand what she wills me to do. I'm trembling, too, and Abby pokes me hard in the ribs and hisses, "Do it."

I scream, "It's too late! It's too late! She's hidden the teat so you won't find it. She removed it with a pin and put it on her head!"

It's nonsense, what I've babbled, but the judge waves a hand to catch the bailiff's attention and says, "Check for it."

Goody Corey wears her hair like my mother does, brushed straight back and plaited into a heavy braid that's coiled and fastened at the nape of her neck, tucked up under her coif. It's held together with hairpins.

The bailiff nods, and Goody Corey says, "But . . ."

He places a hand on the back of her head and forces her to tip her chin to her chest. With his free hand he hunts up into her hair. His eyes light up, and he withdraws a long, sharp hairpin.

The entire assembly gasps.

Abby, sensing her moment, points a vibrating finger at the woman weeping before us, a few threads of gray hair now hanging loose about her shoulders. "She had covenanted with the Devil for ten years! She told me! Six of them were gone, but there's still four to come!"

Judge Hathorne exchanges a purposeful look with the other magistrates who flank him at the bench.

"All right. Let me ask you this, Goodwife Corey. How many persons be there in the Godhead?"

It's a catechism question, one that we all can answer without so much as a thought. But Goody Corey has been reduced to tears and sniveling, and stands propping herself at the bar, alone, shaking her head, and saying, "It cannot be, it cannot be. I? But how could I? I never did. I never would. I'm a gospel woman. I love Jesus." Her speech devolves into gasping and muttering, and the blood oozes down her cheek.

"She's answering but oddly," one of the magistrates whispers to Judge Hathorne, who frowns with his woolly brows knotted together, and nods.

"Goody Corey," Judge Hathorne bellows, and she rolls her eyes at him like a hunted animal. "Do you deny these charges being made against you? Do you mean to say that you're not a witch?"

She sputters. "No! No! Not I, never I!" She chokes back her sobs, and the audience gathered in the meetinghouse blusters with tension, one voice after another raised against her.

The magistrates lean their periwigged heads together while the assembly murmurs among themselves. I spy Abby out of the corner of my eye, and she's wearing a hungry smile. Goody Pope is laughing, her eyes bright. I feel what they're feeling, the intoxicating sense that this squirming wretch who used to scorn us now twists at our mercy, these men with their self-important robes and beefy faces all harken to us, acting at our will. I gaze on the weakened form of Goody Corey, a woman who used to think that she could order me about, could box my ears whenever she felt like it, and as the tears begin to stream down her face, I draw myself up to my full height and I smile.

After that day, I'm empty of pity. Nineteen people mounted the steps to the gallows. Nineteen people heard a final prayer while a mob of friends and neighbors harried them to damnation and threw rotting vegetables at their weeping faces. Nineteen people felt the stool yanked away and their desperate feet kicking at nothing. Nineteen people felt the rope bite into their necks, purpling their mouths, blood vessels bursting in their eyes as the flames of hell licked at their heels. And I condemned them all.

I condemned them all.

CHAPTER 26

DANVERS, MASSACHUSETTS
MONDAY, MARCH 26, 2012

After we got back from the doctor with my prescription, I spent the first three days of spring break asleep. I only got up to go to the bathroom or shuffle into the kitchen looking for something to eat. Once Wheez came in and jumped on my bed, shrieking, "Get up get up get up Colleen get up get up get up!" and I pushed her off with an inarticulate growl and she went running into the other room hollering, "MOM!" but nothing came of it.

Michael had spring break at the same time, but I didn't see much of him. He'd be at the breakfast table with his earbuds in and give me a wave, but that was about it. He was still halfheartedly reading my old copy of *The Crucible*. Turned out they read it in eighth grade at St. Innocent's, so he'd just stolen it to read for school. I considered seeing if he wanted to write my extra-credit paper for me, but then I just didn't care.

I took the pills they gave me. I didn't watch television. I didn't go on the Internet. I told myself I wasn't going to check my phone either, but I wasn't that good. Spence went on a ski trip for his spring break with some kids from his school, and it was coed. I pretended to be totally cool about it and not eaten up with jealousy. I didn't let on. But I confess I liked the text messages he sent, which largely consisted of snowboard reports from Sugarloaf and updates on all the couples who were hooking up. And assuring me that nobody was hooking up with him.

When I finally crept out from my cocoon, my parents acted like it was totally normal for their eldest child to be wearing the same pair of pajama pants that she had changed into several days earlier.

"Coffee?" my mother asked, all chipper.

"Sure," I grumbled, flopping into my usual seat at the breakfast table.

"Linda, it's four thirty," my father said, coming into the breakfast nook from the living room.

"Is it, now," Mom said, pouring me a cup of coffee and adding milk and sugar, the way she knew I liked it. "I hadn't noticed."

I accepted it and took a grateful sip. Feeling started to come back into my hands, and maybe into my mind, too.

"Anjali called," my mother said. "Said you weren't picking up your cell. I told her you were asleep."

I scratched in my nest of sleep-hair and yawned.

"And Deena stopped by yesterday morning. I was going to tell her to go upstairs, but she said it was okay, she knew you were tired."

I blinked in surprise. It felt like I hadn't seen Deena in weeks.

"She said they're going to be down at Front Street this afternoon, hanging out. She's really hoping you'll stop by."

A flutter of pleasure rippled through me. Who would think that the idea of seeing my friends in our regular café would actually be exciting?

"Maybe," I yawned. But she knew I would be there. She knew I was on my way back from wherever I had been.

A while later I walked to Front Street Café, even though I kind of still wanted to be in bed. It was a long walk from our house, but it felt good

382

to be moving, to be out in the air, breathing. Everywhere I looked, spring had planted secret messages for us to find. Waxy green leaves. Daffodils thinking about blooming. The air had that rich, loamy smell that happens when the ground starts to thaw and awaken.

I pushed the screen door of the café open and found Deena, Anjali, and Jennifer Crawford already there, huddled around steaming mugs of tea. They waved merrily at me, and one of them called, "Sleeping Beauty!"

"Psh," I said, stopping by the counter for my own tea and muffin before flopping into the fourth chair at the table.

Deena dropped a newspaper in front of me.

"You're right," Jennifer Crawford said, smiling and elbowing Anjali. "She does have pillow creases on her face."

"Toldja." Anjali grinned.

"Shut up," I said, smiling into my tea.

"Check it," Deena said.

The headline read "Mass. Department of Public Health Clears Sick School." I pulled the paper nearer and peered at the article.

Under the headline was a color photo of the stained-glass window from the chapel, the one of St. Joan looking serene while she's being burned at the stake. The article wasn't very long. It said that while I was drugged out in bed, Bethany Witherspoon released a preliminary report finding that there was no appreciable level of tricoethylene in the grounds of St. Joan's Academy, and that although these initial tests were cause for optimism about the Mystery Illness, she and her team would never rest until the true cause of the Mystery Illness had been found and the proper people held accountable.

I looked up. "So she's gone?" I asked.

Everyone around the table nodded.

"That was quick."

"I saw her on *Good Day, USA* this morning," Jennifer Crawford added. "She said a lot of stuff about increasing government funding for environmental cleanup so that no other girls like us ever have to suffer. Bebe Appleton has started a fund to help with our medical expenses, so you know, that's something. They made a big deal of it, and Clara Skyped in to say thank you on behalf of everyone. Of course."

"Huh," I said.

"Do you think I'll always sound like Emma Stone when I talk, or will I go back to normal?" Anjali wondered while I continued reading. She touched her throat. The scabs around her mouth had started to clear up.

"I bet you'll go back to normal," Deena said.

"Damn," Anjali sighed into her tea.

The article went on to say that the Massachusetts Department of Public Health had consulted with experts at Harvard, Tufts, and Mass General, and their official assessment was that the Mystery Illness had no environmental or infectious cause whatsoever, and that it was instead an unusually widespread group outbreak of conversion disorder. We should all take some time to reflect on the undue stresses placed on teenage girls in America today blah blah blah something blah.

I was distracted by everyone gossiping around the table.

"No way. She's already walking?" one of my friends said.

"I mean, with a cane, but yeah. That's what I heard. And that basically it's just that she's got to build her muscle tone back. She's, like, atrophied or whatever."

"God. Poor Elizabeth."

"Actually, I think her hair looks better now," someone else said, not listening to the first conversation.

"Oh, I know, right? Did you see her on TV? It was, like, already growing back."

"It's really cute short. She should leave it."

The paper did not define what, exactly, conversion disorder was.

The Department of Public Health was leaving a liaison at St. Joan's to coordinate our care, and we were all expected to make a full recovery. The newly appointed upper school dean, Father John Molloy, had no comment at press time, but the paper could exclusively reveal that the original set of girls was already showing signs of improvement.

"What about Clara?"

"I heard her mom's in negotiations to sell the rights."

"Shut up."

"I'm not kidding. TV movie. For, like, Lifetime or something."

"Shut up!"

"Who should play me, do you think?" Anjali asked.

"God, Leigh Carruthers must be freaking out. Does she know?"

"I mean, probably, if I do."

The paper reported that the final tally for the Mystery Illness stood at sixty-two students, or almost a quarter of the upper school student body at St. Joan's Academy. "'We're just excited for everything to get back to normal,' concerned parent Kathy Carruthers was quoted as saying. This has been a terrible strain on her daughter, Carruthers said, and anyone who wants to help or get involved can visit their website at . . ." blah blah blah. I flipped the paper facedown.

I slurped some of my tea.

"So," Deena said, eyeing me.

"So, what?"

"Is it true?"

"Is what true?"

Deena leaned in and whispered, "Did you get it, too?"

I flushed deep crimson and looked at my tea mug while I whispered, "Yes."

My friends' hands found my forearms, piling on in an indistinguishable heap. I couldn't look them in the face just yet.

"Are you okay?" one of them asked.

I nodded. "They've got me on some drugs that made me really

sleepy at first. But I'm adjusting to them okay. My pediatrician thinks it's not a big deal. She said since I got it so late in the outbreak, it shouldn't be too difficult to treat."

I was scheduled to start cognitive behavioral therapy in May, the first date my mom could get me an appointment. But I didn't really feel like telling my friends that. I still didn't feel crazy. The not-feeling-crazy part scared me the most.

"Oh, damn!" Anjali cried, smacking Deena on the arm. "That's not what you were supposed to ask."

"What was I supposed to ask?" Deena asked, feigning innocence.

"Dude! You're supposed to ask if it's set with Spence for spring formal."

I blushed as everyone grinned at me.

"Maybe," I confessed.

We passed the next hour in a pleasant haze of spring formal gossip, discussing strategies to keep Jason Rothstein from showing up in either a tuxedo T-shirt or a gold lamé pimp costume, both of which were on the table, according to Anjali, and whether or not Deena could ask one of the guys she was friends with from St. Innocent's even though she was still talking to Japan Boy on Skype.

Japan Boy, we learned, had applied to Tufts also. I was starting to think Deena had more going on with him than she'd let on. When she talked about him, her smile got big and silly. We were just getting around to what we were all going to wear—Anjali's mom thought she'd look beautiful in a sari, but Anj was having none of it, and I was half thinking of asking her if I could wear it instead—when I said, "So, wait, you guys, is Emma coming?"

A look passed around the table. We all settled on Jennifer Crawford, since she seemed to hear things before everyone else.

"Um. She's got the flu?" she said, raising her eyebrows for confirmation. We all looked at each other and shrugged. "At least, that's what I heard."

"That sucks," Anjali said, toying with her mug and looking at me from the corner of her eyes.

"Yeah," I said, not meeting Anjali's unspoken question.

We hung out for a while longer, gossiping, equal parts Mystery Illness rumors and spring formal scheming, until we saw some guys starting to move chairs around and plug in long extension cords and truck guitar cases from the open hatchback of a car outside.

"I think that's our cue," Deena murmured under her breath.

"Definitely," Anjali said, winding her scarf around her neck.

"I dunno," Jennifer Crawford mused. "The bassist is kind of cute."

Out on the street, in the damp spring night, Deena asked me if I needed a ride.

"That's okay. I'll walk. Thanks," I said, avoiding looking at her.

"Okay," she said, giving me a quick hug. "See you at school."

I nodded, watching her and Anjali walk together under the street-lights to the parking lot. I slid my hands into my jacket pockets and started to walk.

It took me an hour to get to Emma's house, and by then it had gotten dark. I texted with Spence part of the way—he was coming back from Sugarloaf the next day, and he was sorry to have to tell me this, but he took a tree branch to the face and so he was probably going to have a huge purple bruise for spring formal. I suggested he could rent a tux that was the same color. He Snapchatted me a picture, with his eye literally almost swollen shut and his tongue sticking out in a grimace. I couldn't help but laugh. When he finally had to go, I used my phone as a flashlight, stepping around the jagged sidewalk cracks.

The porch light was on at Emma's house, and when I leaned on the bell, her brother, Mark, opened the door. Those Blackburns, seri-ously. With that pale white hair and those oyster-shell eyes. People's genes could not be more recessive.

"Oh, hey, Colleen. How's it going?"

"Hi, Mark. Sorry to just drop in on you guys like this," I said, shuffling my feet on the stoop.

"No problem. Come on in."

I struggled to think of a worthy conversational gambit. I never really knew what to say to Emma's brother.

"So," I ventured. "How's Endicott?"

"Awesome. It's gonna be great, having Em there next year. You'll have to come up. They've got their own beach, you know that?"

"No kidding? That's awesome."

He grinned crookedly at me and nodded. "Yeah. She's upstairs. You know the way."

I did know the way. I climbed up the stairs, my feet fitting into the worn patches on the carpet, comfortable and familiar. I heard voices downstairs in the kitchen, the sounds of dinner under way. Life stirred in Emma's house.

"Em?" I whispered, nudging her bedroom door open with my knuckle.

She was at her desk doing something on her laptop. When she saw me, her eyes lit up.

"Colleen!" she cried, leaping to her feet. Before I knew it, she'd wrapped her arms around my neck. I glanced over at the computer screen, but she'd closed whatever she was working on. "I'm so glad to see you. Did you drive?"

"Nah. I walked. I was down at Front Street with Deena and them."

"Oh, yeah," she said, crawling onto her twin bed and making room for me at the foot. She pulled her old American Girl doll into her lap and toyed with its Puritan hat. It smiled its glassy eyes at me, and I settled in against a pillow.

"I've been so tired this break. It's crazy. I've been sleeping for days," she said, peeking at me over the doll's head.

"Me too," I sighed. "They told me the drugs would do that, but I think I was just really stressed out." We stared at each other, smiling

tentative smiles, wondering who was going to bring up Salem Willows first.

"So," I began.

She looked at her lap. "I'm sorry I didn't tell you," she whispered.
"About Tad."

"No, I'm the one who's sorry," I said in a rush. "It was my fault. I
was so . . . I don't know. Wrapped up in stuff. I should've—"

"No," Emma cut me off, her pale eyes shining in the warm light
of her bedroom. "It's my fault. I wanted to tell you, I really did. But,
I don't know. I was embarrassed. I told Anjali, 'cause I knew she
wouldn't judge me. But I was afraid of what you'd think."

I reached across the quilt and took her hand. She squeezed back.

"It's okay," I said. "I just feel so stupid. My best friend was in love.
And I didn't know."

She smiled and pressed her lips to her doll's head.

"Yeah," she said, and her eyes shone.

"Are you okay?" I asked.

She shrugged. "Um. Maybe? I know it doesn't make any sense, but
he's just . . ."

"I know."

She flopped over on an elbow, taking the doll with her.

"I was over sixteen," she whispered. "It wasn't, like, illegal or anything. But he thinks we should wait. He thinks I should be eighteen."

I nodded. "And what do you think?"

She rolled onto her back. "I think it sucks," she said, laughing.
"But I'll be eighteen this summer, right?"

I laughed, too.

"He's going to grad school next year," she said. "In Providence."

"Oh, yeah? That's not so far."

"No," Emma said. Her smile was hopeful. "Not too far."

I flopped down next to her and took one of her bears under my
arm. "You really thought it was Clara's fault?"

"I don't know." She brought her doll's head up under her chin, crushing its Puritan bonnet to her skin. "It had been, like, three months, and we were seeing each other all the time. I mean, all the time. And then all of a sudden he got all distant. Not returning my texts. Putting off when he was going to see me. Avoiding me at school. He never once looked at me in AP US, not after we came back from winter break. You didn't notice?"

I shook my head.

"I couldn't figure out what happened. And he wasn't saying anything to me at all. Then one afternoon I saw him talking to Clara in the hall. I just thought . . . Well." She smiled sadly. "It's Clara. You know? I mean, what would you think?"

"I know." I nodded.

Emma put her hands over her face, shuddering at the memory. "I just . . . It made me crazy. It made me *crazy*, Colleen. I couldn't stand thinking about him with someone else."

Her voice caught. She shivered, and wiped the wet out from under her eyes with a brave smile.

"Is that why he left St. Joan's?" I asked. "Because of you?"

She nodded. "Well," she said, rolling her eyes. "God. My mom saw texts from him, on my phone. So that's how she found out."

"Emma. Jesus."

"Yeah. She freaked. I mean, *freaked*." The doll kept smiling its doll smile like nothing was amiss.

"God."

"Yeah."

"She said she was going to call the school. And she was going to ground me so bad, I mean, it was going to be school and home and that's it, until, like, graduation. I think my brother talked to her. Made it sound like it was all Tad's fault."

"Did she call the school?"

"I never found out. The next day I got to campus, and he was gone. I didn't know what had happened. If he was sick, or if he got fired, or what. And then, everything started happening, with Clara and every-body. Nobody seemed to care what happened to him. Like we were all too distracted to notice."

"Did you hear from him, after he left?" I asked.

"Um. Yeah." She blushed.

"What's that mean?"

"I maybe stalked him a little."

"Well, duh," I teased, smacking her on the ankle. "Making me your accomplice and everything."

She grinned. "Sorry."

We paused, breathing, listening to the distant sound of the Black-burns making dinner downstairs. I could hear Mark's laughter.

"I was so upset," she whispered. "Colleen, I can't explain it. I thought I would lose my mind if he didn't love me anymore. It's like I would stop being myself. Stop existing if he didn't love me the way I loved him."

I stared at her, wondering. "Emma?"

"Hmm?"

"Do you think . . ." I couldn't make the words come out at first. It was too weird to say out loud. I tried again. "Do you think it was a coincidence?"

"Do I think what was a coincidence?"

"Well," I demurred, "the other day, when I was here. I felt like it sort of . . ."

She watched me, those oyster eyes shining.

"Sort of what?"

"I mean." I was helpless to explain. "I was talking backwards! It's like—that's not normal. Even if I've got conversion disorder or whatever."

"No, you weren't," Emma said easily.

"I was! At the Willows, too. My head was splitting, and I was talk-ing backward . . ." I trailed off.

Emma waited, her almost-invisible eyebrows raised.

"I mean, I'm not saying it was on purpose or anything . . ."

Emma smiled at me and reached over to hold my ankle in her hand. "Colleen," she said, her voice low. "You're going to be okay. Right? They've got everyone on the right drugs now and everything. Everybody's getting better. It was scary, but it's all over! And think what an awesome anecdote this is going to make when you get to college next fall. You're one of the Danvers Mystery Illness girls. That's completely awesome. You'll be, like, famous."

"But—" I started to protest.

"Emma!" her mom called up the stairs. "Dinner!"

We sat up, and Emma set her doll aside with finality. "Coming!" she called. Then to me she said, "I'm just going to finish this one e-mail to him."

"You're writing to Mr. Mitchell?"

"Tad." Her face lit up when she said the name. "Summer's coming. I'll be eighteen. I'll be eighteen very soon."

"Okay," I said. At least my friends still loved me even though I was mental.

Emma wrapped her arms around my neck and squeezed for a long time.

"You're the best," she whispered into my curls.

"No, you are," I whispered back. Some of her butter-blond hair got in my mouth.

When I closed the door behind me, Emma was booting up her laptop, and her happiness was lighting up the room in a soft pink glow.

I was at the bottom of the stairs and almost to the front door when a hand closed around my wrist. I stopped, finding myself held fast by Emma's mom.

"Mrs. Blackburn," I exclaimed. She was obscured by the shadow under the stairwell, and I could barely see her.

"Shhhhh," she whispered. The sound of it raised goose bumps on my arms.

392

"I was just—" I stumbled to explain myself, though I wasn't sure what I'd done wrong that needed explaining.

"Shh," Mrs. Blackburn said again, drawing me closer.

I swallowed, and let myself be pulled under the stairwell.

"My Emma's like me, you know," Mrs. Blackburn said, so quietly that it almost sounded like her voice was happening inside my head.

I hesitated. "She is?"

"Yes."

I waited, unsure what I was supposed to say.

"It's better she stay here. For school," Mrs. Blackburn continued in that nonexistent voice of hers.

I licked my lips. "I guess," I allowed. Mrs. Blackburn's grip on my wrist tightened.

"She's delicate," Emma's mom continued, barely audible over the laughter of her family in the kitchen.

"She is?" I asked. Emma, who sailed and played field hockey?

"She's"—Mrs. Blackburn drew the words out with care—"*prone to spells*. But it can be managed. Helps to have the family close by. I'm only telling you so you don't have to worry."

My mouth went dry.

"But how did you—" I stopped, because it almost seemed as though her eyes were glowing faintly red.

"Anyhow," Mrs. Blackburn said, her smile widening, a tooth glinting in the darkness under the stairs. "They said what caused it, in the news. Didn't they."

"Y—yes." I swallowed.

"Good. So there's no problem."

The hand released my wrist.

"It's always nice to see you, Colleen. Tell your parents hello from us."

Mrs. Blackburn melted away into the darkness under the stairs, and when she was gone, I wondered if the conversation had really happened at all.

EPILOGUE

C olleen! Fifteen minutes!"

"Crap!" I held two nearly identical sweaters in my hands and made an impulsive choice, stuffing one on the top of my rucksack and chucking the other onto the floor of my closet. Downstairs, I heard my father call out, "Is she about ready?"

"Almost ready!" I hollered down the stairs.

Wheez, who proved to be sitting on my bed for I don't know how long, singsonged, "You're going to miss your plane, Colleen."

"I'm not." I was shuffling through a pile of books on my desk, try-ing to decide which ones to bring to England. "Argh," I muttered. I couldn't choose. I wanted to pack enough to read, but I didn't want them to be too heavy.

Deena was meeting me at the airport, and we were going to hike around East Anglia for July. It was my parents' graduation present. Pretty cool. I thought they'd be disappointed that Fabiana beat me out by that tenth. I mean, it was my own fault. Ms. Slater hounded me for weeks, until she finally gave up. I never did finish the extra-credit paper about Ann Putnam. Fabiana deserved valedictorian anyway. She'd always been a teeny bit ahead of me. The real killer was, I didn't even get salutatorian. I know, right? Anjali got it! Guess she wasn't the only one who was playing things close to the chest that spring.

Jason Rothstein dressed in a tuxedo like a normal person for the spring formal, and so did Spence. His snowboarding bruise wasn't even that bad by the time he got back. I don't know what he was so worried about. I still have the picture on my phone. He and Jason pretended like they didn't care about not getting into Harvard. I don't know, maybe they really didn't care. I mean, I know Spence was a legacy, so that might have been kind of hard to take. Not that Spence has anything to complain about, though—he'll be at Yale with Anjali. A good excuse for me to visit.

Deena got into Tufts, and she told me yesterday that Japan Boy got in, too. So that's going to be pretty interesting. I mean, they've been Skyping all year, but she hasn't seen him in person since her summer abroad. It could be weird. But maybe it'll be amazing. Who knows?

I heard that Father Molloy's going to stay the new dean of the upper school at St. Joan's Academy. I don't know if Ms. Slater is going back next year or not, but we all did really well on the AP US History exam, so I think they should really consider keeping her if they can. Periodically we still see something in the news about more testing being done at the school, or experts talking about how common conversion disorder really is, and how it's yet another symptom of how much pressure adolescent girls are under these days. How our childhoods are ending too soon, and we should really look to the example of history to understand how to let children really be children for longer, 'cause, like, everything was better back in the olden days. Whatever. Frankly, St. Joan's is already starting to feel kind of far in the past to me. There's so much more that lies ahead.

Clara's going to Boston College, as we all knew she would. I don't know whatever happened with the TV movie Jennifer Crawford heard about, but probably nothing. Clara's talking totally normally now, like nothing ever happened. The Other Jennifer's kept her hair short, and it looks really adorable. I think she's going to Pine Manor next year. Leigh Carruthers and Elizabeth are both going to UMass, and Elizabeth told me not too long ago that she's being considered for the field hockey team next year, as a freshman. Pretty hard core.

We're all on variations of the same antidepressant. Clara and I had a confessional moment about it in the library washroom right before graduation. It made her really sleepy at first, too. But now it's like our little secret. And it's worked. We're all back to our normal selves.

"Colleen! Your father's in the car!"

"Mom! I'm coming!" I shouted. "Jeez."

My phone vibrated. I grinned.

I'm going to miss you

My grin spread wider.

Me too. I'll call you from the airport. Have news!

The phone buzzed with an instantaneous response.

News?!

I laughed, delighted, and lightning-thumbed him back.

Patience, my young Padawan. Calling in 30.

"What news?" Wheez asked, her nose peering over my shoulder.

"Wheez!" I pushed her way. "Jesus."

But I was smiling too widely to be really annoyed with her.

My news, which my parents didn't know, and which Spence didn't know, and which Deena and Anjali and Emma didn't know, was that that morning I got an e-mail from Judith Pennepacker.

It was about my position on the Harvard wait list.

I know! Could they have kept me waiting any longer? Until now, everyone thought I was going to my safety. Dartmouth was a total bust, and so was Williams. It sucked. Everyone said it was an incredibly competitive year, and that there wasn't anything wrong with going to your safety school, and even students with really top GPAs like mine were still going to their safeties, and it didn't matter and I shouldn't be upset about it. Not that I wouldn't be excited to go to my safety, but . . . I mean. Come on.

Anyway, I'm pretty psyched to be in the same city as Emma. Or near enough. Beverly's not so far at all.

"Hey," Michael said from my door, pulling his earbuds out.

"Hey, Mikey," I said, choosing my last few paperbacks and cramming them into the zipper pocket on the top of the rucksack.

The car honked.

"Colleen!" My mother rattled the handrail on the stairs, her signal that I'd better hurry it up.

"Michael," he corrected me.

"Michael." I grinned, going over to give my brother a hug.

"Hey, okay," he said, nose crushed by my shoulder. "Look, I didn't come here for some big scene."

"Oh, yeah? What'd you come in for, then?" I released him and hoisted my rucksack up. Whoa, damn. So, maybe I packed too many books.

"I just wanted to see if you needed this back. I kind of took it earlier."

He held out my original copy of *The Crucible*. It was all dog-eared and there was a big crack in the spine, and it looked like he'd spilled coffee on it.

"Um." I slid my other arm through the shoulder strap and felt the weight spread itself more evenly across my back. This was better. This, I could carry.

"Colleen, I swear to God, we're going to the airport without you if you don't come down this minute!"

Which was a completely hollow threat, because what would be the point of them going to the airport without me? Just to prove something? But anyway, it was time to go.

Michael tried to put the play in my hands. "I should've, like, asked you. Before I took it," he muttered. "So anyway. Here it is back, if you want it."

"It's okay, Michael." I grinned at him, hooking my thumbs in my rucksack straps. "I don't think I'm going to need it."

Michael shrugged. "Suit yourself," he said, turning to go.

"Can I have it, Mikey?" Wheez asked, trailing after him down the hall. I smiled at her retreating back, but she didn't see.

"Okay," I said to myself, looking around to see what I'd forgotten. Rucksack, check. Hiking boots, on. Hat, rolled up in the outside mesh thing on the rucksack. Passport, in my hip pocket. I was ready.

I stepped through the door of my bedroom, calling "Coming, I'm coming!" and made it halfway down the stairs before I realized that I'd forgotten my phone. Outside, I heard the station wagon engine rumble to life.

Dammit.

I turned and stumped back up the stairs, burst into my childhood bedroom, wrapped my fist around the phone I'd almost left on my desk, and turned to go, this time for good.

I spotted a flicker of movement out of the corner of my eye.

On the tree branch just outside my bedroom window, almost invisible in the shadows of the summer leaves, perched a tiny yellow bird.

POSTLUDE

*A*re you ready, Annie?" my little sister says.
I'm loitering under an elm, hoping for coolness in the shade. It's a scorching day, and the roads are bleached by the summer sun to utter dust.

She holds her hand out for mine. I finger the folded paper in my pocket, pulling it out to look at it, and then thrust it back to its hiding place.

"No," I say, simply.

"Well, it's time to come anyway," she says. Jane was always reasonable that way. She's never been given to fancies at all. She's better than I am in many ways.

My brothers are there, too, but only because Jane asked them to come. They've stayed away from the meetinghouse also, Edward and Thomas and the others. We Putnams don't take humbling well.

The bell tolls in the new bell tower, a merry Sunday morning sound drawing everyone in the village to meeting. The women look fresh and cool under straw hats, and many of them are strangers to

399

me. I've lived in this town my entire life. It's nearly doubled in size in that time. But my shame keeps me low and hidden. I still walk with my shoulders drawn up, warding off the looks I'm sure I'm getting, though Jane tells me no one looks at me anymore.

Jane and I approach the meetinghouse doors, merging with the line of worshippers, all of them gossiping together as we used to do. At the door, Reverend Green greets everyone, wearing the robes of his profession, flanked by his cheerful, robust wife. When he sees me, his entire face darkens.

So does hers.

"Ann," he says, his only acknowledgment.

"Good morning, Reverend Green," I say.

Jane keeps a tight hold on my arm, her eyes shifting to the villagers crowding past us, watching to make sure nothing seems amiss.

"Did you bring it?" he asks.

I nod. Reverend Green holds out his hand, and I put the paper in it.

He leans to my ear and says, "I'll read it for you after the hymn and the prayer. When I'm finished, I'll ask you to acknowledge it. Then we'll pray together, and it'll be done."

I nod my assent as Jane says, "Thank you, Reverend Green. It means so much to Ann and me."

My sister and brothers steer me to a pew near the front, and this time I'm sure I feel eyes on me. When I glance over my shoulder, I find I'm right. Goody Green is glaring at me. A smile fights to bend my mouth, but I vanquish it.

Some villagers who know us stop to greet us, expressing happy surprise at my presence. I see that Salem Village has carried on without the involvement of the Putnam family. My mother's pride would be hurt. They've been more than happy to buy our land off us in parcels, to nod acknowledgment at the market and on the streets, and nothing more.

The opening hymn and the prayer slide past me as I stare at all the

400

faces. They've been happy to forget. Nobody speaks of it. Well, that's not true. People who lost mothers and fathers, spouses, siblings, they speak plenty. They've been petitioning for restitution. I see Dorothy Good betimes wandering the streets, wild-eyed, muttering to herself. After a babyhood in chains and her mother hanged before her eyes, Dorothy Good, always a wild thing, took utter leave of our earth, abandoning a raving body behind. Her father struggles to care for her. There's never enough money.

Jane pinches me, and I return to myself. Reverend Green is talking about me.

"Today, one among us wishes to confess herself. I beg you all to hear her. Listen. Offer her the forgiveness that Christ would offer, that he will offer when she meets him in the next life. Ann Putnam?"

I rise, shakily, to my feet. The congregation whispers. I feel their eyes burning into my back.

Reverend Green unfolds the paper that holds the confession my brother wrote out for me, after Reverend Green's instruction. He skims it, clears his throat, and begins to read.

"I desire to be humbled before God for that sad and humbling providence that befell my father's family in the year about '92; that I, then being in my childhood, should, by such a providence of God, be made an instrument for the accusing of several persons of a grievous crime, whereby their lives were taken away from them, whom now I have just grounds and good reason to believe they were innocent persons; and that it was a great delusion of Satan that deceived me in that sad time, whereby I justly fear I have been instrumental, with others, though ignorantly and unwittingly, to bring upon myself and this land the guilt of innocent blood; though what was said or done by me against any person I can truly and uprightly say, before God and man, I did it not out of any anger, malice, or ill-will to any person, for I had no such thing against one of them; but what I did was done ignorantly, being deluded by Satan. And particularly, as I was a chief instrument of accusing Goodwife Nurse and her two sisters, I desire to lie in the dust, and to be humbled for it, in that I was a cause, with others, of so sad a calamity to them and their families; for which cause I desire to lie in the dust, and earnestly beg forgiveness of God, and from all those unto whom I have given just cause of sorrow and offence, whose relations were taken away or accused."

A leaden silence grips the meetinghouse. I hear a creak of someone's weight shifting in a pew.

"Ann Putnam, do you acknowledge this confession as yours?"

The summer sun slants through the meetinghouse windows, and I open my mouth to speak.

I close my eyes, and think back years ago to something Tittibe Indian said, in the early days of our delusion.

"I'm blind. I cannot see," I whisper. "I cannot see what's real."

AUTHOR'S NOTE

Conversion began when I was sitting in the waiting room at the Meineke, waiting for my taillight to be fixed. It was autumn 2012, and the cable news was on in the waiting room, but I wasn't paying much attention until the news anchor said in passing that they'd figured out what was really wrong with the girls in Le Roy, New York. According to the newscast, the Le Roy Mystery Illness of 2012 was actually just an outbreak of conversion disorder.

"What?" I said to the television, which evoked some glares from the people also waiting for their cars.

In the spring of 2012 a group of sixteen high school girls in Le Roy, New York, about an hour away from where I live, came down with bizarre physical symptoms that no one could explain. They were twitching, and suffering from disordered speech. Some of them, who had been very athletic, had lost the ability to walk. It was thought that they might be having a reaction to the HPV vaccine. Then it was thought they might have PANDAS, or Tourette's. The girls and their parents went on first local, then national, then international television. Environmental pollution was blamed. And while these girls were suffering through this very strange and very public experience, I was teaching *The Crucible* to a group of college students in my sophomore historical fiction seminar.

When the Le Roy story first broke, I arrived in class eager to discuss the parallels between the "afflicted girls" at Salem and these teenagers who lived so close to us. To my surprise, my students didn't see a parallel. After all, the girls in the past were just crazy, whereas the girls in Le Roy had something *really wrong* with them. The more I watched the story unfold, however, the more struck I was by the disjuncture between what the Le Roy girls thought about their own experience and what the assorted "experts" brought in to comment on their situation had to say. I reflected at length about the Salem girls, and specifically about Ann Putnam, who was at the very center of the accusations in the Salem panic, who really did issue an apology (which is reproduced verbatim in this story), and who had been effectively written out of the most popular fictional account of that period in American history, *The Crucible*. In the past, as in the present, the experts had one story to tell about this unique and frightening experience, whereas the girls, I suspected, had an experience all their own, that no one but them could fully understand.

I have taken liberties with both the Le Roy story and with the Salem girls, though many of the details remain true. The progression that I describe with the fictional Danvers Mystery Illness adheres very closely to the progression of hypotheses floated at Le Roy. Similarly, the dates, *dramatis personae,* and much of the dialogue in Ann Putnam's story are adapted from historical records, including trial testimony as well as narratives written by Reverend Deodat Lawson and Reverend John Hale. The episode in which a deacon brings a copy of William Perkins's witch-hunting manual to Samuel Parris the night between Tituba's two confessions derives from a hypothesis explored by historian Larry Gragg in his biography of Samuel Parris, based on a nineteenth-century footnote in the *Proceedings of the Massachusetts Historical Society*. It's unsubstantiated, but highly evocative, and would explain the differences between the real Tituba's two confessions that I reproduce in the book. Further, in 1701 skeptic Robert

Calef wrote that Tituba might have been beaten to encourage her confession. Again, unsubstantiated, but evocative.

Although *Conversion* is in all respects a fictional story, and a product of my imagination, it nevertheless attempts to draw a real comparison between the difficulty of girls' lives in the past and the pressures that teenage girls are under today. I don't think any of us would want to return to a time when slavery was legal, eleven-year-olds were routinely bound out as servants, people could be put to death as witches based solely on reputation and rumor, and social hierarchy was defined unambiguously along race, gender, and economic lines. However, it bears considering why adolescent girls living at the dawn of the twenty-first century, with all of its technological, medical, and social advances, would still be under so much stress that their bodies, quite literally, cannot take it. We look at the afflicted girls during the Salem panic and want very much for there to be one rational explanation for their behavior. Were they faking? Was it moldy bread (the seventeenth-century equivalent of "environmental" factors)? Were they crazy? Part of our desire to identify the one "true" explanation of the Salem witch trials is that we have moved beyond hysteria. If we can consign the Salem episode safely to the past, then such a bizarre, inexplicable, potentially murderous panic can never happen again.

But it just did.

ACKNOWLEDGMENTS

My sincerest gratitude goes to Jennifer Besser, Shauna Rossano, Marisa Russell, and my team at Penguin Young Readers Group for their exquisite support for this novel. My fantastic agent Suzanne Gluck supported this idea from the moment it was a glimmer in my eye, and Laura Bonner, Ashley Fox, Eve Atterman, and all my colleagues at William Morris Endeavor remind me why I am so fortunate to be able to work with incredible people every day.

I would like to thank the girls of Le Roy, New York, for their courage in the face of an experience no teenager should ever have to endure. While they inspired this story, I hasten to add that this story is imaginary. Their experience is theirs and theirs alone.

Many friends have brought their expertise to bear on this manuscript, either by providing comments, reading drafts, listening to ad nauseam brainstorming, or generally cheering me on when I most needed to hear it. My love and thanks to Caroline Arden, Owen Arden, Theo Black, Elisha Cohn, Julia Glass, Connie Goodwin, Bradley Hague, Will Heinrich, Eleanor Henderson, Eric Idsvoog, Emily Kennedy, Kelley Kreitz, Ellen Leventry, Patricia Meinhardt, Jane Mendle, Kenneth Miller, Ginger Myhaver, Mary Beth Norton, Matthew Pearl, Brian Pellinen, Andrew Semans, Weston Smith,

George Spisak, the denizens of End Times Island, and all members of the Third Sarah Battle Whist Club of Boston (Ithaca Chapter).

The first draft of this novel came together in one marathon Writing Lent™, which left me a jabbering mess. My thanks to Stella's Café in Ithaca for feeding and housing me during much of that time, and to Bob Proehl and everyone at Buffalo Street Books for letting me read from this manuscript at an event in which they thought I would be talking about another book entirely.

Richard Trask is the steward of the Danvers Archival Center at the Peabody Institute Library, and I thank him for the vital work that he does preserving the legacy of witchcraft in Salem Village. Thank you also to Ben Ray and the University of Virginia online Salem Archive, which makes the Salem papers available to anyone who wants to see them. And thank you to Jean Marie Procious and everyone at the Salem Athenaeum for continuing the storied literary heritage of Salem, Massachusetts, in addition to providing a beautiful work space for writers like me.

Thank you to the teenagers who let me pry into their worlds, both near and far, present and past, with special thanks to the Snits, to my Cornell historical fiction students, and to my on-site teen accuracy consultant, Eli Hyman. If I were a crueler person, I would put his Twitter handle here.

I am fortunate to have parents who always encouraged me to follow my interests and passions when I was Colleen's age, even when it meant I was too busy reading Sartre to do my French homework. Thank you to George and Katherine S. Howe for helping me become the person I am, and to the Kinkaid School for educating me in spite of my best efforts.

And finally, my thanks as always to Louis Hyman. He knows why.

KATHERINE HOWE

is the *New York Times* bestselling author of the *The Physick Book of Deliverance Dane* and *The House of Velvet and Glass*. She is a lecturer in American studies at Cornell University. She is also a direct descendant of three of the women accused of witchcraft during the Salem witch trials, one who was hanged and two who survived. Her books have been published around the world in twenty-three languages to date.

Visit Katherine online at www.katherinehowe.com and follow her on Twitter @KatherineBHowe